THE PALADINS

JULIE REECE

Month9Books

ISBN: 978-0-9968904-6-5

Published by Month9Books, Raleigh, NC 27609
Cover Designed by Najla Qamber Designs
Cover Copyright © 2016 Month9Books

Month9Books

For my mother who read to me

"If thou thinkest that hell is behind thee, and the devil pursuing thee, thou wilt not loiter. Would the manslayer sleep with the avenger of blood behind him, and the city of refuge before him?"
~ Charles H. Spurgeon

THE
PALADINS

The Before

Cole

It's been four years since I planted the fireworks in Gideon Maddox's locker that burned a third of his face.

Four years since his father took revenge, trapping me with a spell that kept me prisoner in The Void.

Three months since the magic found me again.

Two months since my parents put me in therapy.

One day since my parents left for Paris on a month long business tour.

This morning, a mysterious girl no one else can see beckoned again from The Void.

Tonight, I'm standing on the balcony of my parent's palatial home, buying an airline ticket back to the states—back to Maddox mansion—the heart of my nightmares.

People say the more things change the more they stay the same. I hate them for being right. I lived with the monsters in my prison until I thought I might go mad. Repentant of my past, I made peace with my fate, my eternity. Until the day I was freed, because a stranger had the courage to help.

This time someone needs me.

How can I doom a girl to a fate I barely escaped?

There's only one answer.

I can't.

Chapter One

Cole

A bottle-green fly hums, rubbing his tiny legs together as though he's plotting something. The insect seems a dirty ornament on the shiny desk nameplate he sits upon. Gold on gold, the engraved letters read Navin Cahvan M.D. This is the third psychiatrist I've met in as many weeks. Part of my mother's plan to fix me. Jumpy nerves, insomnia, nightmares about demons when I finally do fall sleep—these are her justifications. Everyone tries to shrink me like a cheap T-shirt in the dryer.

The tawny-skinned man across the desk folds his knotted fingers over his belly and stares. Dark eyes track my movements beneath two bushy white eyebrows. "Mr. Wynter?"

Right. He asked a question. The fly hums again, wings fluttering against his hairy back. My head pounds, my clothes scratch, eyes burn, and my ears are raw with the smallest sounds echoing deep inside.

When Dr. Cahvan shifts, the leather seat groans in protest. "I can help you. But you must tell me the truth."

All I hear is Jack Nicholson screaming the line from *A Few*

Good Men: "You can't handle the truth!"

"Trust me, Cole. Tell me your secret thoughts."

Trust you? Sure. I tell you what happened and you lock me away forever on meds that keep me drooling, while I play dominoes with people who see giant, pink rabbits. No thanks.

He leans forward. His fingers thread together as his hands rest on the desktop. He taps his thumbs together. "I assure you this is a safe place. I call it ... the circle of trust."

Give me a break. You want me to tell you how I was a mean, dangerous kid. Confess that because I tormented a crippled boy, his father used a magic camera to trap me in an alternate universe as punishment. Explain how I lived a half-life in the Maddox mansion for four years until Raven Weathersby rescued me. About how much I miss her and think about going back someday ... Maybe I *am* insane.

"Let's discuss something else."

I find his suggestion amusing since I've barely said ten words in the past hour, and our time is almost up.

The good doctor shifts again. "Instead of talking about the past, why not speak of the present. How are you adjusting to life at home? I understand your parents had a welcome home party when you first arrived. How did that go?"

How do you think? "Swell." I would have preferred stuffing my hand in a high-speed blender. A hundred people that I hadn't seen since I was fifteen—and couldn't care less to see again—showed up to shake my hand and recite all they'd ever read about amnesia, the lie Gideon made up to cover my absence. "I really just need some space."

"And you got your wish, did you not? I understand your parents left town yesterday. How does being alone again so soon make you feel?"

Incredibly pissed. "They've always been busy people. I'm used to them traveling." But I wasn't. I thought with all the time apart, my parents might want to stick around a while. Be a family. Nope. Since appearances mean everything, they threw a party right away to show their friends and colleagues how fine I was. The powerful and highly regarded Mr. and Mrs. Wynter pulled out all the stops to prove their love for their long lost son: fine wine, catered dinner, china, crystal, even a string quartet. Yet, my father couldn't keep the disappointment from his face any more than my mother could drown her misery in vodka.

Perhaps to appease their consciences, my folks hooked me up with doctors and provided for my physical needs before bailing. But a new car and an obscenely padded bank account wasn't what I needed. So easily brushed aside again, I couldn't help but wonder if parts of them were relieved when I'd disappeared four years ago.

Dr. Cahvan's eyes narrow. "So, you remember your life up until your trip to the States?"

"Yes." I'm lying about my amnesia. I know it. He knows it. So do my parents, but it's too late to come up with a better story ... like being the victim of a cult brainwashing or joining a psychedelic commune. I drank a different brand of Kool-Aid in Sales Hollow, South Carolina, and I can never tell a soul.

The fly zings to the window. I flinch as the buzzing is magnified ten times in my head. It takes all my will not to jump up and smash the bug against the glass. The doctor watches me with sharp eyes trained to interpret body language. I hold his gaze, though my skin breaks out in a sweat. A sudden wind rattles the panes, and I startle.

Cahvan's mouth crimps at the corners. "Rather breezy today," he says, glancing out the window at the quiet, blue sky.

Who cares about the weather? I have to give the old guy something before I start whining about magic spells, heightened senses, or worse: how my daddy never loved me.

I blow out a breath. "Look, some things seem familiar, others are confusing. I don't need a doctor. I need time." I only meant to throw him a bone so he'd have something to report when my parents call, but my body heats as I talk. Anger, resentment, and fear all claw their way up my throat and charge out of my mouth before I can stop them. "Time I can't get back where I finish school, date hot girls, and grow up like normal kids do. I'm trying. Doing the best I can, but what I don't need is to sit in rooms with smug strangers who are paid to dissect my brain over things I can't explain, and neither of us will ever understand!" I drag my fingers through my shaggy hair. "That time is gone. I'm pissed off, and I guess I'll be pissed off until I'm not anymore."

Dr. Cahvan rubs his jaw. "That's very interesting, Cole."

My laugh is harsh. Not that any of this is funny. "Is it?"

"Yes. Thank you for your honesty today." His bushy eyebrows push together. "Thank you for entering the circle of trust and allowing me to help you. Please see my secretary on your way out and make another appointment for next week."

Seriously? I stand and head for the door. Oh, I'll see your secretary, all right. I'll nod as I walk right past her. He didn't help me. No one can. There are a lot of things I need. But touchy-feely therapy with Doctor Eyebrows isn't one of them.

After the awkward "circle of trust" episode, I can't decide what to do with myself. I don't want to be around people, but I don't want to go home to an empty house either, so I wind up in the rambling cemetery a couple miles from our house.

I like it here and come pretty often just to think. Crumbling grave markers bear witness to France's rich history, even with the chiseled dates worn and fading with time. Moss, ivy, and ancient trees lend beauty and peace to a place that soothes my soul. I'm not trying to be morbid. I never kept company with the dead. We were the *undead*, in a non-sparkly kind of way.

I'm not stupid enough to think I'll discover the meaning of

life. I'm just trying to find meaning in mine. After surviving a half-death, I've been given a second chance. Trouble is, I don't know what to do with it.

The sun is too hot on my back. No sooner does the thought cross my mind, when a friendly breeze tousles my hair like an old friend. I pull my cell from my pocket and stare at Raven's number. She said to call her anytime, and I do. Gideon said to call her if I wanted my arse kicked. Typical. He's still that insecure kid deep down. Still trying to prove himself, as he tries to control everyone and everything within his reach, just like his old man taught him.

Should have known something was wrong when I first got the invitation to visit Gideon in America all those years ago. My parents were so happy Maddox Senior wasn't pressing charges; they actually thought the gesture was an attempt at friendship. Of course, Mum and Dad sent me packing complete with an olive branch in my mouth. That gesture of goodwill got my picture taken and a trip to The Void with a bunch of vengeful old guys from the early nineteen hundreds and a hot blond with twisted taste in men. We spent our days trying to escape that hell. The labyrinth's ghouls, the surreal existence of consciousness without a physical body, and the constant pain of regret all earmarked a life that wasn't.

Until her.

My fingers comb the grass at my sides. I close my eyes and feel the day's warmth on my face, the wind threading through my thin tee. I may look like a freak, but I can't stop touching everything around me. While I was gone, I missed the sensation of air in my lungs, the taste of coffee, the sweet sensation of a kiss ...

My thumb starts dialing Rae's number.

Cole ...

Shite. Here we go again.

Come to me, Cole ...

I wonder if I sounded this creepy to Raven when I begged for her help.

Veins at my temples pulse. Leaves shake and laugh in the breeze, the echo reverberating in my head. *"Who are you? What do you want with me?"* I want to stand, but my limbs weigh a hundred pounds each. My lungs deflate under the crushing pressure, and I struggle to breathe.

The scenery of oaks and elms surrounding the cemetery blur into a muddy gray-green wall, and I know what's happening. Gravestones push up from the ground like gnashing teeth and recede again until the ground transforms into a smooth, stone floor. The world of pedestrians, car horns, and singing birds around the graveyard fade to a quiet worse than death. My body rejects the idea of gravity. The weightlessness of being sucked back into The Void again invades my person like a virus, spreading into my muscles and bones, my very essence.

I will the door of my mind closed to shut out the transformation. I place a mental shield before the magic so it won't consume me, but magic has a will of its own. It snakes under the imaginary door I've erected in my head, enveloping me. I thrash, but it's useless. My soundless screaming and mind-withering despair only seems to feed The Void's strength.

When I open my eyes, the cemetery is gone. I shift on a cold, damp floor, taking in my new surroundings. I've seen this place before, several times. The space is a circular stone room with two tall, skinny windows allowing diffused light inside. A bed sits across from me. Downy quilts worn and faded with use cover the straw mattress. On the wall, a huge, gilt-framed mirror reflects the room where a pretty blond sits in a hardback chair. Watching me.

I'm familiar with strange, but not with sad, soul-eating eyes like hers.

When she rises, I feel like I should thank her, because light from the window shows her curves through an ultra-thin nightdress. The sight chokes my airflow for a whole different reason.

ThinkofRaventhinkofRaventhinkofRaven.

I'm so not thinking of Raven. For all my faults, I'm not the cheating type, but I *am* a guy, and this girl is seriously fit! I want to touch her in the worst way, but I swallow instead. Attempting to be a gentleman, I lift my gaze and focus on the far wall, yet somehow—because I'm still a guy—I end up watching the way her hair hangs in white blond waves to her thighs. Her rosebud mouth opens slightly. Pleading eyes, more silver than blue, threaten to pull me under and drown me. None of this helps curb my impulse to reach for her.

Then I think about how she brought me here against my will, and that helps tamp down the hormones.

Cole.

What do you want?

Can't you guess?

I can. I pleaded with Raven for the same help not too long ago. Inside The Void, I thought I'd met everyone. The ones that Maddox had imprisoned, and the indigenous inhabitants of the labyrinth. I hadn't known there were any others.

The drip-drop of a leaky faucet is the only sound as I gather my thoughts. "Who are you? *Where* are you? I don't understand what's happening. Where is this place? Did Gideon put you here?" I rattle off my questions not pausing for a response.

She doesn't answer. Maybe she can't.

Wind picks up, whooshing through the hollow room, though the windows are shut. The sound grows, as though someone dropped a microphone in a washing machine. I grit my teeth against the noise. My mind squeezes in the pressurized vacuum.

Cole ... She extends a thin, white hand.

I remember Raven. How she fell to her knees on the floor of the mill house when we first met. Pain rips into my psyche, claws at my sanity. The same way I'm sure it did hers.

"I'm sorry. Forgive me, Raven. I didn't know."

... My name is Rosamond ...

Stone walls smear and fade, the beautiful girl along with them. I can't breathe. Then, the faint outline of tree tops bleed back into view.

... Rosamond Bryer ...

My panting rivals an overheated Saint Bernard. Grass pokes my palms. Rough bark scrapes my spine through my T-shirt. Any trace of the castle turret is erased as the same decrepit cemetery I know solidifies, and the garden is as it was before.

Almost ...

I'm leaning against an old tree, yet my cell and sunglasses still lie next to the rose bushes where I was sitting, almost twenty feet away. I have no memory of moving. How did I get way over here?

Both hands plow through my hair with my exhale. What the bloody hell just happened? Am I imagining this? A nightmare left over from the reality of my imprisonment. Or is the girl real? Trapped like I was and waiting for someone with the courage to free her.

Is that someone me? I've been a lot of things, but brave isn't one of them. To help her means going back to the mansion.

No. I definitely do not need this shite. I'm starting over, leaving that life behind. Yet, the haunted expression on the girl's face tugs at me. Something about her seems familiar. I'm gutted over how she reached for me. Raven doubted, too, but not for long. If the blond is real, then she's really in trouble. *And if she's really in trouble, what, if anything, are you prepared to do about it, Cole Wynter?*

Chapter Two

Gideon

I don't hate cats. Honest. But since my girlfriend Raven's pet is more bear than cat, I might hate this one. She often says a cat will focus on the one person in the room who doesn't want him. That theory appears true, since he's on top of me.

Aww ...

No. Not cute. I tense as the mangy thing marches around in my lap, getting comfortable. His tail swipes my nose, and I sneeze. When his nails dig through my jeans to my thighs, I've had enough.

"My poor baby, come here."

I wish I could say she's talking to me, but Raven's gaze stays on her cat as she walks toward the sofa. She lifts her hundred-pound panther off my lap. Okay, twenty-five pound Maine Coon. Still. She kisses his head, and gently scolds him like a naughty child before depositing him on the rug. Edgar parks his fat carcass in front of the fire and is asleep in seconds.

Raven returns and sits Indian style on the floor at my feet with the slow grace of a dancer. Her chin balances on my knee as she peers up with slate-colored eyes. Unusual, infinite, I will never tire of looking into them. The scent of her shampoo is clean, like the woods after a rain. Her smile distracts me from thoughts of cooking her cat. When I can't stand the distance between us anymore—which isn't long—I pull her closer, kissing her smooth brow, her nose, and neck. I can't get close enough.

"So, Mr. Maddox," she says, clearing her throat. "Where were we?" Her hands fall away from my chest and she resumes her spot on the floor.

She's been doing that more lately, creating distance between us, and not just physically. Raven's never had trouble speaking her mind, yet lately when I ask, she says, "I'm *fine.*" I hate that insipid word. As Artisans, Maddox men are born and bred to act without mercy or hesitation. So, I can't believe I'm admitting this, but I don't know what to do. Cutthroat ultimatums probably aren't the best approach with your girlfriend.

In the past, I dated plenty but seldom saw the same girl twice. I wasn't big on sharing my feelings, and a girl that got too clingy got her number deleted from my cell.

But I'm not that guy anymore. I'm the one people talk about, the sap that changed when he fell for the right girl, and you know what? They're right. I don't give a shit if I'm a cliché. I'm happy, damn it. So, instead of asking why she pulled away, I give her space and answer, "We were talking about your Bug."

Her dilapidated 1973 VW Super Beetle is parked in my driveway. I want to buy her something else. *Anything* else.

Her full lips turn down. "I like my little car."

"That's not a car," I say, still focused on her mouth. "It's rust. Stuck together with more rust."

There's a smile. "One man's rust is another man's classic. Red is my color, and it runs just fine."

Fine.

And so continues our battle of wills. "The car is going. That's done. What about an Audi, or a MINI? You might as well tell me what you'd like to drive, or I'll choose something for you."

"Stubborn."

"Me?"

"Yes, you."

She draws a smiley face on my knee with her fingernail. "I appreciate the offer, I do, but I can't accept a whole car."

Keeping a straight face is impossible. "Somehow, I don't think half a car will solve anything." She smacks my leg. Buying her a *whole* car won't put so much as a dent in my allowance. And it's nothing compared to what I want to give her.

She straightens. "Thanks for the thought. I know you want to help, but a car is too much." Her eyes remain uneasy above a small smile. "You don't always have to buy me things. You know that, right?"

No. This whole conversation is ridiculous. When I found her, she was sleeping on a storeroom floor, surviving by sewing inventive, steampunk creations for a small clientele. If I can afford it and want to spoil her, where's the harm? I recline against the couch cushions with a heavy breath.

Proud and independent, Raven's used to taking care of herself, but all girls like presents, don't they? Then it occurs to me that the VW is a tie to the memory of her stepfather Ben, who recently passed away. Maybe she sees replacing the car as a betrayal. That must be it.

"Raven?" The stiff set of her jaw warns me she's done with the subject, but I press once more. "Your car is old and unreliable. If you were in an accident, Ben would want you safe, and so do I."

Her gaze finds the window.

"I'll make you a deal."

"You and your deals." She doesn't look, but her mouth tips up at the corners. "You're relentless. Like the tide."

I lean forward, lowering my voice, "Keep the Bug. We'll garage your classic. Drive it once in a while to keep the motor in good shape, but let me buy you—"

"Here we are, my lovelies!" Jenny, my housekeeper and part-time surrogate grandmother, scurries into the study through the open door. Her cheeks are flushed, as usual. A sheen of sweat glistens on her ruddy skin, and the starched collar of her powder-blue uniform has begun to droop.

She sets her overloaded tray down with a final rattle on my desktop. "Who makes s'mores in the fireplace? In June, no less? Why, I've never heard of such a thing." Facing the desk, she clucks like an old hen as she sets out the necessary supplies.

I give Raven a reassuring wink.

"You know I'd make you lambs anything you want for a late-night snack." Jenny pauses, looking up. "All you need do is ask. It's no bother."

"S'mores are a childhood memory of Raven's," I say. One of the few happy ones since her mother died leaving Rae to nurse an alcoholic stepfather. "I intend to indulge her wishes."

She jumps up and heads for the desk. Holding a bag of marshmallows in the air, she shakes them like a little kid. "Do you want me to make you one, Jenny? You have to be careful to get the mallow brown without burning it."

My housekeeper's eyebrows climb for her hairline. "The idea! Guests do *not* attend servants, Miss Weathersby, no matter how charmingly they may offer." Jenny pats Raven's cheek, and then glances over her shoulder. "Gracious, child, will you look at this room. What a green thumb you have. I confess the plants in the house have fairly doubled in size since you took to watering them. And so green!"

Raven follows her gaze to the potted jungle growing near the window and smiles. "We never had many plants around our house. I didn't know I'd like it so much, but there's something sort of therapeutic about gardening."

"Well, they're better off with you minding them." Jenny steps toward the various containers, examining each one. "Now isn't this is strange ... See how they're growing?" Raven joins Jenny at the window, her hand gently running over the glossy ficus leaves. "Look here, see how the stems bend *away* from the sun. That's odd."

It is odd. I hadn't noticed until now, but the growth is uneven. All the new leaves sprout on one side growing away from the light and toward Raven's favorite chair in the darker corner.

"No matter, dearie. I suppose the plants know best what they need, eh? And now ... " Jenny's chattering stops for a gulp of air. "Will there be anything else for you two this evening?"

I glance at my new Rolex surprised it's nearly nine o'clock. "No, thank you. Please get some rest."

"Very good, sir. I hope you have a pleasant flight to New York tomorrow, and a nice ..." She shrinks as Rae cheerfully impales a plump marshmallow with her skewer.

I lift my chin. "Night, Jenny."

Once the door clicks shut, Raven moves to the fire. "Remind me to ask for some of her chocolate chunk cookies this week. I don't want to hurt her feelings."

Concern for others is a constant of Raven's. It was she that agreed to take the place of her ailing stepfather last year and make restitution for his gambling debt against my family. Little did she know I'd exact payment by insisting she move in with me.

I scoot over on the couch and prop my feet up. As Raven stretches over the fire, her sleek black hair swings forward. The color picks up a red glow from the hot coals beneath, her eyes reflecting the low burning flame. The sight speeds my pulse.

After she moved in, I became obsessed with the girl who sacrificed her dreams for someone as unworthy as her stepfather. Weeks passed, and I studied her habits, watched as she created the beautiful designs that saved my father's failing clothing line. She worked for me, her enemy, endured my temper, kept her grades up, even befriended my lonesome housekeeper.

"Oh, ouch!" Raven blows out the flame charring her marshmallow and plucks it from the prongs. "Dang it."

I'm off the couch in a blink. "Careful, you'll burn yourself." Taking her hand in mine, I guide the scorched sugar to my lips and devour the whole thing.

"Gideon! That one's ruined."

I release her fingers and laugh through the mush. "But I wuv the burnf wons."

"You do?" Her little frown destroys me.

"Mm-hmm."

Her glaze flits to the fire and back. "Okay, here's an idea. Don't go to New York tomorrow, and I'll make you as many charred s'mores as you can eat."

I gulp the last of my marshmallow, confused by her request. "I'd love to, but you know I can't." Truth is, I'd avoided half a dozen meetings in the last two months. Art Windsor, my father's longtime business associate, and the nearest thing to a friend I have on the board, called this morning. First, to check on me, as it's out of character for me to miss so much work, second, to warn me that tomorrow's meeting is mandatory.

She slides her empty skewer onto the mantle. "I know. I'm sure it's stupid paranoia, but I have a really weird feeling about this trip."

My head lowers. "I don't." Kiss. "Want you." Kiss. "To worry." Our lips are warm and sticky with sugar. My hands drop to her hips, and though I meant to distract *her*, it's my pulse that's revving. "I'll be back in two days, three at most. Deal?" When I slide my arms around her ribcage, she melds into me.

Her hands move up my back. The contact energizes me. My heart pounds harder. When her lips part for me, I deepen the kiss, making sure she understands what she means to me, what she *does* to me. My fingers dig into the fabric of her blouse. Her answering whimper drives me half-crazy with wanting. I never knew it could be like this with anyone. And then I realize, it *wouldn't* be like this with anyone but her.

My head spins. Thought goes up in smoke, replaced by need, yet I can't help but notice the increasing heat from the hearth. The warmth becomes uncomfortable, then unbearable. Edgar's hiss unhinges something in my spine.

Breaking the kiss, Raven balks at our little fire. Only it's not so little anymore.

The color is wrong. Blue flame licks the interior brick walls, flaring up the chimney. My head pounds, hearing sharpens as the wood snaps and crackles. There's an odd hum coming from the grate.

Tiny nails scratch the floor as Edgar squeezes his bulk under the couch. I step between Raven and the fire, but it seems I've overreacted, because the blaze lessens. Colors gradually change from blue to a natural orange and the flares shrink to their former size in seconds.

When Raven presses her cheek to my shoulder, I turn, drawing her under my arm.

"Wow," she says. "What was that about?"

"I don't know, sap or something flammable on the log." There's no reason to worry, still my arm tightens around her shoulder.

We watch the log burn, and when nothing else interesting happens, Raven slides away from me, taking a seat on the couch. "Phew, it's gotten hot in here." She fans herself with a hand. "Do you still want dessert?"

"Hm." Moving in her direction, ten inappropriate replies to her question file through my mind, but I leave them alone. The mood's suddenly heavier. Tomorrow will come soon enough and with it, our separation.

Whipped much, Maddox?

I don't much care.

Raven's head tilts. "What?" Her smile grows unsure and becomes a squeal as I lift her into my arms, take her place on the couch, and settle her in my lap. Her laughter fades under my steady gaze. When the light in her eyes dims to a smolder, I cover her mouth with mine and kiss her until we're both breathless.

Chapter Three

Raven

A quick breeze whips the leaves of the trees outside. Like thousands of blinking green crystals, the foliage quivers, reflective emerald flashes in the afternoon light become nature's chandeliers.

Mind racing with thoughts I can't shut out, I shift on the second of two twin beds in my best friend Maggie's fuchsia bedroom and stare out her open, double window.

Taking an adult role at a young age kept me focused, driven, so I don't know why I'm so freaked out about starting school in the fall. It's stupid, since it's all I've ever wanted.

No matter what, I've always been tough, tenacious. And I sort of liked that about me. Now, I'm more like a flat tire with all the air sucked out of a big hole in the rubber—that hole being the death of my stepfather. Sure, our world before was chaos, but it was chaos I understood.

After being held captive in the Maddox mansion, after Ben died of cirrhosis, after Gideon said he loved me, I needed time to deal, get my head on straight. So, having no other family, I moved in with Maggie Wilson and her parents. I couldn't very well keep living with Gideon—not that he didn't try and convince me.

The plan we settled on was that I'd stay here until college started in the fall. Then Maggie and her boyfriend Dane would head for Armstrong Atlantic, and I would go to SCAD in Savannah. Gideon would attend at College of Charleston to be near me, and that was that. But plans can change. No one knows that better than I do.

The cell on my bed chirps signaling another text. *Speaking of change* ... Cole and I have been talking on and off all morning. Actually, we've been talking ever since he flew home to France eight months ago.

Cole: I'm in hell here, Raven. Another bizarre nightmare. I miss you. Wish we could meet for coffee.

Raven: Me, too. I'm sorry, Cole. Hang in there. Life will get better.

I don't know if it will or not, but I send him what hope I can. Poor Cole. In light of all he's been through, it's not surprising the guy suffers from bad dreams.

The Artisan curse that left him haunting Maddox mansion drove him to ask me for help. It took months to unravel the mystery that threatened my sanity and my life. With the help of my friends, Jenny, and finally Gideon himself, we went to the mansion's cellar where we performed the ritual that set Cole free.

Life altering, supernatural events tend to blow your mind, then bind you irrevocably to the people you went through them with. At least, that's what happened to me.

My boyfriend doesn't like my friendship with Cole, but he tolerates it. In time, I hope he'll accept that while I'm drawn to Cole, there's no one else like Gideon Maddox.

Still, I can't deny the strain between us, and I know he feels it, too. We came together like two speeding trains, barreling toward each other with opposite goals ending in a fierce and fiery meeting. All the ugly, painful parts of our lives spilled onto the ground for the other to inspect first. How does a new couple rewind to small talk and seemingly unimportant details after *that?* We've both lived crisis to crisis for so long, I'm not sure we know how to live without one.

Maybe it takes time to adjust. And maybe there's not enough time in the world to adjust to what we've been through. But no, I can't let myself think that way. We'll work it out. We have to.

Edgar meows and bumps my hand with his massive head. I stroke his soft, black fur and peer out the window again. A jet parts the thin clouds overhead. Gideon's plane will have landed in New York by now. He's traveled much less lately, and I suspect that's because of me, but I miss him anyway. I've never been the doe-eyed, clingy-type. Then again, I've never been crazy in love before, either.

The wind blows the arms of the oaks outside, and I swear they call my name. I'm mesmerized, can't stop watching. This fascination with fauna is new. Growing. And honestly, a bit disconcerting.

I spot Dane in his red T-shirt coming up the sidewalk. His stride is uniquely him, athletic with a little gangsta-strut thrown in that I'd recognize anywhere. Not that anyone could miss the long russet dreads that hang like macramé cords from his head. Just the sight of him cheers me up. I grin as he strolls through the yard and up to my window instead of going to the front door like normal people.

Two years ago, he was the new kid at school. Quiet, brooding, but one day he complimented my clothes. I said I liked his hair. He told me I could dance—for a white girl. Another smile breaks free at the memory of us debating everything from movies to whether or not rappers are poets. Boom. A friendship was born. Always there for me, Dane protected me those nights when I used to hunt the bars for Ben, and I stitched him up whenever he'd come over after a fight with his dad and needed a place to crash.

He stops in front of my window and speaks to his shoes.

"Hey, little Rae."

"Hey, yourself." He tends to use my nickname when he's worried—about me, or himself. Based on this afternoon's activities, I'm betting on the latter.

"Will you walk in with me?"

"Chicken?"

He nods. "I ain't even gonna lie."

I sympathize. When I introduced him to Maggie, lightning struck. His feelings were instant and obvious, at least to me, and he carried that torch in silence for a long time. In Dane's mind, his poverty and past next to her middle class status made her as unreachable as a star. That is, until we knocked some sense into his hard head a few months ago. He still gets nervous around Maggie's parents—especially her dad.

As for Gideon, his parents passed away when he was young. I never had to face them, but since Dane and I are from the same (wrong) side of the tracks, I can imagine quite a scene if I had.

"No worries, bro. Meet me at the door, I got your back."

I grab my sketchpad, and bounce off the bed. When I get to the front door and swing it open, Dane's face is riddled with anxiety. I pull him inside and loop his arm through mine with a gentle squeeze to bolster him. Arm in arm, we make our way down the hall, through the living room, and head for the back door. I'm grinning because pretzel-walking in tight spaces with someone is awkward, yet my friend grips me like a life preserver. His skin grows clammy, and his complexion exchanges color—cinnamon for green. He's stiff as a ruler.

"Try and relax," I say. "They're good people and so are you. Just be yourself."

Dane snorts as we push past the screen door and step onto a rambling two-tiered deck.

The Wilson's backyard is a fenced quarter-acre of suburban normalcy. Dogs bark, birds sing, and neighbors swear at their burning bratwurst while little kids squeal and play on their swing sets.

Mags's father stands in one corner, grilling burgers. He waves his spatula, and I lift my chin in greeting. I'm sorry to say he wears a white chef's hat and a chartreuse "Kiss the Cook" apron that I plan to burn later. Maggie's mother sets the picnic table for five. It's like Norman Rockwell threw up out here, and I love it.

Dane takes an unsteady step forward. "Sup, Mr. Wilson?"

Poor guy.

I wink at Mags as I head for the big maple tree in the center of the yard. Sketching until dinner's ready will give Dane some time alone with the fam, and Maggie can more than handle his frayed nerves.

Easing my back against the tree, I sketch a new design for my steampunk timepiece line. The breeze is warm for early June, and I predict a blistering summer. Dandelions dot the yard in need of mowing. Cirrocumulus clouds cover the hazy blue sky. I'm proud I remember that handy tidbit from science class, they are also nicknamed Mackerel because the clouds look like fish scales. So, why can't we just call them that? Why do scientists always have to name everything such long, stupid names that no one can ever remember for a test?

Except that I just did. Gah! Shut up, Raven! Sometimes I can't turn my rambling brain off.

Maggie giggles, and I watch the foursome on the deck, enjoying the day. Simple gratitude wells up inside me until the feeling spills over. Thankful for the sun, the shade that a faithful, old tree provides in summer, for the strength of its support, the music of fluttering leaves in the breeze.

The ground jumps and rumbles beneath me.

Startled, I glance around, but there's nothing to see.

Another rumble and energy infuses my nerves, sending a shock through my body.

I drop my pad and pencil. My palms press the grass on either side of me, fingers digging into the soft soil for balance.

Then the shaking stops.

On the deck, Maggie tosses her head back and laughs as her

father points the nozzle of the ketchup bottle her direction. She begs Dane for help, but he puts his hands in the air, as if to say this is between her and her dad. Mrs. Wilson frowns, warning her husband to stop his teasing.

No one seems alarmed by the fact a small earthquake has just taken place. No one seems to notice at all.

Does a power line run under this tree? Maybe a neighbor dug in the wrong place. Lawn mower run amok? Sink hole? I wait, rooted to the spot, but nothing else happens.

My muscles relax as another soft breeze floats by. I shake my head at my overactive imagination, and settle against the tree. Slowly, I'm eased forward and back again. As a child, I often fell asleep on Ben's solid chest. Gentle swells and contractions of his ribcage forced me up and down in a steady rhythm like a lullaby with each breath. The tree trunk *breathes* the same way—like a giant lung. Shivers wrack my body. I force myself to sit still as several limbs bow low. Leaves gently caress my face and neck sending little jolts of energy skittering under my flesh. As the maple rolls me forward again, a warm sensation fills my mind with a sense of awe and wonder. And power. Light floods my eyes in a brilliant flash. I scramble to my feet with a shriek, and, too fast to track, the tree limbs retreat to the canopy above.

"What's wrong?" Maggie yells over her father's shoulder. "Ew, is there a bug?"

"Uh … " How do I explain? I stare at my friend, unable to answer with a single intelligent word.

Worry, fear, and doubt weight the air easing from my chest. When Gideon and I broke the curse last year, I thought the ritual would end our troubles—the supernatural ones, anyway. Suddenly, I'm not so sure. And if the magic's retuning, how in the world do I tell my beautiful, strong-willed, and overly protective boyfriend?

The Middle

Chapter Four

Cole

It's two in the morning and Rosamond's spirit still haunts my dreams. She's appearing more often, making her pleas that much harder to ignore.

I'm supposed to be going through the stack of tutoring resumes my parents left behind. A year of catching up on my education, and I'm off to Uni. Carving out a worthy career path is a task expected of every *decent* Wynter.

Instead, I'm standing on the second floor balcony watching a fox dart across our moonlit garden. Trees, flowers, expensive wrought iron furniture—everything's washed in an effluent glow.

Life is peaceful in this moment, or could be, if not for the mysterious blond whose image won't fade. I tell myself the visions aren't real, and then she appears again. The more I say she isn't my problem, the heavier my soul feels. How do I live with myself if I walk away? Yet, the bigger question may be … how can I possibly help?

My hands grip the balcony railing. As far as I know, the camera hidden in the Maddox mansion was the only way into The Void. While our physical bodies were stored in coffins in the

Maddox cellar, our spirits walked the grounds between worlds. Never in my years of banishment had I seen Rosamond.

Were there other coffins? More people that the Artisans punished whom I'd never met? Gideon never mentioned anyone else. In fact, when Raven convinced him to free us, all twenty-four souls were accounted for that night. So, where did Rosamond come from?

Even if I knew, would Gideon help me free her?

Memories can haunt a person as effectively as ghosts. And considering all I'd done to him, I highly doubted that he would …

At age fifteen, I remember waiting outside the headmaster's office at Malcolm College, listening to my father rant. Mottled glass panes in the oak door gave me a decent, if blurry, view of the uncomfortable scene unfolding within.

Headmaster Stewart (Stewie or Stewmeat, as we liked to call him) Allen Gamble was about as tough as boiled noodles. Confrontation with my father was best handled as you would an attack dog. Speak with a clear and firm voice. Never show fear. Never run.

Who knows how Stewie achieved his high rank? It hardly mattered. If my father had much to say about it—and he did—poor Stewmeat wouldn't have his job much longer.

As Father spoke, the volume grew. Cold and hard as the steely, blue barrel of a gun, old man Wynter leveled that voice at his victim and pulled the trigger. "This is absurd! No one expels a Wynter. It doesn't happen. So, a few boys played an innocent prank that went awry. The burn was an accident. Hell, didn't we all do a little hazing of the new chap when we were in school? Young master Maddox needs to toughen up anyway, I dare say."

My father's tone held a hint of pride mixed in with his superiority. As though my chosen method of torturing Gideon won me points for ingenuity. My stomach soured. Teeth ground to the point of shattering. I never meant to hurt the kid, not really. The plan was to embarrass, and maybe scare him a little.

Back then, Dr. Greene, my therapist, said I did shite like that as an outlet for my anger and for attention. Maybe that was true. Or maybe I was the biggest monster of all because I'd seen the hospital photos of Gideon's burns collected by case investigators.

Scanning the photographs, I can still feel the way my eyes stung, and throat swelled shut. I wanted to shout, say I was sorry. But how could anyone apologize for something like that?

All Maddox wanted was to fit in.

My father might have disowned me if he knew how sick I felt. A Wynter is never wrong, never apologizes, or shows regret for his actions. That's weakness.

But as I viewed the evidence of my crimes against Maddox, my hands trembled, and I knew I was the weakest boy on the planet, because I cried like a baby—but not until I got home and alone behind the closed door of my bedroom.

We weren't so different, really, Maddox and me. I wondered if he'd seen that, too. Wealthy, overachieving, only sons with assholes for fathers. We were polished, clever, and fairly miserable, trying to be something we would never be. Acceptable. The difference was I'd learned to play the game and Gideon hadn't. He still cared, and I hated him for it.

Students thought of me as popular, funny, and charismatic. Gideon wasn't. Awkward and self-conscious, the boy drove me and my mates crazy with his wretched slide-stop gait—gimping down the hall on his crutches. Head always hung a little too low, back a smidge too bowed. He never looked anyone in the eye, excluding our professors, naturally. He ate by himself, studied alone in his room, yet there was something about him. A gleam in his eye at times that hinted at promise, winked at hope. That look made me want to knock him down.

That and the fact he wasn't completely barking yet, either. Not like the rest of us. Time changed all that, of course. Eventually, Maddox surpassed my reputation, and that's saying something.

"My dear, Mr. Wynter!" Stewmeat's shocked tone drew my focus to the heated conversation in the other room. "The Maddox boy was seriously injured. The board is furious. Cole's actions are without excuse and cannot be swept under the rug this time."

Through the glass, I watched the headmaster's shoulders hunch—probably withering under the glare of my father. I knew the feeling well.

The door swung open, Father hesitating just inside the room. His face an angry shade of purple—just a screaming, giant blue grape jutting out of his shirt collar where his head should've been. I'd have laughed if I wasn't so close to vomiting.

"My son doesn't need this third rate institution of incompetence. The board doesn't scare me. If you people had done your job and given these spirited boys proper supervision, the accident wouldn't have been possible. It's your fault, Stewart. None but yours. No need to expel my son. I withdraw him. This isn't over. Mark my words, you sniveling coward!"

As he left, my father slammed the door shut with a shuddering bang. How the glass didn't break is still a mystery. He stalked to the leather chair in the hall where I'd sat perched like a goose awaiting beheading. Hands knotted at my sides, I couldn't look up, and then I did. He's not a large man, my father, yet the fury in his eyes made him seem eight feet tall. "You!" he growled, pointing an accusing finger my direction. "I'll deal with at home."

I glanced over at Stewmeat hovering in the doorway. He never spoke, but his expression softened to what I believe was genuine pity.

Pity. Something a true Wynter abhors, and yet the emotion sat on my chest like a hundred-pound weight.

An owl screams in the forest behind our home, drawing me from bad memories. It's just a bird, but the cry falls like an accusation. A flash of wings against the night and the owl is gone. Only the moon remains, enduring, strong. Faithful to pull the tide, first to light the way ...

I've been fighting the truth, but I can't deny what's happening anymore. Once, I hurt someone just to impress my friends, then sat by and did nothing to please my father.

The guilt almost killed me.

If I fly to South Carolina, Gideon may refuse to help me ... or call the cops. He might grin as he socks me in the nose. Yet, in this moment, I lean on the balcony rail, pressing numbers on my cell phone to buy a plane ticket.

Rosamond's freedom is worth the risk.

Chapter Five

Gideon

Maddox Industries occupies an entire floor at 32 Old Slip in Manhattan's financial district. My father's expensive leather chair squeaks as I redistribute my weight and stare out the wall of windows. To me, sunset makes the hard edges of New York's uneven horizon appear more like an erratic EKG tape than a big city skyline. My view is crystal clear, yet I can barely function inside the cloud of shock suffocating my brain.

My gaze shifts to the grandfather clock in the corner, to the walls covered with paintings depicting my father's favorite generals and historical battle scenes ... and down again, to the stark paperwork awaiting my signature. How many Maddox men have worked at this ancient desk? My great-grandfather first, and then my grandfather, my father, and finally, me. All gone.

Who could have guessed that when the executive board called an emergency meeting, which happens from time to time, they'd have an ambush waiting? I'm out on my ass, thank you very much.

I got lazy. Distracted. Soft. Apparently, our tax attorneys had embezzled obscene amounts of money before disappearing last week. The board found out, took a look at our holdings, and panicked before our stockholders could. Restructuring to save what's left of the institution my ancestors built was swift, and lethal. Also, it does not include me.

So be it.

A year ago, I was just as ruthless. Their decision is exactly what I would have done in their place. Feeling altruistic, the board left me the mansion, and the country house in Grey Horse, but no cash, stock, art, jewelry or any other real estate holdings my family had acquired. Art Windsor, my father's most trusted advisor, was the only one to stand with me in today's meeting and contest the board's decision. Afterward, he told me not to give up as he took my company credit cards and promised to investigate the matter. He means well, but I know there's nothing he can do.

In front of me sits a document. The board's offering to pay a small annuity for the right to retain the name of Maddox Industries. The name is prestigious and well known globally. As much as I'd like to tell them where to shove their offer, I can't refuse. The money covers upkeep on the mansion and will pay the salaries of Jamis and Jenny until their deaths.

Nothing more.

No meetings, decisions, responsibilities, or business trips for a job I don't have. Jetting to glamorous cities for concerts, dinner, or just for the hell of it is a thing of the past. Gone are the luxury cars, clothes, and toys. A Maddox without money? My father is probably rolling over in his grave. Once again, I am the weak link in our family chain bringing the company to ruin because I was too distracted to notice we were being robbed blind.

Raven ...

The thought of her slams into me like a cannonball. Well, not the thought of her, but *about* her. Without money, how will I make her dream of becoming a world famous designer a reality? All I promised, all I hoped to give her is gone. My hands fist on the desk. Thankfully, her college tuition is in an account in her name—a scholarship the board can't access. Too bad I didn't do the same for myself. I never thought I'd have to.

Our joint clothing venture Raedoxx Apparel dodged a bullet, as well. I developed the company last year when I blackmailed Raven to work for me. Before I fell in love. Now the company's safe, but not because of any strategic move on my part, and not because the board didn't try to include her designs in the takeover. Saving Raedoxx was a lucky, sentimental accident. I put the company in her name with me as acting CEO thinking I'd present it to her as a wedding present or some other ridiculous display of affection someday. That desire inadvertently protected the newly formed LLC from the board. The parent company absorbed the initial costs of production—and the profits. We planned to grow the company together, so while the money's gone, at least her designs are safe.

With a roar, I grab the expensive vase on the corner of my desk and hurl it against the wall.

My attempt to blow off steam doesn't help. Instead, it leaves a pile of shattered glass on the carpet in a million irreparable shards that someone else will have to clean up.

I'm nothing. And tomorrow, I'll have to fly home and tell the girl I love.

How could I have been so stupid?

As I move along a darkened hallway, the fishbowl echo and blurry edges of memory let me know I'm dreaming. At eight years old, everything looks bigger, but our lake house in Grey Horse is vast by anyone's standards.

The rubber soles of my new shoes squeak against the highly polished wood floors. I pause, wait a beat in case I'm discovered, but no one appears to condemn me. Creeping closer to the forbidden room, I nudge the mahogany doors open and peer inside my father's study.

One sharp breath and I hold it in. Consequences for appearing in this room uninvited may be severe, but I want to be near him so badly, I ignore any possible repercussions. The smell of earthy, wood spice and tobacco tell me he's close. I exhale, then breathe more deeply of him. Confident. Powerful. A scent all his own and my favorite in the universe.

A great man, perfect in ways I will never be, my father stands before an enormous, gilded mirror, taller than a giant, and wide as ten windows. He stares into the glass, eyes moving back and forth as though he's watching a soccer game on TV.

"Come here, Gideon."

Caught spying, my young heart hammers away. "Father?"

"Come, boy. Look here with me. Tell me what you see."

See? I'm not sure what he means. Historically, my father's questions involve some trick or riddle assuring both my failure and his wrath.

As I draw near, I study the reflection of my father. Tall. Athletic. His dark hair is pulled into the neat ponytail he wears for work. The silver streaks at his temples are thickening of late. Firm chin, straight nose, lips pinned together in impatient anticipation. My father's green eyes miss nothing. The orbs glitter, deep and penetrating as the facets of an emerald.

I glance at my image in comparison.

My body is frail. Crooked. One blue eye stares back. My hair hangs in messy curls over my forehead hiding my green eye. The one I got from him.

"Observe closely." Father's fingers clutch my shoulder. He squeezes to the point of pain, lessening his grip with my flinch. "Look past the obvious, son. Past this crude flesh," he says, pressing my arm. "What do you see?"

Instinctively, I know he's not referring to the ordinary items surrounding us. Rich, leather chairs I'm not allowed to sit on. Heavy, cherry desk with drawers I mustn't open. Persian rugs I dare not tread upon. Tension electrifies the silence as I hesitate. My mind casts about desperately hoping to grasp his meaning. Earn his approval.

"Look, damn you!" he says. "Inside the glass. Magic is elemental. It's in the earth, the water, even in the air we breathe. Magic is in the fire of a man's will. Understand?"

I jump at his hardened speech. Breathe in. Breathe out. My lids lower by half, as I squint at the mirror. Slowly, the shiny surface dims, replaced by a swirl of gray clouds. Shadows deepen while lighter fog clusters and takes shape. There! I see ... what are those ... trees? Yes, and hedges. Tall as the mirror itself, forming what appears to be an endless maze. Color bleeds through the black and gray scene. A stone footpath lies at my feet, disappearing into the maze running left to right. Blue leaks into the sky. I lean forward as the space in the center of the shrub before me rustles. The temperature drops. I breathe out a fine, white mist, but my eyes continue tracking the quivering leaves.

Something draws nearer. Twigs snap. Leaves shake more and more vigorously. I gulp my breath as the hedge parts, and two pale horns push from the maze like a birth. I stiffen, terrified of what's on the other side.

Does my father see? If so, he doesn't say anything, doesn't react in the least.

But I do. Fear ticks down my spine as the horns extend through the leaves followed by a broad forehead. Golden eyes glint in the darkness, hard as two unseeing buttons. Above us, a crow screams. I spring back, and the horned creature withdraws. In an instant, the hedge is gone. The maze is no more. Only a pair of reflections are left in view—mine and my father's.

"What did you see?" His tone is insistent, almost desperate.

I crane my neck. My father's stern glance beats down on me, harder than a strong wind, unforgiving as the desert sun. He knows I saw something, yet I doubt my senses, and when I do, truth withers on my tongue. I can't tell my practical, no-nonsense father that a goat with scary eyes came out of a bush and tried to get me. He'll hit me;

call me a stupid boy, or worse, he'll laugh.

Maybe there really is a horned demon hiding in the mirror, but my father will never believe it, so I panic. Play it safe. I lie. "Nothing?"

A muscle in his jaw jumps.

I squirm, toes bunching inside the ends of my tennis shoes. "I'm sorry. I tried, but—"

"Worthless," he says.

My chest depresses with the realization that I failed him again. "Father?"

No reply. His heels click on the hardwood floor as he exits, leaving me alone in his study. I face the mirror, wish, will, and try again and again, but my long wait is in vain.

The only one who looks back is me.

I wake with a violent twist, jerking a knot in my neck. As I rub the painful kink, my mind ruminates on my dream. I haven't thought of the lake house in years. The mention of it in my severance package probably provoked my nightmare. I'll find a realtor and get the house listed. The money will help, and I have no love for the place, that's for sure.

My bedside clock reads 3:17 a.m. I'm more wired than sleepy, so I walk to the window and stare at the lights of New York. There's no way to look at this scene without remembering my trip with Raven. We flew up for a fashion show and spent the first night sightseeing on the deck of the Empire State Building. She was so beautiful under the city-lit sky, dark hair flying in the breeze, talking about life and the possibilities ahead. The sight of her stole my breath. Still does. Every single time.

What are the possibilities now? She needs revenue—a lot of it—and the connections to reach her true potential, not to be shackled to a penniless, crippled, recluse with nothing left to offer.

I run a hand through my hair, pressure building in my chest like an overheating boiler. All my life, I've strived for two things: to become a fully functioning Artisan, and successfully run my father's company. Once Raven helped me understand the harm my Artisan legacy caused, I gave it up willingly. I let that part of me die and became the whole of the other—steward of the family business. Now that's gone, too. So, if I'm not an Artisan, and not a businessman, then who the hell am I?

Light flickers from the bathroom doorway. I don't remember leaving any lights on, but something's off and I decide to check. As strange as my childhood was, you'd think I'd have been afraid at night, but the opposite was true. I still need full dark to fall asleep.

When I peer into the bath, flame spurts from the electrical socket near the sink. The buzzing sound coming from behind the plaster doesn't bode well, and neither does the sudden pop and spark that scares the shit out of me. Adrenaline floods my system. I flip on the overhead light and grab the first thing my fingers touch. In this case, a hotel robe hanging off the hook on the back of the door. I smother the flame, but when I remove the fabric, blue sparks shoot from the outlet. Swearing, I press the material over the plate, waiting longer this time before checking. When the fire doesn't rekindle, my lungs depress with relief.

Between my nightmare and electrical problems, I feel a nasty migraine coming on, and I'm ready to get out of my luxury hotel suite. I lift the handset and dial 0 for the front desk with a smoky odor still in my nose. The mishap in the bathroom is a safety issue. Management will comp the bill if I complain, which works for me now that I'm poor and on a budget.

I laugh, but it sounds a bit unhinged, just like the rest of my life.

Chapter Six

Raven

*M*other holds my hand as we stroll along the path in Sales Hollow Park. "Raven, remember that the oak is your best friend, strong and faithful," she says. "Maple, pine, and ash are also our friends, but beware the hemlock, for he is cunning, and the alder cruel.

Though I'm a small child in this moment, I know my mother is long dead so this must be a dream. Her memory rose to comfort my restless sleep, yet my heart warns it's much more.

Dark hair falls in luxurious waves around Mother's shoulders as she kneels before me. "This is important, sweetheart. Beware Miss Willow. She will seem a friend and refuge at first, but do not trust her. She is selfish and unhappy, and will betray you if she can. In the end, you must bend them all to your will."

I nod with no understanding of her words.

"Remember what I've told you, Raven. It's important." Her eyes sparkle with intensity, yet her voice is kind and gentle.

I'm confused, but not afraid. "Yes, ma'am."

She smiles. "That's my good girl." The pupils in both her eyes grow bigger, black bleeds into the whites, spreading like ink over a page until the entire space is filled. "A storm is coming, baby. You will need the help of your friends in order to defeat the coming evil. My girl is brave and strong. You can overcome her if you don't lose heart."

Her? Who her? I focus on the woman who looks like my mother—the one with obsidian eyes. There's a millpond to our right. Prickles rise on the back of my neck, and down my arms. The scene mirrors the place where Desiree drowned last year. A sense of evil overwhelms me. The same darkness I felt when she tried to strangle me in Gideon's attic.

My gaze darts past my mother to the shadowed crevices and thick hedge between the trees. I'm searching for danger, trying to identify the threat. My heart beats like that of a little bird, thrumming to the point of arrest. The oppressive feeling grows nearer. It's almost upon me. Help. When I try to speak the words, none form. "Help me, Mother. Don't let her get me!"

Mother still kneels at my feet. Tiny, green tendrils, no wider than a piece of string, slither from the corners of her eyes. Another root sprouts from her nostril, more from her ears. The foot of a tender, new vine blindly feels its way across her shoulder, down her arm to her hand. They multiply and grow thicker, stretching every orifice to capacity. Crawling over her skin, the vines swell until Mother's face splits open. Her flesh tears and reknits, changing form.

She is the tree.

Her roots reach for me. I squeeze my eyes shut, bracing myself as the tentacles make first contact.

They tickle. My eyes pop open, but Mother is gone. Nothing remains but an ever thickening system of heavy vine coiling one over the other. Slowly, my legs are encased in soft leaves, my body, arms, and face. I giggle as I imagine myself a small pea hiding inside a pod. Butterflies live inside a cocoon before they hatch. Do they feel like I do—safe, warm, and protected inside a fortress of ivy? Strong as iron, smooth as velvet.

Sleep, my child.

"Yes, Mother," I whisper.

Chapter Seven

Cole

Lyon to London, then to Dallas, on to Savannah, if not for the first class seating that set me back seven grand, my legs would have permanent pretzel bends.

I lift the shade and stare out the plane window though there's nothing to see. My hands fist on my lap as I stretch again. Fatigue covers me like an itchy, woolen blanket. Instead of making me sleepy, I'm tense and restless.

Head crammed with scenarios for when I reach South Carolina, I practice my speech asking Maddox for help. Picture Raven in my mind over and over as I ask her how she's been; gauge her reaction to seeing me again. I've missed her, but does she feel the same? I used to be confident with the girls at school. Flirting was easy then, snogging at parties ... and the rest. Then, four years of my life were erased.

I rub my dry, tired eyes. Everything's changed. Raven means more to me, has done more for me, than I can ever repay. One day, I vow to show her my thanks.

Cole ...

Rosamond? How is this happening here, at thirty thousand feet? Maybe it doesn't matter.

Come to me, Cole ...

Somehow, I don't think I have a choice, though I hope this visit to Rosamond won't cause a first class scene that ends with me getting cuffed by the air marshal. The cabin spins. Seats, floor, windows, even the little, blue-haired lady sleeping in the seat next to me smears as I'm sucked into a timeless vacuum.

I brace for the weightlessness that's always present in The Void, but it doesn't happen. Rosamond glides toward me. Curiosity, compassion, lust, fear, countless emotions fill me as she draws near. Her hypnotic eyes lock with mine as she hovers before me in her gauzy white gown.

I can't imagine what this ethereal creature did to earn imprisonment. Not too long ago her circumstance was mine. Claustrophobia threatens to unravel me as I contemplate getting stuck in here again. No matter how much I'd like to help her, I can't go back.

Below her knees, there's nothing but air. She floats more than walks, the way I did when I was a prisoner here. Moonlight leaks though the small window in the stone tower, her hair shimmering in the soft glow. Silver eyes remain riveted on me. The hold is strong, as though I'm iron and she's magnetized.

She reaches for me, but halfway between us her hand stalls.

I make up the distance, my fingers gently wrapping her wrist. I expect to pass right though her ghostly form, yet my jaw drops as solid flesh stops my momentum. Her eyes widen at our contact. She's substantive, skin like cool silk. Below us, her feet materialize from nothing.

Rosamond's brow creases, confusion contorting her flawless features.

I withdraw my hand and her feet disappear. Lightening quick, she grips my hand and her legs form beneath her again. Dainty white feet stand firmly on the ground. Bare toes grip the floor for balance. The action seems so innocent and unaware, and completely adorable. She's whole and corporeal at my touch, but as soon as she releases me, everything below the knee disappears again.

"What's going on?" Rosamond asks.

Good question.

"Who are you, Cole? Why is this happening?"

I'd hoped she knew, and said as much. "How do you know my name? How did you find me?"

"I saw you." She glances over her shoulder at an ornate mirror on the wall. Two spots of color rise on her cheeks. "Through there, in the magician's looking glass."

Pan. The magician. Man. Monster. The one we feared above any other. Master and keeper of The Void's labyrinth.

She raises her hand and pauses, as if she wants to touch me and changed her mind. I wish she would change it again. "I used to see other places through it, other worlds. Your photograph hung on a wall across from my mirror for a time." She stares at the floor where her feet would be if she had any. "Pan's idea of a joke, I think, torturing me with a picture of a handsome boy. You were the symbol for a relationship I can never have."

However shallow, my mind replays the part where she calls me handsome. I don't know what to say. I'm afraid my voice will crack anyway, so I don't respond.

"Your photo was moved after a time. I was blind to you, and that left me lonelier than ever. The whole point, I guess. I see the outside world through there, but so does *he*. There's a network of mirrors connected to this one. He's always watching."

Icy cold and foreboding, a shudder runs though me at the thought of him spying on her or anyone else. Somewhere, the sound of water trickles over hard stone. I wonder, and not for the first time, what part of the labyrinth she's hidden in. "Rosamond, how do you reach me? How is it we're talking?"

Pale lashes fan her cheeks as she looks away. "I don't know."

She's been through so much, and still going through it, a mystery that needs solving. Her accent is American, possibly from the southern states, yet more formal than Rae's. Maybe she hasn't been here that long, but who took her picture?

She leans forward. "Can you get me out?"

Her question launches ten more in my head. They zing through gray matter like arrows, embedding themselves in a flurry of conflicting thoughts. "How long have you been a prisoner, Rosamond?"

"I ... a year, maybe more? I'm not sure."

Her gaze darts over my face, and I think she's waiting for me to respond, but what do I say? Releasing someone is complicated for more than one reason. If she's been here too long, she'll die outside these walls. Somehow, I don't think hearing that will help her anxiety level, so I say the only thing I can.

"I'm sorry you're here." Her little hands clasp like she'll pray. I have the strangest urge to gather her into my arms and hold her against me. The temptation's strong enough that I cross my arms and tamp the impulse down. With a baseball bat. "Try not to worry. I'll figure something out."

Pressure builds around us as the walls start to blur.

"Looks like times up."

Rosamond lifts her face and smiles. "So, I'll just wait here then?"

The fact she has enough fight left to joke about her situation loosens something in my throat. I cough as the room swirls. Her eyes soften with something like longing. I wonder how long it's been since she had someone to talk to, since anyone touched her?

"I'll try. I promise." The turret disintegrates. My head snaps back against the cushioned seat of the airplane. I can just make out the soft edges of platinum hair as she fades from view. The old woman in the seat next to me rematerializes in Rosamond's place. "I'll try."

Thank you, Cole.

Chapter Eight

Raven

I wake with Maggie's screech.

"Rae? Oh my lanta. What, in the name of photosynthesis *hell,* is going on with you?"

My eyes snap open. The first thing I see is my best friend's face mere inches from mine. A green, leafy veil partially obstructs my view, but she's too close, and surrounded by vines. When I twist, I can't move more than a few inches in any direction.

She's not the one encased in roots the width of my arm. I am. The smooth bark doesn't chafe, but the vines hold me closer than a botanical MRI machine. Panic dries my mouth. My muscles go rigid in a fit of claustrophobia, and I wonder if I'll have a heart attack and die right here and now.

"Mags," I whisper. "Help me." One minute, I'm having crazy dreams about my mother going all "Poison Ivy" on me, the next my nightmare morphs into reality.

Edgar yowls from my bedside. He paws at a leaf before touching the leather pad of his nose to mine. His whiskers tickle, but I can't move my arm to scratch his ear like I normally would.

He sits and cries again.

"I know, honey," Maggie says, soothing my unhappy cat.

"Um, little help?"

"Right, sorry." Tentatively, Maggie reaches out and strokes her fingers down the foliage attached to my shoulder. "I'm open to suggestions."

I wish I had one. "I had a nightmare, about my mother and a tree."

"And did this tree try and eat you?" The question sounds sarcastic, but the look on my friend's face is deadly serious. Her fingers curl around the nearest vine. She tugs, but it won't budge.

"Not exactly. It was trying to help, I think."

"Well, think again." She digs her hands between me and the sturdy roots, puts her foot on the mattress, and yanks. Noisy grunts underline the effort she's expending, but the plants won't move. A head toss sends her platinum bob swinging. "Seriously ... " She pants. "They're like freaking iron." Her voice hardens, losing some of the fear I heard earlier. Her eyes narrow. I know that look of stubborn determination. Without warning, she scrambles over top of me and the pile of roots.

Air rushes from my chest as I'm squeezed under her hands and knees. "What are you ... doing?" I groan. "What do you see?"

"The vines. This is so weird ..."

Which part?

"Okay, let's think this through. The vines obviously grew in through the window overnight, but I never heard a sound." As if to emphasize her thought process, she climbs down and faces me from a few feet away. "When I stand back and look at you from a distance, the vines are like a jail." Her head tilts. One hand rubs her jaw. "Actually, it looks like you're stuck inside a giant ribcage, eaten by a huge plant skeleton—"

"Mags!" I shudder. "So not helping."

"I have more, eco-burrito?"

"You used to be a nice person."

"You used to have a sense of humor." She stops and frowns.

"Sorry. I'm sorry! You know this crap stresses me out. Okay, we have to get you out before my parents get home. Mom will freak out and spray you with weed killer, or call the fire department."

"No she won't. We'll explain it." The idea sounds ridiculous, even to me.

"Have you met my mom?" Maggie's head snap clears the hair from her eyes. "Remember the time she told our neighbors she was growing Chlamydia under the mailbox. Chlamydia, Rae. Not the *Clematis* actually potted in the container. Everyone thinks our front lawn has a venereal disease."

"Okay, you may have a small point there." Initial panic subsiding, I still want out of jail. "Just help me, please."

She chews her thumbnail, and then says, "I could text Dane that we have an emergency, but he doesn't check his phone much at work." She squats to make eye contact. "Hey ... *should* I call the fire department?"

Confined by the ivy, my headshake is a complete fail. "We can't have this on the six o'clock news, Mags."

"Right. You're right." Maggie swipes a pair of sweatpants from the floor and pulls them on under her thin nightie. "My dad has an ax in the shed. That's what firemen use anyway. It'll have to do since we sold our 'Jaws of Life' bolt cutters in the last garage sale."

"Ha. Ha." She's just trying to keep things light, but my heart sinks. I don't know how my friend thinks she'll hack me out without chopping me to pieces, and oddly, that's not even my main concern. I called the plants my jail, but a cage shields too, right? Protects, provides safety.

Hurting the vines feels like a betrayal. It's stupid and illogical, but it's also strangely true. Withering leaves, roots hacked and dying, it all makes me queasy, and I find myself wishing I could save them.

Maggie leans over, hands clutching her knees. "Wait here. I'll be right back."

"Oh, funny." I glare at her through the leaves, but she's already jogging out the door. "You should do stand-up!" I yell, hoping she'll hear down the hall.

The longer Maggie takes getting the ax, the more uncomfortable I am with the plants' impending doom. No matter how irrational, I can't stand the thought of their destruction. A total reversal considering the claustrophobia I felt minutes ago. What's wrong with me?

My head pounds with quick and sudden pain. Nausea worsens. The ground shudders and floorboards creak. Bed legs scoot and stutter with the mini-quake. I should be terrified, yet I'm suffering more for the plants that will soon die.

Then suddenly, like a snake waking from a long sleep, the vines begin uncoiling from around my body. Edgar hisses. I hear the thud as he jumps to the floor. Claws scratching as he scurries away. Starting with the thinnest ends, the roots loosen, leaves retract. Inch by inch, the vines unwind from my limbs. Released from my bonds, I arch to see the plants scuttle over the sill, retreating out the open window.

"What. The. Hell?"

I turn as Maggie drops the ax. The metal head hits the floor with a clang. "Rae … ?"

"Shh, I know." Fearing any distraction will stop the migrating foliage from vacating our room, I plead with my eyes for her to keep still.

Leaves brush noisily against glass panes with the vines' exodus, the sound lessening as the stragglers slide out and away. Once they're gone, I roll to my knees and poke my head out of the window. Maggie joins me on the bed, and, side by side, we watch the last of the roots burrow into the ground of her parents' yard. The soil isn't disturbed. There are no holes, tunnels, or furrows to prove that what we just witnessed was real.

HO-LY CRAP.

"Raven?" Awe, fear, and disbelief leak though her tone, heightening the same feelings in me.

I stare at the dirt that swallowed the roots and feel a little like *Jack and the Beanstalk*, but in reverse. "They left when I told them to."

"What?"

"At least, I think they did. When you went for the ax, I felt sorry for them. I wished they would leave so they didn't have to die. And then they just … went."

Maggie pinches the bridge of her nose with her thumb and forefinger. Her exhale's long and dramatic before meeting my gaze. "You felt sorry for the killer weeds?" I nod. "Honey, did you call the plants here in the first place? Lord help me, what am I even saying?"

"I was dreaming about plants, so I guess it's possible." Somehow, I'm now convinced the invading plants meant me no harm. In my dream, the connection between us let me know they were there for my protection—but from what? I'm thinking like a crazy person. Plants aren't dogs. They don't come and go on command. Or spring to life, cage humans, and then slink away again.

"You could have been killed. Strangled. Why would you bring them here? Or better yet, *how*?"

"I don't know." We're both quiet, and then I add, "It's happening again, isn't it? The magic. Or I'm finally completely insane."

"This wasn't a nightmare, Rae. I saw it, too. If you're crazy, I'm right there with ya."

We stare out the window until my neck stiffens and my thighs go numb. Nothing happens. The roots don't return. No giant Venus flytrap comes calling. "I think I'll head over to Gideon's and hang out." I need to see him, feel his arms around me. Hear his smooth southern voice telling me we are going to be okay, and that we can have a life that is normal. If normal exists. "He'll be back this afternoon."

Her red hair stripe swishes with her nod. "Excellent notion, Rae, but I'm going, too."

I wasn't going to argue. No one stops Maggie once she's on a roll.

"If you think I'm going to sit here all day waiting for a *Little Shop of Horrors* rerun, you really are out of your mind."

Chapter Nine

Gideon

Another glance at my watch confirms Dane and Mags have been gone fifteen minutes. The same amount of time Raven's been staring out the dining room window. Not that I'm complaining. While she watches the oaks in the garden, I get to study her. After a while, though, I miss the sound of her voice.

"Rae?"

No answer. Not even a blink. She's growing more preoccupied, and I'm pretty sure she's hiding something.

The hypocrisy isn't lost on me, because I still haven't told her about the Maddox Industries takeover and resulting financial ruin. Nor did I mention that I caught an earlier flight home to meet with Jenny and my butler Jamis. My staff accepted the bad news with their typical stoic dignity. Regular fixtures in the Maddox household, the pair assured me they would stay on indefinitely, even if I couldn't pay them a dime. While Jenny cleared her throat and hurriedly left the room, Jamis—very uncharacteristically, I might add—seemed anxious to speak to me. We'd barely begun when Raven and Maggie surprised us at the front door and we had to postpone.

For now, Raven continues watching the yard. I follow the angular lines of her face and throat. Track her long, graceful fingers to their talented ends. I was supposed to have all the answers ... take care of *her*. I can't pretend that New York didn't happen, much as I try. If I ignore the wall rising between us, brick by brick, fear and doubt will divide us. The thought of losing her hurts like a kick in the teeth.

I have to tell her, and I will. Tomorrow.

My lungs slowly fill. Even breathing seems more difficult with all the stress I'm under, and these daily headaches don't help. I need time to sort everything out. Maybe Rae needs the same to work through whatever's bothering her.

"Where are you today, woman?"

Did I mention patience is not my best quality?

She shifts to face me. Her black hair dips over one shoulder. I drop my pen to the yellow legal pad below me on the mahogany table. She smiles. I fake one in return, eyes narrowing playfully with an unapologetic grin. A challenge for her to deny me what I need.

Her gaze drops. She blushes with no idea how the pretty color affects my heart rate. When she looks up, I crook my finger, urging her closer. I'm sick to death of thinking, and plotting, and planning my way out of the next disaster. Holding her makes me forget.

Gray eyes flash. She meets my gaze with a slow, tantalizing smile. As though a bolt of lightning hits my chest, a feeling of wanting pumps from my heart, electrifying my veins.

"We're working," she says. "You promised to behave."

I chuckle at that. "Does *behave* sound like a promise I'd make? You asked. I said nothing." I jerk my chin toward the window. "Besides, you're not working. You're daydreaming."

She glances to the trees and back. "No, I just ... took a break."

"Mm-hm. You realize you've already completed the designs for Raedoxx's spring line, pre-orders are off the charts. Leave your new ideas for the fall." She glances at the sketchpad on her knee, and my conscience pokes an accusing finger. The poor girl designs for a company with no financial backing, but we're not talking about that. Not yet. "Stop for a while. Be with me." I stand and lean over the table, fingers stretching toward her in a predatory manner.

"I can't believe I'm hearing this from you of all people." Her expression turns indignant, but her tone is playful. "The great and powerful Gideon Maddox, workaholic tycoon."

Was. Was a workaholic. The words cut, but it's not her fault. She can't know how her appraisal has changed.

Her gaze slides to the open books on my dining table. "Dane and Mags will be back from the kitchen any minute."

"No, they won't."

I'm right and she knows it. They're off somewhere making out. It doesn't take this long to grab a snack from Jenny. If she thought we wanted anything at all, she'd have been in here ten minutes ago with enough food to feed an army.

Slow and easy, I make my way to Raven's side of the table, as if she's a bird that's easily startled. "See what you've done to me? I'm actually the victim here. One woman cuts Samson's hair and saps his strength, another seduces Mark Antony, or launches a thousand ships and starts a war ... now, there's you."

The sound of her laugh warms me. "You stuck me in the evil woman category? How nice."

My smile feels crooked. "You're not evil." I lean in, gripping the armrests on either side of her chair and trapping her between my arms. "Not entirely."

"You think *I'm* trouble?" Her laugh is nervous and unsure this time. Good to know I still have that effect on her.

"Oh, I know you are." I reach for her wrist, my fingers skimming her flesh. The feeling is incredible, like satin under my palm. Gently, I lift her to a stand. When my arms encircle her waist, her little shiver fans the embers inside me, sending my pulse into overdrive. "I think you enjoy torturing me, just a little." Our proximity affects the room's temperature. Or mine.

"I'm not trying to." Her tone is serious. "We—"

"Shh, I know. I'm just messing with you." My fingers brush her chin. "I understand." And I do. She wants to wait. I respect that and her beliefs. Her teenage mother had an affair with an older guy, resulting in pregnancy before he abandoned them both. After losing so much, she needs security. Once again, I bury the knowledge that I can't offer that anymore. My arms tighten around her. "I'd like to kiss you now, Raven, if that's okay." I'm proving a point. The attempt is untried and clumsy but sincere.

Her body relaxes into mine and she lifts her mouth. "Definitely okay."

My lips capture hers in a soft, sensual taking. One arm flexes around her waist, while the other moves up her back, between her shoulder blades. The exotic, lotus scent of her hair intoxicates my senses. The person I was before wants to crush her beneath me, consume her, brand her with my love so she knows who she belongs to. But I don't. Because what I need more than to fulfill any selfish desire is her confidence—for her to feel safe and protected with me.

My hand slides to her neck. Fingers thread through the hair at her nape, curling until they're secured at the roots. I send my message of need and devotion through my touch, hoping it's clear.

When she parts her lips, my tongue sweeps her mouth gently probing, exploring. Her hands inch up my arms to my shoulders, finally clasping around my neck. I absorb the heat from her body, raising the temperature in mine.

Capturing her bottom lip between my teeth, I worry the tender flesh with gentle violence until I feel her body weaken. She whimpers as I pull away. "Say my name," I whisper against her neck. Her erratic pulse thrums beneath my lips, ramping my own heartbeat still higher.

"What?" The word comes out shaky, breathless.

"My name," I urge. "Say it." I pause, lowering my forehead

until it rests against hers. *Calm down, Maddox. I guess the beast isn't completely gone …*

"Gideon."

I raise my head. Energy builds inside me as I follow the curve of her lips with my eyes. Kissing Raven is unlike anything I've ever felt before—with anyone. Lately, though, it's different. If my mouth is made of gasoline, she's the match. I'm a hot, exposed wire, and her touch is water. As I cover her mouth again, heat pours from my throat. My lungs expand, burn. I'm on fire.

"What the heck is going on in here?"

Raven's hands find my chest. A hard push creates unwanted distance between us. My gaze darts between Maggie and Dane, who are standing in the doorway, and the fire blazing away in the middle of the dining room table.

Fire?

Sure enough, one of Raven's thick sketchpads is engulfed in blue flame. Smoke curling toward the ceiling.

I sweep Raven behind me with one hand, and snatch my jacket off the back of a chair. As fabric smothers the burning book, Dane tosses whatever liquid is in the pitcher he's holding over the small inferno.

The flames die. Smoke chugs a few gasping puffs before sputtering out. Everything's done in seconds, but …

"What the hell?" Dane asks.

Exactly.

I stare at the table, as though it's capable of explaining how a book spontaneously combusts. Scowl firmly in place, I pick through the scorched items on the table: pens, paper, a magazine, some junk mail. "There's nothing here to ignite, nothing electrical, no accelerant."

I've seen my fair share of magical happenings in this house, but I'd hoped breaking the curse meant an end to the supernatural.

Maggie's erratic glance darts from Dane to me. "It was a fluke, right? Please say I'm right. I can't take any more today." The words spill fast and urgent. The death grip she's got on a tray of cookies bleaches her knuckles white.

Dane pries the tray from her hands and places it on the oak credenza behind us.

"My poor sketchpad … all that work." Rae sneezes repeatedly. "Sorry. Soot up my nose."

Maggie stares at the charred remains. "Ohmigosh, I know, but how weird. Rae, don't you think this is getting scary?"

Her nervous chatter grates on my last nerve. No longer ignorant of ghostly specters, she and Dane were here the night my stepmother Desiree tried to strangle Raven with her undead hands.

Rae grabs my arm. "It's like the other night in your study … "

Her pained expression twists my gut, knowing how badly she needs peace. Paranormal activity seems the antithesis of all things peaceful, but the past year taught me that while a person's mind can deceive them, truth is constant. Reality can't be changed or manipulated just because you don't like it. When Raven finally broke through my denial, we acted together based on facts.

And the fact is this isn't our first unexplained fire.

"What happened in the study?" Dane is all hard angles with an even harder head. He doesn't trust me, and though Dane's with Maggie, he and Raven share an iron bond of friendship that I'm forced to acknowledge.

I don't take orders, I give them. But for Rae's sake, I ignore his demanding tone. "I kissed her."

"*So* not the part I meant," Rae says, a blush creeping over her skin.

Dane rolls his eyes, which I find both amusing and patronizing since he and Maggie rarely come up for air.

"We had a fire going in the fireplace. I just wanted one for fun, and for atmosphere."

I grin. "And s'mores."

"That, too," she concedes. "The room got super hot, and the fire went crazy. I didn't think any more about it until today."

Now might not be the best time to mention the mysterious burning light socket in my hotel room.

Dane studies the soggy, ruined sketchpad. His long dreads hang down his back in thick ropes. "Weren't you two at it again, just now?"

I bark out a laugh. "You think my kissing Raven starts fires?" She focuses on the toes of her boots, an act I find both sexy and sweet.

"Why not? You're the one with the voodoo, man."

My smile hardens.

Maggie slides a hand under Dane's arm. She's petite and fair next to his dark and obviously annoyed body.

Rae sends me a pleading glance, and I relax my shoulders. There's a point at which the beast inside may lose patience, but not today.

"Excuse me, sir." Jamis appears in the doorway behind Dane and Mags. My employee is hunched, bald, covered in liver spots, and about a hundred and fifty years old, but there's no one more loyal to our family. "There's a gentleman here to see you."

"Not a good time. As you can see, we've had an accident. Will you ask Jenny to step in please?"

"Yes, sir. Of course, but … " The guy has so much white hair sticking out of his nose, he looks like he's sneezed a scrub brush. "If you'll forgive my insistence, I think you'll want to see this visitor."

Exasperated, I pause. No doubt my impatience is clear in my heavy exhalation. "Oh? And why is that?"

"Because the gentleman is Master Cole Wynter, *sir*."

Chapter Ten

Cole

I freely admit I'm not the bravest guy ever. Walking up to Gideon's house earlier today produced a coughing fit, dry heaves, and finally my lunch. There's some small satisfaction in that, I guess—defiling Gideon's manicured bushes with my vomit. While the act of returning to the place of my imprisonment makes me physically ill, the thought of returning to France without answers is unthinkable.

Nerves scramble over my skin like tiny spiders as I wait for Maddox in his imposing library. The room is unchanged. The smell of age, and dust, and pipe tobacco permeates leather book covers and antique rugs. Light streams in through the window at my right. It's early summer and bright, but the weather does nothing to ease the chill in my veins. I'm here as a flesh and blood human this time, yet the Déjà vu is even weirder than I'd anticipated. That's saying something, since I've become quite a coinsurer of weird.

A grandfather clock in the corner of the room marks the time. Amplified ticking drills a headache into the base of my skull. Maddox's decrepit butler Jamis only left ten minutes ago, but it seems an eternity.

Multiple footsteps echo down the hall and my stomach cramps. I'm waiting for Raven, but it's Gideon who enters first. His blue and green eyes focus on me the way a gambler watches another man's cards. He steps aside allowing a tall black guy and tiny blond girl to saunter in. I remember these two. Dane and Maggie, friends of Raven's who helped me escape The Void last year. Taking seats in the wingbacks across from me, they stare as well.

Cozy.

I nod to the room in general. Dust motes flit behind my host as he moves across the room to the heavy walnut desk. He leans lightly on his ornate walking stick to hide his limp. Springs creak as he settles into a brown leather chair. The lion head on his cane snarls at me over the edge of his desk. "Why are you here?"

No hello. No welcome, or greeting, or pleasantries. I expected as much. Dane's hard gaze rivals Gideon's, but Maggie grins as though I'm today's guest of honor.

When I unfist my hands, my knee bounces instead. I focus on Rosamond. I'm here to help her, and if I can, save myself as well. All I want is freedom, real freedom this time. Well, and maybe to leave with Raven.

And then she's here. A chain on her boot jingles with each step. My eyes follow her long legs until they disappear under a leather miniskirt; linger over her red mouth and spooky gray eyes. Seeing her again blows the doubt from my mind, breathes fresh air into my lungs. I'm out of my seat before I know what I'm doing. Her hand is small inside mine. "Raven." The name is healing, her gentle touch medicinal.

She throws her arms around my neck and hugs me tight. "I'm so glad to see you."

Whoa, me too. "Hello, duck."

Our embrace is awkward, but the clumsiness is all on my end. I curse my rusty skills as I pat her back. The motion feels wrong, like something you'd do with your sister. *Damn it.*

She smells like flowers and rain. Clean, like a baptism, or a new beginning. I feel Gideon's eyes boring into my back and resist the impulse to flip him off. Raven should have the choice of who she dates—more choice than Maddox, anyway. This girl isn't another possession to flaunt. She's smart, and kind, and generous. She deserves the moon, and I doubt Maddox cares.

I hug her a few seconds too long, mostly because I'm hoping it will piss him off. When I release her, instead of sitting near me, as I'd hoped, she inches her pretty derriere over the edge of Gideon's desk.

"What brings you here, Cole?" The guy's nostrils flare as though he'd like to break my face. I imagine he would, too, if not for Raven's influence.

I retake my seat, rubbing my hands down the legs of my jeans. I assume it's okay to talk in front of the others. If he's got no objection to his friends hearing about our collective oddities, I shouldn't either. Maybe they can help. "I've got a problem." My gaze darts around the room. "Actually, I wonder if *we* don't have a problem. And I need your help."

"Something that couldn't be handled with a phone call, I'm guessing?" Gideon takes a large, gold coin from his pocket and rolls the piece through his fingers. A habit I've seen him perform many times.

For the sake of the lost girl haunting me, I hold my ground. "Not a chance, mate."

Raven leans forward, interrupting our stare-down. "What's going on?"

The words "you won't believe me" die in my mouth. If anyone will understand, it's this crew. "First, I've been experiencing … it's hard to explain. There's new energy, a strange force that's been building inside me for weeks until I feel ready to explode."

Dane's head angles with his snort. "You need a girl, dude."

Maggie punches his arm.

Neck stiffening, I refrain from glancing at Raven. "That's

not what I need." A deep breath steadies me. "My hearing is unnaturally enhanced. I feel everything more distinctly. On the way here … " I fall mute, afraid to voice my worst fears—that the magic of this house followed me home.

"Maybe its stress," Maggie offers. "Adrenaline overload. That's a thing, right?"

Dane rubs her arm. "Definitely a thing, baby." He plants a soft kiss on her mouth.

Really?

Gideon ignores them, and for once, I'm in complete agreement. "And second?"

"Second, there is someone else in The Void … Rosamond Bryer. She's been visiting me in visions."

Dane straightens. "Say what?"

At the same time, Raven leans forward. "What's a void?"

I'm not sure who to address. "The Void is what I call the in-between place where I was banished. The place inside the camera, behind the photos, hell I don't know where it is." I swipe a hand through my fringe, pushing it from my eyes. "I can't remember if I made it up or if that's the real name. After a while, we all called it that."

"Who are *we all*?" Dane asks.

"The others. The people the Artisans imprisoned. Until they were released and went up in smoke, that is."

Gideon's gaze drops, and he repositions in his chair. A few months ago, he discovered the magic salts used for developing the film in the ancient camera were also the key to breaking the curse. At Raven's urging, he sprinkled the bodies stored in the cellar with the substance, but the years lost in The Void were cumulative upon their release. People were swallowed in hot blue fire as the missing decades came rushing back to consume them.

"Everyone died but me," I continue.

Raven's shudder is visible. I want to hold her, but it's Gideon who captures her hand. His gaze lifts. "Who's left in The Void, Cole? We released everyone with a coffin."

I'm still watching their fingers thread together—it's impossible to tell where one ends and the other begins, and I force my gaze away. "That's just it. She wasn't with us. I've never seen her before, and the curse bound us all to either The Void's labyrinth or the Maddox property as far as I knew." That's not entirely true. Only Desiree, Gideon's deranged stepmother, dared to cross the boundary into the human world. Though she's dead now, too.

"Let me get this straight." Maggie's bob swings across her cheek, more tassel than hair. "A girl shows up in your dreams and you want us to ... what exactly?"

Isn't it obvious? "Get her out. Help her the way you helped me."

"Impossible," Gideon says.

My eyes narrow. "Why?"

"I'm sorry for her." He glances to Raven. "I really am, but it's too dangerous. Even if we wanted to, the salts are gone, and—"

"Make more," I say. "Your father left you the recipe in the armoire." There's little I don't know about the mansion. After all, I spent years haunting this place.

"It's not that simple. How much do you know about her, Cole? She might incinerate upon release, and we don't have her coffin, or her body. You said yourself she isn't on the grounds anywhere, so where is she? Freeing you was a lucky guess, do you understand? A one in a million chance."

Raven taps her chin, eyes glittering with what might be a dozen unanswered questions. "We need more information."

"No!" Dane and Gideon echo.

"Hey." Maggie leans across the rug and pokes my knee. "If you live in France, why do you have an English accent?"

"Pardon?" What my accent and family origins have to do with rescuing Rosamond from The Void, I have no clue, but I answer just the same. "I was born in England. My family moved when I was eleven."

"Brothers and sisters?"

"Only child."

"Parents?"

"Away on a business tour." I lob my answers back as though we're matched at Wimbledon.

"Girlfriend?"

"No!" My face heats at my explosive response, but I can't believe little Ms. Nosey Parker is asking me about my love life right now. What's worse is admitting what a loser I am in front of the girl I most want to impress.

I hate Maggie! Or at least, the pitying look she wears while inspecting my face. Then, as if my silence suddenly explains everything, she stands. "All right, then. We can't just leave Rosamond in there, can we?" *I love Maggie!* I want to applaud as she exits her seat and steps to Dane's chair. "No one should be alone like that," she says, settling in his lap.

I guess she means Rosamond, but she's looking at me.

Solitude is a common theme among the people in this room. In my mind's eye, the lonely, silver girl from The Void rematerializes. I can see her mournful eyes, her thin, pale shoulders as she turns toward me. The air is dank. Her prison smells like water and peat. Nothing but cold, damp stone and broken dreams.

Thoughts of her forever cursed make me ill all over again. "Someone has to help her." I stand and face Gideon.

"No," he says. "I won't risk … " His gaze cuts to Raven. "No."

"For once, listen to me."

He lifts his head, expression unyielding as ever.

"What I did to you was wrong. I deserved the punishment your father gave me, but I'm not the guy I was, and neither are you. There's more to The Void than you know. Darkness lives there, monsters more lethal than Desiree, crueler than our fathers. I can't damn anyone to that hell. If you truly understood, neither would you."

He pauses, taps the gold coin on his desktop. "I will provide supplies and whatever information I can to help you get started, but no more than that." The words fall hard, resounding like a judge's gavel. Final. Resolute. He eases back into his seat. Raven's lips part as if she'll say something but doesn't. "Come here, Rae." Silent as her cat, she slides off the desk and into his lap.

They murmur together. Does she argue or agree? His arms wrap her like two bands of iron, and I don't blame him a bit. Maddox isn't stupid. He knows the risk involved in helping me. And if he had a clue what I'm really asking for, he'd throw me out and lock his woman safely away.

Which brings me to my next confusing question: why put the girl I care about most in danger for one I don't even know? Yet, God forgive me, I would. Rosamond and I are connected by experience and something deeper. I've been where she is, been *her*.

Cole ...

My fists tighten. Hang on, Rose. I'm coming for you.

When I first arrived in South Carolina, I hailed a cab and came straight away to the mansion. I assumed Gideon would banish my arse to the nearest hotel. Instead, he asked if I'd be comfortable staying here. In his home. What the what?

Since that time, I'd been shown to an immaculately clean guest room and taken a hot shower. The jeans I wore on the plane are clean, but I changed into a comfortable, faded blue T-shirt. The plump and ever-friendly Jenny brought a tray to my room, stuffing me with chicken salad sandwiches, coleslaw, brownies, and enough lemonade to drown a man. Meanwhile, Jamis delivered three cardboard boxes filled with leather-bound journals, old ledgers, and dog-eared letters for me to sort through.

The considerations probably came from Rae. Even so, I'm shocked Maddox agreed. Of course, it's fairly impossible to say no to Raven.

Books and paperwork lay sprawled all over the king-sized bed where I sit. The records Raven found in the Maddox's attic last year document decades of Artisan activity. Gideon's long and distinguished lineage of county judges handed out harsh sentences like sweets. The answer to Rose's freedom must be in here somewhere. My newfound goal makes me feel more alive, more hopeful than I've been in months.

The enthusiasm I have delving into the ancient texts surprises even me. I've made rescuing a girl I don't know from a turret I've never seen my top priority.

Words, names, and dates blur against cream pages as I scan the lists in the journals. My finger hunts for the name Rosamond, or Bryer, and while I find neither, I don't stop looking. With all we've been through, and all that may still be asked of us in order to free someone else; I have to believe in a good outcome.

Outside my window, a squirrel and bird argue territorial rights for the tree limb they occupy. My annoyance builds, but a sudden gust of wind sends them both packing.

Hours later, words jumble as I read the same sentence a third time. The excitement I felt at the beginning of my task wanes with the fading sun. Shadows gather like restless spirits in the darkening corners of the room.

My headache returns to punish the base of my skull, while my eyes are dry and strained with prolonged concentration. Walls spin and smudge as I'm caught up in the coming vision. The heavy oak door of the guest room melds with the bureau, absorbing the ceiling and the floor until my room is gone and replaced with one of damp stone that's becoming all too familiar.

"Hey, Rosamond."

Cole? Oh, you're here! Her voice is high and breathy. Her eyes shine as she clasps her little hands together.

Guilt stabs me in the throat. I understand about loneliness, but I don't control how often I visit her. "Rose, how did—" My mouth stops working, and my face burns. Up to now, I've kept her nickname to myself, but her delighted smile suggests she doesn't mind a bit.

"Yes, Cole?"

I swallow and start again. "Do you … bring me here, to The Void?" I almost use the word summon, but catch it in time.

"No. But I can sense when you're close." Her gaze drops. "Just as well. If I could wish you here, I might abuse the privilege and keep you with me."

Keep me? I cough into my fist to hide my shock.

An epic fail because her hand shoots up. "Hey, I'm kidding! It was a joke." A sigh. "I'm not very good at this, am I?"

"Good at what?"

"Flirting." Waves of platinum hair ripple over her pale shoulders with her head shake. "I would never, ever, force you to stay. I wouldn't know how even if I wanted to. And I *don't* want to. Not for real."

"It's all right," I say, trying to erase the awkward moment.

"Do you want to sit down for a while? We could talk." She floats over to a tiny end table and gestures to the only chair. "I have a chess board, but I'm pretty bad." She laughs. "Whoops, I guess I shouldn't admit that before we start, should I?"

Her chatter is nervous and endearing. She tries so hard. Too hard. So, I don't mention my loathing for the game. Or how my father insisted that I learn, and not just play but excel, compete on a team, as he had. "Let's talk."

"Okay, yes, good." Rose wanders to the bed and, settling against the backboard, faces the empty chair like she expects me to sit there.

Instead, I take a seat across from her at the other end of the bed. The straw mattress gives under my elbows as I lie back. I stretch my legs out, boot heels scuffing the flagstone flooring as I cross my ankles.

A lengthy pause electrifies the space between us. I wonder who she is, how she came to be here, and about the spell she's casting over me.

Rose leans forward, delicate hands clasped in her lap. A blink hides her silver eyes for a moment before recapturing my gaze. "Touch me, Cole."

"What?" Shite. My voice actually cracks. I panic imagining the supremely uncool sweat rings that are surely spreading under my arms. I'm looking for a rock to crawl under when she lifts a hand to mine. On contact, her weight presses the blankets beneath her body. Her legs and small white feet materialize.

Gravity. Of course, she touched me to feel like her old self again. I swallow my bruised pride and squeeze her hand.

Her smile is shy and unsure. "Thank you, Cole. I know I'm asking a lot, but if there is a way in for you, there must be a way out for us.

Us?

"I appreciate everything you're doing. Maybe if you—"

The room jolts and pivots as sudden and violent as a carnival ride. Like before, the walls run together. I can just make out her blond hair flashing in my peripheral vision every so often as the whirling room brings her image round again.

Soon, Cole ... I know you'll find a way.

Oxygen expands my lungs to bursting and then exits in a rush as the walls condense around me. My body is torn from the room. I'm blown through the window, away from her world, and back into mine.

Chapter Eleven

Raven

Gideon's arms slide around my waist as I stand at the kitchen sink with my snack. I'm trying to work up the courage to tell him what happened in my room this morning. All day I've avoided delivering the news that may derail our careful plans for fall semester.

Warm breath lingers on the back of my head sending delicious chills though my body. His fingers gently brush the skin on my stomach beneath my blouse, and I fight the urge to turn and leap into his arms. The guy emits more dangerous energy than a leaky power plant. Still, I hold back.

I was the one who wanted to go slowly. Like, first gear slow. Maybe just idle. Call me old fashioned, but I always dreamed that my first time sleeping with a guy would be with my husband on our honeymoon. I still want that, and him, but I just turned eighteen.

The muscles under his golden skin ripple as they tighten around me. How does he make me feel safe and nervous at the same time? His nose parts the hair above my ear. Steady breaths, finally drive me to place my cookie on the counter and face him. My hands slide around his neck, fingers playing with the silky curls at his nape. I love the spicy scent of black licorice that's distinctly his.

He lowers his head, nose rubbing mine before he lets his lips drift over my mouth. Whisper soft, his hesitant touch is an excruciating tease. Always, there's curiosity and the promise of more to come.

My fingers untangle at his neck and drop to the bulge in his biceps. I can't help enjoying the way they bunch when he holds me. My legs lose strength, knees weaken. There's every possibility the boy will kiss me into unconsciousness. Can that happen? He must know because he holds me so close I hardly have the air to speak.

"So, how 'bout them Panthers?" My sarcasm's an attempt to diffuse the sexual tension between us.

He chuckles as I wriggle free of his grasp and reface the sink. He knows exactly what I'm doing but allows it.

Focus on your sugar craving, Raven. The whole room smells of butter, and chocolate, and peanut butter goodness. Lifting a cookie over my shoulder, I ask, "Want a bite?"

Ignoring my offer, his teeth graze the bare skin of my shoulder, and I gently bump him with my elbow. "Bite of *cookie.*"

"You're all I want." His feet shift. "Hurry up and eat those, so I can kiss you. I'm losing patience."

I smile. Did he ever have any? Too lazy to get a plate, I stick two more cookies on a paper towel planning to eat them over the sink. If Jenny saw me, she'd fuss and insist on china and a linen napkin.

The treat is halfway to my mouth when I glance through the window and spy Cole outside on the lawn—except, he wasn't there a second ago. He *appeared.* As in, out of thin air appeared.

I drop the cookie in the sink. "What in blue blazes?"

Cole tries to stand and falls. Not a second passes and he vanishes, materializing again near the large maple tree clear across the yard.

"Come on!" I fling my napkin and bolt for the door. Without a word, Gideon follows me outside. I love how he doesn't ask what's wrong. In this house, anything from homicidal poltergeists to random fires could be the culprit, and maybe he's beginning to trust my judgment.

My feet pound the earth as I race toward Cole's prone body in the grass. To my rear, Gideon's uneven gait keeps pace. The leg damaged in a fight with childhood cancer hardly slows him.

I drop to my knees beside Cole, terrified he's stroking out in the heat. "Hey, can you hear me?" One careful nudge with my palm to his shoulder. Two. Three. Panic takes over and I'm shaking him until his teeth rattle. "Wake up!"

"Easy, tiger," Gideon says, easing me aside to get a better look before placing two fingers against Cole's neck.

"Do you know what you're doing?" I ask.

"Probably not."

I watch as my boyfriend checks Cole's airway, presses an ear to his chest, lifts each closed eyelid to stare at his giant pupils. Gideon's expression stays serious and focused while he does what he does until I can't take the silence anymore.

"What's wrong with him?"

Gideon straightens. "Nothing. Not that I can see. He just ... passed out."

"Well, that's not normal. I mean, there must be a reason."

Cole seizes violently, then he's gone again, his whole body vanishing.

Gideon jumps a foot. "The hell?"

We glance across the lawn and find Cole's body sprawled on the grass by the back door.

"Just a wild guess here, but I'm going to assume *that's* your reason. Whatever *that* is." It takes less than a heartbeat for Gideon's careful reserve to slip back into place.

I confess I don't have his discipline. Nervous energy courses through my veins. My head aches, and I'm strangely lightheaded. The ground rumbles beneath us sending pings of cold fear skipping down my spine.

"There, do you feel that?" I ask. "The ground shaking?"

"Yes." His eyes narrow, I think suspicion flickers behind

them, but I'm not sure.

Drat. "I was hoping it was my imagination."

When the tremors stop, my feet scramble for purchase on the dry grass.

Steady fingers wrap my wrist before I shoot off toward Cole. "Wait. It might not be safe."

I haven't been safe since my mother died, but I don't point that out right now. My gaze focuses on Gideon's amazing eyes. One blue. One green. The sight calms me, if slightly.

Sudden wind blows up, weird since it was still and ninety degrees a minute ago. The powerful gusts nearly bowl us over. I push the hair from my face and yell, "Can you bring Cole into the house? We have to figure out what's going on."

Despite the crazy winds, Gideon rises with the graceful ease I'm accustomed to. He tucks a hand beneath my arm and helps me to my feet.

"Hang on a sec!" Cole's thin, but tall and solid—enough to be a handful in this gale. I leave the boys, run in through the back door and holler for Dane.

"What's wrong?" His answer comes fast enough to tell me he wasn't far.

"Did you see?"

"See what?" Maggie asks, bouncing into the kitchen from the butler's pantry where they were probably making out again.

If only Gideon and I could be so carefree. I wonder if life will ever slow enough for us to have a simple relationship.

I point toward the backdoor. "Can you help us with Cole first? We'll go from there."

Positioned on the sofa in the study, Cole lies pale and still as a corpse. I flash back to the cellar where his spellbound body lay in a straw-lined casket next to two dozen others. It's not a nice memory.

As Mags enters with a basin of water, I quickly fill her and Dane in on Cole's disappearing act outside. Gideon sits in a chair nearby and watches the sky through the window. He adds nothing to my story, only rolls the old coin his father gave him between his fingers.

Maggie places the bowl on the end table at the head of the couch, and hands me the washcloth. She settles herself on the floor in between Dane's outstretched legs, while I apply a damp cloth to Cole's forehead.

We're waiting for Doctor Dave, Gideon's eccentric, private physician who's paid well to make house calls, treat bizarre injuries, and ask no questions.

"Do you think it's the curse from before?" Dane asks, nodding toward Cole. "Or is this something else?"

"Dane," Maggie hisses. "Don't ask things like that. You'll scare everybody."

Like disappearing bodies, rouge plants, and fires won't?

"Oh come on. This place was jacked up long before Wynter got here. I used to think horror movies were hilarious before I knew the shit was real." He palms Maggie's cheek. "I don't want you around it anymore."

"You talk like it's a disease I can catch."

"I'm not sure it isn't. Seriously, I've thought about this a lot lately, and I think we need to be careful. Now, I don't know that I believe everything Rae does about God or heaven and hell, but I *know* the things we do follow us. Good and bad pieces of the past stick to us and affect the future."

I've never heard Dane get so philosophical, but I see what he's getting at. Cole's choices, Ben's, mine, Gideon's, they've all had consequences—and Dane watched it unfold. His father beat him pretty often before he moved to the garage apartment offered at

Maggie's aunt's house. He's had no one of his own until a few months ago when Maggie realized she'd been in love with him all along. He won't risk her.

Maggie plays with the collar of his shirt. "Don't you think—?"

"No," Gideon says. "I agree with him." He looks pointedly at Dane. "You're not wrong."

Dane nods like a whole lot more just passed between them in the guy-non-speak we girls don't understand.

"About … ?" Maggie asks.

"Protecting the people he cares about." Gideon rubs the dark gold stubble on his jaw, his gaze drawn back to the world outside the window. His savage expression makes my stomach flutter. I'm ridiculous, but I never get tired of watching him, or fail to notice how spectacular he is doing the simplest things.

"I woke up the other night with a memory I haven't thought about in years, and it's been haunting me ever since." His fingers stop moving, and the gold coin disappears into his palm. "Simply put, Artisans are guardians of a magical power handed down through generations. Though my father taught me some about the Artisan way of life, Desiree killed him long before he finished. There's little written down, but I knew a few details: the importance of secrecy, and I remember the idea of commerce attached to his explanation of magic, something about cost and checks and balances. He used to say magic is everywhere, but the world can't see it. And it doesn't die." Gideon faces us. "Actually, his words were, magic *never* dies."

Dane lifts his chin from the top of Maggie's head. "So, when a magical curse is broken … "

" … Where does the magic go?" I finish.

"The plants!" Maggie says. "Raven, did you tell him about—"

Cole's timely groan saves me from the explanation I've dreaded all day. His lids crack open and he lifts a shaky hand, examining his fingers as though they're brand new. "What happened?"

I remove the soggy cloth from his head. "We were hoping you could tell us." Though I don't look up, I *feel* Gideon staring a hole through me. Of course he'll want to know why it's taken me all day to bring up the plants. I wish the reason was more interesting than plain old denial.

Cole's eyebrows crunch together. "I was in my room reading through an old diary. I must have fallen asleep when Rosamond broke through again. One minute we were talking, and the next, I'm caught inside a bloody hurricane. I can't explain, but it was a little like flying."

"We found you out on the lawn. You were there and just like that," I snap my fingers, "you were gone and reappeared twenty feet away."

His eyes widen. "You're barking. I didn't—"

"We aren't. And you did." Gideon palms the lion head of his cane. "The question isn't *if*. It's why?"

Mounting tension ramps my pulse. Fires, rogue plants, Cole's arrival along with the mysterious girl … it's obviously connected, I just don't know how.

Gideon's gaze meets mine. His head shakes, no more than a hairsbreadth, and I get that he wants to talk in private.

"I need to get up." Cole's shoulders lift, but my body blocks his path. "Raven, you don't understand. Rose told me things about Pan, the magician who rules The Void, and the mirrors he's watching us through."

Hair prickles on the back of my neck.

"Let me up." Cole pushes past, swinging his feet around me to the floor. "The answer could be in the journals." His face is drawn, but the resolve in his dark blue eyes is undeniable.

Gideon's bloodless knuckles grip the lion head of his cane, and he stands. "I'll have the books brought to the dining room. We'll spread everything out and hunt together."

Hunt. Interesting word choice.

Determination sharpens his features as he strides toward me. "Rae and I will be there in a minute, right after we chat."

Chapter Twelve

Gideon

Raven avoids my gaze choosing instead to employ the nervous habit of plucking at a hangnail.

I lower to the seat beside her, enclosing both her hands inside my larger palm. She stills. I swear I feel her pulse slow down, but that's impossible, isn't it? Heavy lashes fan her smooth cheek. Silence becomes a living, breathing thing between us.

"Will you look at me?"

Eyes, gray as a summer storm, search my face for answers I'd rather not give. Our breath mixes, heartbeats align. She pulls a hand free and runs her fingertips over my mouth. I kiss the tips before pushing my cheek into her palm.

"It's all going to change again, isn't it?"

"Yes." I say truthfully, and consider breaking up with her. Letting go might be the right thing to do. My life endangers hers, and it's been a hell of a long time since I did anything unselfish.

"What's happening to us?"

I'm not ready for that conversation yet. Taking a lock of her hair, I rub the silky strands between my fingers. My stomach knots knowing it's a privilege I may not have much longer.

Neither of us wants to reopen the newly formed scab of hope we had on life, so I don't tell her that I suspect we're only beginning another chapter of supernatural horrors. I also don't say that I've never loved anyone the way I love her. That I would die to protect her, or that I would marry her tomorrow if I could. We had no financial constraints to keep us apart, but that's not true anymore. So I keep my mouth shut, because these are things you can't tell the girl you're planning to leave.

Since my hypocrisy only goes so far, I'm not angry that she's keeping secrets. "What happened this morning?"

Raven's gaze cuts to the window. "Remember I told you about the breathing tree in Maggie's backyard? You said that I'd probably fallen asleep or imagined it."

I nod, fear an invisible fist in my gut.

"I didn't."

"Why?" I trace the delicate lines in her palm. Each crease is supposed to mean something, but I don't know what. I do it mainly to keep sane while I listen.

"Last night, I dreamt my mother was talking to me in the park. Warning me actually, about good trees, and bad trees, and I can't remember what all. Then these vines started growing out of her body, and when I woke up … *voila*, real plants." She slides her hand from mine. "Gideon, this is going to sound insane, but Maggie thinks I called them, and I think she's right."

Wait … "What?" I feel my expression hardening. "I don't understand."

"I mean I woke up literally covered in these huge, thick vines that encased me like a mummy. Poor Edgar went ballistic trying to get me out. Maggie, too. I don't know how I did it, but I'm pretty sure I wished them there. And then it got weirder."

How the hell can this get any weirder?

Her gaze flits everywhere but my face.

"Because … " I prompt. My fingers wrap hers, both to stop her trembling and keep me grounded.

"*Because*, when Maggie went for an ax, I felt sick that the plants would die when they were only trying to help. I wished they would save themselves, and Gideon, they did! Wound out the window as easily as rolling up your everyday garden hose."

On instinct, I cup her cheek. Her belief in me, in us, is so solid, right or wrong; I question my ability to leave.

"The magic is still here," she says, finally pulling away. "Maybe it's different, but it's alive."

A glass-shattering scream sends Raven bolting into my arms. The cry came from the dining room down the hall. In seconds I'm up, and with Raven safely behind me, we're racing out the door.

Wind roars as loud as any locomotive.

Another scream. Rae's fingers are a vice on my hand as we run up the long hallway. Ahead, closed double doors rattle on their hinges. White light shines through every gap around the dark oak frames.

It takes all my strength to force the doors open. Once I do, wind blasts the hair from my face. Sheer drapes snap and blow around closed windows as though a hurricane were unleashed, yet outside the leaves on the trees are calm and still.

Wall sconce lights flicker. Dane holds a hysterical Maggie near the fireplace, while Cole sits in a chair at the far end of the ten-foot table. Vibrating.

"This way!" Rae's panicked shout eclipses mine. When she steps toward Mags, I fist her flimsy blouse and draw her back.

Dane meets my gaze, but Cole grabs our attention as his choppy, broken movements increase in speed. Something makes my old schoolmate's body jerk wildly. His image blinks on and off again, as grainy as bad TV reception. And then he's gone, reappearing two chairs away.

He's standing by the window, then the doorway, on top of the table, under a chair, knocking it over. Now he's nearly on top of Dane and Mags. I can't keep up. Both hands cover his ears. His chest pumps up and down as though he's hyperventilating. And he's screaming.

Doors on the buffet slam open and shut. A vase blows off the mantle, smashing on the glossy wood floor. Glass shards fly through the air as jagged missiles.

"Bloody hell, make it stop!" Cole bends at the waist, arms wrapping his torso as though that will keep his quaking body from coming apart. He looks across the room and just that fast, he's there.

This is more than being tossed around by a storm. Cole's completely vanishing and reappearing in other places. Raven believed she *called* the vines. That she wished them into being. Could Cole be doing the same without knowing it?

"Calm down!" My words die in the gale. Wind rocks the chandelier overhead. Another chair topples, blowing across the floor and into a window with a crash. "You're doing it yourself!"

"I'm what?" Cole vanishes only to appear halfway up a paneled wall. His body falls to the floor in a heap of arms and legs.

Driving against the wind, I deliver Raven into Dane's arms alongside Maggie. My head throbs, chest squeezes too tightly as I pivot back and forth, tracking the ever moving Cole. I sound like a lunatic, but I'm determined to try Raven's theory. "Try to relax!"

"Sod off," Cole shouts, before disappearing again. He pops up behind me, nearly knocking me down. I whirl, grabbing both of his arms. "Tell the wind to stop."

"Are you mad?"

"Take deep breaths," Rae volunteers. "It helps."

That's my girl.

The doors swing open behind us as my employees enter. Jenny shrieks as she's flung against a wall, her enormous bust bouncing on impact.

Jamis totters like a drunkard in the swirling gusts. "What shall I do, sir?"

"Help me hold him still!"

Jamis digs his ancient, claw-like fingers into Cole's shoulders.

His body rattles beneath our hands, energy rolling off in constant waves. My chest grows uncomfortably warm, then hot in response, as though I'm absorbing his energy. A powerful current zings down the veins in my arms to my fingertips, fans through my legs burning the soles of my feet. "I think it's you, man. You're controlling the wind!" A sudden gust nearly bowls us over.

Or not controlling it.

"Shite!" Cole's gone again, popping up a few feet away. His back is hunched, head hanging below his shoulders with his palms pressed flat on the floor.

The chandelier swings so hard, it hits the ceiling. Crystal shatters to swirling white dust. Snow in a snow globe blizzard. As the chain snaps, my arms rise just in time to shield my face. What's left of a hundred-year-old light fixture cracks the top of my dining table and rolls to the floor.

Cole has digressed to the fetal position, his lips moving continuously. By degrees, the lights stop flashing, and the wind slows until the room's curtains hang beside blown-out windows in limp tatters. One has caught fire.

Abandoning the girls, Dane bolts across the room, tears the sheer from the rod, and stamps the fire out.

Cole rolls on his back with a groan. "Am I dead?"

"No. Are you all right? Did you break anything?" Raven asks.

"Everything, I'll wager."

"I meant bones," she says, breaking from Maggie's hold. That's when I notice the red welts running the length of her cheek.

A sudden shriek trips and crashes down each vertebra in my back like an old man falling down the stairs. Jenny's pointing to the far wall where the words "Wednesday's Child" are scrawled near a portrait of Mathias Maddox. Crimson drips down the cream plaster forming a garish puddle on the floor, but whether paint or blood, I can't say.

"Saints preserve us," Jenny breathes.

"Wednesday's child is full of woe," Jamis says, quoting a children's verse I've heard before. Fear and warning reflect in his rheumy eyes. "The message is meant for you, master. Born on a Wednesday, you were. Like every male Maddox before you. The magician sends a taunt."

I swear the room is colder, now. My bones crust over with frost. "What do you mean?"

"The words appeared before, the last a challenge to your grandfather."

I've read the ledgers mentioning a magician, but that was over a hundred years ago. "Are you sure?"

Jamis lifts his chin when annoyed, which is pretty often. The old man has been with us forever, but his comment goes way beyond the general knowledge I assumed he had of the curse. I'm ashamed I never bothered to learn anything about him personally, Jenny either for that matter.

"Of course you are, Jamis. Forgive me."

A curt nod suggests my apology is as obvious as it is overdue. It's true. No one's going to nominate me for boss of the year.

"Let's everyone calm down and think." Raven's walk is a bit uneven. She rights an overturned chair and sits unceremoniously, keeping her knees pinned together like a small child. Her gaze flits to the words still bleeding on the wall. "From the beginning, can someone tell us what happened?"

Maggie pipes up. "We ... we'd just started looking though some books. Dane and I here," she points to two chairs as she and Dane sit, "Cole over there."

Jamis helps a shaken Jenny slip quietly out the door, and for now, I let them go.

Cole resumes his seat at the far head of the table. His hair juts out in static, black spikes reminding me of a towel just removed from the dryer. I take my regular place at the other end. Our eyes meet and hold a tense moment before he glances away.

"I'm sorry. I never meant ... " Cole jerks his thumb indicating the sum total of my newly destroyed dining hall. "Maddox, what you said during the storm. I thought you were crazy, but I would have tried anything to make it stop. It took a while, but once I focused … I found, no I *felt* my connection to the wind. Everything stopped *when I told it to!* How's that even possible?"

"How is any of it possible?" Dane asks.

"Hang on." Cole peers under the table, searches the floor around his chair. "Everything started when I read, uh … Here!" His fingers grasp a crumpled, brown leather diary from amongst the debris. "All right, just let me find it again." He straightens, thumbing through the yellowed pages until finding the passage he wants.

Maggie snaps the hair from her face. "If you're going to read that, stop short of another *X-Men Apocalypse* episode, okay?"

"Right." His voice clears.

Spring, 1865
Today, Gordon confided, while dressing me for dinner, that he overheard the cook and delivery man discussing the death of Mrs. Lawrence. Her bruises apparently so plentiful, she was rarely seen in public this season. Having missed her presence at both the Sales Hollow Christmas Ball and the Johnson's cotillion, I believe it must be true. My poor, sweet Emma …

"He blathers on about his long lost love, yadda, yadda, yadda … " Cole runs a finger down the crinkled page. "Here's where he plots his revenge against her husband Jonathan Lawrence, the man who killed her." Cole's head pops up. "I knew him by the way, old man Lawrence. Met him in The Void."

My eyebrows hike.

"Real wanker, that one." Cole returns to the journal.

I traveled to The Grey Horse Saloon again two weeks prior to this entry and met with one Professor Pan, the magician. No price is too high. He will give me the means to avenge her death, though the path gives me pause. It is a clever plan, to send Jonathan through the rabbit hole where no one may follow. Were I to make a bargain with this devil, Pan, I would be trading one evil for another, even risk my

*soul. Yet your blood calls to me from the ground, dearest Emma, and
I cannot bear the sound. Take heart, beloved. Jonathan is as vain as
a peacock. The whole of Colleton County knows he cares more for his
white gelding than you, my darling. Let them rot together then.*

*I will stand in the graveyard of Pan's ancestors and speak the
words he gave to me. Those with power enough to unlock the door
between worlds. To bring justice. To be together again.*

Cole lifts his head again. "Mathias is talking about The Void
here. He made a deal with Pan for some magical verbiage and
poof, the door to the labyrinth was opened."

"What sort of deal?" Dane asks.

"Doesn't say how much he paid, just goes on about a 'rabbit
hole' and the means to avenge Emma's death being the catalyst
for the whole mess. And here's the bit about the pictures …"

*One simple photograph with the enchanted camera traps him for
an eternity. A gilded frame will be his cell, the walls of my house, his
jail. He will spend his prison sentence ruing the day he hurt you and
crossed the man who truly loved you. The one whose heart you hold
for all time.*

Mathias Maddox,

"The more I read, the more agitated I got. My head hurt. The
pressure was crushing, and just when I thought I couldn't bear it
anymore, everything blew apart." Cole peers at the surrounding
chaos. "And I'm no closer to helping Rose." His gaze finds
me, eyes hard and accusing. "Your people did this. Punishing
criminals is one thing, but she's innocent."

His anger sparks mine. "How do you know?" Cole might be
right about her. He's definitely right about my family, but loyalty
makes me defend them anyway. The last thing I need is a lecture
on morality from the guy that made my life at school a living
hell.

Cole stands. His face wads up, muscles twitching like an

angry squirrel. Not the harmless type old people feed in the park. He's the annoying, bushy-tailed rats we southern boys like to shoot out of trees. Gut them, peel their skin ... cut off their heads. *Where's my rifle?*

"You guys, quit it," Maggie says. "We've got enough problems without ya'll fighting, too."

When Cole and Raven share a look, jealousy threatens my plan to let her go. If only I didn't want to squeeze his tiny British brain until it popped.

"He's right," Rae says. "About the headaches, I mean. I thought it was sinus, or summer allergies to pollen. But after this morning's scare with the plants, my head was hurting."

Cole perks up. "Hang on. What plants?"

While Rae retells her story, my mind drifts. Cole's mention of a mirror mixes with the dream I had in the hotel.

"Look, damn you! There's magic. Inside the glass. Magic is elemental. It's in the earth, the water, even in the air we breathe. Understand?" My father's words hammer through my head, battering open the memories I'd shut out for so long. *Magic is elemental ... elemental, elemental ...*

A prickle of awareness creeps up my neck. If trees are perhaps a symbol for earth, Cole's uncontrollable shifts could be wind. The fires ... What if elemental components are somehow erupting through the three of us? However farfetched, it's the only explanation that makes sense. The idea's worth exploring, anyway. The strange occurrences are an outpouring of elements, each of us representing a different aspect.

My hands fist and release with pent up energy. "I might know what's happening." The room goes quiet. "I'll have Jenny box these books to bring with us. Get packed everybody. It'll be tight, but we'll go in my Jeep."

"Road trip," Dane says.

I catch his eye. "Can you get away from work for a few days?"

"I'll manage."

"Why? Where are we going?" Raven asks.

"I'll explain on the way." Or try my damnedest.

My mind's made up. Much as it kills me, I might have found a way to provide for her future and defeat The Void at once. All we need is a miracle. Or ten.

Dane answers to no one, but the girls need an alibi. "Clear a camping trip with Maggie's folks. Tell them I've rented a cabin or something somewhere in North Carolina. We're going to my lake house—in Grey Horse."

Chapter Thirteen

Cole

To say I'm unhappy stuck in the back seat of Gideon's Jeep with Dane and Maggie, aka the "love-fest" twins is an understatement. Raven rides shotgun. At least I have an unobstructed view of her, and my eyes stay riveted to avoid watching the mauling of Maggie by Mr. "Happy-hands" Dane.

The injustice.

The smell of petrol mixed with Maggie's indulgent use of perfume turns my stomach. I'm carsick, heartsick, stressed-out, and hatching the mother of all headaches. Hopefully, I won't jettison outside the vehicle to become its unwilling hood ornament.

My legs are too long for the space behind the seat. I shift and squirm, but we're lemmings back here. I'd rather be up front with Raven. The wish gels into more than vague thought, and before I know what's happening, I'm vibrating like a guitar string. The pressure in my head expands. *Shite. Here we go …*

I blink to clear my vision of the lovely throat I'm suddenly staring at. Nope, still there. Somehow, I've transported myself into the front passenger seat facing the dashboard with the incredible Raven Weathersby situated directly on my lap.

Fist bump. High five. *Yes!*

"Cole!" Raven punches me in the shoulder, and though it doesn't hurt, I believe she put some force behind the blow. She wriggles in my lap, which isn't helping my focus *at all*.

I can't help my laugh, half glee, half shock.

"What the hell, Wynter?" Gideon growls. My body jerks as his fingers clamp my shoulder.

I'm unsuccessful at shrugging him off. "How should I know?" *Which is true.* "It's not like I asked to be up here." *Which is definitely not true.*

He releases me to change gears, and we pass the slow moving Toyota stalling our progress.

"How did you get up here?" Raven's voice has a hypnotic, natural rasp. The scent of her cinnamon gum fills the air between us, drawing me in, but if I kiss her, Maddox will toss me out of the window arse over elbow. I might do it anyway.

I'm at a loss as to where to put my hands. They end up clutching the seat at my sides, but I can't avoid the pair of bright gray eyes inches away. "I get carsick riding in the back. When I thought about sitting up front, I started—I don't know—buzzing, and poof, here I am."

My heart tips over when she laughs. "Poof?"

"Yeah … " I grin. "Poof."

"That's enough, Wynter," Gideon warns. "Off you go."

I'm in no hurry to respond. Especially since the prat's ordering and not asking.

Raven angles toward him. "I'll ride in the back, he can stay."

"Not happening," he says, then under his breath, "Not yet."

"You're cranky, Maddox, even for you." I shrug at his trademark scowl. "Fine, I'm going."

Easing Raven aside, I crawl over the seat. The job's a challenge, trying to keep from jabbing Raven with my knee or kicking the gearshift with my combat boots.

Relegated to the backseat again, I try for conversation. "Oi, Maddox. Now might be a good time to clue us in on your theories."

Gideon's eyes meet mine in the rearview mirror before glancing at the lip-locked pair beside me. A smirk emerges.

"You're a right foul git, you know that?"

"I know."

"What's a git?" Raven asks.

"Anything related to Maddox."

"Moving on," Gideon says. "Here's the deal from my perspective. Either our collective sanity's gone to hell, or we're creating our own problems this time."

Dane and Maggie separate and face front. *Thank you, God.*

"In the library, when Cole mentioned the mirrors and Pan, I remembered something from when I was a kid. We have a country house in Grey Horse. I hadn't thought about it in years since I've only been there twice in my life. Citing historical significance to the family, my grandfather bought the property and built a house on the exact site that used to be a saloon. That's about all I knew."

"The same Grey Horse Saloon mentioned in the journal entry?" I ask.

He finds me again in his mirror and nods. "The very same."

"Well, that's no coincidence, is it?" Maggie asks.

"Unfortunately, no," Gideon admits. "Like I said, we didn't spend much time there. I'd forgotten about the afternoon I spent with my father in his office until a few days ago. Remember when I told you that my father said magic never dies? If that's true, then when one source of power is cut off, the properties of magic must transfer somewhere else."

I snort. He's trying to make his explanation sound important and scientific, but I doubt he knows what the hell he's saying.

Raven tucks a lock of hair behind one ear and leans forward. I swallow the barb on my tongue meant for Maddox, because if his words give her hope, who am I to rob her of them?

Gideon downshifts behind a slow moving semi. "That got me

thinking. What if they did go somewhere? The night the curse was broken, three people in that cellar survived. Me, Raven, and you, Wynter. Maybe we absorbed the magic. It makes sense with what's been going on, only I didn't see it until now.

"My father said magic is born from the elements, earth, wind, water—"

"And fire," Rae finishes. "The fires, last week ... and again today. Gideon, was that you?"

"I think so. What you and Wynter described with headaches and odd dreams, the same physical symptoms have bothered me, too, lately."

"Why didn't you say something?" Raven's voice is so low I can hardly hear her over the noisy engine.

He runs a finger down her cheek. The gesture is tender and guts me to watch. "I didn't want you to worry, and I could be wrong."

"What if you're not? Anyway, that's not really the point ... " He pulls sharply away, and she looks like she might cry. "I wish you'd told me."

"There was nothing to tell," he snaps. "I'm theorizing, but my best guess is the night the curse was broken, the magical elements re-homed themselves in us."

I hate eating my own words. It sucks, but I have to admit I agree with him. The evidence is overwhelming.

"Whoa," Maggie says. "You guys are, like, crime fighting, superheroes, now. You can have your own secret hideout and catch bad guys, like on *Arrow*."

"Stop it, Mags, you've seen what's been happening." Raven's eyes shine. "We don't control the elements. Right now, they control us, and there's no one to explain how it works. If Gideon's right, then we could hurt somebody or ourselves."

"No, we can figure this out." Gideon says, shifting again. "We'll have to test my theory, of course, but personally, I hope I'm right. I wouldn't mind having a little lightning in my veins." His eyes brighten at the prospect. I can't tell if he's kidding or not, but Raven's not smiling.

She glances out the window. "Then you're just trading a camera for fire."

I'm not sure anyone else heard until Maggie's cheeks puff up. "Again? This is just so typical of you, Rae."

"What is?"

"You're always … freaking Princess Gloom and Doom, aren't you? Last year, when you found out you had to move in with the big, bad Maddox heir, you and Dane were all like, ahhh! And I was like whoosah, children, he's not *that* scary." She waves a hand. "No offense, dude."

Gideon grins. "None taken. I am *that* scary."

I roll my eyes.

"If you recall, that situation turned out fine, and I'm predicting this will, too. Promise." She crosses her chest. "I have a feeling."

Her words are full of confidence, but I wouldn't take those odds. Raven's prediction we'll end up offing ourselves is more believable. Though the image of Gideon's perfect hair catching fire is brilliant.

"Mags, you can't promise something like that," Dane cautions. "What if they accidently blow—Oof."

Maggie shoves him. "Don't be a downer, dude." The girl is C-4 packed into a tiny five-foot frame. "You'll make them feel bad. Try to stay positive, please." Her little arms fold under a disproportionately large chest rendering her push-up bra unnecessary.

"Hang on," I say, trying to wipe Maggie's cleavage from my mind. "Let me get this straight. Elemental magic is divided into four: wind, earth, water, and fire. So I'm what, wind?"

Gideon nods. "Probably, yes, and if Rae is Earth, then that explains her connection to the vines."

"Our little *Poison Ivy* is just a wee bit intimidating when she gets going," Maggie jokes.

I snort, but Gideon doesn't even crack a smile. "My point

exactly," he says. "So, if it's true, I've clearly absorbed the fire element."

Maddox and fire's a sobering combo. "What about water?" I ask. "Anyone have a tidal wave in the bath?" I have nothing to tell. No one else speaks either, but Gideon gives Raven a sideways glance. The accusation in his eyes has me betting she's been less than forthcoming about her recent tree hugging experiences. Good.

"Maybe water hasn't shown up yet," I offer. Frankly, I hope it doesn't. Wind is more than enough.

"Maybe not," he agrees. "But there are four elements, and four of us initially survived the curse breaking ceremony."

"Right, Desiree. That's must be it." Raven says. "But then she died."

Dane leans forward, his brow tied in knots. "You said if the host dies, the magic latches on somewhere else. So, where did it go?"

"Hell, I don't know!" Gideon barks. "Who knows if she had it to start with? Maybe it's in the bottom of the pond, waiting for you. Or there's a big ass, water-wielding alligator in my backyard." He pauses, angling his neck until it cracks. "Like I said, I'm guessing as I go. I could be wrong—"

"I don't think you are," Maggie says. "Honestly, I wish I had water, because this could be amazing." She cuts a quick glance at her boyfriend. "Eventually."

"If we're voting, I say we walk away." Dane ignores her frown. "Superstitions, wives' tales, all the warnings make sense to me now. Playing with supernatural shit is unnatural, gives me the heebie-jeebies."

I have no earthly idea what heebie-jeebies are, but they sound freakish coming from an African American redhead with dreads.

"Dane," Raven says softly. "I agree with you. But how do you walk away when magic shows up on your doorstep, or in this case, in your mind, uninvited? I never went looking for trouble, but I can't regret helping people either." She sighs heavily. "It's too late. We have to see where this goes and hope for the best. What else can we do?"

It's too late. My fists ball on my knees. I needed Gideon to be wrong, but since I've turned into some sort of wind-riding teleporter, the evidence seems irrefutable.

I wanted to help a girl—a sweet, pretty girl. Our transformations aren't her fault.

Last year, I told Raven that The Void saved my life. In a way, that's true, because the time I spent there humbled me. I thought I'd dealt with my anger, forgiven my parents for their neglect, Nathan for banishing me. But something acidic still gnaws at the lining in my gut.

Maybe it's me I can't forgive.

My head rests against the glass. Exhausted, the subtle vibration relaxes me. I feel myself drifting off, and with that, a vague hope that Rose will show up. Funny how often my mind turns not to Raven, but Rosamond.

Chapter Fourteen

Raven

Stiff and keyed up, we pile out of the Jeep at the infamous lake house. Five of us stand in the circular driveway, staring up at a huge, two story, Cape Cod style dwelling. Gideon glares at the front porch as if it told him off. When I reach for him, he moves away. Maybe he's dealing with the same nervous tension that's inside me, but the brush off stings. In the past, I'd call him out on it, but lately, I don't have the energy. It's easier to stuff the hurt. Pretend I misunderstood him.

"You forgot about this place?" Dane asks.

"Not forgot." Gideon stalks to the back of the vehicle and swings the tailgate open. "It's just not on my radar. Like I said, the place was my father's getaway." He riffles through a box of ledgers. His clipped tone makes the distinction between Nathan Maddox and himself very clear.

A single crow flies across the sun.

One for sorrow ...

The first line of the childhood poem I've always loved seems a bad omen today.

Gideon thumbs through one of the journals and then snaps it shut. Satisfied he's found what he needs, he stuffs the volume under one arm and starts walking. "The graveyard is this way. There's a clearing in the woods over that knoll, about a twenty minute hike."

My feet remain cemented to the ground. No one else moves either.

Gideon is several steps out before rounding on us again, his expression one of annoyed confusion. "Well?"

Cole fidgets, pushing his hands deep into his jean pockets. "You want to do this *now?*"

As if unified in thought, the rest of us sneak a glance at the beautiful, old house. I need to pee like a racehorse. I assumed we'd go inside. Get a drink. Eat. Change. Regroup. Talk. Stall. I don't know …

"You don't?" Gideon asks, eyes glittering fire under the sun's rays. "The girl's counting on you, Wynter."

And with that one statement, I get it. I know why he's angry, and hurried. Why he did a one-eighty agreeing to help Cole when at first he was so reluctant. He's not here for Cole or Rosemond—though I believe Gideon would have helped them anyway—he needs answers for what's happening to *us*.

"You came all the way from France. What's another mile?"

"Keep your hair on, mate. No one said anything about quitting. We only want ten minutes inside."

Gideon looks from us to the wide, wraparound porch. His expression softens, shoulders relax. "Sorry, you're right." A smile emerges with his headshake. I love it when he does that, keeps a sense of humor when he realizes he's been wrong. The old Gideon would never admit it. "Ten minutes … and then we go." Walking toward the steps, he pulls a key from his pocket and amiably tosses it to Cole.

Catching the brass chain, Cole's lips curve up. " … And then we go."

En masse, we follow our fearless leader into the forest. I'm thankful to discover the temperature's several degrees lower in the shade.

Power from the surrounding foliage infuses me with energy, yet I'm calm. At peace. Moss, bark, pine, and honeysuckle mix to fill my nose with a woodsy aroma. A bird cries in alarm as we trespass. *Shhh, it's okay, little man.* He immediately quiets and settles, but I don't mention the coincidence to my friends. It's a ridiculous thought, right? Birds don't read minds.

Twigs snap in the underbrush. Ahead, Gideon clears several fallen branches from our path. His blue, button-down shirt stretches against his broad back. A ray of light breaks though the canopy overhead, catching in his curls and turning them yellow-bright before falling into shadow as he pushes forward. Nothing stops him once he's decided.

Assess. Choose. Act. A maxim brought to you by Nathan Maddox and family. Arrogance and ruthless discipline taught the Maddox heirs to manage both the Artisan legacy and their business holdings. Gideon was nearly destroyed by his father's cruelty.

It's hard not to hate him for it.

Despite the heat, the soil beneath the leaf litter is damp and squishy. Maggie trips and swears.

"You okay?" I ask.

"Always." She smiles, but it doesn't light her eyes.

I've known her long enough to recognize when she's nervous. Back in the day, she, Dane, and I were the Three Musketeers. I leaned on her in between caring for my stepfather, sewing to earn extra money, and the pressures of school. For Dane, she was the dream girl and mental escape from troubles at home. Of the three of us, Maggie was the only one with a "normal" life.

But that was before paranormal events stole our innocence, before I made the deal that put me under Gideon's roof for a year in exchange for Ben's rehab costs. And while I lost his body to addiction, our relationship healed and his soul was restored.

I owe Gideon so much. Odd how the one I vowed to hate is now the one who owns my heart. As if he can hear my thoughts, he glances over his shoulder. I'm confused by his frown until Cole falls in line beside me.

He shoulder bumps me with a grin. "How much farther?"

"Not much more, I hope."

Cool indifference back in place, Gideon faces front, plunging up the next steep bank.

Sweat spikes the hair on Cole's forehead. "Your sunshine beats our fog, but this heat is melting the skin off my face."

It's a handsome face with fair skin and dark blue eyes. His lanky frame has gained muscle since I last saw him. The years lost in The Void are catching up—and in a very good way.

"Our summers are famous for face melting. Afternoon rains will cool it off soon. Then you'll just be sticky."

"Humidity is my second favorite; did I mention that?" He shoos the horsefly at his ear. "That and bugs the size of pigeons."

"Our state bird." I smile and he does, too. It's nice, this carefree moment where we're not worried or afraid. "Hey, I know. Why don't you work us up a breeze?"

Both eyebrows wing up, and I'm sure my big, stupid mouth just ruined a perfectly nice time. He's quiet so long that I worry I've offended him. Finally, he says, "I'm not sure I can do it on purpose."

Guilt has me backtracking. "I'm sorry. I was kidding, and I shouldn't—"

"No, I'll give it a go." He grins like I've challenged him, and I suppose I have. "If a tornado shows up, remember this was your idea."

Super. "Think very small thoughts about wind."

"Mm-hm." We stop, and he closes his eyes. Lips move without words, both hands lift shoulder high.

We wait so long I'm about to interrupt, when the hushed whisper of a breeze kisses my damp skin, cooling my face. My body begs for more, and I get it. Leaves rustle in the canopy above. Growing in strength, wind dashes to the ground wrapping us in a tiny vortex of velvety relief. And then it's gone.

I lunge, throwing my arms around his neck. "You did it! Oh, my gosh, Cole. You controlled the air!" I hit octaves nearing G7#, but I'm too excited to care. I release him and grin. "You have to tell me how you did that. Does raising your arms help?" When I mimic his actions, he grins.

"Nah. I'm hoping it makes me look badass."

I laugh, enjoying his accent. "Seriously badass." Cole is funny and sweet and deserves to be happy. Gideon not so subtly called Rosamond "Cole's girl." My boyfriend might as well pee a circle around me as territorial as he gets—and he'd for sure push Cole in any direction but mine—but that doesn't necessarily mean he's wrong about Cole liking her.

"Can I ask you something?"

"I don't know how I did it. I just … did."

"No, not that—" My toe catches on a root, and I stumble right into him. "Oh! Sorry."

He grabs my elbow, shoring me up. "Don't be sorry, Rae."

The way he's looking at me, the tenderness in his voice makes me unsure. He flirts sometimes, but I'm also the first girl his age he's talked to in four years. We're friends, we get along—but that isn't love. I think I'm a placeholder for someone else. A girl he hasn't met yet, at least, I hope so.

"It's sort of personal."

"Even better." He wiggles his eyebrows, and grins like a wolf.

Uh oh. "Can you tell me more about Rosamond?" His smile fades. I wince inwardly, but push ahead. "How often do you see her? Has she said who put her in The Void? What does she—"

His palms face me. "Whoa. Hang on." He busts out with a hearty laugh.

"What?" I don't know what's so funny, but I'm laughing because he is.

Once he gets control, a grin continues at the corners of his mouth. "I'll always tell you anything you want to know, but one thing at a time, all right?"

I bite my lip to keep the next three questions from spilling out, and we end up laughing again. Gideon watches us over his shoulder. Instead of the scowl I expect, he looks interested, thoughtful. I'm not sure if that's a good sign or bad.

"I've seen Rose a dozen times," Cole says. "She's locked in a room, some sort of castle by the looks of it. Last time, I even tried physically hanging on to her as I left The Void. To pull her back with me as I woke up." He wipes his face on the bottom of his T-shirt revealing a set of lean abs. "Didn't work, obviously."

Mags and Dane step nearer without any attempt to hide their eavesdropping.

"She's young like us. Lovely, all silvery and fit." Cole's face reddens, but I pretend not to notice. "Rosamond's never said who put her in there, but she talks about Pan. How he holds her prisoner in the maze. She's terrified of him."

Weighted by sympathy, my chest compresses. "Was it like that with you, too?"

"I never met him myself. A few others daft enough to enter the labyrinth—namely Desiree—told us stories, though. I don't know why, but Pan and his monsters never leave the maze, which is why I mostly kept to the mansion."

Mostly. I can't imagine years of hiding and the constant threat of darkness.

"What sort of monsters?" Dane asks, formally joining the discussion.

Maggie smacks his tattooed arm. "He doesn't want to talk about it." Then to Cole she adds, "You don't have to talk about it. I'm sorry for you. And sorry for Rosamond, too."

Grass pokes through the pine needles in lone patches of sunlight. The trees thin out revealing glimpses of a meadow ahead.

Cole gives us a one armed shrug. "Thanks, but it's all right. Somehow, I don't mind so much. Telling you three."

With permission granted, Dane doesn't miss a beat. "So what's the difference between the maze and labyrinth?"

"Same thing. I avoided the place, but there was one time when I—"

"We're here," Gideon calls. "Grey Horse Cemetery, in the flesh—so to speak."

The five of us pile onto a flat, green carpet. Headstones punch through the soil in the little clearing like broken bones from a shallow grave. There are as few as thirty markers here.

A cloud glides over the sky casting bleak shadows, and it seems even the sun hides from this place.

Gideon extends the open diary in his hand to Cole. "You're up, Wynter. Page thirteen."

"Me?"

"It's your show."

Cole's tentative fingers hover above the book before taking it. "What will happen?"

Gideon glances around the graveyard. "I honestly don't know. Since that book is all we have to go on, I guess we do what they did. Stand in the graveyard, read the words out loud ... I'm thinking if you rub the lamp, the genie will appear."

"By genie you mean Pan?" Heavy braids stick to Dane's glistening skin. "We're going to summon a dead magician, and then what?"

Cole scratches his nose. "Er, the book never quite explains the details, mate."

"Fantastic. And say this does work, are we sure we want him here?"

"No." Gideon drags his fingers through his hair the way he does when he's frustrated. "All my life I've known, as fact, what the rest of the world rejects—and now that power is inside of us.

We can't call the Feds or convince Homeland Security to help." The look he gives us is weary. "So, what do you suggest we do instead?"

No one answers at first, so I'm surprised it's Dane who finally says, "Do it. Just get it over with."

Cole nods. "Right." He takes a step or two and turns. "Which grave? What page again?" He continues, mumbling in French. I suspect the anger in his tone is really fear, and he's not alone.

"Easy," Gideon says. "I bent the page."

Nervous tension swamps me, as we back off, leaving Cole to his task. I wait for Gideon to take his place next to me, wrap a comforting arm around my shoulders the way he always does. Instead, he chooses a semi-solitary spot near Dane, of all people, and leans forward resting both hands on his cane. He calls to Cole, "Is anything marked?"

Okay, wow. A feeling of dread drops like a boulder in my stomach. He never even looked my way.

"Did you two fight?" Maggie whispers.

Throat too dry to answer, I shake my head.

Cole steps between the graves, searching for the one we need. Kudzu blankets the clearing. Thick ropes of ivy climb the gravestones, choking the marble. He stops in front of a tall, crumbling headstone and kneels. "This is pointless," he grumbles. "Half the writing is worn off. The rest are so overgrown; I can't tell who's who."

Maggie gives a meaningful look from Gideon to me before taking Dane's hand. "C'mon, handsome, let's help the boy."

My friend means well, but a graveyard full of spectators isn't the venue for a relationship status talk. At the same time, wherever my lady-balls have been hiding the past few months, I think I found them, because I'm more pissed off than scared.

Mags is at work in front of a large headstone. Her short fingers thread the twisting bands of ivy and tear at the tiny roots. I need to keep busy until my showdown with Gideon later, so I move toward her.

A wail halts my steps. I can't see anyone, but the crying grows.

Muscles clench against the sudden war in my abdomen. A dull ache starts in my jaw and spreads. Maggie rips a vine from the headstone and tosses it behind her. With every leaf she damages, my stomach twists. A moan rolls up my throat. "Wait, Mags. Can you stop a minute?" Oh, God.

"What's wrong?"

Gideon's gentle hand on my back steadies my wobbling, but I'm breathing too fast. The plants, I can *hear* them. "Make her stop."

"Stop what, tell me?"

It makes no sense, but whatever is happening to the plants in the clearing affects me. I *feel* them being torn apart, dying, and that freaks me out worse than the pain. "The vines." Another wave of nausea crashes through me. I double over, fall to one knee. "Leave them ... "

"Everyone stop!"

The pain instantly lessens. My breathing slows. When I dare to lift my head, my three friends hold statue-still. Every eye fixed on Gideon while he watches me.

Maggie brushes her palms together. "Rae, what's the matter, hon?"

I straighten. "I don't know why, but when you pull the weeds, it hurts. I've got some kind of connection with them."

And that connection births an idea. The roots in Maggie's room left when I wished them gone. If Cole can create a breeze to cool us, maybe I can make our search easier. "Ya'll, give me another second; I want to try one thing."

My eyelids seal shut, and I focus on the ivy covering the markers. Silently, I ask them to leave. My mind pictures their green leaves, black roots down to the tiny white feeder shoots. *Move away, guys. Climb down from the gravestones.* My nausea subsides, while my headache grows.

"Holy freaking cow ... "

Slowly, I raise my eyelids. Vines slide over the ground like a thousand lime-green snakes. Leaves shiver, creating a loud drag as they retreat to the tree line.

And all at my request.

"That's great, guys," I pant. "Far enough, you can stop now."

Maggie's eyes bug. She stares as though I've grown a second head, and I realize I just spoke out loud to a bunch of Kudzu. Chatted with everyday vegetation like they're close personal friends of mine. Creepy much?

"How did you … *do* that?" she squeals.

"I have no clue. I just asked nicely and they seemed happy to go. I think they knew I didn't want them damaged. When you pulled their roots out, it made me so sad, I felt sick."

"Then Gideon was right." Dane's teeth are snowy white against his dark skin. His eyes light up like the Fourth of July. "Ha! You've gone green, Raven, a tree hugger for realz." His humor earns a solid punch in the shoulder from Mags.

I rub my arms against a nonexistent chill. "I don't know how much "earth" I control, but the plants *did* move when I asked." A reality that's freaking me out more by the minute.

"Do something else!" Dane looks around, twisting on the balls of his feet. "Make that tree bow, or that bush walk. See what else you can do." Excitement sharpens his voice as he speaks. Mr. elemental-power-equals-heebie-jeebies is now asking for a showy demonstration. No talk about how unnatural it is now, I notice. "Do it, little Rae!" He squats and hunts for something in the grass. I wince as he picks a dandelion and holds it up to me. Another big grin eats his face. "Come on, make it dance."

He's so cute. Like a little kid, but I can't do what he asks. My heart senses the life leaving the little flower, and a breath leaks out in sympathy. My fingers wrap Dane's hand, and I ease him to a stand. "It won't work now, bro."

"Yes you can. I know you can." His smile weakens as he studies my face. "Why not?"

"Our connection broke when you picked it. He's dead." The truth of my words hit me as I say them. I don't know how I know, but somehow, I'm sure. Whatever it is I control, it's not life. I can't bring the flower back or prevent death. I glance at a hundred other blooms sprouted at his feet.

Dane drops the yellow flower to the ground. A crease forms between his eyebrows. "Sorry."

"Rae." Cole appears my side. "That was bloody brilliant. Let's practice. Try something else, whatever you feel."

"What, you mean right now?"

"Yes." Dane looks me square in the eye. "I can't believe I'm saying this, but Cole's right. You should all get comfortable with the changes happening in you. Might as well know what you can control. If anything."

Out of habit, I look to Gideon for guidance. Alone. Silent. He nods in agreement.

A chill grips my heart, though it's ninety-eight degrees outside. Everything in his manner reminds me of the cold, aloof boy I first met, the one with haughty eyes and a cruel mouth.

The broken one.

Chapter Fifteen

Cole

Maggie yells, "God bless your pea-pickin' little heart, Cole Wynter," once more as I send another cooling breeze over the glen. I laugh at her enthusiasm, and for my new ability to conjure wind. It's getting easier, and I'm actually enjoying myself.

Transporting is another matter entirely. My body hums with energy as I pick a point in the grass on the other side of the cemetery. Again and again I try, and nothing happens. I give up, frustrated, then … *Whoosh.* One tick and I'm standing twenty meters from the spot I'd wanted. No control but, *What a rush!* If only the shakes and headaches would stop.

Under our feet lies a thick floral blanket of yellow and purple. Apparently, Raven chose to practice her element by forcing blooms over a three-acre spread. She runs around, jumping and spinning like a little kid. When she laughs, it's like Christmas.

I don't know what good a plethora of flowers is against an evil magician. Unless he has massive allergy issues and can sneeze to death, her gift, while entertaining, is useless.

I keep my thoughts to myself however and glance at our host. Gideon has rarely been what I'd call a fun guy, but today he's acting a complete wanker. I've never seen him so foul. He hardly speaks and refused to make fire. Blamed it on dry field conditions. *Sure.* With everyone watching, my bet is he's having performance issues.

We've been out here for hours. Thanks to Rae's trick with the ivy, I located the headstone twenty minutes ago. "You ready to start?" I ask Maddox.

"Been ready. So, whenever you two are done playing games ... "

Rae stops twirling, her cheeks color bright and hot. Clearly embarrassed, she removes the ivy and flowers from her hair and places them gently on the ground.

Tosser. We all agreed to test what we could do.

Gideon keeps off to the side, while Raven joins Dane and Maggie. They regard her with something nearing pity, and Mags gives her a quiet pat on the arm.

Honeymoon over already? What could the poor girl have done to piss him off so badly?

The tension is palpable. Anger sours my stomach, and I want to hit Maddox. Even with his bum leg, the defensive training classes his father paid for means I'm no match for him, but I know who is. And I privately wish Dane would break his nose.

Whatever. The stupid plank doesn't deserve her.

I force my gaze from the hurt in Rae's eyes, and remember how she picked him over me. While I'm glad his idiocy gives me another chance, I can't stand her suffering.

Everyone stands a few feet away, watching me, waiting for something to happen. Every hardened muscle in Dane's body tenses, the whites of his eyes brighter against his dark skin. For a big guy, he clutches his girl as if she'll save *him* should our attempt to reach Pan backfire.

Get on with it, Cole. I scan the words on the page, wondering how simple script on paper can hold any power. Only one way to find out, and though I feel ridiculous, like a cheesy actor in some daft school play, this is real. I believe it. So, I clear my throat, keep my voice loud and clear, and read.

"Deep within a shadowed wood
Old bones yearn as if they could
Revisit passions of the living
Taste past years from the beginning

The filmy moon doth rise and fall
O'er my labyrinth paying homage to all
Who come in pain, in bondage, or need
We welcome thee; yea our hearts swell with greed

For we know of thy jealousy, rejection, despair
Take rest from thy envy, worry and care
I'll cure thee of vice in the place of forgetting
Seek ye help in the land of promise begetting
Thy secret desires.

Caught between feelings of fear, awe, and total wankerdom, I let the last words trail off into the wind. The whole scenario is as absurd as it is terrifying.

Despite the fact that I put great gusto into evoking a real-life boogey man, nothing happens. We stand together, five living statues in a desolate field. The lot of us eyeing each other, cold dread etched on our faces. Yet, there is no clap of thunder to announce our enemy. No tempest whisking us over the rainbow to a foreign land. A drop of sweat trickles down my back while I wait, stuck in tortuous anticipation.

After a few more minutes of uncomfortable silence, I snap the book shut. "Not much of a poet, was he?" My joke falls flat, even as my nerves still tingle. "Sounds like a lot of rubbish to me." I hope the others can't detect my lie.

"I don't get it," Maggie says. "The words don't even make sense."

"I know that's right." Dane has the decency to give me an apologetic grimace. "Sorry for Rosamond and all, but no one dying today is a win."

I exhale, my thoughts on Rose. Our trip ends in a spectacular fail, and I don't know how to tell her.

"We're standing in a graveyard, reading dumb-ass poetry like a bunch of girls trying to scare each other at a slumber party." Dane walks over and claps a hand to my back. "No offense, man. Calling you a girl."

"None taken. You called yourself one, too."

His brow furrows as he works that one out.

"I thought we'd made a believer out of you." Gideon says, stepping nearer.

"I only meant—"

"Oh right," Rae says. "Why hope dumb-ass poetry could help those of us who *talk to plants!*" With a swish of her hand, dandelions bloom, covering Dane's black trainers. Green tendrils lace back and forth over his feet and ankles with dizzying speed until he's sewn to the spot.

"Nice." He jerks without gaining his freedom, "Yo, call 'em off, Rae!" At her command, the plants recede as fast as they grew. "I'm not saying you don't have a problem, but tell the truth, do you really want to ask some dead guy that's crawling out of the ground to solve it? We tried. It didn't work." He reaches for Maggie's hand. "Now, can we go home?"

The sky darkens. Several heavy clouds blow in burying the late afternoon sun.

"Cole?" Raven asks.

"It isn't me." A drop of rain hits my eyebrow. Cold engulfs me like a winter frost—from the *inside*, slowing my heart rate, stiffening my joints. Absolute silence presses on my ears until the quiet is as deafening as orchestra cymbals, until ...

A hysterical laugh echoes from somewhere in the trees. If I'm not crazy, and I can't argue that point right now, I swear I hear a flute playing.

"Monday's child is fair of face."

Another mad giggle filters through the forest.

"Tuesday's child is full of grace,

Wednesday's child is full of woe.

Thursday's child has far to … here we gooo … "

Gideon curses as he steps in front of Raven. He lifts his cane, fingers gripping the lion head as though poised to unsheathe the dagger hidden inside. "Pan?"

Yellow tints the light around us a sickly, artificial hue. "Of course it's me, stupid boy. Who else would it be?"

"Where? *Where* are you?"

I glance around, but no one's hovering. Clouds build at the same rate as my confusion. With a push of my mind, wind punches the sky faster than a military jet leaving black clouds curling in on themselves.

"We're looking for a girl, Rosamond," I say to the nothing in the sky. "We think she might—"

"Imbecile, I am fully aware of what you want!" The voice shrieks, high and wild. "Do you think I don't know who you are?"

Unable to answer, we turn in slow circles, focusing on the detached voice in our midst. Our gazes slide from one to another, utterly confounded.

"Young Master Maddox … " Pan says. "Weak leg, and a weak mind, you've been crippled in more ways than one, eh? What a crushing disappointment you turned out to be, yet you tried so very hard, didn't you? A worthless failure, your faith curled up. Despite your pathetic pride, and your great show of rage, you were unable to keep people away, as you'd hoped. Now you've gone and lost what matters most, as did your forefathers. Congratulations, lad. You finally measure up."

Thunder sends a jolt through me, but Pan's speech goes on unabated. "Ah yes, next we have Mr. Wynter … displaced, lonely, boring, forgettable. No family to care, no woman to love, no loyal friend, not even a dog. But you'd change that, wouldn't you, son? Just add water." His giggle is a fierce and careening sound. "Busy-busy becoming anyone but dear old dad, are you not?"

Every word is like a knife thrust in my chest as he so accurately describes my existence in a sentence or two. I only realize I'm backing up when Maggie holds out a gentle hand to stop me running into her.

"Moving on, may I present the very troubled Dane, pitied and pitiful, written off as an unfortunate loss by the good people of Sales Hollow. Receptacle for a father's shame, punching bag for his resentments, scapegoat, sin eater, a sad and broken past keeps your soul a withered, bloodless organ, doesn't it? Why, you're barely breathing. Ha, ha!"

Maggie clings fiercely to the wiry giant beside her, and it's a good thing. Color drains from his face, and his eyes glaze with shock.

"Doubt, anger, insecurity, fear, you're perfectly lovely, Dane. Yes indeed, but not nearly as lovely as our Raven here. Such a pretty bauble, no more than a broken doll, really. Why, the pair of you could satisfy me for years with your tortured memories, regret, and guilt. Drowning in uncertainty, aren't you, my dear. Loss, death, betrayal, lies, broken dreams, fading hopes ... I'm quite enraptured."

"Stop it!" Maggie shouts.

"Mm, yes of course. Last and certainly the least of these, we have Miss High and Mighty Margaret. Queen of the mundane. Small, chubby, plain, loud, pushy, and supremely annoying, you're as tiresome as any fly, buzzing, buzzing in my ear. No one likes a bossy little know-it-all, now do they?"

Maggie blinks as though she's been slapped. Dane hugs her close and glares at the sky. If expressions could sucker-punch, Pan would be in deep shite.

Though not inaccurate, his insults seem a purposeful distraction. And since we're not getting anywhere as his verbal dartboards, I speak to the disembodied voice. "We came to talk about Rosamond Bryer. The girl in your maze."

"No need to shout, son. Nothing's wrong with my hearing. What about her?"

His words are overly eager and cheerful, as though he's

waited all his life to have this conversation; however, it's having the opposite effect on me. His tone cloaks and bewitches—the quality hypnotic in texture. I swallow against the dryness in my throat, and try to shake his voice from my head. How in the world do I convince a madman—that may not be a man at all—to let Rose go?

There's always the straightforward approach. "She's visiting me in dreams."

"Really? Bully for you."

"And she'd like to go home." This is going too well. He's not arguing, and he's too damn happy about our little visit. Warnings ping my mind like rain off a windshield, but what can I do? It's why we're here, so I dive back in. "We were wondering if ... is there a way to make that happen?"

"Perhaps. What will you give me in return?"

A deal? "I have money—"

"Pfft. What need have I for your coin, boy? I grow weary of this. Give me something I can use or we're finished here." Someone brushes past my arm. Gideon leans forward on his cane, chin jutting upward.

"Not the time for games, Pan," he snarls. "Name your price. Tell us what you want."

Gideon's spent his whole life negotiating. Maybe I should have let him do the talking from the start, yet I know this guy, watched him for years. A big risk taker, no one likes a deal better than Maddox. He won't back down once he's started. It's not in his nature.

"How about a trade? One of you for her."

"No." Sweat darkens his hair. An impatient head toss removes the curls threatening his odd-colored eyes. Unlike mine, his manner is restrained, calculating, and I hate him the more for it. "Choose something else."

"I don't want anything else. You decide who it will be, pull a stranger off the street for all I care, but I won't be robbed of all my treasures at once."

Gideon pauses, concentrating on the puzzle in his head. We wait in silence until his face brightens. "Really, Pan? Your demand lacks imagination and hardly seems sporting. How about a wager, instead?"

Shite! I should have known. Who am I kidding, I *did* know. I grab Gideon's arm but he shrugs me off.

Raven steps forward. Her hand slides up his back, but whether in support or to shut him up, I can't guess. He responds by wrapping her waist, but it's only to push her off toward Dane.

I'd ask what the hell he's playing at, treating her this way, but I have a life to save. And Maddox's big mouth might have just thrown a spanner that will get us all killed.

"Give us a chance to free her," he says. "A fair option without an automatic sacrifice of ourselves."

"Oooh, intriguing ... Yes, whoever wishes may come and visit, by all means. I could do with some fine, new company." The cavernous voice magnifies, bouncing off the surrounding forest. A murder of crows erupts from the treetops, filling the sky with ebony wings.

Everyone rallies closer. *Us.* The small army of misfits choosing to fight a spoiled, self-indulgent god from another world. Are we mad, yes, but at least we're no longer alone.

"Marvelous! I'm rather excited. Come along then, children. Come and find me, if you dare. Enter the labyrinth, locate the girl, and find your way out again. If you do that, you're free."

"Wait!" Gideon cries. "That's not what I—"

"I always did like a challenge," Pan says. "And when I'm through, I'll glut off your bloated misery until I'm fat and sated. Find me through the looking glass. Gideon knows the spot, don't you, boy? We'll be waiting ... "

We? When did it go from one psychopath to *we?*

Gideon lifts his face to the sky. "Pan, wait! We haven't discussed the rules."

"There are none. Do it or don't. Get yourselves in and out and you'll win the princess. Alive is preferable to you, I'm sure, though I'll be entertained either way." Maniacal laughter clogs the air again, congealing the blood around my heart. "However, should you lose yourselves along the way, well then, I suppose the rest is self-explanatory."

Oppressive shadows retreat as clouds pass from the sun. The evil that haunts the graveyard slinks into hiding. Cicadas sing. Birds chit and tweedle again in the trees.

"Pan!" Gideon tries again, but it's clear he's gone.

Dane clings to Maggie like he'll never see her again. When their eyes meet, his eyebrows knit together. "Maddox," he whispers, still looking at Mags. "I can't." The intensity radiating from that one word rivals the damn sun.

"It's all right, Dane. I understand." Gideon's jaw clenches hard enough to shatter bone. His gaze drifts over Rae, and quickly moves on. "We'll meet in my father's office at nine tomorrow morning. Until then, shower, change, eat, sleep … whatever you want. Each person must decide for themselves if they intend to travel into The Void, so consider the consequences carefully. No one here will think any less of you if you choose not to go."

No one responds. There's nothing to say. *Each person must decide for themselves if they intend to travel to The Void* … I'm going. Mind made up in an instant. For better or worse, I've committed myself to Rose's freedom. As far as the others, I have no idea what they'll do.

Dread fills my chest knowing that the only one who may pass through the mirror tomorrow is me.

Chapter Sixteen

Gideon

Dry drowning occurs when a person's lungs become unable to extract oxygen from the air. That's the official definition from Wikipedia. I don't remember how or why I'm familiar with the term, but it comes to mind because that's what's happening to me as I look into Raven's beautiful gray eyes and lie.

"You're breaking up with me?" she asks. Her voice holds a note of stunned defeat.

"Yes."

"I'm confused. You said ... " Her gaze drops. "We had all these plans."

I clench my fists, fighting the urge to reach for her, plead temporary insanity and kiss her senseless. Instead I say, "I know, but everything's different now." I can hardly believe the curt, unemotional words are mine. "The Void is dangerous. I can't do my job if I'm worrying about your safety. Or Wynter's, for that matter. I'm sorry, but—"

"You're *sorry?*" The sheen in her eyes might as well be a scythe for how deeply it cuts. "And you're telling me you want to go in there alone?" She doesn't wait for my answer. "First, you're adamant only Cole goes into The Void, and we stay behind. Now, no one should go *but* you. What changed?"

"Is that an actual question?" My laugh is dry and tight, but she merely stares. "You want plain talk? All right then, here it is. I'll need to make spit-second decisions in there, and I can't afford distractions or to carry any dead weight. We need fighters. You grow flowers. You'd only be in the way."

Two spots of pink rise under her perfect, bloodless cheeks. If I have to watch her suffer a minute longer, I'll crack. So, I face the window, study the forest beyond our property, keeping my back to Rae. From the sunroom where we stand, a massive screened porch opens to a three tiered deck, and further down, the lake. My father doesn't do anything small. After Maddox Industries gave me the boot, I thought of selling this place and using the money for tuition. Yet, once I suspected the magic hidden in my father's office, selling the house was out of the question. What if an innocent family moves in? I can't have anyone accidentally sucked into The Void.

No. I'm out of options.

"I've finally accepted my responsibility, Raven. My family opened the door between worlds causing *decades* of suffering. It's my problem to fix, undo those wrongs, and close the portal forever. I won't leave someone else to clean up my mess. Not this time." I'm convincing myself as much as her, but it sounds right. Confident my plan will protect her while providing the excuse I need for breaking up, if she'll just …

"Not happening."

… stop fighting me.

"You actually think you can do all of this by yourself?"

As of about an hour ago, yes. I hadn't considered destroying the portal, but why not? Hell, who knows if it's even possible, but my life here is over and if I'm going in there anyway, I might as well try. Salt fills my throat as I turn and face her. "Wynter just got his life back. No need to make him a martyr. He needs to move on." And take care of you, whether or not I come back.

When she nods, I think I'm finally getting through until that stubborn chin of hers sets. "Fine, we'll bring Rosamond back for him."

"No," I say. "You misunderstand. There is no we anymore." She blanches, and I want to punch myself, but I've come too far to stop. "You're going to stay here, *with* him."

She steps forward, placing a palm on my forearm. My skin scorches under her fingertips, my heart pulsing with need. It kills me that her touch is so tentative. She's unsure because I've made her so. All I want is her—all I've wanted from day one—but that's impossible now. Words strangle in my throat, so I glare at her little hand on my arm until she withdraws it.

"Why?" she whispers. "What did I do?"

The question knifes me. "Nothing. I'll always be your friend." It's the truth. I step back, still tethered by her mist-colored eyes. Resilience lights inside them. The strength I've always admired in her—gone missing these last few months—reappears now in force and works like liquefying flame against my waxy bones.

"You want to be friends?" Something between a laugh and sob escapes. Her hands spread in a helpless gesture. "Are you doing this to protect me? Is that it?"

"Partly." Completely. I feel my will crumbling under her pleading gaze, and that won't do. "I told you, everything's changed."

"Including your feelings for me?"

"Yes." It's only one word. Though I feel my soul blackening around the edges before turning to ash the way paper does as it burns.

She's not listening. I can see it in the stubborn set of her mouth. Her fingers climb my arms, slide over my shoulders until her hands clasp behind my neck. My eyes roll back as she presses her warm lips to my jaw. "Raven ... please don't."

Apparently, my words aren't convincing, because she pulls my head forward. How is it that when my lips touch her skin, it's my lungs that catch fire? Heartbreak knocks furiously at the door of my chest. My body responds to her against my will, muscles tighten and ignite.

"Tell me what's really going on … " Her voice, a soft hum in my ear, drives me crazy with wanting. "Whatever it is, you can trust me."

Her lips skim feather light over my mouth. I feel every breath, each nuance. The way her nose nudges mine and her eyelashes flutter against my cheek. She teases, nips at my lower lip, then drops soft, maddeningly gentle kisses across my throat looking for a response. My brain is an oven. Heart, lungs, arms, all of me screams for relief. I want to douse the pain of losing her with the truth and beg her forgiveness, but then it becomes about what's good for me again and not for her.

"Stop it, Rae!" I hate how the gritty sound of my voice reveals my weakness for her. My hands grip both her arms, and plucking them from around my neck, I complete the herculean task of setting her apart from me.

I search her filling eyes. Would she stay if I told her everything? I fear she would, but without her dreams, she'd never be satisfied. Never truly happy, and she'd end up resenting me. I wouldn't survive that. "This isn't working anymore. Please understand that I can't be with you. Not in that way."

"Can't or won't."

Her tears break free. Each one mirrors a punishing lash across my back. I hide my pain in a shrug. "Believe what you want, but we're over."

Raven's lips part, but she doesn't speak. She's backing away. Faster. She turns. Runs. As she flies out the door, she barrels past Dane who's standing just outside. He calls after her, but gets no response.

Dane angles toward me, hands fisted. His stride is heavy with purpose. "What did you do?"

I don't even try to block the punch that's coming. In fact, I hope he hits me with everything he's got. And he doesn't let me down.

Red stars explode behind both eyes. My jaw may be lying on the floor somewhere, but I hardly care. Pain radiates down my neck and shoulder as I await his next blow. Disappointment consumes me when it doesn't come. I want to fight, to black out. Forget who I am, and what I've done, if only for a moment, but I don't.

"What's up with you, asshole?"

This seems to be a recurring theme today. I palm my jaw where the swelling has already started. Calming my churning insides, I answer with a cool I don't feel. "Eavesdropping?" I pick up my cane and struggle to my feet. Leaning against the window to my rear, I wait for the throbbing to subside.

"With all that yelling, who could help it? Tell me what the hell is going on."

"I'm not doing this with you, Dane."

"I didn't ask you to dance. I want to know why you're being an ass."

"It's none of your business."

"You're hurting Rae."

His accusation works like a shiv between my ribs. "I know." The last person on Earth to deserve such treatment is wounded, confused, and angry—because of me. I glance into a corner. There, a tiny moth tries to free himself of the sticky web. As I focus on his struggle, a heavy breath leaks out along with my resolve. "There was a meeting in New York last week. The board took my company."

Several expressions scroll across Dane's face as he processes what I've said. Not that I give a shit. I don't need his approval.

"They've taken everything." Admitting the truth out loud is freeing while making me angrier than I've ever been. "I let her down, *and* my father, *and* everyone at Maddox Industries. I'm broke, Dane. Does that clear the situation up any?"

He's quiet for a long while and then says, "I'm sorry, man. I really am. Does she know?"

Words that flowed so freely moments ago stick as my throat

clogs with shame. I shake my head.

His eyes light with accusation and then sharpen into understanding. "So, your answer is to end it?"

"She won't be alone." Just the thought of her with *him,* and I press my lips to a line.

"Aw, dog." Dane bumps my arm. "No way, you're talking about Cole? You are! It's all over your face." He laughs without humor. "Nah, man that's … "

Cold? Cowardly? He doesn't use words, but his expression sends the same message.

"Dude, that's twisted, even for you." He rubs a finger beneath his nose. "Rae's not a puppy. You don't find your girlfriend a new owner because you're moving or lost your job. I thought you were smarter than this."

Dane's intuitive, blunt, and honest. Qualities that make me like him more than I'll admit. I move my jaw from side to side, wincing as I test its capabilities. "Nice left."

His smirk is cocky. "I'm aware."

"Listen, I'm not naive, but Raven's happiness as a person depends on her art. It's in her blood. She's ambitious, worked too hard, and put up with too much shit to have that chance taken away. The girl is worth any sacrifice I can make. Hell, you said yourself, I'm an ass. It probably won't take her long to figure out she's better off. Cole's rich. He knows her history, and he loves her."

"Are you sure?"

I feel my brow wrinkle. "You're not?"

Dane takes a quick glance back, thick dreads drifting over his shoulder. "Don't get me wrong, I'm Maggie's for life, but I get what's cool about lil' Rae." He rubs his chin. "Especially from Cole's perspective. She rescued him, right? She's mysterious in a way that makes guys notice. Cole admires her. That ain't the same thing as love."

"He'd do anything for her."

"Maybe. Look, I'll admit I didn't trust you in the beginning, but Rae's been … better with you. Happier than I've ever seen her. You too, right?"

I stare him down. My feelings are obvious enough, and though I'm interested in Dane's opinion, I'm not spilling my guts for him.

He doesn't blink. "You're just going to walk away without a fight?"

Yes, I am. She's hurt now, but Wynter will pick up the pieces. I promised I'd never leave, and I won't. She'll recover, and when she's ready, we'll be friends again. "In the end, she's better off." As for me, I'm used to being alone. I'll get used to it again.

"You should tell her about the money, and let Raven decide what's right for her."

I lean forward. "No. And you're not telling her either. You don't have to understand—"

"Never said I didn't understand; I just think you're wrong."

My muscles relax. "It's for the best. Trust me, it's easier this way."

He frowns, expression dubious, but his hand finds my shoulder and he gives me a squeeze. "Rethink your plan, Maddox. I seriously doubt it's for the best. And it damn sure isn't going to be easy. For either of you."

Chapter Seventeen

Cole

As I face the mirror that leads into The Void, two dark blue eyes look back. They have a lot to say, the first of which is: *Are you completely mental? Rose must be some special girl to tempt you back to the hellhole you barely escaped.*

My reflection is wise enough not to answer.

The snick of the door handle has me whirling around. Gideon was here in his father's study when I arrived, and after a quick hallo, we've ignored each other ever since. He wears his khaki cargo pants and black button down effortlessly. Leaning against a bookcase reading, he looks more like some GQ model on a safari photo shoot than crusader. I think of a first meeting with Rose, and glance down at my faded jeans, black boots, and T-shirt. For a moment, I consider heading upstairs to change before wondering when I became a bloody girl.

I head for the couch and flop onto the downy cushions to wait. It's nine a.m. when Dane and Maggie walk in together, each holding a ridiculous, American-sized coffee mug. A pang of jealousy hits as they laugh, so easy and comfortable with each other. Still dressed in drawstring flannel, I assume they've just rolled out of bed and opted out of our little adventure. Under the silhouette of a semi-automatic gun, Dane's T-shirt reads: *Southern Men own the Zombie Apocalypse*, while Maggie's declares: *I'm not fat, I'm poofy*.

All right then.

Dane strolls over to Gideon. My heightened senses make their hushed whispers easy to hear. Not that I'm trying. Okay, I'm trying a little bit. They're discussing Gideon's "redefined" relationship with Raven and how he intends to get Rose out of The Void alone.

Over my dead body.

Maggie makes her way over and sinks into the cushion next to me. "Hey."

"Hello," I answer, still distracted by the pair near the bookshelves. Dane squeezes Gideon's shoulder. When did those two get so chummy? "What's happening over there?"

"Hm?" She glances over her shoulder, expression darkening. "Oh. Gideon's leaving us some instructions for Jamis and Jenny while he's away."

I guess that confirms they aren't coming.

" ... and for Raven. He's hoping you'll help us look after her, Cole." Maggie's head tilts. Her questioning gaze roams my face, but I'm not hiding anything.

"Always, but I won't stay behind." My muscles tense, answering questions she hasn't asked. "I'm over the moon Rae's not going. She has you, and Dane, and I know she'll be okay. Rose has no one, nothing but a small hope that I might come for her. I can't let her down."

A smile threatens. "Raven felt that way about you, you know."

"I know. That's why she'll understand." I nod toward Gideon. "He's the one that should stay. Tosser. First, I can't even look at her he's so jealous, and now? He's already bored, moving on to the next conquest." Typical Maddox asshattery. "She's better off without him. And maybe one day ... "

"Maybe what?"

I don't know what holds me back. Raven was everything. *Is.* Is everything I ever wanted, yet I can't quite say so. She's had enough loss and hardship to last two lifetimes, and Maddox just dumped her. If I promise to come back and then don't ... No. I won't do that to her. "It isn't fair."

"What isn't fair?"

Did I say that out loud? I need to relax. Thankfully, Raven walks through the door and saves me from talking more rubbish.

She spies Gideon and Dane in the corner. Their heads bend toward each other conspiratorially.

While she's distracted, I watch her. I can't help myself. Black combat boots, gray camo pants, and tank so tight its likely illegal in seven states. A black satchel dangles from one shoulder. Her long, dark braid casually hangs over the other, Laura Croft style. Everything about her screams defiant badass.

My gaze slips to Maddox for his reaction. She doesn't resemble the jilted little woman *or* one likely to stay behind.

Raven strolls to the sofa. "You've got that look."

Maggie's eyes dart around their sockets like pinballs. "No I don't. What look? There's no look."

She smiles. "It's going to be fine."

"Of course it is. Who said it wouldn't? I'll take care of everything. Edgar will be fine, spoiled rotten. I'll handle the explanations with my parents. You'll be back in time to start school in the fall ... " She bites her lip, eyes shiny and full.

"Oh, Mags, don't." Raven drops to her knees. Taking Maggie's hands in her own, she pulls her friend close. "We agreed on a plan last night, remember?"

Maggie glances up as Dane nears. "Maybe we should go with them. What if something happens and they need us? I think we should go." She snorts, sucking whatever's clogging her nose back into her sinus cavity. A noise to make any Viking proud. Or nauseated.

"Oh, no you don't. I need you and Dane to manage things

here, for peace of mind. Besides," Rae smiles, slinging her braid over her shoulder, "you lack the necessary superpowers to take this joker out."

Oh hell yeah!

Maggie's eyebrows spring up. "Who said anything about taking anybody out? Don't mess around. Get Rose and come home. That's enough."

"We're going to be epic. You had a feeling in your gut about this trip, so listen to yourself and wish me luck."

"No one is wishing you anything, because you're not going." Gideon towers over her bent form. His stance looks about as pliable as granite.

Raven is dangerously slow to rise. When she does, she allows the full force of her anger to shine from her face. I feel every volt of her one hundred watt I-don't-give-a-shit-what-you-say-I'm-going glare.

Gideon's Adam's apple bobs with his swallow.

Message received.

I fight a smile. While I don't enjoy seeing Raven nurse a broken heart, observing the great Gideon Maddox reduced to jelly by a mere mortal is extremely satisfying.

"Last night, you clarified we aren't together anymore," Raven says. "That choice removes you from influencing me. Understand?" She bends, retrieving her leather bag from the floor, then faces me. "Ready, handsome?"

I grin. *Oh yeah.*

"Raven ... " Gideon's tone is soft despite the warning in it.

She ignores him. "Hugs?" Throwing her arms around Maggie, black hair mixes with blond. Tiny sniffles are followed by whispers that turn into uncontrollable giggling. "And find Mr. Mouse. You know Edgar can't sleep without his mouse."

Maggie's laugh ends in a sob. "It's wrong to keep that animal hopped up on catnip all the time."

"I know." Raven gives her a last hug. "But listen, if I don't—"

"Nope. You'll come back. You'll go to college, and movie stars will wear your clothes on red carpets."

"I'll be back before you have time to miss me."

Maggie mumbles, "Damn straight you will," but Raven's already extracting her arms and moving on to Dane.

Gideon paces in the background. I'm confused because he could try a lot harder to stop her ... unless he really wants her along. But then why the big show?

"Take care of our Mags?"

"Always." Dane lowers his head. "*You* find this Rosamond chick and git to home, hear?"

"Yes, sir." She runs a hand down his arm and squeezes before letting go. Once her back is turned, Dane's expression goes feral. I've seen it before, a mask to hide other emotions. Still, he's a force to be reckoned with, and I wish he was coming.

Rae adjusts the strap on her pack. "Let's go, Wynter."

We move to the gleaming sheet of silver hiding a portal to the world I loathe. I raise my hand, fingertips gliding across the smooth surface, but feel nothing unexpected. "How does it work?"

"Is there anything I can say to convince you to stay?" Gideon asks.

Raven finds his eyes in the glass, her determination palpable.

His lips twitch. If I didn't know better, I'd swear he found something funny. "My father said to look *through* the mirror, beyond the obvious reflection to what's on the other side."

My chest rises with a deep inhalation as I focus on the glass.

The glass shimmers, wavy lines on a bad TV screen. Fuzzy, gray-green smudges bleed though my reflection. As I concentrate, the image sharpens to a line of hedges across a stone footpath on the other side. I *hear* water, smell the wind through the trees.

My hand stretches out, and this time, it passes easily though the mirror's surface. The sensation is not unlike Jell-O—until my fingers start to burn. Growing suction prevents my attempts to draw back.

My mouth dries, but I can't stop sweating. *Stop being a bloody coward and just go,* I tell myself. I let the mirror consume my arm, suck me deeper inside its icy cavern. I close my eyes as my knee follows, then my foot. Once inside, I can't breathe. It's as if I'm trapped inside a water balloon, except this one's filled with freezing cold oil. Blind, my fingers press against a slick, rubbery substance. Elastic walls give under my hands, but I can't break through. My lungs tighten. Claustrophobia grips my throat.

I'm about to lose my shite, when following too closely, Raven steps on my heel. She reminds me that while I'm no expert, I know more about the labyrinth than anyone else. People are counting on a leader that can hold it together, not a cowering Nancy-boy.

With renewed determination, I shove forward, really put my back into it. The barrier spreads thinner and thinner, but I'm desperate for oxygen, now. At the point of either this wall or my lungs blowing apart, elastic snaps, spitting me high into the air. My arse smacks the ground, driving needle-like pains into my tailbone.

Sludge coats my face, fills my eyes. As I dig it out with my fingers, I notice my feet first. Am I supposed to have those? Last time, my legs remained a foggy enigma below the knee. Now, my heels dig at the earth. *Yes!* I'm completely solid, corporeal.

I don't know what I expected. Since we entered by way of mirror, maybe we keep our physical bodies. On impulse, I send a request out to test for wind and am immediately rewarded with a light breeze. In this moment, I sense more of its properties than I ever have. Currents hug the landscape in every direction. High, low, differing patterns skim across lakes and ponds, dip between hilltops, glide over forests. They're ready, listening and waiting, for me.

Mind blown.

As my companions break the boundary between worlds, their bodies land with a thud and roll past in the chalky dirt and leaves.

"Ugh!" Raven's fingers pinch at the thick, yellow mucus

covering her clothes. "That was … this is beyond disgusting."

"Not unlike pushing out of a placenta, I imagine," Gideon announces, with his usual charm.

She stops cleaning and glares. "I didn't need the visual, too. Thanks."

A laugh rumbles deep in his throat.

"I'm glad somebody finds this amusing." Raven wipes more slop from her arms and legs. We all do. "It won't come off! And I smell like a Porta-Potty."

"A *what*?" Now I'm laughing.

"Don't you have those in Europe? It's a portable … You know what, never mind." She stands, stamps her feet. "Got to admit, I don't feel much like a ghost."

"Since we didn't use magic salts or enter through the camera, I think our bodies came with us." I shrug.

Gideon doesn't correct me, so I assume my hypothesis works for him. A quick sweep of our surroundings shows we've landed in some garden pathway. Two rows of hedges dense as brick walls and twelve feet high run in both directions with a familiar cobblestone path in between. In front of us, the hedge breaks into a half circle to accommodate a small pond and garden, definitely inside the maze.

"A lake? Thank all that's clean and goo free," Raven says. Before I guess her plan, she's sprinting toward the water.

"Raven, wait!" Gone.

Gideon's on his feet. "What is it?" He must hear the panic in my voice, but it's too late. The girl of our dreams dives into the murky pond and disappears. I'm up and running with him at my side. "You can't do that shite here," I pant. "Nothing's safe."

His eyes widen with understanding. While she's splashing around, oblivious to possible dangers, we race to the water's edge and throw ourselves in after her.

"Rae!" Gideon's usually steady voice cracks. "Get out of the damn water."

Our yelling gets her attention. She faces us, waves and smiles like the fecking Queen. We're halfway to her when I see a shadow break the surface. Dark and spiny, a fin cuts the water, winding its way back and forth from the shallows.

"Rae—"

"Almost done," she answers, turning aside. She can't be serious. This is no time for stupid, girly hygiene.

"Do you know what that fin's attached to?" Gideon addresses me, but his eyes stay fixed on the thing in the water.

I shake my head. "Nothing good." Little in the maze is.

Finally, Raven tracks our gaze to the shiny, blade gliding toward us. Her cry shrivels my pod faster than the cold water. *Don't panic, don't panic.* "Don't panic!" Is that my voice? I sound like a nine-year-old girl.

"Get her out of here!" Gideon orders. He veers away from me. "Rae, go with Cole." He shouts and splashes before swimming the opposite direction.

"Wait, what … ?" My brow smooths. A decoy? Right! As I lunge for Rae, the fin angles his direction, just as we hoped. Except now he's screwed.

Raven's protesting, but I keep focus on the threat. The simple winds I conjure can't stop something that size, but I have to try. My fear already has the sky reacting, darkening with my mood. Ignoring the nausea roiling in my gut, I continue swimming, dragging Rae behind me. It isn't long until I touch bottom, and plant my feet in the muck. I start slow, nudging little breezes with my mind, gathering them together to make stronger gusts.

A glossy back erupts from the churning water, pushing the fin higher. Only it's not a fin, it's a shell. Black armour connects the beast in three places. Giant claws with razor sharp pincers lift from the muddy depths. Dripping water, they snap and bite at the air. Scorpion.

Wonderful.

I grab Raven's wrist. She wrestles against me, screaming for Gideon, but he's too preoccupied with a stabbing tail and menacing claws to answer. Two unblinking eyes pivot in their ebony sockets. This thing has a face uglier than a dog's arse.

My free hand juts out, and I drive the winds I've collected forward, straining until I have decent force blowing against the water. The resistance is like pushing down a wall, but I manage to get a sequence of waves going. They crash the monster's body. I hoped to knock him over, but he's too strong. And now he's good and aggro. Angling toward us, it moves quickly. The tail rises, deadly stinger poised to strike.

We're so dead.

Firelight flashes. I fall forward as Rae stumbles into my ribs. When I get to my feet, a ball of flame pelts the scorpion's side. The fire bolt bounces off the armor and drops hissing into the water. Another missile hits, then another.

One by one, Gideon lobs small flares onto the scorpion. Not powerful enough to kill, but they might scare him off. Sure enough, the animal lurches away before darting under the water. We track his tail hovering above the surface until it submerges completely.

I ease Rae toward the shallows with Gideon lagging behind. A patch of thick reeds slow our pace. We're making progress when a splash disrupts the water. Gideon shouts. Raven gasps. And I'm nothing short of frantic as the fin rises on our right. The black tail arcs over its back, water trickling from the stinger. My arms shoot out on instinct. Our doom is ten feet away. Nine. Eight. My heart races, head pounds. I can't see the claws and pull my feet up, tucking my thighs into my chest. Seven feet away, six … I'm practically hyperventilating as I wait for the scissoring mandibles to sever a leg or slice me in half below the surface.

Somewhere behind me, Raven screams. "Don't, don't, don't!"

Using my fear as fuel, I call the winds. Power infuses me, shakes my body. "Fight me, then. C'mon, damn you!" I send the tempest out as he lunges. The monster smashes against my barrier as though hitting a glass building. When it staggers, I press my advantage. The gale blows so hard, water shoots away from his skeletal frame until he's writhing on a mud floor.

A blast of fire pounds the scorpion's side. Bigger, more explosive, the improved firepower Gideon's launching proves he's learning fast. Sparks fly, shell smokes and chars as a firebomb tunnels into the animal's head, finishing it.

Exhausted, my hands drop causing the winds to slow, then cease. I can barely make out the creature's dark outline sinking as the now freed water rushes over it. With what little strength I have left, I head for shore, Raven's hand limp in mine.

My slick hand loses its grip, and I slap at the water tying to reclaim her. A bout of vertigo blurs my vision. Water laps at my neck, rising to my chin. I'd fight but my muscles cramp, and I go under. I'm floating, or maybe I'm drowning.

Someone yanks my arm. Raven's pale face appears almost white against her dark hair, braid hanging limply down her back. The sight fades in and out. She's slipping away.

Gideon swims into view, fingers straining toward me. Two hands hook beneath my arms before clasping together across my chest. My head sags as we stumble out of the water.

"You're no feather, are you, England?" Gideon grouses, hauling me up the soggy bank. "But I think you'll live."

I nod, because I'm breathing too hard to speak. My boots drag the mud. Then I'm rolled onto my back, and someone brushes the hair from my eyes.

Raven crouches beside me. Her small hand closes over mine, warming my skin.

I watch her knees sink into the soft soil. When my breaths finally slow, I say, "Are you … okay?" The question liberates her smile.

"Never mind me, how are *you*? I thought you'd drown."

"I'm fine," I wheeze. "Never better." My gaze finds Gideon. "Thanks, mate. Really, thank you."

He looks from me to Raven with relief and something else. "I should be thanking you."

All that matters is she's safe, which reminds me. "Rae, you can't just … run off like that." I suck in another lungful of air. "I wasn't kidding about monsters."

"I'm sorry. That was incredibly stupid, and selfish, and ... stupid. I didn't think past getting the slime off. It won't happen again."

My hand rotates until we're palm to palm, and our fingers thread. "You're forgiven."

"Come on." Gideon's voice is quick and tight. He snaps his head, clearing the dripping hair from his eyes. "We need to keep moving. Let's find Rosamond and get back before dark. I have no desire to spend the night inside Pan's nightmare."

His estimated timeline is a bit optimistic, but I keep mum. The guy's as irritable as poison oak, but he just saved my arse, so I won't provoke him.

Raven helps me up, and I throw an arm over her shoulder as casually as I can. She's been through a lot and needs my support, right? Sure, we'll all buy that.

Maddox stares at the pond, his mismatched eyes riveted on the gray-green water. The corners of his mouth bend. I can't see what's amusing, considering any one of the three of us were almost impaled on the end of a giant scorpion's stinger, but his smile stretches to a full-on grin. When he chuckles, it's contagious and dammit, now I'm smiling too. He looks over at me and laughs. We're both whooping it up, by God, because nearly dying is just hilarious. My arm is around his ex and he's probably going to change his mind, want her back, and stab me in the heart. Brill. I only laugh harder.

Raven watches us. I gather she's wondering if we've finally cashed in our sanity chips by the confusion etched on her brow. "What's so funny?"

I have no idea, but tears threaten the corners of my eyes. Raven throws her hands up which Gideon must find comical, because he claps me on the back and leans over, shoulders shaking with his big guffaws. I've never heard Gideon's laugh before. It's deep and hearty and makes the corner of Raven's mouth curl up. All reasons to hate him more, but I don't. Instead, I break into a new fit of hysterics, because I need this release.

Raven tries again. "What am I missing?"

Gideon straightens, his laughter subsiding as his usual reserve regains control. He watches my arm tighten on Raven's shoulder and does nothing. I don't get it. "We're alive," he says. "Don't you see? We used the elements to fend off a homicidal insect and survived."

We did. And it felt good. Important. Maybe for the first time, I have hope we can actually get Rose out instead of the bull I've been shoveling in the hopes someone might believe me.

"Do you know where we are?" Gideon asks me. "There's a tower over there."

I spot the structure beyond the hedge. "It's farther than it looks."

"Is it hers?"

"Possibly." I can tell by his frown he doesn't like my answer. I didn't spend much time in the labyrinth, but I know we won't just waltz in here and take Rose out in a day.

We'll have to spend the night.

Chapter Eighteen

Raven

The sky is heavy and gray with thunderclouds. Gale force winds howl and moan around the white clapboard siding of the tiny church building in Sales Hollow. My hair escapes its bonds, whips my face. The thin white nightgown I wear flaps against my calves as the first raindrop falls.

"Mother!" I call. "Mother, where are you?"

As a child, I had a lot of nightmares. I recognize this as one, but that doesn't stop the images from coming. Rain falls harder, soaking my gown, turning the fabric sheer. My flesh pebbles under the freezing water. Somewhere, a door slams. Reedy trees bend to breaking in the storm. Yet here I stand.

"Mother?"

The trickle of water at my feet widens to a stream, quickly rising to my knees. The runoff carves a ravine in the ground between the church graveyard and the gate. Guess which side I'm on? Along the hillside, gravestones tilt in the washing soil. They slide and slip away completely as rain loosens their footers. A mudslide exposes a dozen coffins at least. Slim wooden boxes that house the dead careen down the steep bank, overturning like cars in a soapbox derby pileup.

Corpses, dressed in their Sunday best spill out into the rushing water. Arms and legs akimbo, red clay stains their finery. The same mud holds me in place, an unwilling spectator to a mass unearthing. Bodies bunch behind a fallen tree like a pile of discarded mannequins. Limbs joined at unnatural angles stick out from behind a fallen log. In time, the coffins come apart or sink but not the remains. Those shrunken forms work themselves loose and float along the current. Bobbing driftwood made of dehydrated bone, and flesh, and muscle.

A scream tears from me as the first body bumps against my hip. The man's lids are open. One cloudy blue eye stares without seeing. Looks at me. Accusing. His lips have rotted, exposing long teeth in an angry grimace. As if I'm the one who dug him up and threw him away.

The dead wash past me, directed by an unfeeling current toward an unsympathetic sea. They plunge and reemerge in the churning water.

Another whimper escapes as they crash into me, one gory corpse after another. An object snags at my feet. The bulk skitters and stalls against my shin bones, but won't pass by.

A body? I shudder. Tears stab my eyes.

Something long and soft snakes up my calves, tickling the skin. Hair?

I jump as lightning flashes. Thunder booms overhead before echoing in the distance. I strain with effort. Struggle to free myself from the mud, but its hold is iron. Through it all, the unseen something softly jostles at my ankles. It won't go away. Can't move on. Not without help. Water streaked and murky with clay makes it impossible to see what's down there. Or who.

I bend, dipping my hand under the boiling river, my hair drags in the flow. Uneven heartbeats play a staccato tune in my ears. Hesitant, my fingertips pull back a beat before I plunge ahead.

My fingers wrap a branch or stick. It weighs nothing, yet when I lift, the source moves two or three inches and snags. Gauzy fabric flutters against my hand. Someone's dress? Definitely a body.

Shivers wrack my frame. I bite back a cry, applying more force to what I assume is a bone. I yank and rotate until I feel a snap.

An arm, thin as a broom handle breaks the surface. I gag, throw the limb away, and dive again with both hands. I'm not so tentative now, frantically pulling until the body gives and rises—spine first. A pink dress hangs against an emaciated ribcage. Bleached skin still clings to bones in patches. Long dark hair parts against a white skull. I turn her over because this is a dream. The place where you do things you wouldn't normally do.

The nose is gone. A fleshy nub of skin dangles in the hole once occupied by cartilage. One ear is missing which strikes me as incredibly sad. Lips torn away, her mouth is a narrow hole. Her eyes are muted orbs, but I imagine them gray as they once were. The dim irises sway back and forth, as if she's searching for someone. For me.

My gaze drops to the amethyst pendant at her throat.

"Wake up, Raven," my mother says. "This is no place for the living."

I shake my head. I don't want to argue, but I have questions.

Rain falls harder. The water rises to my waist, my chest, bringing my mother's face ever nearer.

The river gives up her dead. Braced against the current, they stand before me in varying forms of decay. Tattered clothes hang from sagging shoulders. Bony fingers point. "Go home, Raven." Their words mock me.

My grip tightens on my mother's sharp frame. "You were my home!" Water laps my chin. I press my lips together to keep out the toxic sludge. The river bloats, brine and mulch and waste fill my nose. My face tilts up, but the swell covers that, too.

Mother slips away.

I can't do this without you.

Water slides into my mouth, fills my lungs, and clogs my windpipe. I'm surprised to find drowning doesn't hurt the way I thought it would.

Mother's face appears under the filthy water. Her milky eyes dull in the gloom, her nose an ink spot. "Don't give up, child. Fight for what you love."

Pressure builds in my head, around my heart. Wait for me, Mother. I'll be with you and Ben soon.

"Raven."

Gideon? His voice floats above me, vacuous, unattainable as air. Be happy. I loved you so much.

"Raven, wake up!"

A gentle hand smoothes the hair from my forehead, the motion's warm and comforting. This time, my name's no more than a whispered breath in my ear sending a shiver through me. When the scent of spicy black licorice tickles my nose, my eyelids flutter open. It's still dark. I'm flat on my back, the air cool and dewy on my skin. My boyfriend's face swims into view surrounded by a starry night's sky. Ex-boyfriend. Guess I haven't gotten used to thinking of him that way yet, and my chest cramps painfully when I do.

Behind him is the clearing where we made camp. Skeletal trees skirt the boundary of a small circular lawn. I'm lying on the leaf-littered ground and not in the tree where I fell asleep. We tied ourselves to sturdy limbs to pass the night, away from the dangers Cole's always warning us about. I heard several screams while trying to nod off, followed by grisly sounds of flesh being ripped apart. Perhaps that's why I had the nightmare.

I push up on my elbows. "I must have been sleepwalking again." Nighttime weirdness I'd done on and off since I was a kid, unfortunately.

"Hm, yes, so I gathered," he says, still running calloused fingers up and down my arm. "I recognized the signs, though you didn't end up in bed with me this time."

"Oh, uh ... " He chuckles, and I'm thankful the dark hides my blush. Because I'd done *exactly* that, sleepwalking into his room on multiple occasions last year. "No. See, I was actually dreaming about my mother. She was telling me something ... " Like a lot of dreams, it seemed so important at the time, but the urgency fades as soon as you wake up. "I forget now." Glancing around, I remember our goal here and pass from one nightmare to the reality of another.

His fingers stop moving against my skin. "I'm sorry. Are you all right?" Gideon's handsome face leans in, lines etched deeper with concern.

At first, all I want is to alleviate his fears. Then I remember how he dumped my butt not twenty-four hours ago with no better reason than to say life is "complicated," and *Have a nice day!* That can't be the whole story, can it? After promising not to leave, maybe he can't bring himself to admit his feelings faded after all. The thought flips a switch inside me and I push my nightmare aside.

I made of fool of myself kissing him yesterday. Throwing myself at him is more accurate. I played every card I had, laid all my stupid feelings on the table. So when he kissed me back, I thought maybe … But my very short experiment as seductress was a humiliating fail, because in the end, he had no trouble walking away.

"Wait a minute, you broke up with me." I say, scrambling to stand.

He rises with me. "What?"

"When you break up with somebody, you don't get to say stuff like 'I'm sorry' or listen to their dreams or ask them how they are." I hate that I sound like a petulant child, but my heart is bleeding, and the hurt makes it easier to speak without filters.

"I'll never stop caring about you, Raven."

His words hold no meaning. Even so, I'm distracted by the planes of his chest showing through his unbuttoned shirt. How the dip between his pectoral muscles rises and falls with each quick breath, how the waistband of his khakis rides too low on his hips while his shirt is hiked up enough to see a swath of golden skin. He looks so good, and that makes me so mad, I want to yell.

"You can't break up and then act all … "

"All what?"

Nice.

It makes everything harder. I stare a hole into a nearby tree trunk to keep from crying. He might feel guilty over breaking my heart, but it occurs to me he may have confused pity and love from the beginning. Either way, I need space. "Thanks for checking on me, but I'm good."

"Rae." His tone is incredibly soft. "Don't do that." His fingers stretch toward my cheek. I've never wanted something so much, but I turn aside. He can't have it both ways. My heart can't take it.

"Do what?" My arms fold creating a tiny wall between us.

"That. Shut me out. Can't we find a way to be friends again?"

"See, that's the thing," I fire back. "We were never friends. Never took our time getting to know each other. We went straight from enemies to madly in love. Well, at least one of us did. That was my mistake." Thank you, sarcasm.

He blanches like I slapped him. I actually feel bad for a minute until his nostrils flare. A sure sign his patience is waning. I can't imagine what right he has to feel frustrated. And if he is, that's his problem. "I don't want to fight."

A sad smile leaks out through my pain. "You love to fight, Gideon ... debate, win." I watch his lips turn down, think about how they feel on my neck, and mentally pinch the crap out of myself. My head knows we're finished but not my soul. Sure, he's being a contradictory ass right now, and he's still the most fascinating person I've ever known.

Wind kicks up, rustling the leaves above us. I peek up at our wind maker, but Cole's still asleep high in a tree. My empty bunk is on the limb right next to his. Where Gideon put it. I swear, it's like he's forcing me on Cole. "You like bargains, so I'll make a deal with you. We're here to rescue Rose, right? Arguing the whole time will only cause problems. Not to mention be awkward for Cole, so let's both suck it up and move on."

"Oh yes," he snarls. "Let's make sure Wynter's happy. I'll make it my top priority."

From the first, Gideon's moods were unpredictable, but the

last few days, he's off the rails. "You want to tell me what's going on with you lately, Jekyll?"

His eyes narrow as he steps closer. "Want to elaborate?"

He's inches from me, but I'm not backing up ... or down. Not this time. "Well, first off, you're acting like a lunatic." His mouth opens, but I talk over him. "You won't tell me why you've been so upset lately. Or explain how you and Dane suddenly became the brotastic duo." I pause looking into his moonlit eyes. It won't make any difference. It might even hurt more to know, but I plunge ahead. "Or give me a real reason for breaking up." I didn't plan to cry, yet a tear breaks free, falling into darkness.

His hands frame my face, fingers threading the hair at my temples. His breaths heat my skin, and I swear I hear his heart pounding, but it must be mine. "You did nothing wrong. It's me."

I sob-laugh because I'm actually getting the it's-not-you-it's-me speech.

Standing together in the dark, we cling to each other acknowledging a chance taken that wasn't meant to be. My pulse quickens as the wind whips through the trees, gusts around our feet. With his blue and green eyes blazing down on me, I could almost believe it's desire instead of guilt that drives his tortured expression. Almost. But then he's always been unpredictable, and I can't say he didn't warn me.

"So, that's it," I say, though I think I'm talking more to myself at this point. "You don't want me anymore."

He won't even look at me. "I'm sorry, but no. Not like that."

"Wow, that's a real no, isn't it?" My voice is calm, strangely resigned. Hard as it is, I step away. His hands drop, and he looks as miserable as I feel. While he doesn't love me, it's clear he hoped to stay in my life. That would be great if I were capable. I'm not. Maybe one day. Right now, I can't handle watching him move on with someone else. Or worse, withdraw into that lonely old house. Destroy himself with bitterness and hate the way he used to. He's better than that, even if he doesn't think so.

Why can't girls come pre-wired with memory card delete buttons for ex-boyfriends? Why do we spend hours planning improbable, imaginary solutions for bad breakups? I'd heard it a hundred times in school. Girls wishing out loud their ex would be hit by lightning while simultaneously checking their cells every ten seconds for apology texts where he begs to get back together. I never understood their paradoxical thinking—until now.

"Okay, I call a truce." I take a deep breath, refocusing on the bigger part of what brought us here. "We'll work together, get Rose, and go home. But afterward, I'm gone. We won't ever have to set eyes on each other again. Deal?"

His stare is savage, jaw clamped tight enough to crack bone. With a sudden lunge, he grabs my arms, fingers digging in. "I never wanted this." His breath catches with intention. "If you … God, this is killing me."

I wrench free of his hold. *Killing you?* Anger finally boils over. "You say you won't leave and then you do. We break up, but you look at me like you're looking at me right now. I can't do this anymore."

"Raven, will you—"

"They're coming. Run, Rose!"

Our heads swivel up. Whatever Gideon planned to say next is lost as Cole shouts from his nest in the tree.

Seems I'm not the only one suffering from nightmares tonight.

Chapter Nineteen

Cole

Tied into my makeshift hammock on a tree limb, I can't help listening to Rae and Gideon's post break-up spat. *Right.* Okay, maybe I can help it. I'm only half-ashamed to admit my curiosity to know what killed their relationship rivals a forensic coroner with a dead guy on the slab. After a few minutes, I have new insight on the couple-drama happening below. In fact, I'm about to pull an optic muscle with all the eye rolling I'm doing.

A knot in the branch digs into my spine. I shift to my side, and just that fast, I'm sucked into another dream state. The lull is so powerful, not even a good fight keeps me awake. As I enter the mysterious space holding Rose captive, I no longer fight against it.

The turret room materializes, solidifies. Moonlight streams in through the window. Dim candlelight glows on the table by the bed.

I've barely taken a breath before the lovely blond is in my arms. Rose is instantly corporal. I reject the idea she's holding me for any other reason than to feel the weight of her own body.

"I've missed you so much, Cole."

Okay, until she says that. There's no guile in her. No games or coy talk. Just, "I missed you." My arms cinch around her frail shoulders. Her cheek nuzzles my chest making me feel strong and needed.

"I said I'd be back."

She takes my hand and gives a tug, leading me to the open window. Without releasing my hand, she presses her thighs against the cool stone and leans out to gaze at the courtyard and surrounding labyrinth. "He was here again today: Pan." The name slithers though my mind like a curling viper. How often does he come to see her, and why? "He knows you're coming for me. Be careful, Cole. He's planning something bad."

"Define *bad*."

"I can't." She shakes her head. "I mean, I don't know, maybe a trap." She shivers and I squeeze her hand.

"We expected a fight, but thank you for warning us."

Her smile is quick before fading to a frown. "Don't thank me. I'm not a good person."

"Of course you are. Why would you say that?"

"Because I'm turning out just like my uncle. I swore I wouldn't, but I am." Her eyes continue scanning the courtyard as though she's lost someone.

She's different tonight, distracted and pensive. My finger slides beneath her chin, and I force her gaze up. "I'm sorry, Rose, but I don't know what you're talking about."

"You always call me Rose now. I like it."

Her comment is deflection 101. Used it myself, which is why she won't get away with a non-answer. "Why don't you think you're a good person? What happened with your uncle?"

When she bites her pale peach lips, I realize I'm staring like a perv. *Focus, Cole.*

"Talk to me."

"I'm here because my uncle wanted Pan to rig a big game he had going in Las Vegas. Poker."

"He lost?" I ask, but I already know what she'll say, and my stomach sinks.

"Yes, and no. More like *I* lost." Her features harden with a look I've not seen before. "Pan used magic to ensure my uncle won. In return, Pan asked for a percentage of the winnings. His *treasure*." But my uncle was sick, he couldn't stop gambling. He lost everything he'd won the following day. Pan took me instead, and I wound up here."

"Which was likely his plan all along." I surmise.

"Exactly. See that mirror on the wall?" When she releases me to point, her feet disappear in a white mist. I touch the fabric of her gown and bring them back. "Pan's enchanted other mirrors in different places that connect to the labyrinth. He left that one here on purpose. So my uncle could see into my jail and suffer with what his choices had done to me. He fell into a deep depression, before he hanged himself."

"That must have been—"

She waves me off. "Ask me how I know." Her tone's sharper than the ragged edge of a broken bottle.

There's no need to ask her anything. I know she watched her uncle kill himself through the looking glass. "I'm sorry."

"I'm sorry, too." The anger dies from her voice leaving it tired sounding instead. Lines mar her smooth skin. Her pain is pure and authentic. Listening to her story feels like spying, even though she invited me in. "I can't bring him back, but I don't want to die never having lived."

At the catch in her voice, I reach for her but she tears herself away. Fully ethereal, she hovers at the window, facing the garden again.

"That's why I'm bad. I wanted my life back so much; I risked you and your friends for the slightest chance." Her fingers play with her hair. "It's hopeless. No one beats the magician. And you'll hate me, and I'm sorry, and I wish I could take it all back, because you'll be stuck here. I don't want you of all people to hate me."

Why me of all people? But that's not what comes out. "I could never hate you." I asked Raven to risk as much a year ago myself. "We're not as different as you might think."

Silver-blond hair stirs with the faint breeze, and a strand floats over her eyes. The silence between us stretches, yet I've never felt closer to anyone. My body leans in. I'm going to kiss her. She lifts her face like she'll let me. We barely know each other, but I don't care.

A hiss brings me up short. I glance out the window, and in the yard, dozens of glowing orbs gleam like animal eyes watching from the forest.

Never mind the kissing now. "What the hell are those?"

"The Draugar," she whispers. "I knew he—"

"What's a Draugar?"

"The undead that roam these woods."

I stare as though she slapped me. "Vampires?"

"Zombies."

"Impossible."

"Except it isn't. My grandmother told stories. Old Nordic women used to threaten us kids into good behavior with scary fables about black monsters who ate naughty children. The legend says they are mound dwellers, shape shifters. Ones who walk after death. The stuff of nightmares, but in this place, our worst fears become real."

She's right. The eyes in the forest grow brighter. Skulking, black shapes draw near the tower. "What do we do? How do we kill them?" I'm yelling my head off. Not that I'm blaming her, of course, but damn, zombies?

"You don't." Her little hands clutch my chest. "Cutting their heads off will slow them down for a while." I stumble back, as her silver eyes latch onto mine. "They aren't fast, but they don't stop. You have to get out of here. Go! Save yourself. Warn your friends … "

"Cole, wake up. Can you hear me?"

Though I'm still inside the turret, Raven's urgent call penetrates the stones themselves. "Rae?" My head swivels. "Where are you?"

"Oh for crying out loud, will you just wake up? We have to get out of here!"

"Out of where? What the hell?"

Rose ignores my crazy conversation with an invisible Raven, choosing to shout at the ceiling instead. "Pan, don't hurt him, please. I'm begging you, anything but this. Leave them alone."

I throw my hands up. Torn between two worlds, it's obvious something scary is also happening on Raven's side of my trance, but I've no idea what. Voices blend, each shouting their own agenda until I can't tell who's speaking to whom.

The room blurs and it no longer matters. I spin out of time and function. The turret disappears. Rose is gone. And I wake in the tree where my night started.

Raven's fingers bite my shoulders. "For the love of Pete!" She gives me a good shake. "Wake up before those *things* get us."

"What things?" My eyes blink open.

Rae balances her weight on the thick limb at my head while Gideon squats at my feet.

"Those," he answers, pointing to the clearing below.

Yellow lights shine from the surrounding wood, filling my stomach with sick dread. I have no idea how they got here so fast, but the zombies I'd seen from Rose's tower now plod toward our campsite.

I sit up too fast and lose my balance. Arms flailing, my hand knocks Raven over, while my feet sweep Gideon's boots. He swears an oath, and then we're falling. Wind whistles past my head, Rae and Gideon alongside me.

On instinct, my hands fly out. Wind might cushion our fall, but in my panic, I send mixed signals to the east and northern currents with no time to correct my mistake.

I land so hard, it's a miracle I can still breathe. If I'm going to wield air for our benefit, I'll need to be faster. A lot faster.

Maddox groans and staggers to his feet in a very un-Gideon-like manner. I don't see his cane until Rae steps from behind me and hands it to him. He grasps the handle, planting the other end in the dirt. One arm wraps his waist. He curses again, raising his gaze. "Is everyone okay?" It strikes me we should be asking him that question.

"I think so." Raven says, rubbing her dirty shoulder.

The hissing grows louder. Pale yellow lights move closer on all sides, and I guess the Draugar are roughly forty meters away.

Gideon steps forward, leaning heavily on his cane. "What's out there?"

"Zombies," I say, forcing my feet under me. My legs shake, but I'm up. "Saw them from Rose's window."

"Wait, what?" Raven winces. "Real, brain-eating zombies?"

"I don't know about the brain-eating part, but yeah."

"God help us."

"What do we do?" Gideon's asks. Moments of indecision feel like hours. Through the shadows, a few misshapen silhouettes threaten the clearing.

"Their heads have to come off." Nerves tingle down my arms. Wind sweeps the leaves around in gusts. Unfortunately, it's an involuntary response to my fear and not a sign of my controlling anything. "Or we can run. Personally, I vote we run."

Gideon grabs Raven's arm and sends her barreling into my chest, followed by her backpack. "Split up. Take Raven with you."

Her headshake is vehement. "No, we stick together."

Gideon jogs the opposite direction, his limp definitely more pronounced. That's when I see the blood spreading on his T-shirt under his arm.

"You're hurt?" Rae asks this as though her eyesight is lying.

Instead of answering, Gideon stares me down. I get it. There's no time to debate with her.

The first Draugar enter the clearing. Moonlight washes the dark monsters blue. The non-humans are tall and emaciated. No flesh, just shriveled leather stretched over bone. Each mouth is a flapping black hole, their teeth clack in a terrible, steady rhythm.

And they keep coming.

"He's bleeding." Raven wrestles free of my grip. "We need to stay together."

"No!" Gideon and I yell at once. More zombies lurch from the forest cutting us off.

We're running, within view of each other at first, but after a few minutes of dodging trees and monsters—more popping up at every turn—the landscape and zombies force us farther and farther apart.

A mad giggle echoes from the treetops.

"Pan, please don't!" Rose's ethereal voice floats through the wood followed by a sinister laugh. I spin, watching for a flash of silver, but see nothing.

"Dry your tears, Rosamond angel, delicious though they are. I'm only having a bit of fun with our new guests."

"Don't do this." Rose's desperate pleading leaves me gutted. "This is my fault. Please don't punish them with my nightmares."

"What's her fault?" Gideon yells from somewhere in the black.

Pan ignores him, continuing the eerie disembodied discussion. "If you won't share your night terrors, sweet Rosamond, I'll simply have to improvise."

A woman sobs, volume increasing until her weeping rolls like thunder overhead. I cover my ears but still hear Pan's cruel mimic. "Oh, boohoo. Please don't hurt them."

I grind my teeth to shut out the noise. His voice is so loud my ears may bleed.

"Keep going, children." Pan's laughter twines with the hissing Draugar. "Run for your lives. Since our dearest Rosamond is unwilling to share, feed us with your fear. Face the terrors within."

Whatever Pan is threatening, there's no time to ask. As more zombies break from the tree line, I zigzag around saplings and bushes.

Raven calls and I answer. At least I think it's her, she's too far ahead to see. Roots snag my bootlaces. Branches scratch my arms and face as I tear through the underbrush.

My foot sinks ankle deep in mud. Hissing follows a hair's breadth behind. Always advancing. Gaining. I'm sure I catch a glimpse of Gideon as he fades into the murky shadows ahead. Freeing my boot from the muck, I startle, imagining the twig brushing my shoulder is the rotting claw of a zombie. Every thud and bump echoing in the night becomes a monster's footstep announcing my doom.

I run until hard clay softens to swamp, and tall leafless trees surround me. Stripped of bark, they glow white in the moonlight, their knotted roots still stab at the saturated ground that drowned them long ago. My tread slips in the damp, the earth sucking with moisture and slowing my pace. "Rae? Gideon? Where are you?"

No answer.

Another misstep has me tripping over a taut vine. I stumble, splashing down hands and knees into a foot of dank water. "Bloody horror show, isn't it?" I whisper to no one. Vines litter the swamp. They float across the bog dotted with big purple blooms. Several flowers spring open when jostled. With each move I make, more petals unfurl, the flowers, one by one, shuddering and sifting open along the cluster of vines I've disturbed. All at once, yellow pistils secrete a cloudy mist that fills the air.

"Bollocks." This can't be good. Plus, I'm talking to myself.

My eyes sting and tear. I hate on the flowers. Curse the dust in my nose, because I'm choking on it. I'm too loud, but can't stop. The flowers blow more powder, and I hack and wheeze, waiting for the next coughing fit to produce a lung.

A hiss goes off in my ear. Shudders crawl under my skin as I twist away. I'm up and jogging, but my boots lose traction on the boggy leaves sending my feet flying out from under me yet again. I land hard on my back. Peering into the canopy of crippled tree branches, a single Draugar is here, looming overhead, arms outstretched. I scuttle away, palms and feet to the ground like a hermit crab. My shoulders smack the broad trunk of a tree, and I can go no further.

Misshapen legs shuffle toward me. He's on me in seconds, and when the zombie clamps his dry, rotting fingers around my neck, my airway closes. Rough bark digs and scrapes my spine as I grapple with the stony bones at my throat. The eyes are nothing but gouged-out holes that go on forever. Desperate to free myself, I kick both feet up, but instead of throwing him off, my boots punch straight through his sunken chest. The laces snag somewhere inside his ribcage.

The Draugar stands, releasing my throat, but with my feet attached to the skeleton, I'm drawn upside down like a rabbit in a snare. Engulfed by panic, I scream and shout obscenities. My eyes bulge and heartbeats gallop. I strain and stamp and punch at the stinking carcass, breaking him to smithereens and freeing myself.

My chest heaves as though I'll never draw enough air again.

Storm winds bend the young saplings in the glade, plucking sparse leaves from their branches like feathers from a dead chicken.

All around, pieces of the zombie I just destroyed twitch and jump all by themselves. Slowly, ruined limbs inch toward each other. I cringe watching old bones snap into place and knit together again like grotesque puzzle pieces. The creature struggles to his feet, shoulders hanging at odd angles. A hiss that sounds a lot like my name draws my gaze up. The creature has donned a thin, black robe that I recognize from my father's dressing closet with its expensive satin sheen and rich, scarlet lining. The edges flap in the gale I'm creating with my fear and desperation. The robe's collar droops, and inside, I see a young girl with platinum hair cradled within the heavy folds.

"Rose?"

The sight of her pressed against the mephitic flesh of the zombie turns my stomach.

The scene smears with my fury. I rub my eyes and look again, but this time I'm drawn to the zombie's face.

Dead, black eyes clear and turn bright blue. Healthy flesh

forms over bone, and the citrus scents of home replace that of rot and decay. Shining, black hair, a perfect match to my own, grows from the misshapen skull.

Father?

He sets Rose aside and comes for me.

I'm weak, helpless. I don't even fight as his palms resume the unrelenting pressure on my windpipe.

Icy breath leaks from his open mouth in a cloud of mist. I blink, but slowly. Purple lines streak across the backs of my eyelids. My head spins. I'm sinking as he forces my head down and underwater.

Waves close over my nose. A few bubbles escape my mouth, and I watch them travel lazily to the surface and burst.

The muscles in my father's face flex with effort as his hands continue crushing my throat. The heartbeat echoing in my ears slows to nothing. My vision darkens, lungs heat to burning.

You always did want me out of the way.

Ah, there ... my father smiles at me, perhaps to say goodbye. But no, I see now it's merely a grimace from the sheer force of his exertion on my neck.

My hands go limp and fall to my sides.

So, this is what it's like to die.

Chapter Twenty

Gideon

Over and over, my cane snags in the undergrowth, and my boots stick in the sucking mud. The wound in my side is screaming, slowing me down. Because my pace is slow, I'm falling behind. Falling behind means I've lost sight of her. Losing sight of her makes me insane with worry. Insane worry makes me rash and incredibly stupid.

"Raven!"

The thought of her in the hands of those *things* makes me see red. Literally. Like the blood I long to spill stains the sky, drips from the trees. Everything I look at is inked crimson. My thoughts are murderous as they turn to Pan, the board at Maddox enterprises, and myself. For once, life was good. I was happy. How did everything go from amazing to screwed so quickly?

My foot goes out from under me, and I'm on the ground, covered in swamp. Wet and rotting, when the forest exhales, its foul breath permeates my lungs. The dozen flowers surrounding me open and vomit pollen. Swearing an extra painful death to Pan, I shake yellow powder from my hair. When the dust settles,

I glance up and detect a clearing just beyond the haunted wood.

It's not the lake house that lies ahead in the distance, but Maddox mansion. I briefly think that's impossible, but Jamis and Jenny's safety trumps logic. Old as they are, they're no match for Pan's creatures. Like a fool, I must have led them all the way home.

I search through the muck with my fingers, grasping for my cane but can't find it, and I'm out of time to look. The house needs warning, so I gather my legs beneath me, muscles burning as I rise. My exhaustion makes sense, but not the labored breathing and blurry vision. Everything hurts as though I finished a triathlon, but it's the sharp pain in my ribs that has my attention.

Eight inches of tree branch protrudes from my side. I clench my teeth knowing it has to come out. Trembling fingers grip the stick's end. I tense, ready my mind, and ease the wooden stake from my torso. My lips press together to gag the cry in my throat. Sweat beads on my forehead. Breaths pant from me in noisy, broken puffs.

I can't control my shaking hands. Red runs down my fingers, splattering the leaves below until, inch by inch, the stick is out. As I examine my skewer, it tips forward from my too loose grasp and falls to the ground.

As if someone slashed a tire, dull hissing leaks through the forest behind me.

I ignore the pain in my gut, forget my cane, and limp toward the house. There's plywood stockpiled near the garage, left over from repair work we did last month. If I can get everyone inside, perhaps we can bar the windows. Create a barricade. Once the zombies lose interest, I can slip out again and look for Raven. Not much of a plan, but it's all I've got. She's strong. Smart. She can hold on until I find her. I force myself to believe it's true.

I head for the detached garage. Though I'm constantly watching the house windows for my employees, I alternately scan the woods for Draugar.

And then the first one breaks from the tree line. More follow, slinking along in their relentless pursuit. The zombies' mouths hang open, no more than cavernous black holes. With their weird, hobbling gate, the things look like mummies wrapped in tobacco leaves.

Shudders wrack my body, but I keep moving.

A new group pours from the trees opposite, thick like a trail of fire ants between me and the house. Rapid heartbeats slap at my aching ribs. I'm breathing so loud I fear they'll hear me.

Slipping through the side door of the garage, I search for anything that will make a decent weapon. The place reeks of gasoline and sawdust. Moonlight streams through rotted shingles in the roof. Between the junk piled in here and my father's old '57 Corvette rusting under its cover, there's nowhere to step without making noise.

I dare a glance out the dirty window and come face to face with a zombie. Ducking, I bump the rear fender of the car with my ass. My elbow knocks a paint can over, and the hissing outside increases tenfold.

Shadows play on the cover of the Vette, staining the old, blue plastic darker. I know a dozen zombies congregate just outside. Sweat creeps down the back of my neck, dampening my collar.

Glass breaks. The door on the far side of the room creaks open. Frantic, I scan for a way out and catch sight of the rafters and damaged roof beyond. The hole may be too small to fit through, but if zombies can't climb, this is my chance.

I'll have one shot. Placing most of my weight on my good leg, I launch toward the lowest beam. Arms stretched to capacity, my fingers bite onto the rough wood. My injury stabs white-hot as I pull myself up, just as the door smashes inward.

Zombies burst into the room and swarm the car. One spots me, alerting the others with his shallow wheezing. They reach for my legs, but my feet scrabble up and over the beam to safety. I never find out if zombies climb—because they jump.

Crouching like spiders on the floor, they shoot upward. Limbs flailing, they windmill through the air before clinging to the beams. One grabs my boot with a hiss, its open mouth moist and foul as the pit of hell.

With surprising ferocity, I'm yanked from my perch. My body rockets toward the floor. My lids slam shut as I brace for impact. The fall lasts longer than I think it should, and my eyes open again.

Then I hit.

Pain blisters my knee, hip, and shoulder where I make contact.

Looking up at the Draugar, the distance seems wrong, and I realize I've fallen into a pit that wasn't here a minute ago. My fingertips graze concrete block. Cold and damp, it surrounds me on four sides.

Above, the creatures watch. They bob their hideous heads, pace to me at bay, but they don't attack. I'm almost afraid to know why. Then the grinding starts.

A slab of concrete at least a foot thick inches its way over the top of the pit. Only it's not a pit.

It's a tomb.

No vault exists in my garage. No crypt or mausoleum is kept anywhere on our property. At least, not one I know about. Yet here I am. About to be buried alive.

What are the last thoughts of a dying man?

Memories flit through my mind, but fear scatters them until I can't hold on to any one image. I need more time. My voice rings out and returns to smother me. Reason is quickly wiped clean by the panic filling my brain. Questions knock against fear with no time left to consider anything but ...

Raven. God, how I love you. Did you know?

The question will remain forever unanswered as I suffocate here alone in the earth. God help me. No, no help *her.*

She's all that matters. All I ever wanted. And hers is the name I call as the lid slides shut on my grave with a final, echoing boom.

Chapter Twenty-One

Raven

The night enveloping me is silky and unpleasant, like suffocating inside black satin sheets. Darkness presses in, wrapping my arms and legs in an unseen bond until I can no longer move. I trip and fall into a yellow mist as cold as winter's breath. Coughing only brings a burn to my nose and lungs.

Last I knew, I was running in the woods, away from actual zombies. Separated in the swamp, I lost sight of Cole and couldn't find Gideon no matter how I tried. And I tried. I'm still looking. Seems I can't turn my feelings off the way he apparently can.

I sneeze a disgusting clump of gold dust. A snap and rustle in the swamp's undergrowth gets me to my feet. With the fear of monsters clinging to me, I call for my friends just in case, but no one answers.

A quiet flutter pulls my gaze up. Four baby owls cluster together in the crook of a dead tree. Squat and wide-eyed, they stare as if I'm a threat. "It's okay, boys," I soothe. "No one's going to hurt you."

As I step nearer, their little, round heads bobble. Heaven help me, they aren't owls at all, they're children! Smooth skin shines with oil, and dirt, and grime. Dark, greasy hair plasters to their swarthy foreheads, while round eyes grow ever bigger inside emaciated faces. What's wrong with me? I don't know how I ever mistook these pitiful little kids for birds.

Metal clinks. My heart twists as moonlight reflects off the manacles attached to their ankles, the chaffing skin beneath raw and wet with infection. Tiny feet clutch the tree bark so tightly, their toes appear to be white and bloodless worms.

One child picks at a scab on his knee until a red trail leaks from the wound. The next in line flinches. I think he's in pain or afraid, but he repeats the awkward motion several times over. He gurgles, the sound of mucus thick and uncomfortable in his throat. I think he might choke, but no he suffers from some odd, gulping tic.

The wind brings the scent of illness and decay. My skin crawls at the sight of them, and then I scold myself. They need help.

When I raise my palm, the group huddles closer together.

"It's okay," I say.

The boys hunch and scowl with black eyes so round, I can't see any white.

My hand inches closer. "Hey, I'm not going to hurt you."

The children's mouths yawn wide and they screech as a unit. One ducks low, the youngest on the end. Little square teeth gnash. *Click, click, click.*

I stumble back, struggling to regain my balance, and when I look again, four baby owls shiver on a tree limb.

What … ? Taking an uneasy step, I push the panic down. A dreamlike quality affects my mind until I'm dizzy. No longer sure what's real, I turn. Run.

The ground is soft and damp, giving beneath my pounding tread. My lungs tighten in the humid forest, but I don't stop. Perspiration glues my clothes to my skin. My progress seems slow and heavy, yet I jump at every leaf rustle, twig snap, and bird call.

I run until I can't run anymore, and then I walk. A glow burns faintly up ahead, growing brighter as I near. Flame lights the uneven, narrow path before me that might be a deer trail to a watering hole. I'm wishing, since I'm parched.

Something hits the ground nearby with a thud. "Gideon?" I hope it's him, but I'm met with silence.

My feet hit water, squishing in ankle deep mud. I *feel* the swamp beneath me, brackish water, and loamy, rotting debris. Yet when I glance down, the ground is as dry and cracked as Georgia red clay in August.

Or is this another of Pan's tricks, a hallucination?

The smell of wood rot and moss surrounds me. Orange sparks fly up in the distance, tiny fireworks against a velvet blue sky. Smoke tickles the back of my throat. I pause as something whisper-soft touches my arm, like the brush of fabric. Crystal clinks. A woman giggles somewhere deep in the wood. Impossible, but I swear I hear music, an orchestra playing some classical tune I've forgotten the name of.

I jog down the path toward the fire. The pop and crackle of wood increases, and, as unlikely as it is, I pray the boys are together, and safe, and made camp while they waited for me.

But when I reach the spot, I find it's more than a simple blaze. A wide band of flame divides me from my destination. Behind me lies the deadly swamp full of zombies and wrapped in the darkest night.

On the other side of the firewall, the sun shines brightly. A lush field of spring-green grass opens onto a rolling meadow. A brook lined with pretty brown stones cuts through the middle. There are maple trees and gray mountains in the distance. Cirrus clouds appear as checkmarks in the azure sky, marking off each perfect detail of the pastoral scene. The fire seems the division between day and night, two distinct and separate worlds.

And I'm on the wrong side.

More laughter trickles through the forest. I turn, seeing no one, but I smell them. Men's cologne and a woman's heavy perfume mix in a sickeningly sweet aroma that irritates my nose and throat. The gentle murmur of a man's voice is answered by more giggling.

"Who's there?" My gaze sweeps the dank, empty forest. I'm

brushed aside as an unseen force jostles me in the dark.

Another glance at the meadow shows a group of people gathering on the hill. As they move closer, I count three heads. Four. Five. Backlit against the bright summer sun, their silhouettes are familiar to me.

Dane's swagger is unmistakable, and there's Maggie with her cheerful bounce following close behind. Gideon is here, his golden hair gleaming, radiant under the sun's rays. He smiles, lifts his chin in greeting. Oh my gosh, that's Ben! And my mother beside him. The parents I miss so much.

Emotion thickens my throat. When I blink, I'm surprised to find my lashes are wet. I laugh and wave, joy filling my soul to overflowing as I shout my hellos.

Until I remember that they're dead.

Words strangle and drop off, dissolving in the sudden wind. Another pulse of fabric against my arm, a flash of purple, and suddenly, the scales fall from my eyes.

Dancers. I'm surrounded by a sea of waltzing men and women dressed in exquisitely designed formal attire. Silver, black, plum, and midnight blue, I've studied fashion enough to know the styles date from the year eighteen sixty or earlier. The animal masks they wear suggest a masquerade. Never mind we're out in the open and cut off by a ten-foot wall of fire. Crazy? That's just another day in the neighborhood for The Void.

I'm caught between the swirling partners, edging me farther away from the pretty meadow. People spin and whirl, the heavy scent of perfume, sweat, and oppressive heat nauseate me. I'm bumped again and long for the cool brook on the other side of the firewall.

"Not so fast, pretty bauble. I'm all alone here, so you must be my partner."

A handsome young man appears dressed in a top hat and black coat with tails. I don't know what he means saying he's alone inside this strange mosh pit. His face is powdered white with makeup. Long, black diamonds are painted over both eyelids like a harlequin. His coffee-colored eyes sparkle with humor, yet I sense something cautionary within. Brown hair spills from under his hat to his shoulders. His skin is tanned and smooth below the paint line.

"Thank you, no." Why am I being so polite? I point to the pasture. "Can you take me to my friends, please?"

"In heaven? Oh, I'm sorry, didn't anyone explain? You won't be going. We're your family now, aren't we, pets?" The crowd gathers around us, laughing. It's an eerie sound: hollow and empty as the deepest well. "I'm afraid you weren't good enough."

Everywhere I look, beautiful, white faces press closer. They leer at me with their dull, cold eyes. Red mouths smile cruelly. No, he's wrong about heaven, isn't he? It's faith that saves you. Cut off from the people I love, I swallow my doubt like a dry pill. "It's not what you do that gets you in; it's about what you believe."

"Not in your nightmares, my sweet." He glances at the meadow, a sardonic smile tilting his lips. "And I'm weaver of the very best."

"I don't understand."

"Of course not, but you will."

A puff of silver smoke, and I'm face to face with him, a cluster of purple orchids clutched in my fist. I peer down through a dark veil and find myself wearing a black ball gown. Or … oh, God, a wedding dress? I drop the flowers and toss the square of lace covering my face aside.

"You are intoxicating, aren't you? Plenty of darkness … hmm, and pain. Quite lovely." He pulls me roughly to his chest. "Dance with me." His nose grazes my temple. Despite the heat of the fire, his breath frosts my cheek.

"Not a chance." I shove his chest, and he plows into a fish-eyed girl in purple taffeta. "Dance with your groupie puppets, and let me go."

"But can't you see that's all they are." Pan seizes the girl's hand. With vicious force, he rips ball from socket, tearing her arm off.

My hand flies to my mouth. Wires hang loose from the hole in her shoulder to the limb in Pan's hands. Sawdust and newsprint protrude from the tattered openings. She stands blinking stupidly, feeling nothing. Puppets.

He is alone.

"You see?" He stands motionless, aside from his gaze currently sweeping my body. "Worship me, Raven" he says. "Rule by my side. We'll have such fun. Neither of us will be lonely, and we'll play games and kiss every day. Love me, and I'll protect you. You'll never want for anything, I promise."

I'm already backing away. He talks like a child. Bargains and makes promises like a little kid, which almost scares me more. "I don't need you or anyone else taking care of me."

"Be careful, girl. I won't beg."

"It wouldn't do you any good." My chin comes up, punctuating my message.

"Pity," he says. "Have it your own way, then."

The ground rumbles and cracks before spreading open beneath us like a zipper. I sink into the deep crevice, slip through the loose soil away from my tormentor and into darkness. As the earth swallows me, immense pressure squeezes every wisp of air from my lungs. Dirt presses into my nose, and ears, against my closed mouth. My nails claw at the dirt making tiny, ineffective furrows. It's a toss-up whether the ground will crush me before I suffocate. Claustrophobia grips my mind as my lungs plead for oxygen. I thrash and jerk until my legs suddenly kick free.

I feel a cavernous space widening beneath me as I'm sucked deeper. My body breaks loose of the earth's hold, and I free fall.

Pain radiates up my spine as I land on a tile floor with a crack. When I glance up at the dirty hole I've just come through, black earth retreats, plaster repairs itself perfectly and without blemish. I watch it all happening as though a demolition video is set on rewind. The damage transforms into a seamless, high ceiling, painted dull white.

The room is large and rectangular. Most of the bulbs are smashed, but a few fluorescents still hum and flicker. Weak lighting washes the room in a sickly glow revealing peeling green paint and the gray cinder block beneath. There's a double door across from me and two tall windows to my rear with mostly broken panes. When a bolt of lightning flashes, it highlights the sharp angles, turning shattered glass to gruesome fangs that mean me harm.

"I'm trapped in a horror movie."

Leaves have blown in and gather in the dark corners of the room. Cobwebs cocoon the abandoned wheelchair sitting in an otherwise empty space. I must be in some defunct hospital.

Wind moans as it wraps the side of the building making me jump. The cold voice of dread whispers my name. A shudder wracks my frame.

On the other side of the room, arrays of medieval-type torture devices materialize like old props from a haunted house. They weren't there a minute ago, I'm sure. At least, I think I'm sure. Who knows in this place, but I've got a real bad feeling about it.

An iron cage hangs from a heavy bolt in the ceiling. Wide metal bands arc down from a domed lid to a flat bottom big enough to house a man if he scrunched up knees to chin. The floor is littered with iron masks, manacles, pliers, and prongs. A collection of large saws hang off peg boards on the wall. Jagged teeth spread in a rusty grin. The adjoining wall hosts a coffin lined with protruding nails. There's a rack with leather tie bands, and a large wooden wheel studded with foot long spikes around the circumference.

"Who could do such a thing?" I ask no one.

I jolt as lightning flashes, and a man is here. Hooded and cloaked, he turns the crank handle of the monstrous wheel. The quick image of his victim impaled on the cruel spikes spins round and round. I gag as liquid splatters, glistening off the walls and floor. The cloying scent of salt, and rust, and iron fills my nostrils with a foul aroma.

When I scream, the hooded man disappears, and only a dusty wheel remains—dry, empty and immobile. This isn't real.

Another clap of thunder bowls through the flashing sky. I smother a sob as a new victim appears ten feet away on the cold floor. The man wears no shirt and only threadbare trousers. His hands and feet are shackled. An oversized head cage is secured at his neck with a padlock dangling at the back. Blood smears his throat and chest. Fear pricks my skin like needles as the poor soul thrashes and shrieks.

I don't understand what's happening to him until I see the hungry rat trapped *within* the wire. I turn away, sickened by what hate and madness inspire men to do to one another. My eyes shut to the ghostly visions, mirages—whatever they are. Witnessing their pain makes me feel like an accomplice to the disgusting acts, however unwilling.

A bang sends my already panicked heartbeat whipping into Mach speed. Two men dressed in solid white scrubs burst through the double doors. This is no hallucination, because they grab my arms and lift me. I can't see their faces, then I realize that's because they don't have any. Like bandits with tan stockings pulled over their heads, no mouth or eyes are discernible. There's only a bump where their noses should be.

I'm slammed onto the gurney. One end is adjusted and locked to keep me in a semi-reclined position. Velcro straps secure my wrists and ankles to the metal bed frame. I scream until a gag is inserted into my mouth and tied behind my head.

Down a hallway we go. Wires hang in knotted clumps from the ceiling. Half the lights work and those flicker on and off like an SOS that won't be answered. Maybe a dozen doors pass to the left and right. Black mold chews at the baseboards and framework.

An exit sign glows red over another doorway, but we don't stop. My attendants move quickly, their feet tip-tapping with purpose on the gray linoleum.

Strong antiseptic doesn't quite cover the smell of urine. Or fear. When my mother died, I grew accustomed to the distinct odors that death and sickness carry, and again in the hospital ward of my stepfather's rehab facility.

Only I wasn't bound and gagged then.

Struggle is pointless. My cries are muffled by the cloth bit in my mouth. Adrenaline shoots through my veins, lighting me up like a Christmas tree, but it's not enough to break my bonds.

Another set of double doors snap back as the end of my gurney rams them. The orderlies on either side of me stop under a spider web of domed lights.

My stomach plunges.

The room appears to be some sort of operating arena. On one side is the door we just entered. On the other is a long, glass window, lined with more featureless faces poised to watch. Stainless steel tray tables cluttered with scalpels, forceps, and other panic inducing instruments form a barricade between me and my audience.

Why am I here? I wasn't injured, and I don't feel sick. The bedside manner of my attendants suggests this isn't a real hospital, and they aren't here to help me. Terror grips my throat, squeezing until I can't breathe. I feel my eyes stretch to capacity, and I groan through my gag.

A man in tie-dyed scrubs enters the room. With both hands held high, he makes a big show of putting on a pair of latex gloves. He lifts an electric hair clipper from the counter and faces me.

It's the harlequin boy.

Pan.

A tear slips from my eye.

"I'm awfully sorry," he says. "You've been exposed."

Exposed? Exposed to what? I have a feeling it doesn't matter.

"We'll need a closer look." He giggles, addressing the faceless man nearest him. "Maestro, would you do us the honors?"

The orderly takes the shears and flips the switch. I glance up as Faceless Man leans over me. On closer inspection—not that I wanted one—smooth skin covers the spaces a nose and eyes would occupy. Black thread sews his mouth shut in a series of crude X's.

Blades vibrate against my skin as he draws the clippers along my skull. Ropes of dark hair drop into my lap. The urge to pick them up and hold them overwhelms me. My restraints make sure I don't.

"Marvelous," Pan says, rubbing his distended belly. "Her

agony is delectable. I hope it lasts."

His associates mimic the action, each movement small, stiff, and robotic. It's as though they're playing a sick game of copy-cat. Every stomach bloats to capacity, human balloons filling with air. Pregnant monsters.

"I'm almost too full to continue," Pan snickers. "But I will. How shall we produce a second course, gentlemen? Hm."

Wait ... Produce? An idea surfaces too horrible to contemplate, and yet I can't stop the thought from forming. *You eat feelings?*

"Yes!" he answers excitedly, though I never spoke aloud. Or did I? "Yes, that's it exactly. Oh, well done, you. I'm rather proud. Audience?"

The faceless men in the window applaud.

"Though I suppose I should correct you, we're only interested in the negatives—physical pain, mental anguish, all your scrumptious miseries ... "

My gag disappears. A breath of relief escapes as my mouth closes. I moisten my lips and rest my aching head against the gurney. "You trap people here and live off their suffering." It's a statement, not a question. I understand him now. Should have guessed from the beginning, the signs were all there.

He might have me, but Cole and Gideon are still out there. *You think you've won?* I shake my head. *Not yet, you son of a—*

"My, my, aren't we the optimist."

I can't remember speaking, but I must have. *They will beat you. Gideon will beat you.*

"Gideon is an arrogant boy."

"How ... " *He hears my thoughts.*

"But I suppose you reference your newfound ability?" he asks. "Some believe human beings only use three percent of their total brain capacity. Did you know that, Miss Weathersby?"

I say nothing, trying to block my thoughts from my enemy. Movement draws my gaze to the attendants arranging scalpels by size on the nearby trays. I can't control my shudders.

"It's a myth, of course," Pan goes on. "The actual number

is twenty-seven percent. Humans have an unlimited capacity to feel, and learn, and understand, but they can't access the power inside them. Power suppressed by years of over reliance on machinery and technology. People have 'evolved.'" He makes his point with air quotes. "So much so, no one believes in good old magic anymore, and that works in my benefit. The word *magic* has bad connotations in the modern age. Yet true magic is nothing more than utilizing brain capacity to manipulate the elements, deconstruct matter and rearrange atoms and molecules to suit our needs. As you are learning, elemental manipulation isn't that difficult once you access the part of your brain controlling it. The ability is no different than exercising a leg muscle that's been dormant too long. A little physical therapy and the muscles remember and function properly."

"Wait, you're equating therapy with starting fires?"

"Yes, and not at all. You're rather dimwitted, aren't you?"

I ignore his jab. "If what you say is true, then why can't I summon fire? Why can't Gideon control the wind?"

"Why can some sing and some dance? Why can't I paint like Leonardo da Vinci? Why are there only some who succeed in mathematics, while others play professional sports, or invent?" His eye roll is dramatic by any eight-year-old's standard. "How incredibly *boring* to be exactly alike, Raven. We are unique as individuals. And in that uniqueness lies our separate talents and aptitude levels. Understand?"

I'm beginning to.

"And of course, initial power must germinate from somewhere."

The Artisans broken curse. Gideon was right all along.

"Indeed, he was. Though it won't save him."

We'll see. Maybe Pan isn't perfect either, just had more practice. He must have a weakness. Maybe one we can use to our advantage. The idea gives me hope. Shores me up for what's ahead. I need to tell Gideon what I've learned. If I get the chance.

"Now, let's see what's going on inside that teeny-tiny, little mind of yours, shall we?"

Pan's eyes remain lifeless for someone who sounds so over-the-top perky. His faceless attendant holds something resembling a miniature saw blade.

I fight the restraints until my wrists burn. My heart races; the muscle knocks against my ribs as though trying to free itself, because the rest of me is finished.

I love you, Gideon. Always.

Pan leans over, inspecting me like a culture in a petri dish. I freeze, blood chilling under his evil smile. I can't control the terror widening my eyes while his are relaxed and unmoved.

Somewhere outside, maybe down the hall, I swear I hear Gideon's voice. Desperate, he calls for me, screams my name.

My mind reaches out, feeders of thought and feeling search for him through space and time—somewhere in The Void. He's close, calling to me just ahead in the shadows, but the closer I get, the more he slips away. I'm desperate to find him, and when I can't, my hope fades along with his voice.

Pan touches my cheek with his gloved finger. The smell of antiseptic and latex triggers my gag reflex. He runs his lips gently over each of my eyelids. "I gave you every chance, sweet Raven. We might have been together, lovers, but now ... "

Any bravery I had evaporated the moment that fleeting connection with Gideon broke apart. I'm about to die, and all I can think about are the people I saw in heaven across the divide. The ones I couldn't save, or control. Gideon is right; people can't be collected and stored. Protected like priceless heirlooms or rare birds in a cage. Humans have freewill. And when they choose, do I judge them? Love them unconditionally?

All this time, maybe it's been me that was lost.

Tiny teeth from the saw blade bite my forehead. My courage bleeds out as screams flood the auditorium. My will to survive leaks away, drips down my face. An angry, red river flows over my chest and arms and onto the floor, seeping into the drain under my bed.

As Pan continues to cut.

Chapter Twenty-Two

Cole

When I wake, my mouth is crusty and tastes like feet. Lips smacking with the worst case of cotton-mouth ever, I rise up on both elbows and spit. What comes out is mulch and not dirty socks. Still tastes like feet.

I thought I was dead, but dead guys don't hurt this much.

The swamp scene where I fell last night sharpens and comes into focus. Smooth, white trees tower up from the murky water. They raise their spindly branches to the sky in a hallelujah choir, but I'm not rejoicing yet. Light filters through the leaves in long strips highlighting patches of bog. Around me, the purple lotus-type flowers lie spent. Their delicate edges, darkened with poison, curl in the sun.

The yellow powder is gone. A hallucinogen, I'm sure of it.

My aching body reminds me of my first trip to the labyrinth. No picnic then, either.

Not long after I'd been banished by Gideon's father, I was floating around Maddox's garden, minding my own business, doing my ghostly thing—which is not much of anything—when a woman approached and asked if I'd like to go on a "quest."

I don't know about other guys, but to me, the word quest evoked the idea of a noble adventure, especially when asked by a gorgeous, older woman. I'd never been off the Maddox grounds before. In fact, I'd been warned by the others against it. Still, one look at her baby blues and I answered as any hormonal, bugged-eyed boy of fourteen would. "Hell yes."

My first night in The Void I experienced a darkness unlike any other. Rather than the absence of light, the dark there ate it like acid. The notion of peace or happiness drained from my soul as if it never existed to begin with. Unfortunately, I remember every detail …

"Cole, you idiot. Don't stand on the pathway in plain sight. Why not invite the Minotaur down on our heads?"

I curse myself and the pretty blond who's yelling at me. Turns out her name is Desiree. She's Gideon's step-monster, fellow prisoner, and not remotely nice. Her talk about a deal with the magician to escape brought us to the center of the maze tonight. Who knows what she thinks she has to trade, but it takes balls of brass to enter the labyrinth. Mine must be made of lesser stuff.

"Get over here!"

I join her in the copse near the center of the maze. In part, because I don't know what I'm doing, the other part being her balls are still bigger than mine.

"Do you even know where to find him?" I ask.

"Of course we do." Jonathan Lawrence steps from the shadowed hedgerow. Trapped here as long as anyone, he smells of things long forgotten: dust, and dry rot, and the attic you're too scared to visit. I'm fascinated by the constant swivel of his fat head, and I'm pretty sure at least one of his parents was a cobra.

Desiree peeks at a white tower above the bushes. "Pan spends most of his time here. Follow me and keep quiet."

Cobblestones, bleached pale with moonlight, guide the way. I bring up the rear in our skulking band of three.

The air is cool and unfriendly. Things I don't want to think about rustle the shrubbery. An animal squeaks followed by the sickening sounds of flesh tearing. I should have kept to the mansion. Monsters don't hunt outside the maze.

"There," Desiree says.

Craning my neck, I follow the tower spire jutting up beyond the bushes. We turn the corner around a twelve-foot hedge trimmed to resemble a phone booth. Before I remark on this oddity, we pass more sentinels. A rowboat, fox, and giant clown all constructed from shrubbery. The clown smiles, and I shrink from the fangs more vampirish than circus performer.

Only fourteen-feet of courtyard lie between us and the tower door. A shadow moves near the archway, and I get a really bad feeling.

Desiree pauses. We stop behind her as she calls, "Pan?"

There's a dry scrape against the pavers. The movement is clumsy. Slow.

Icy prickles pelt my spine. "Let's go," I warn, but it's too late.

Two horns emerge from the inky dark. Moonlight falls, inch by inch, unveiling the body of a man with the head of a bull. Muscles more pronounced than a top bodybuilder tense and bulge with each steady movement. His eyelids rise exposing two glowing red fields where eyes should be. Instead of a foot, a cloven hoof paws the ground.

Is it terror or stupefied wonder that keeps me frozen in place? The man-beast tosses his head. When he snorts, the sound echoes like a thunder clap.

Shite on a biscuit!

It's not until my partners give me a look somewhere between shock and fury that I realize I've spoken out loud.

"Run. Run!" Desiree cries.

Believe me, I'm going!

The Pamplona run has nothing on us. We streak down the path toward the mansion where some magic boundary keeps the monsters from crossing over. Ever the fool for a pretty face, I was the bigger idiot to follow Desiree in here.

The ground shakes as the Minotaur gives chase. Old man Lawrence puffs louder than the bull.

Sure, our tactile functions are diminished in The Void, but that doesn't mean we won't feel a fifteen-hundred-pound Minotaur standing on our heads. I've heard the stories. And since our spirits are temporarily separated from our bodies, we can't die. Meaning we'll have to endure Mr. Moo back there, and his mauling, until he exhausts himself or gets bored.

No thanks.

Desiree sprints alongside me, blond hair glowing in the dim light. Her white evening gown doesn't slow her one whit. Jonathan, I'm sorry to say, is falling behind. The guy runs like a bloated woodchuck. He's about to be trampled, and there's no way to stop it.

Desiree must see that too, because she darts left toward a break in the hedge. "Separate!"

Her plan comes too late to save Lawrence. The Minotaur slams into him, and they roll. Bull and man legs tangle, bones crack and snap. Lawrence cries out, but Desiree's abandoned him to the whims of a psychotic man-animal.

Will I do the same?

I veer around a clump of bushes to catch my breath. It doesn't take long. I'm a quasi-spirit after all.

The Minotaur grabs a handful of Jonathan's hair before whacking his skull on the path below. Cranial plates split. Blood seeps from the back of his head staining his gray hair crimson, the ground a gory red. The bull's hands are slick, his breathing is labored, yet he doesn't stop smashing.

Something pink and jellylike collects on the stones. Though I know the spell that binds us to this world will heal him in a few hours, Lawrence's screams for help turn my stomach.

I crouch, pick up a small rock, and lob it. "Leave him alone!"

My rock pelts the bull's mucus-slathered nose. Minotaur lifts his head and sniffs. Jonathan's crying, pleading for mercy, but it isn't necessary anymore. The bull's moving on.

Toward me.

Brilliant.

I'm off, but running blind without Desiree's guidance. Bloody traitor. I don't spend time in the labyrinth, and the ton of thundering bison behind me is a good reason why.

I dart around hedges, but there's no break in what seems like miles of maze. I'm so dead. Well … more dead.

Just ahead, a small stand of trees grows up through the hedge. Vines hang off lower branches like lifelines. The ground trembles, evidence the bull is on my heels. I have a minute, maybe seconds before he catches me. Then it's my head battering the ground until my brains scramble.

Heavy breaths warm my neck. I leap for the clump of dangling plants. Wrapping thick coils around both wrists, I hoist myself up. Climb higher in the web of tangled runners. A tug on my waist nearly tears my arms from their sockets. I'm barely hanging on as the bull beneath me snorts and pulls again. I kick my invisible feet. He stumbles, and my knee connects with a bright, red eye.

The bull bellows and covers his eyes. Then his hands drop and he charges. Clutching one of my dangling legs, the Minotaur wrenches until tendons rip and my bone cracks with a wet pop. I scream and he trumpets. Our struggle loosens a vine that wraps his neck.

Now, I have an idea. One chance to keep the rest of my appendages in place.

I fight the pain and throw my legs over the bull's broad shoulders. He bucks, and I ride while wrapping more vines around his impossibly wide neck. He stops jumping when I cinch them tighter, cupping his throat with his stubby, human fingers.

Thank God for pro wrestling and sleeper holds. If I can cut off Minotaur's airway, maybe he will pass out long enough for me to get away.

I tug the vines until my muscles cramp, but my arms alone won't exert enough pressure to drop this monster before I tire out. Keeping the vines taut, I slide my body over his shoulder, and down his back, adding the whole of my dead weight to the pressure on his windpipe. I hang there, limbs shaking with fatigue. I bite my cheek against the pain until the taste of copper floods my mouth.

Finally, the beast sags. His knees buckle, and he crashes to the ground. I leap away to avoid being crushed. My busted leg won't hold, and I roll several feet, cursing loudly at every turn.

I swear vengeance on Desiree, Maddox, my old man. Everyone.

Thanks to the curse, I'll heal, but tonight it's a long hike to the mansion on one leg. As much as I hate it there, I'm not signing up for more midnight meetings. Desiree be hanged. The woman's certifiable, and from now on, completely on her own.

The underbrush rustles, pulling me from horrible memories.

I jump, thinking the zombies have come to finish me off. Pain stabs my trapezius as I twist for a better look. "Damn it, Maddox," I say, as he limps from behind a tree. "What the hell? I thought you were … something else."

"I missed you too, Wynter. You look like I feel."

Comedian.

Gideon's slides to a sit and rests against the tree trunk, knees pointed at the sky. Shadows collect under his legs, darkening the molding leaves beneath him. As his lids slide shut, my gaze follows the dark blood trail on his shirt connecting ribcage to waist.

"Are you all right, mate?"

"Fine."

"Where'd you come from?"

One eye opens. "Hell if I know." Both eyes. "I woke up half-dead and face down in a ditch. Started walking. Found you."

Always chatty, Maddox is.

"Have you seen her?"

"Seen who?"

"*Who?* Raven!"

Oh. "Right, right." As I stretch, each vertebra in my back snaps louder than mallets on a xylophone. "Not yet. She ran a different direction than you and I did, but she can't be far. Likely we were all sent on Pan's little Peyote party last night." I jerk my chin toward the black flowers.

Gideon nods. Lips pressed to a flat line as he cradles his injury with one hand. "My supplies are gone, cane too. Do you have anything left?"

I glance about. "Nah, probably dropped my satchel in the woods."

He accepts or guessed as much because he's staring off into space. "We have to find Rae. She needs ... you."

I palm my neck, rubbing stiff muscles loose. "Er, yeah." The turnabout still mystifies me, since only a few days ago he wanted to cut my heart out for smiling at her. I should be thrilled, and I am, I guess. Yet an uneasy thought hides in the shadows of my mind. I can't seem to focus, and then it's too late.

A wail rolls out from the woods shattering the stillness.

"Come on." Gideon's already moving, struggling to stand. "Can you walk?"

"Yeah." I force my body vertical. "I'll live. What about you?" I'm staring at the blood on his shirt again.

He gives me his back as an answer, boots shuffling over the uneven ground.

As we hurry toward the cry, I expect to see someone behind the first tree, or the next, perhaps the one after that. Hope keeps us tromping through the swamp, but we don't find anyone. One hour. Two. We walk until the earth dries and hardens. With no more cries to guide us, we continue in the same direction.

The forest thins, then stops altogether on the edge of a rolling meadow. Vegetation changes color from sickly gray, to yellow, to green. One last, scrawny tree bends to greet me like a withered, old man. My steps slow. A cluster of three knots located on the trunk's center suggests a nose and eyes. A bunch of protruding moss mimics a perfect goatee.

"Hey," I say, stopping to catch my breath. "Doesn't that tree look like old man Arnold, our professor of literature at Malcolm? He was always going on about dead poets and moldy Greek gods."

Gideon halts giving the tree his full consideration. "Actually, it really does."

The tree is a distraction from what neither of us wants to admit. We've lost her. We've lost Raven, and we both know it. I'm thirsty and hungry. My muscles ache, and my head thumps with constant, magnified sound echoing in my ears.

I don't care that I can hear where a creek blends with a stream, or that a bird has caught a grasshopper in its beak. I just want the noise to stop before I go mad. Gideon trudges on, but I stay put. We don't have a clue which way to go and this aimless wandering isn't helping my mood.

I have a better idea.

"Wait," I say.

Gideon stops, though his glare indicates he's not happy.

"Hang on." My eyes close. I concentrate, asking the wind to send me noises.

Unidentified birds scatter in the breeze, the haphazard wing pattern of a bug flitters. Maybe this is a stupid idea, but I specifically ask the breeze to carry the sounds of humans. Gideon waits as I listen. Moments pass. Every second ticking by seems an eternity. Then I hear voices.

"Girls," I announce, pointing. "And they aren't screaming, they're laughing."

Our boots explode over the dry grass of the glade and pound up the knoll opposite. We break over the crest and find a large valley on the other side. No people, but to the right is a lake with a small island in the center. A white stone temple of impressive size sits at its peak, glinting under the hot sun's rays. Proud columns surround the structure but fail to hold the crumbling porch roof. As a boy, I accompanied my parents on a trip to Greece. The site seems plucked from a postcard and placed here in The Void.

"Heh, that's funny," I say.

"What is?"

"We were just talking about the tree and old man Arnold. Remember? He was always on about Shakespeare, and Dickens, and Zeus. Anyway, I was thinking that structure would be a great set for Battle Medusa. Did you see *Clash of the Titans*?"

"Original or remake?" Gideon doesn't miss a beat.

"Either. Both. Which did you prefer?"

"Remake, no question." His expression is resolute. "Better special effects."

"Yeah, they were cool, but I'm into cult films and old school claymation, myself."

More laughter breaks across the valley.

Our heads jerk up as three teen girls skip in the hollow below, a blond, brunette, and a redhead. No one was there ten seconds ago and now it's a flaming party. The girls wear little more than scarves made of sheer, gauzy material that flutters as they run. Not that I'm complaining.

There's more giggling as the trio points in our direction, followed by friendly waves and outright beckoning. Desire flares in my chest at the same time warning bells ring in my head. Apparently, Gideon hears no such bells and is already plowing down the hillside even as he says, "Something doesn't feel right about this."

I'm about to ask if that's true, why is he practically running to meet them. Until I realize I'm doing the very same thing.

The redhead is first to greet us, every curvaceous feature bouncing as she does. She touches my arm, and I feel the heat in my toes. Whispered breaths, as sweet as cherries, fall on my skin. Her soft hair sweeps my face, snagging on my unshaven jaw. "Hello, handsome." The girl's lips are full with a hint of bronze glow. Hazel eyes flash under dreamy, come-hither eyelids.

I'm in so much trouble.

She kisses my cheek, my lips. Blood sloshes against my eardrums. My heart rate climbs, chest pumping up and down like a jackhammer.

Ho-ly shite! You'd think I'd be happy. Didn't I just win the lottery of impromptu dates? Getting attacked by beautiful, mostly naked girls is every guy's dream, right? *Right?*

Back in the real world, sure, but not in the labyrinth. I'm not an unattractive guy, and I get my share of appreciative "looks" from the ladies, but even I have to admit, this is suspicious.

As the redhead slides her blood red nails through my hair, I'm one hundred percent sure there's nothing I can do to stop her.

"Come here, baby. Give us a kiss." She puckers those pillowy lips and plants one on me.

Sparks zing up my spine igniting my brainstem. *Is my hair on fire?*

For a moment, I forget where I am. And that I came here to rescue a sweet and innocent girl from the horrors of this place. My name slips from memory. Where I came from, who I was, and who I'm trying to be. Pleasure in the form of color explodes against the backdrop of my brain. A mysterious tune plays, washing me in soothing sound, like waves caressing the shoreline.

Then a tiny sliver of reason separates my mind from the euphoria my body wants more of.

I seize my moment of clarity and call Gideon who's standing not six feet away. A voluptuous blond whispers in one ear, while the sexy brunette on the other side toys with the neckline of his shirt. He's got the stupidest grin I've ever seen smeared on his idiot face. I swear he looks like a hound getting his belly scratched.

I shouldn't judge. I'm pretty sure my expression is equally knobbed.

"Psst … Oi, Gideon!" I feel my grin widen, as though I've inhaled too much gas at the dentist's office. My glee devolves into a fit of chuckling. "I think it's a trap."

He tears himself from the lips of the blond inhaling him, and answers. "Heh. You think?" His guffaw thunders across the meadow.

"Listen." The gravity of the situation isn't lost on me, yet I can't stop giggling as the redhead nuzzles my ear. I want to fight, get angry, but her spell is too strong. Escape seems impossible, but if I'm going down, there's something I have to do first. "Gideon."

He lifts his head. The sun reflects off his golden hair making him appear like damn Apollo himself. I mean to frown, but I smile. I want to scream, except I laugh. "I think you're great. Brilliant." *What the hell?* So not what I meant to say, nor do I care to sound like a twelve-year-old girl. If I could punch myself in the face right now, I'd be only too happy to oblige.

"You're all right, Cole." Gideon staggers, and the blond catches him. "At least you try and help people. You were right about Raven. She deserves better than me. Take her. It's what I want." The brunette silences him with her ruby mouth.

"But I don't waaanna be with Raven anymore," I whine.

I don't? Where did that come from? She's all I've wanted since I left The Void. Now I'm not so sure. Maybe it's the spell, but the need to explain myself takes priority over anything else. "Gideon, can you hear me?"

His head lifts, though his lids are mere slits. His smile is a runny egg sliding from his face.

"I'm sorry for dragging you here, for risking Raven's life and yours. I'm sorry for burning your face all those years ago at school ... " Another giggle rips from me as the redhead stuffs her hand up my shirt.

The other two girls continue mauling my friend, kissing and fawning all over him. I feel sick, yet I laugh until my sides ache. Did I get through to him? I need his forgiveness, but nothing I say sobers the idiotic grin on his mug.

"Gideon?"

"I know." He stumbles, laughing again. "Water under the bridge—and I'm sorry too, Wynter."

He's sorry? Emotions running full throttle, I can't stop the words from tumbling out. "You're the best friend anybody could ever have." And there it is. I said it. More like slurred it, but the words were audible. Can someone please shoot me now?

"No, just no," he mutters. Hope spikes at the nasty edge in his tone. For a moment, he sounds like the old, embittered Gideon I know and count on. He shrugs the brunette off, but her arms lasso his neck, drawing him back. He trips, face plunging into her ample cleavage. All hope dies as his head lifts and the simpleton smile is back in place. "We're done for." Tears stream from his eyes, he laughs so hard. "I ... I can't."

Can't what?

The blond pulls at his earlobe with her teeth. Gideon shrieks. Peels of insane laughter roll off of him. "Get free," he says. Wrapping his hands around the blond's neck, his fingers flex and tighten on her throat. "I'll try and ... "

The brunette shuts him up again, but not with a kiss. She hammers him with a dead tree branch, and Gideon topples like a felled oak.

"Poor old sod." I shake my head and smile. *What a shame. A terrible end for such a lovely, sensitive guy.* I watch his still body lying in the grass—right before orange fireworks explode behind my eyelids and it all goes dark.

Chapter Twenty-Three

Gideon

The back of my skull bumps a hard surface, pinpointing the exact location of blunt trauma. I picture my gray matter swelling, cerebral plates pushing maximum capacity until my brain explodes in a fine, pink mist. *Poohft.*

How does a person go from zombie apocalypse, to seduction, to the world's worst hangover? I can't remember, but pain drills my head so incessantly, I hardly care. My tongue is thick and gummy, lips dry as ash. I'd kill for a drink of water.

My eyelids crack open. The scene blurs and refocuses. While the space is dim, light shines from an opening at the other end of what appears to be a small cave. I shift but can't move more than an inch or two. My ankles are tied, wrists bound behind my back. My fingers extend against cold, damp stone.

I fist and release my hands to get the blood pumping. No telling what's happened to Raven by now, I have to get to her.

A foul odor attacks my sinuses. I've never snorted dead rat rolled into a dirty diaper, dipped in pus and sardines. If I had, I imagine it would smell like this.

Embers glow from a small stone pit in the center of a dirt floor. Lumps of things stuffed in burlap sacks sit in odd groupings here and there. One jiggles and rolls over, but whatever lurks within stays hidden. I shudder, wondering if it's causing the stench.

Propped next to me on the same stone bench is Cole. Bound, listless, and out cold.

Fantastic.

I let my eyelids slide shut. Where are you, Rae?

Injured, lost, afraid and hiding somewhere in the woods?

She has to be okay. Every curve of her face is etched in my brain. Her smile when I'm teasing, the flash of her eyes when I've pissed her off. *God, I miss the girl.* The memory of her satin lips pressing my cheek threatens my sanity. I'm torturing myself, but can't stop the flashbacks. Her voice is forever burned into my mind as though she were here. Right now. I feel her hands in my hair, quickening heartbeats, soft breaths in my ear.

If Pan hurts her, I'll—

You'll what?

My eyes snap open. Anger kindles in my chest, and I strain against my bonds, but it's no use. Nothing. I can do nothing.

You let her go, remember?

For her own good.

And look where that got her.

I tell myself to shut the hell up. To help Raven, first Cole and I have to get free.

He snorts and smacks his lips but doesn't wake.

Yeah.

I'm stuck here with Wonder-Wind Boy, while Raven is God knows where. The Void is a hellhole, nothing but mind games and death traps. What if she's facing the same trials we are? Did some mythical Greek god try and seduce her; abduct her to a cave like this one? Suddenly, I'm shaking with rage. *I'll kill him.*

Cole's head slides against the wall and comes to rest on my shoulder. A healthy string of drool glistens on his chin, and he's snoring like a blender full of nails.

I shrug. "Get off!" Shouting actually hurts less than I feared. My head begins to clear. The ache lessens, if slightly. Still, I lower my voice. "Wake up, Wynter."

Cole's head flops forward. A groan escapes from under his greasy, dark hair.

A breeze sends the stink of ammonia wafting from a corner. No sooner do I mumble about this being the perfect spot for a colony of blood-sucking bats, and a cloud of sharp black wings swoop from the ceiling. Their high-pitched keening deafening as they dive.

My heart jolts, pulse goes supersonic as my spine presses the wall, but there's nowhere to go. Wheeling in unison, the animals head straight for us, consuming Cole and me within their black hive of terror.

Cole wakes, hollering like a deranged Tarzan. Bound and immobile, we're unable to shield ourselves from the onslaught.

Needle-like claws slash my arms and face. A bat lands on my chest; his nose shrivels exposing small, white teeth. I buck and squirm, but the devil digs in. Using its wings like hands, the bat crawls commando-style over my torso.

I'm not usually one for hysteria, but I'm petrified he'll head for my junk. Instead, the little bloodsucker hones in on the hole in my shirt. His snout roots at the blood-stained fabric until my wound is exposed.

There's a nibble, then a sting as his needle-like fangs embed themselves in my flesh. My stomach lurches with my revulsion as the animal feeds on me.

In my panic, I call to the embers in the pit. Fire responds with a golf ball-sized cinder levitating two feet up. Keeping my focus on the widest part of the rodent drinking my blood, fire blasts the target. One screech and the animal darts away leaving the scent of singed fur in its wake.

Blue flame burns the ropes at my wrists and ankles. I feel no pain. It's a heady feeling, willing fire to do my bidding. Too bad I can't enjoy the moment.

White smoke billows up, adding to the chaos. A cough rips from my chest. I'm choking when a breeze clears a path around me. *Cole.*

I'm done with this cave. Whoever tied us up will be back, and we're wasting time. Rage burns like the fire I'm controlling. I fight like a madman against the ropes, aiding the flame until the fibers break loose.

A garbled scream sends my already racing pulse toward the checkered flag.

Through the flurry of dusky wings, I spy a bat hanging from Cole's mouth. How he caught one with his teeth I'll never know, but like a dog with a sock, Wynter shakes his head before slinging the limp creature to the floor in a heap.

He gets full props. Bat biting is some badass shit, and must send a message, because the rest of the bat cloud retreats to the cavern's roof.

Cole's eyes are round, red rimmed, and shining. We're both blowing like marooned fish. "What the hell?" he pants, shaking the hair from his eyes.

I wish I knew.

Three silhouettes, backlit from the morning sun, enter the cave. Curvy figures hint these are the girls from the meadow.

"Sirens," Cole whispers.

I search my memory, but can't recall much about sirens—other than I thought they drowned fishermen at sea. I angle toward Cole, keeping my voice low. "They don't have fins."

"Those are mermaids, mate."

So, I'm not versed in fairy tale trivia. I risk a quick glance at the whispering shadows.

"Can you get loose?" Cole asks.

"Shh." I keep my wrists and ankles knit together, feigning restraints for our jailors. No sense tipping our hand.

"Hush, sisters, they're awake."

Damn.

We've barely recovered normal breathing from the bat horde,

making my desire to fend off another love-trance right up there with root canal. I'm not confused about who my heart belongs to, but our bondage suggests the girls have something more sinister in mind than forced make-out sessions.

Somewhere in the twenty-foot walk between us and them, a metamorphosis occurs in our captors. Several inches of height disappear and their spines bend. Breasts swell and sag, waists thicken and bulge. Deep lines mar their youthful skin, while three heads of luxurious hair fade and tangle, as if someone rinsed a bright dye job from cheap gray mops.

I'm equal parts disgust and fascination as their long fingers curl to knotted talons at their sides. Eyes blend and sink into one empty, dark hole in the center of each forehead.

"Who has the eye?" one croaks. Faint traces of blond hair distinguish her from her sisters.

"I have it ... here in my pocket." The brunette fishes in her tattered coat and produces a single, naked eyeball. She holds the slimy orb in the air like a trophy.

"Give it here," says the blond. She swipes blindly for her prize and misses.

"No," the redhead answers. "My turn, it is." Grabbing the eye from her sister, she twists it into place in the middle of her face. A milky secretion drips from the socket to her lip, and I smother a gag.

"Who are you?" Cole demands of the three crones before us.

"Can you not guess?" the redhead answers. Her once ruby lips have deepened to an ugly purple, much like two fat worms. "T'was you that called us forth. Woke the Weird Sisters, you did."

Who is this chick, Yoda?

"Me?" Cole answers. "You're mad. I did no such ... oh, wait."

"Wait?" I ask. *Wait for what?* My anger redirects to the idiot beside me. If he did call these creepy old hags, I'll break his little French face. "What's going on?"

"Weird sisters, weird sisters ... " Cole chants, and I think he's finally lost it. "You're the Grey Witches."

"Careful, sister," says the blond. "He's not as stupid as he looks."

"Hey!"

The redhead nods, smacking her bloated lips.

Revulsion slithers across the membrane of recent memories. I lean aside. "You kissed that, Wynters?"

Cole shifts against his bonds. "So did you."

I glance from blond to brunette. He's right. My soul withers a little.

The brunette feels her way around her sister to the forefront. "Enough of this, I'm hungry."

"Yessss," the blond answers. "Let's eat the plump one."

I hope they mean Cole.

Coincidentally, he starts vibrating beside me. "Get ready," he whispers, then louder, "and get *the eye*."

"Right!" Wait, do what?

Cole rattles like the tail of a snake and is gone. Nothing left but a few ropes in the dirt.

He reappears in the midst of the witches, bowling them over like ten pins. The eye is knocked to the floor and rolls under one of the mysterious burlap lumps. Of course it does.

Get the eye! I'm up, charging ahead.

Witches curse, scrambling to their feet. Lights flash followed by a roll of thunder. I swear a bolt of lightning hits the center of the cave. I suspect the weather connects to the sister's anger somehow. Or Cole's.

The brunette follows him. Every time she gets close, he vanishes, reappearing a few feet away. Hissing like a cat in a dark alley, the brunette asks her sisters for help. I'm hopeful they'll be distracted by Cole's diversionary tactics, but no dice.

The pair dives for the eyeball. Nimble moves for old ladies, but I'm already there. I plunge my hand under the burlap sack. Damp soil greets my searching fingertips, and the bag squeaks. As I reach further, the damp changes to thick slime. What the hell is this stuff? Maggots, troll snot, frog eggs? Whatever it is, it smells like death. I've hit a new level of putrescence.

The witches crawl forward and grab my boots. I toss the bag away and balk. Mice. Thousands of naked, pink mice squirm blindly in a sea of gray mucus, and the witches' eye sits dead center.

Veins fork over the orb, pulsing up the sides with tiny charges of light. The iris moves as I do, watching me. I swallow my nausea and scoop with my palm.

Searing pain shoots up my calf, and I howl. The redhead's long yellow teeth embed in my calf. I kick her off, then plant my heel directly in her hooked nose. Cartilage snaps and she wails.

The blond scuttles over her suffering sister with zero compassion and comes after me. Her sideways crawl is crab-like and just as fast. There's no way to outrun her, and I can't teleport the way Cole does to escape.

Desperate, I scramble for the fire and suspend their precious eye over the heat. "Get back or I'll drop it."

The sisters stop, heads still waggling on their wrinkled necks. They scratch at the air and whine, exposing broken teeth, but no one takes a step. Lightning flashes like a strobe sending off round after round of thunder, but these women don't scare me anymore. I have something they want.

"Brilliant, Maddox! Good thinking." Cole materializes beside me. "So, ladies, tell us how we beat Pan."

I'm lost as to what he's talking about, and say so.

"Perseus," he says from the corner of his mouth. Like I should know what the hell that means. "Remember? Professor Arnold told us the story in class. Perseus took the witches' eye and they did whatever he asked to get it back."

The redhead licks her lips. "Clever, the lad is."

The brunette crosses her scabby arms. "Yesss, sister, very clever indeed."

Chapter Twenty-Four

Cole

The nerves under my skin tingle with anticipation. Later, I will be tired, allow myself to feel scared, or worried. Right now? I'm brassed off and ready to plant the three Weird Sisters six feet underground.

"Clever he may be," the blond observes, "but, will it save him?" She pauses, head poking up in curious bird fashion. "If we answer your question, you will give us the eye?"

"Of course." Gideon tosses me the eye. *Blech.* Oh, this is bloody disgusting. Sticky with gooey shite all over it, the thing must have a lot of power for them to want it so badly. I hold the desired object near the pit, ready to be rid of it. The fire flares higher, flames reaching for the eye. Gideon's theatrics, no doubt, and very effective.

"Do not singe the eye!" the sisters plead. "He mustn't have it, *nooo.*"

The blond steps nearer. With one hand outstretched, her mouth parts as if she'll speak.

A sudden flash and lightning explodes in the cave, temporarily blinding me. I whirl, but the blond is on me. Attached to my back, she weighs nothing, and beats my head with both fists like a tyrannical child.

Gideon stumbles, nearly knocking us over as the other two attack him.

I twist round, grappling with the creature clawing my neck, biting my shoulder. She lets go only to sink her teeth into the shell of my ear. I shout, and double over, letting loose with a string of obscenities.

The eyeball is plucked from my hand. Victorious cackling echoes off the shimmering cave walls.

When my fingers slide over my damaged ear, the top half is missing.

This isn't remotely how the story happened with Perseus.

And that bitch is going down.

My body hums with energy as Gideon and I face the snarling threesome.

His head tilts, keeping watch on our enemies. "Forget the eye. I'm thinking barbeque, southern style."

I smile. Though we didn't have good old-fashioned pig roasts in the UK, I'd spent enough time in the south to get his meaning.

While the Weird Sisters are laughing it up over their win, Gideon pulls fire from the dwindling pit. He molds the ball of flame in his hands like Play Dough. His lids lower to slits. Jaw clenched, back ramrod straight.

I don't know where he learned that trick, but I'm glad he's on my side.

Boom! Gideon slams the fireball to the floor.

The witches recoil in a chorus of shrieks.

The three separate in an attempt to flee, but fire races around the sisters creating an inescapable prison.

Except for me.

I concentrate on a spot in the middle of the fire ring. Muscles shake and then I'm there. The blond growls as I relieve her of the eye. Sharp teeth protrude from sickly, white gums—the same teeth that took my ear, and yeah, I'm vain enough to hold a grudge. I teleport to the space behind her. One good shove on her bony spine, and she topples face first into the blaze.

Her rags catch fire. The fabric blackens as the flames lick higher, igniting her long, knotted hair. The spectacle is terrible and (I'm sorry) fascinating. I can't look away. Apparently, the woman was never taught to stop, drop, and roll in school, because she sprints around the circle, knee action higher than an Olympian.

Her sisters plead for mercy. They aren't talking to me but to Gideon, who stands as stony faced as an Egyptian sphinx. In either desperation or a gleaming moment of stupidity, the burning blond leaps onto her dark-haired sister who will share her fire and her fate.

"Gideon! Hold up. We need one alive." I teleport from the ring to my partner's side and finish my thought unbroken. "She may know something about Pan."

The redhead kneels. Bony hands clasped together, she begs for her life even as the blond falls to the ground in a smoking heap. The brunette staggers about, a wheeling inferno. Gideon waves a hand and the fire dies allowing the last witch her freedom.

The survivor creeps nearer, clothes blackened by the fire that incinerated her sisters. I'm ready for anything, but she doesn't rise from her knees. Her face lifts, the hole in her forehead a filthy, dark void. "Mighty paladin, spare me."

I don't know what a paladin is, and right now, I don't care. "Tell us about Pan."

Her head retracts into her shoulders. "Very well." She coughs and spits farther than any fútbol player I've ever seen. "He is not indestructible." Thankful the woman needs no more persuasion to give up her secrets, she spills like a broken dam. "I know not how to kill him—my oath on the eye. Yet, he may be weakened. His power to see you lies in the ability to see himself. Destroy his sight to earn your freedom."

"Bloody munter, you want us to dig his eyes out?" Nerves

tweak my spine all the way to the end.

She cackles. "Fool. That simple, it is not."

"Explain! Destroy it how?" Veins bulge in Gideon's neck as he shouts. A ball of flame leaps from the fire into his hand.

The witch cowers with a cry. "Your weakness makes him strong. Grow stronger yourselves. Destroy his way to see!" Her fingers splay in the dust as she dissolves into tears. "I speak true, I speak true, oh great paladins ... "

Gideon's eyes roll with typical impatience.

I lift a shoulder. It's clear the witch is terrified. I sense no lie, but he's right, her blathering doesn't help us.

I kneel before the witch, and pull the manky eye from my pocket. "Hag." The gray head wobbles on her flabby neck. Her breath holds the stench of a thousand dumpsters as she whimpers, and I wonder if she senses the eye is near. "I will give you your sight, if you tell me how to take his."

"He seeks the living, only the living, so you must pollute the silver circles of sight. The dead may not enter there, no, no. It is forbidden. Therefore, use the dead. Only then will you be free. Blind Pan with the dead and he can seek you no more."

Gideon curses. "Leave her, Wynter. It's useless."

Barking? Yes. Useless? I'm not so sure. I rise and toss the eye to the other side of the cave. The old bat scampers after it, faster than what makes me comfortable.

Gideon and I beat a hasty retreat to the mouth of the cave. Out of the den, down the hillside, to the valley, heading the opposite way we came through the swamp. We walk in silence for the first twenty minutes. I drag my weary feet, so it's no surprise when my toe catches the edge of a rock, and I stumble. Gideon shoulders me up, and we press on. Minutes, hours, it's easy to lose track of time here. And all the while, my mind's fixated on the witch's puzzling words ... and Rose.

Maddox glances over and frowns. "We need to do something with that ear soon. It's still bleeding."

Hurts too. I glance at the white sun hanging just past noon

in the sky. I know its position is merely a suggestion of time. "Thanks. You can have a look when we stop, if you like."

We round the next bend, then another. I chew on the inside of my cheek, sizing up our journey so far. Rae's missing, no sign of Rose, zombies, poisoned flowers, and then I go and make a bloody fool of myself when the sisters hexed us, espousing all of Maddox's fine qualities. I need to clear that up right now. "Listen, mate, the other day, I said things … "

Gideon gives his standard expression for get to the damn point. Or better still, don't, and just shut up.

Right. "I was under a spell, talking rubbish the way a person might if he'd gotten rat-arsed at the pub, or gone completely mental. So—"

"Stop. I'm begging you."

I do—both my feet and my mouth.

"Look." Gideon's fingers snag in his matted curls. "This place is cursed, so nothing makes sense. As far as I'm concerned, we worked well as a team today. There's no need to discuss what either of us said back there. *Ever.*"

I nod, but my grin is hard to suppress. Not surprisingly, Maddox can't deal with bromance. "Suits me, mate," I say, clapping him on the shoulder. And for the first time since I've known him, he doesn't shrug me off.

Chapter Twenty-Five

Raven

My eyes won't open. I panic that I've gone blind, until I realize I'm face down on the ground, and my lids are crusted shut. I rub them clean and roll onto my back. Leaves crunch beneath my weight, or maybe it's my spine snapping.

Every bone in my body aches like I've been beaten with a shovel, run over by a car, and then dragged by a horse. I think that about covers it.

I pry my lids apart. The scene above focuses into gray sky pierced with naked tree limbs. As I force myself to sit, my teeth clench against the strain of sore muscles. My filthy hair falls across my face, and that strikes me as odd, since I remember Pan shaving my head. His strange, faceless men torturing me until I passed out, it all comes rushing back.

My battered skin is black and blue. I'm covered in deep cuts and scrapes, proving at least part of the nightmare was real. A gash on my calf peeks through the tear in my pants. I wonder if there is any part of me left untouched.

My trembling fingers thread my hair. I pull at the roots hard enough to know it's still attached, not clogging the drain of Pan's operating room. I search along my forehead for the wounds he inflicted while I was bound. The blood that I expect to coat my fingertips doesn't materialize. Confusion mixes with hope as I hunt amidst my hairline and find nothing wrong.

Was it real? I blow out a breath. It *felt* real enough.

A bird cries, and I survey the sickly trees surrounding me. The boggy soil turns their roots white with decay. Black flowers dot the landscape; those at my feet are open and withered. Poison?

That explains a lot. All of a sudden, I'm Dorothy and the Wicked Witch has sent orchids instead of poppies to keep me from the Emerald City.

No sooner do I murmur of my beloved children's story, than a shriek echoes somewhere deep in the swamp that sounds eerily like a monkey's scream.

Fear covers me again with her dark cloak, and I'm so very tired of being afraid. My backpack is gone, lost or left with Pan in his creep show asylum. All my supplies were in that bag. Searching my boot, I find the knife I brought is missing as well.

Great.

My feet curl beneath me as I push to a shaky stand. My throat is dry, my head fogged with the aftereffects of Pan's toxins, and I'd kill for a hot bath. Trees stretch out around me in a tangled maze, disappearing into shadow and the unknown.

Utterly alone, I think of Gideon, and I hate the need swamping my heart. The memory of old habits haunt me, routines and familiar patterns that make a couple unique, transforming two people into one. I miss the feel of his strong arms around me, ache for the sound of his voice. I close my eyes and listen, because I'm that pathetic. His tone is soft and low as he tells me everything will be all right. My chest rises as he says he loves me. Exhales as he vows he won't ever let me go ... but he did. Tears sting beneath my lids. I swallow both the longing and the salt in my throat.

Don't even go there, Rae.

My eyes flash open, hands unfurling at my sides. There's no time for jilted ex-girlfriends indulging in self-pity meltdowns. *Suck it up and find the guys.* If Pan tortured me with medieval visions, no telling what he's done to them.

I trudge through the forest and away from freaky monkey noises. I'm not exactly the rock-climbing, fire-starting, outdoorsy type of girl, and I have no idea where I'm going. The best I can do is pick a direction and try to walk a straight path.

Nothing moves but the gentle rocking of tree limbs and an occasional startled squirrel. Hours pass without incident. Landscapes shift from sparse swamp to shady forest. The monotony is a welcome change and beats facing Pan, his games, or his zombie squad.

The problem is all this blank time keeps me focused on Gideon and Cole. And Gideon.

Attempts *not* to stress about them are useless. In fact, their possible wellbeing, or lack of it, utterly consumes me. I count my steps, sing, play *I Spy* with myself, and recite the words to my favorite Edgar Allen Poe poems.

In the end, nothing cures my anxious mind. A hundred scenarios play concerning what really happened last night: how long we've been in The Void, if the boys are together, if they're hurt. Worry is poor company but effective motivation. What if they need me? My feet move faster.

Another hour, maybe two, passes. Eventually, my legs grow heavy, slowing with each step. The wound on my calf throbs. Fresh blood leaves a wet sheen on my pants.

A vine snags my boot, and I trip. My palms shoot out, smacking the earth, and my knees follow. Sharp spikes puncture my flesh. The vine is covered with thorns a half inch long.

I pivot and sit on my butt in the dust. Hot tears cut trails in the dirt on my face. *Oh, Gideon, why? Where are you?* My chest squeezes painfully. I should have known. I *did* know. And I ran. He followed me to Maggie's house last fall. Practically tore the door off the hinges to explain that, though he couldn't promise not to die, he'd never choose to leave. He meant what he said then, I'm sure. My reluctance probably pressured him into swearing his oath to stay.

Relationships don't come with money-back guarantees. You aren't given a warranty like you get on a car transmission or appliance. Life is messy, unpredictable. So you guard your heart and make peace with loneliness, or you take a chance and risk a broken heart. If I'm truthful, I wouldn't take any of it back. I'm not sorry we tried.

After we broke up and Gideon asked to stay in my life, I think he was trying to keep his promise—but as my friend. I lean, draping my scratched elbows over scraped knees. Yeah, I'm angry, but I don't hate him. I wish I did. Life would be easier. He still cares, and it obviously hurts him to hurt me, so he wouldn't unless ... *We really are over.*

I lift my palm, study the throbbing holes in my skin. Nothing I've endured aches as much as Gideon's admission that he doesn't love me.

I don't want to do this anymore.

The sun smears under a hazy swipe of cloud. The ground is hard and dry. Gone are the drowning, bald cypress trees, replaced by a dozen different species. The leaves are familiar. My mother used to point them out on our walks together in the park.

"Remember the Oak is your best friend, strong and faithful," Mother said.

My mind seizes around her message, the faded dream I had days ago suddenly clear.

"Maple, Pine, and Ash are also our friends, but beware the Hemlock, for he is cunning, and the Alder cruel."

Nervous, I scan the area, I see no alder. No hemlock either, but I spy an oak nearby. Can I make contact through my element? "Er, hello?"

Nothing happens, and I'm almost glad no one's here to see this.

"Hey, can you hear me, anybody?" I wait, but all is quiet.

How do you talk to trees? What good would it do if I did? "Can you help me? I'm lost."

Nada.

This is just sad.

You were wrong, Mother. "They aren't listening!" There's little point yelling at a bunch of trees in the woods, but I'm past caring, and it makes me feel better. "We aren't superheroes, Maggie. We're more like super zeroes. Wait, I've got it. How about, Not-so-Super-Girl."

I laugh at my own lame joke and then question my eroding sanity. It must be stress, but I can't stop until my giggle ends in a choking fit. I wipe my streaming eyes. My hand burns, and I glare at the swollen marks in my palm, then at the purple thorns on the ground that made them. "I thought you guys were supposed to be my friends." Some wielder I turned out to be.

"You must bend them all to your will."

My mother's words repeat their challenge in my head. In the cemetery, when I asked the vines to move, they obeyed. Why can't I do that here in the labyrinth?

Focusing on the prickly vines at my feet, I ask them to move. My heart rate slows. I feel it beat, hear the blood inside my chest rushing from one chamber to the next. The vines shiver, just a bit at first, then more. They retreat under my gaze. Not just the ones I fell on, but all of the purple-thorned ivy.

Emboldened, I ask for help. I have no plan, no idea who I'm addressing, or even what I hope for. Still, I send out wave after wave of general truths. I hurt. I'm tired. Thirsty. Need Gideon. Find Rosamond ...

If nothing else, the thoughts are cathartic. The list delineates what I need, and gives me focus. I can't quit, not with my friends still out there and maybe in worse shape than I am. *Suck it up, Rae. Fight!*

Timber groans. I whirl trying to pinpoint the noise. My pulse doubles. Then my chin drops as the trunk of a nearby oak bends at his would-be waist.

I fear he'll topple and crush me. Instead, two huge limbs reach down and the tapered branches near the ends encircle me. My feet leave the earth as I'm lifted up. I take a breath, hold it in, and wait to die.

Like the actress in the clutches of King Kong, the giant oak hoists me into the air. Wind blows my hair back. We're moving too fast, and my stomach dips roller coaster-style. I squeeze my eyes shut as my body rockets into the canopy above.

What have I done? God save me!

Is this tree my friend or enemy? I haven't figured it out yet, and it may not matter, because at any moment, the Tree King could hurl me to the ground from spite or accidently drop me trying to help.

A scream strangles in my throat. I pray and plead. Send my fear out to the tree on waves of emotion hoping he'll understand. *Please. Don't hurt me.*

The oak doesn't seem to hear. He sways back and forth, though there isn't a stitch of wind. Limbs creak with his stretching. Thin branches extend as human fingers and strain until they're leaning far enough to meet with the tree nearest us, a mountainous sycamore.

The sycamore sways as well. Branches from both trees work like careful arms reaching toward each other, leaves mesh to become quiet hands. The hand-off from one tree to the other is smooth. It occurs to me this might be cool, if it weren't so brain-obliteratingly scary.

Remembering to breathe, I shuttle air in and out of my spastic lungs. I'm not relaxed, exactly, but not completely petrified anymore either. In fact, I keep my eyes open as the sycamore rocks.

He swings forward, depositing my body into the arms of the smaller maple next door. Slowly, I begin to grasp they aren't plotting my death. They're moving me.

The dance goes on from tree to tree. Wood moans as the forest sways, heeding my call for aid. Their song closely resembles a pod of whales as they communicate.

I have no idea where they're sending me, but I trust them. What choice do I have? They are as kind and attentive as if I'm a baby in a swing. I send them my gratitude. Respect and thanks flood from me to each tree as I cross the miles by way of the fearsome wildwood highway.

Over time, the trees and I come to an understanding. As I travel among them, I relax, and our connection improves. I'm learning to listen instead of screaming emotion at them out of panicked desperation. And the trees have a lot to say.

It's funny because they don't talk. Not in the traditional sense. Trees emit feelings that leave an imprint on my mind. Like hands in wet cement, when I open myself up, trust them, I receive their messages as an impression. My brain discerns their meaning, translates it somehow, and boom, I comprehend.

The longer I'm passed along, the bolder I become. There's no question the trees are friendly. Powerful, regal, wise. I've always loved trees, but never guessed they were quite this awesome. Their energy rubs off on me. A steady breeze brushes my skin as I travel. Instead of cowering in a ball as I'd first done, I stretch out, experiment with balance, actually assist in my hand-off from one set of limbs to the next. First, I'm on my hands and knees, crouching like a toddler. I think of my kitty Edgar, remembering the time we got stuck in a tree. If he could see me now!

Each tree has a definite rhythm, slightly different from his brothers. Once I'm comfortable, I try and stand. The oak gently steadies me as I wobble and trip. Working as my spotter, if I lean too far one way, the oak gently corrects my balance. An hour or two later, I'm running down the heavy limbs, leaping into the waiting arms of the elm ahead.

This is magic I can handle. No way could I ride the treetops without the Earth element imparted to me.

My feet slide across the bark of a maple, and I'm in the air again. A laugh escapes. I'm both exhilarated and scared to death. I wonder briefly if this is how it feels to leap from a plane, or BASE jump. A jumper must trust the equipment and instructor to risk so much. There's faith and belief involved. That's how I feel anyway, as I land in the soft needles of a pine tree. Adrenaline blocks any pain.

My tree hopping might be more accurately described as surfing. I'm high as a kite, and I'm not talking feet in the air. The woods share their knowledge. Infuse me with energy, life, and power. I'm one with the forest, me and not me all at once.

As the woodland thins, a meadow and lake loom in the distance. Willows crowd the left bank, their greedy roots snaking into the water, drinking their fill. I slow, asking the one closest if she'll receive me.

She will. I leap falling several feet from the taller elm to the willow below. She raises her wispy-thin arms. Bands of skinny branches wrap my body, curl around me like ropes and deposit my feet on firm ground. She's all grace and beauty as she straightens, and I tell her so.

Thank you, I say, feeling the loss of her energy immediately. I'm tempted to climb right back up into the safety of the trees, but this is where the forest ends, and I still have to find Gideon. Tall, yellow grasses swish against my legs as I wade through the dense foliage toward the water. Sparrows dive for the bugs leaping from my path. Crickets saw their legs together in sing-song chirps. Frogs burp. The scene is deceptively pretty.

Yet, having left the trees, the ache returns to my muscles. Pain keeps me tethered to our reality. I'm filthy, caked in mud from the swamp, sweaty, bloody, and very sure I stink. Mother always said you know it's bad when you can smell yourself.

The lake shines as clear and blue as a postcard from the Mediterranean, but the last time I wanted a wash, things got ugly.

Now, I have allies. I face the trees. *Is it safe?*

My impression from them is yes, but with hesitation. Unsure what to make of their answer, I go with the yeses. Piece by piece, I strip to nothing, groaning inwardly at how freeing it is to have everything off. My toes hit the icy water first. *No time for complaining*, I warn myself and dive in, bringing my dirt-stiff clothing along for a rinse.

I dunk my head under and find the murky water surprisingly refreshing. Next, I rub my clothes against my skin to shed the blood and grime from both. Any degree of clean is better than the filth I dove in wearing.

Weeds tickle my feet on the gloppy lake bottom. My heart jolts as the plants wind their long tendrils over my ankles, and climb my calves. I gasp when they reach higher. *Whoa there, that's getting personal.* I jump aside, but the bottom is covered in the strange vegetation. It suctions onto my stomach and thighs, it doesn't hurt but freaks me the hell out. I'm sloshing through the water toward the bank, lake weed grabbing at me as I pass.

"What do you want?"

Peace, be still …

The impression presses in on me. I take a breath, and try to relax. The oak helped when I trusted him, so I choose to trust again.

Peace …

I allow the mushy, green plants to creep over me. The trees were cool and helpful, but this is just gross. I feel beyond awkward standing naked in waist-deep water while some kinky pond scum feels me up for kicks.

As I wait, my skin begins to tingle, then burn. Cuts and scrapes sting as though doused in antiseptic. My mind opens to the plants, and at last I understand. They're healing me.

Time passes. I lose track of how much as the lake weed

soothes my injuries. While my hair dries under the fading sun, my mind strays to Gideon, as always, and then Cole. Finally, the lake fauna is done with me and retreat to their beds in the mud.

I climb out of the pond and dress in my soggy, albeit cleaner, clothes. The cuts and scrapes don't hurt as much and appear less red and angry. The stiffness in my body is all but gone.

Wielder of the Earth Element, huh? Not bad. I like my new title better all the time.

Chapter Twenty-Six

Cole

Silent as a pair of foxes, Gideon and I put as much distance as possible between us and the last surviving Weird Sister. I turn her words over in my mind, searching for answers.

"Pollute the silver circles of sight. The dead may not enter …
Therefore use the dead."

Silver circles … What does that mean? Does he own a pair of magic glasses, or crystal ball that we need to steal or break? How do we pollute them? If it's a metaphor, she could mean water or the moon. A lake can be polluted *and* silver, especially if it ices in winter. And her suggestion to use something dead leaves me dischuffed, to say the least.

I rub my grumbling torso as if that will stave off the hunger gnawing my gut. At this point, I've gone so long without food, I think my body's eating itself. Trapped here before in spirit form, we never ate. Who would have guessed there were perks to being a ghost?

Tired as we are, we bash on. Gideon keeps company with his own thoughts, which I suspect are half-crazed over Raven. His jaw clenches so tightly, I wonder how his teeth don't crack. Could be his injury, fatigue, or both, but his limp's more pronounced and he slows our pace. Not that I'm pointing it out. I adjust my gate to match his while trying not to appear patronizing. Life was easier when I was a prat, but not very satisfying.

Now, I fantasize about playing the hero, rescuing Rose, reuniting her with her family. Of course, they'll go wild with gratitude. Her mother will probably cry and hug me. Her father will shake my hand and call me son. Rose and I will date. I'll take her to the cinema, buy her presents, and do all the corny shite normal couples do. We'll take our time getting to know each other. Life will move on, unfold as it should.

It could happen.

A flash draws my gaze to Gideon who's casually squeezing a glowing sphere in his palm like a stress ball. Dark veins run over its orange base reminding me of cooling magma. He doesn't appear to feel the heat. Nothing burns his skin. The ball slides up his hand to his first finger, and he spins it like a basketball.

"Nicely done," I say.

He smiles.

"When did you learn that one?"

"Not sure, but it's all coming easier. It's as much about respect and listening to my element, as it is giving orders. We're partners. Does that make any sense?"

"Yes." It's the same for me.

Curious, my mind summons wind, and a stiff breeze immediately answers. The unseen force bounces around my body like a happy dog, waiting for instructions. I wasn't sure how the elements work for the others, but I feel at one with the air. My breathing slows and the temperature drops. As I concentrate all my efforts on the flame under Gideon's control, I cover the sphere in a frosty gust. Wind encircles the ball until it freezes over, cracks, and shatters in a puff of steam.

My grin is checked by Gideon's narrowing eyes. His nostrils flare. *Uh oh.* I was pissing about and now he's cheesed off again.

It doesn't take much. Maddox has all the patience of an injured wolverine.

Surprise lifts my eyebrows when one side of his mouth slides up. "Oh, it's on, Wynter."

I'm up for some sport. "Yeah, well good luck, yank. You'll need it."

I dive as Gideon chucks a flare at my head. *Oh, no you didn't.* I roll and hop to my feet in a ready crouch. To answer his challenge, I summon winds from every direction, gather the power at my torso, and shoot. The gust blows so hard, it knocks Maddox on his arse.

As much as I enjoy the sight, there's no time to gloat because he's already rising, and more than that, his hands are glowing. The grin on his face is pure revenge. Odd yellow light shines from his chest, growing brighter. This is bad. Very bad.

The blast shakes the ground as if a furnace exploded. My frame trembles a fraction of a second before I teleport to a safe spot behind him. The grass where I stood a moment ago is scorched and smoking.

Impressive, but now it's my turn.

The sky darkens as clouds gather at my beckoning. Thunderheads build, fierce and angry. Power courses through my limbs to my fingertips. The sensation is both exhilarating, and I'll admit, a little frightening. I don't have a headache, and I'm not the least bit tired.

Energy fills me with a capability that I didn't earn and don't fully understand. What if we can't control what we've started? Toying with the elements like this is madness, but the temptation is too strong. Like telling a boy he can't ride his new bike on Christmas Day.

Whatever I imagine, the wind obeys. Wielding my new power is becoming as effortless as breathing, the energy as much a part of me as any other limb. I feel free enough to fly. No sooner do I *think* than I'm rising on the wind, hovering a few feet off the ground. Another neat trick I had no idea I was capable of.

Gideon whirls to face me and glances up. "Wha ... "

Pride swells as his eyes bulge. I must be damn imposing, floating in mid-air like the Egyptian god Amun. Hell, maybe he had the same gift.

Energy particles circle the atmosphere above us where I've collected it. My mind reaches out to stir the air, and the storm obeys. The full force of a hurricane waits in the heavens for my command.

I lift one eyebrow. "Give up?" I hope he's intimidated enough to back down, but this is Gideon.

"Ha! You wish." He raises a fire at his feet. Feeding off the dry grass, it doubles in size, quadruples. Flames bend and twist, weaving together until they take shape.

My brow creases as I struggle to identify the still knitting form. The fire moves as though alive, finally consolidating into the head of a giant wolf. The warning I ignored earlier resurfaces. Fun? Hell yeah, but the situation could easily get out of hand. "Maddox, c'mon, mate enough."

"No. Let's see what happens."

He stands on the far side of his burning creation, and while the heat doesn't affect him, I'm sweating. Hovering two feet above ground, a wave of my hand drives me beyond the too-warm blaze into cooler territory.

"Let's not." I hate that I'm the disapproving parent in this scenario telling a kid why it's not cool to play with matches. Responsible behavior is the antithesis of my old MO, and I'm no choir boy, but I didn't come this far to end up dead.

"Do it!" he shouts.

"No."

Coward. The word is in his eyes.

Resentment blows through me like a chill wind. *Golden boy. Teacher's pet. Always getting his way.* "You asked for it."

Pressure builds, and my chest tingles with expectation. Electricity in the air makes the hairs on my arms stand on end. When I drop my hand, wind falls from the sky like a hurtling locomotive. I'm not afraid. Somehow, I sense I'm protected, and I am. When the force strikes, it separates, flowing over me the way water parts around a rock and heads straight for Gideon.

Air hits the earth like Thor's hammer. And his fire responds. Darting over Gideon, the wolf shields him, enduring the brunt of my attack. Lifting his smoldering muzzle, the beast opens his mouth wide and I see my mistake.

Wind feeds flame.

When my airstream collides with Gideon's fire-beast, the animal … eats it. I don't know how else to describe what's happening. The more forced air the inferno consumes, the bigger it grows. Fifteen feet. Twenty.

The heat is unbearable. I glide further away to avoid incineration.

The wolf gulps air. His head bloats as he ingests more oxygen, expands to bursting. "He's going to blow!" The words have barely left my mouth when an unseen force punches my chest like a giant fist. I'm a daredevil shot from a cannon, first I fly, then I fall.

My head smacks the ground hard enough to make my ears ring. The sky above darkens, but it doesn't matter since my lids slide down. Breaths come in shallow pants. I'm sure I'll pass out, except I don't. Waves of pain radiate throughout my skeleton. My ear hurts again, and I can't move, but then again, I don't really want to …

"You awake?"

Gideon. His voice is muted, as though a blanket covers his mouth. I'd like to hit him, but I can't lift my arms. "Tosser."

"Excellent. If you're strong enough for insults, I expect you'll live."

"Sod off."

"Only proving my point, Wynter."

When I open my eyes, Gideon lies flat on his back next to me. I struggle to sit up. Everything spins, and I groan.

Fully night, the moon is up in a clear sky that sheds plenty of light to see by. The fire is out. The air cool and crisp. I glare at the perfect, silver orb as if she's responsible for the ache in my head.

" *... you must pollute the silver circles of sight. Only then will you be free, for once blind Pan can seek you no more.* "

I massage my stiff neck muscles. "Shut it, witch."

"What?"

"Nothing. How long was I out?" Talking creates white mist in front of my mouth. It's colder than I thought. When I touch my torn ear, there's fresh blood on my fingertips.

"No idea. Woke up just before you did." He sits up, wrapping his arms around his knees and drawing them in.

I don't remember blacking out, but I must have done. "We never should have fought like that."

"Why not? We're getting stronger. We need to test our abilities." He grins. "Besides, it was—"

"Stupid?"

"Necessary. In all likelihood, we'll face Pan soon. We have to know what we're capable of. Understand the weapons at our disposal."

"Weapons? Will you listen to yourself? What about Rose and Raven?"

"This is for them." His voice rises. "I'll do whatever I have to, anything, *everything* to protect Rae. You still don't get it, do you? We have to use our powers to even have a chance of winning."

I see his point, but it's not enough. "And what chance do you think Rose and Raven have if we kill each other *practicing* for a fight? Pan wins them both." I'm surprised how rational I sound. Although, I guess four years left rotting in The Void will change a bloke.

"Then what do you suggest we do?" There's defeat in his tone that I don't recognize.

"I'm not saying don't practice, just maybe not on each other." My head falls back, and I stare at the moon. Stars dot the velvet sky, but the constellations are unknown to me. I shiver, rubbing my hands together to ward off the chill.

Gideon snaps his fingers, a small fire flares. With the added light, I note hundreds of fine, red scratches covering his skin. "You look like chickens danced on your face."

He glances at both arms before sliding a hand down his throat. "Windburn, I think." He readjusts his weight. "Hurts like a bitch."

"Sorry?"

"Don't be. *You* have no eyebrows."

"What?" My fingers roam my forehead. The hair over both eyes feels patchy and thin. I palm my jaw searching for the five o'clock shadow I've started. It's barely there, the skin beneath raw and painful. "What the hell, Maddox?"

Humor carves a mean smile in his face. "You've been singed, my friend."

Panicked, my fingers grip my hair. Most of it seems intact. I think. A breath hisses out between my teeth as I glance around. I'll smash his goolies with the first stick I find. We'll see if he thinks *that's* funny. "Arse."

"Never knew you were so vain." His grin fades. "I very much doubt Raven will care."

"Look, mate, about that." I pull a few blades of grass and toss them into the fire. "For now, let's focus on Rose and Raven. It's not that I don't appreciate the support—"

"You keep saying Rose and Raven not Raven and Rose."

"What? So?"

"*So*, first name implies preference."

He's right. Raven is kind and brave, but I'm not in love with her. If I were, I wouldn't spend all my time thinking of Rose. Not that I'm in love with her either, but I could be. One day. "It's not going to work between me and Raven. At least, not the way you mean."

A headshake whips the hair from his eyes. "The witches confused you."

"No, I know what I'm saying." I lower my chin and look him square in the eye. "Raven gave me back my life. A life I didn't appreciate before. It's like being born all over again to do everything differently. Can you understand?" Maddox watches his fire. "I'll help her get a start. Anything I have is hers, but—"

"She'd never take your money."

I smile. "No, probably not, but the offer stands." I can't call her sister ... or maybe I can now. She's the sister I never had. The friend I never was to anyone before this place. That's all changed because of her. "I'll always be there for her. She's ... well, I don't need to tell you all she is."

"No." The fire changes from orange to blue. "You don't even know this Rose person. I'm sorry, but she might not survive the extraction."

I hide my chill behind a weak smile. "Extraction? Is that what we're calling it now?" He doesn't answer. "What's important for this conversation is that I *want* to know her. When I get home, I'm moving out of my parents' house. Starting my life over, and this time, I won't waste it."

The fire glows hotter. "You've got it all figured out, haven't you?"

"I'm beginning to. I'll go to university, buy a fast car, maybe I'll meet a girl—somebody like Raven."

"But not Raven?" He says it like a statement.

Guilt tightens my chest knowing I brought her to this hell while convincing myself nothing would really happen. If it has, another piece of me will die, but—"I won't pretend I feel something I don't. Not even for her. Especially not for her. She deserves more than lies."

His head jerks as though I punched him, and he's given himself away.

"That's it! You *lied* to her, didn't you? Mr. Judge and Jury Maddox told a fib." It isn't funny but the hypocrisy is unbelievable.

"What'd you do, Maddox, cheat, run over her cat?"

He blows me off with a snort.

"Seriously, what? You're obviously still strung out on her." It's all so clear. I suspected something the night they argued, but I wasn't sure until right now. "You open your mouth for two reasons: to threaten someone, and to talk about her. Did you know that?"

"I'm not doing this with you."

"Sorry, mate, it's too late for that."

"Fine." The fire blazes higher and I lean away. His laugh is hard and out of place, and I wonder if he's finally gone off his trolley. I sit silent as a stone, giving him time.

When he finally lifts his gaze, his eyes aren't angry as I expected. They're hollow. "The board took control of Maddox Industries, and shut me out. I can't take care of her, Cole."

Cole. Not Wynter.

"I thought maybe you could look after her. She'd be safe with you."

In his way, he's put her first, and I'll be dammed if I don't admire that. "That's almost noble, Maddox, if it weren't so misguided. In fact, it's the most asinine reasoning I've ever heard of." I pause, in case he wants to deck me.

He doesn't.

"Who else knows about this?"

"Besides you?" His lips meet his knuckles as he considers. "The board. Jennings. Jamis. Dane, which I'm sure means Maggie by now. That's it." He finishes like he's correctly completed the word *anthropomorphic* at a spelling bee.

"For someone who keeps his business private, that's quite a few names." Gideon's wearing his get-to-the-damn-point face again, so I do. "Tell *her*, idiot. The worst that happens is she rejects you, but what if she doesn't?" His features set. "Uh huh. See? That's what scares you most, isn't it? The worst scenario for you is if she says *yes,* because it means you'll start off with nothing—together on even ground."

Tiny flames thread his fingers, highlighting half his face,

eclipsing the rest. "You still have money, Cole. You can't understand."

But I do. "Have you lost your experience, your instincts? Did your brain blow out your arse when they took your company?" The words pour out and in talking to him, I liberate myself. My volume increases with my conviction because I know him.

He's me.

"You can't buy her. Your mistake was thinking you ever could. Raven doesn't *need* either of us, mate, but she chose you. Use what you've learned to your advantage. Sure, you'll have to earn everything back, be poor, *and* a Maddox at once. The pair of you will struggle together to build your lives and careers like most people do, but so what?"

The question hangs in the air as the fire burns low. His head drops into his palms.

"Guys like us live in the shadow of our fathers. We think money and power is all we are because of who they are." I lean back on my elbows. "We don't have to be like them."

Gideon straightens and faces me. "So, what do I do?"

He's asking me? He may regret it, because I don't hold back. "Swallow your pride, and tell her the truth. Then, *don't* tell her what to do about it. I've watched you for years, remember? Making corporate decisions, doing whatever the hell you wanted without answering to anybody, manipulating people to do your bidding." His mouth opens like he'll argue but he shuts it again. A minor miracle. "Let Rae make up her own mind from now on."

His cheeks puff with a held breath. "Okay," he exhales.

Was that as painful for him to admit as I think it was? I can't say a word; though I'm pretty sure hell just froze over.

"No, you're right," he says. Though I don't know if it's to convince himself, or in response to the shite look I must have on my face. His mouth crooks on one side. "I'll talk to her."

I nod. "First we have to find her, eh?"

"Both of them. So, let's kick some ass and get our girls."

I can't stop my smile though every muscle in my face hurts. Gideon 2.0.

Chapter Twenty-Seven

Cole

This time when I end up in Rose's bedroom, I don't hesitate. Once I feel my feet beneath me, I lunge for her, drawing her into my arms.

Her form coalesces with my touch. "Oh, Cole. It's been so long. I was really worried." She fidgets like a frightened bird.

"Shh, I'm here. Everyone's safe," I lie.

"When the Draugar came, I thought ... " She lowers her voice to a whisper, "Pan says if I leave the tower, they will kill me. It's my worst nightmare."

Her admission echoes Pan's threat.

Since our dearest Rosamond is unwilling to share. Feed us with your fear. Face the terrors deep within your own minds.

He's using our fears against us? *Cheap shot, you dirty bastard.*

She holds me tighter. "I'm so happy you're here. I wish you could bring your friends, next time. I want to meet Gideon and Raven."

"I know. You'll meet them soon." I slide my first finger beneath her chin, remembering the crushing loneliness here.

Water gurgles nearby. I briefly wonder if a stream runs under the tower.

"I've been so curious about them, you know? And, of course, I need to thank Gideon for all he's done for me. He must be pretty special." Her words hit a sour note, which must show on my face because she quickly adds, "Oh, gosh and Raven and you, too, of course. Everyone's been wonderful."

Her eyes brighten with a smile so sweet, I forget what I was about to say, and my mind takes a different tack. "I'm going to kiss you now, Rose."

Her breathing accelerates with her *Ooh*. The apples of her cheeks pink, but she doesn't resist.

As my hands slide down her arms, my heart rate surges. It may have been a while, but I definitely remember this part. I lower my head, brushing my lips against her closed mouth. She's trembling, so I assume this is a first for her.

She leans into me with a sigh and stumbles a little. We smile against each other, all lips and teeth and bumping noses. I pull her body closer and try again. This time, she responds with less awkwardness. I raise my hand to cup her cheek. Her hands encircle my neck. Nudging her lips apart, I slip my tongue inside. The taste cool and rimy with a bite like January.

Suddenly, Rose fists my shirt with both hands, while her tongue plunders my mouth like a pro. My lids fly open, but arousal soon overcomes surprise. I close my eyes, and match her enthusiasm.

I'm aware of everything and nothing at once. The press of her fingers on my shoulder, her soft hair brushing my skin, thundering heartbeats, mixing breaths heating our faces. When I finally break away, we're both panting.

Rose steps aside, feet disappearing to mist. She raises the back of her hand to her swollen lips. As she looks away, her lashes create a veil over her eyes, as though she's keeping secrets. "I guess we got carried away."

"I guess we did." Either my Rose is a very fast learner, or that wasn't her first kiss after all. Not that I care.

She glides to her little chair by the window and sits.

The lure of more snogging lodges firmly at the forefront of my mind, but I take the hint and sit several feet away on her bed. "Rose?"

"Hm." She pulls her attention from the window and smiles. "Yes, Cole?"

"I met someone here who mentioned a connection to Pan and silver circles. Have you ever heard of them?"

"Silver circles? No, I haven't."

Her dismissal is so fast, I'm not sure I have her full attention. "Are you sure? It could be important. Does Pan wear glasses, or own any silver jewelry? The smallest thing could—"

"No." Her eyes sharpen to something hard and immovable. "I'm sorry, but I don't know what you're talking about." She's so agitated that I suspect her, but of what, I can't say. Immediately, I feel like a prat for thinking the worst. She could be afraid or simply telling the truth, or both.

As always, the room spins without warning. Pieces of me wear away as my tie to her severs. I curse myself for wasting our last moments on Pan. For making her uneasy, but we really need some answers.

Rose slouches in her chair, expression full of longing. I know it so well, the ache of waiting and wanting.

"Hold on," I tell her. "We'll be together soon."

Soon …

Chapter Twenty-Eight

Raven

The sun sinks even as the moon rises. Like two sentinels switching places for guard duty, the change signals the coming of night. I hate The Void under any circumstances, but the dark here is a separate, singular terror.

Forest to the south, nothing but open meadow lies ahead to the north. Even though I came from the wood, I'm tempted to return—ride the trees again and rely on their direction to lead me to my friends. I square my shoulders when a willow bough brushes my arm. She caresses my skin with her leaves, and gives me a little push urging me toward the meadow. Assurance and a strong vibe of confidence accompany her entreaty. Without a better plan, I obey. After all, she helped me at the lake. The trees have been nothing but good.

There's a gentle slope on the hill to the top of the ridge. My muscles tingle as I jog, pulling energy from the grass below to power me forward.

I sense pain, not mine, but emanating from somewhere nearby. A tiny wail stops me. Panicked, I glance over my shoulder and notice patches of yellowed grass on the path I just trod. *No!* I kneel, placing both palms on the soft ground. A pang of guilt stabs me. Greedy to maintain my stamina, I absorbed too much fuel from the soil and hurt the delicate plants. "Sorry. I'm so sorry."

Armed with new information, I rise. As bad as I feel, there's nothing to do but continue, though I carefully adjust my intake of nutrients so the life around me thrives. My green friends are generous, their power so potent my head swims. Stronger than any chemical, vitamin, or adrenaline burst, the earth's energy buzzes within me.

My confidence soars. I've totally got this. We can win. Then I hit the crest of the hill, and my feet stop dead.

The hill below harbors more than a dozen, freestanding doors. Surrounded by air, they're planted in the ground like brightly painted headstones. Tall, wide, short, narrow, the entryways stand alone and vertical, attached to ... nothing.

Who put them here? Why?

Curiosity tugs me like a tractor beam. I shuffle down the steep hill, angling for the closest door. Painted bright red, a masterpiece of ornate millwork adorns the top, while carved, wooden roses cascade down the sides, punctuated with twigs and ivy. Birds hide within the sculpted edges. On several leaves, tiny tree frogs bunch as though they'll jump to life. And then one does.

The door swings open. Cold filters from the entrance, swirling gray mist leaks from the deep black beyond. I step back and meet with a solid barrier. One glance up and I know I've been punked.

My mother's voice whispers a reminder.

"Miss Willow will seem a friend and refuge at first, but do not trust her. She is selfish and unhappy, and will betray you if she can."

If only I'd remembered an hour ago. Willow branches secure my arms and legs. How the heck did a tree get up the hill? They're rooted to the ground for crying out loud. No less weird than trees that bend and hand me off to one another, I suppose. I didn't mind the impossible as long as it helped me.

I plead, and when that gets me nowhere, I swear, and finally fight. The willow ignores me, tightening her cable-like branches until I can't move. Wasn't that me trekking up the knoll a minute ago all cocky and thinking I had the whole super-power thing down? *Dummy.*

Once more, I jerk my head and beg the willow to let me go, but she won't listen. I struggle against my bonds, but it's hopeless. She's too strong. There are probably smarter choices than hysteria, but I can't think of one.

"You must bend them all to your will."

I try, but my concentration sucks. The only one that's bending is me as the willow shoves me into the cavernous space on the other side of the yawning doorway.

Once again, I'm free falling. Too dark to see, my arms flail searching for anything to cling to and find only dead space. I slam onto hard ground, elbows cracking against an unyielding surface. I cry out as my body bounces and hits again. Blood fills my mouth where I bit my tongue.

Son of a … I lift my aching head. Shout up the tunnel I fell through, telling the willow exactly what I think of her.

Above, the sun is setting. Here, a cloud slides off the fading moon as the first glimpse of morning light reveals a pretty courtyard. Perfectly manicured hedges run in every direction, dotted in places by shrubbery trained in the shape of objects, a penguin, bear, even an open book. It's cool, or would be if I saw the botanical creations anywhere else. The courtyard is paved in cobblestones. No wonder my landing hurt.

In the center, a tower made of gleaming white stone rises into the sky.

Rosamond!

There's a single door at the base painted emerald green with a brass knocker shaped like a bull's head. A pale flash draws my attention to the lone window three quarters up the structure. I squint and the outline of a face appears, disappears, and pops into view again.

"Hello?" I clamp my lips shut. The urge to speak was impulse and quite possibly stupid. I have no idea if who or what I saw up there is friendly.

"Raven?"

I blink. *What the* ... A girl pokes her head all the way out the window. She's young, about my age, and very pretty. Her blond hair tumbles past the sill. I swear all I can think of is Rapunzel. The thought is laughable, but this is so not the venue for humor.

"Are you Rosamond?" I stage whisper. "How do you know me?"

"Oh. M'gosh! I'm so glad you're here!" Is she blind? Why is she talking to the shrubbery way over there? "Call me Rose, okay?"

What I'd like to call this chick is noisy. I'm sure she's excited. I would be too if I thought I was getting out of this effing madhouse, but her girly squeak is practically a shout. And I don't exactly want my arrival broadcasted. "Okay, Rose. How do you know me?"

"I would know you anywhere, Raven." Her tone hardens as she says my name. It's odd, but she quickly resumes her high-pitched excitement. "Where's Gideon and Cole?"

"We got separated. Can you come down?"

"Sorry. Pan locks the door and has the only key."

When her gaze doesn't leave the hedge, fear pokes my ribs. I pivot to watch with her. "Is he coming?"

"Who?"

"Pan."

"Oh. I don't think so, why?"

"Never mind." I scan the courtyard for something to jimmy the door open with. This isn't like opening a hotel door with your keycard, or even using a Slim Jim on a car—not that I have either of those items anyway.

The tower door is thick, old wood, the wrought iron hinges are massive. Finding nothing useful near me, my hands settle on my hips. I blow out a long breath.

"What are you doing?" Rose asks.

I step back and look up. "Trying to get you out."

She's sitting on the sill with one leg dangling down the wall, or half a leg. Her foot disappears in mist. "I need tools that I don't have to get you out."

Her leg swings. "Hmm, hang on a minute!" I'm standing right here, but she yells as though I'm a mile off. Inside the turret, several crashes—not unlike those of a major car accident—bounce off the stone. When she reappears, she tosses something out the window.

Heart in my throat, I jump back to avoid having my head bashed in. Metal clatters on the pavers. "Hey!"

"Will that work?"

A three-foot bed slat lies at my feet. I swallow, and count to ten until I'm calm. Cole's girl is cute, adorable even, and ... I'm sorry, but first impressions indicate she's as helpless as a newborn bunny and just as bright.

"Thanks," I mumble, lifting the slat.

"Oh no, Raven. Thank *you!*"

Lord, help me. I walk to the door and wedge the end of the bar against the handle. I apply steady pressure, left, right, up, down. It won't budge. I try again with the hinges, finally resorting to whacking them with all of my strength. The cool air doesn't prevent sweat from beading on my forehead.

"Did you get it open yet?" Rose's voice floats down from her perch on the sill above.

Seriously? I pause in my battle with the stubborn door. My shoulder slumps against the wood in defeat. "I promise you'll be the first to know." I hear the terseness in my voice. My frustration isn't her fault, but my patience is wearing thin. I need help. *The garden!*

"What's funny?" Rose asks.

I didn't realize I'd laughed out loud. "Hang tight, Rose. I've got an idea."

"Oh, good. Me, too."

I don't know what she's talking about, but I'm too absorbed with the jasmine I see climbing up the stone arch to ask. *Can you pick the lock? Open the door ... ?* My lids shut. I send my request out with thanks for whatever they might do to help us.

"Raven? What are you doing? I can't see you. Are you still here?"

I don't answer, keeping my connection with the plants strong. As my lids open, the vines are already at work. The delicate roots stuff into the keyhole. Busy with their task, they squirm and rotate until I hear a soft click.

You're amazing, thank you. Thank you, Jasmine.

With the job done in less than sixty seconds, the vines retreat to their home as though they'd never moved. I'm thrilled different varieties of plant life respond to me the same way. Who knew this incredible link was even possible?

Pan, that's who.

I shrug the thought off like a dirty coat, turn the handle, and push. "Rose, you can come down now, I—"

Bushes rustle behind me. I hesitate, afraid to look. Tingles cross my scalp as more leaves swish, twigs snap, branches break. For a brief moment, I pretend its Gideon, or Cole. I turn, praying it's them.

It's not.

Two shiny horns push through the hedge, swiftly followed by the rest of a bull's head. Fear balloons in my chest. The beast snorts and thrashes, crushing the shrubbery under his enormous mass. As the rest of his body emerges, logic disconnects in my brain.

The charging body of the bull I expect is replaced by eight-pack abs and the bulging pectorals of a *man*. He walks upright and sports two gigantic human arms, with human hands and fingers. Below the waist, skin becomes fur with a tail and bovine legs ending in cloven hooves.

What is this thing?

In one fist, he carries a weapon. Half sword, half ax, the medieval looking blade is a fusion of two things, just like him.

The bull-man bellows, and paws the ground with his plate-sized hoof.

My lungs smother. Breath comes in shallow pants that I can't slow. I throw myself at the door and find it closed. Frantic, I jiggle the handle, but it won't turn. "Rose?"

There's no reply, but I didn't speak above a whisper, not

wanting to draw the attention of ... er, whatever the heck that is.

Perspiration turns cold and clammy on my skin. I jerk the door handle again without success. "Rose!" *Where is she?*

I flatten myself in the corner of the doorway where shadows are deepest. There are no trees near enough the tower to climb. Asking the hedges to fight a slobbering mound of angry beef would mean their senseless deaths.

While Sales Hollow is a small rural town, I grew up inside the few city blocks of our downtown. I don't know much about farming and less about bulls. I own a cat. What calms Edgar might not work on a bull-man.

Steam rises above his muzzle as he sniffs the air. His movements are slow and cumbersome.

Is he real, like the tower, or an illusion, like the mental hospital?

Last year in Gideon's mansion, his stepmother Desiree influenced my dreams. Created frightening visions that felt incredibly real, like Pan's. I pray the bull is another illusion.

The monster snorts, then angles toward the door and my hope disintegrates. *Oh, God. Can he smell me?*

If I stay, he'll kill me. If I run, he'll kill me.

Animals sense fear, right? I know Edgar does. Right now, I'm sweating fear-bullets so big, that thing could track me through raw sewage. As a last resort, I close my eyes and slow my heart rate. I emit a sense of peace and calm, and ask for help, though I'm not sure who would answer.

Hooves scuff stone as the bull draws near. I imagine his shadow falling over me, the heat from his body warming the space between us. Does the hand holding his weapon lift, blade pause above my head ready to strike?

Eyes pinched shut, I feel him. Steamy breath blows warm and wet on my face. I'm certain it's snot that dots my skin. The scent in my nose is fur and earth, and musk.

If you're real, don't hurt me. I pray he isn't, and ask God to bail me out, like He's done so many times before.

The snuffling continues. So do my thoughts of, *I'll-be-your-*

best-friend-if-you-don't-squash-me, and *Nice bull*.

Seconds tick by with an occasional scratch of hoof, maybe he shakes his head or shifts his stance.

What's he waiting for? I crack open an eye. Not a foot from my face is a broad, furry brown head. Both my eyes open and I follow the line of his two thick horns to sharp points—perfect for stabbing. Shining brown eyes situated on either side of his head watch me.

"Hey," I say, clearing the frog from my throat. "Aren't you just the biggest, um … guy? Listen, I don't want to hurt anyone, but Rose, up there in the tower? She's my friend. I came to help her, not fight with you. Do you understand?"

He stands there, unmoving, as I babble. I get nothing but long breaths and phlegm. Much more of this and he won't need to stab me. I'll drown.

He shuffles his feet. Shoes. Hooves. Whatever. His nose stretches toward me. I hold my breath as his muzzle slides over my head. The bull-man sucks a breath, snorting my scent (and, I'm pretty sure, hair) up his nose. Mucus drips with a splat onto the stones below. I can only imagine the disgusting souvenirs he leaves on my skin. When he drops his nose to my shoulder, I press my lips together, sure he'll rip a chunk out of me with his big bovine teeth.

After nuzzling me a moment, he sighs, then bends lower, running his forehead up and down my pants leg. Up and down, up and down. Holy freaking cow. *Heh, cow.* No, really. The bull is scratching his face on my thigh!

"What's wrong?" I ask. Carefully, I place my hand on his head between his horns where the hair is longer and curls. "Can I help?" I give him a rub, and he leans in. I press harder, and he groans. The bull isn't angry, he's itchy. He butts me, demanding more attention, and I oblige him. Whatever he wants, he gets, as long as he's not goring me with those horns.

Like with the oaks, I sense the bull doesn't intend to hurt me. I relax my neck muscles, but stay alert. Change happens fast here.

I'm not taking any chances.

He grunts again as my nails rake his face.

"You're just a Ferdinand, aren't you?" I glance at the ax still gripped in his hand. Okay, maybe not, but he's not a mindless killer either.

Now that I know I'm not going to be skewered, I glance at the door. Somehow during the confusion it relocked. Rose must be scared to death.

Eyeing his weapon, I say, "Ferdy, do you understand me, bud?" His head lifts, and my hand falls away. "Can you help me open the door? It's lock—"

In one smooth motion, his fist flies out sideways. Using his knuckles as a battering ram, I didn't even finish asking, and the door is decimated with one blow.

Day-aam.

His head swings round to face me. I feel a question reaching from his mind to mine. As with the trees, the idea of his intended meaning comes through, and it appears I communicate with animals, too.

"That's exactly what I needed. You did an awesome job." He snorts and steps back.

I poke my head through the shattered door. The space is narrow, but torches mounted every few feet up a curling stone staircase cast a steady glow. Like a bisected seashell, the spiral ribbed steps wind up and around, disappearing behind the bend.

"Rose?"

"Raven?"

"Yeah … " Who else would it be?

"You're alive?"

"Er … yeah." The shock in her voice is understandable, considering I'm standing next to a drooling, eight-foot tall freak of nature. Now that we've established I'm not dead and we've reacquainted ourselves, there's one more introduction to make. "Come on down, okay? You're free. And there's someone here that I'd like you to meet."

Chapter Twenty-Nine

Raven

Lilac scents the breeze sweeping over me, diluting the pungent scent of cow. I keep watch over the bull-man, but he stands perfectly still and waits with me. I assumed he'd wander off after satisfying his curiosity. Never assume.

Rose materializes next to me. "Raven?"

I jump a foot, hand covering my hammering heart. "Whoa!" I forgot how these ghosts make no noise. Cole used to scare the crap out of me every time he popped up in the mansion last year. "You surprised me."

"Sorry." Her big blue eyes rivet on the bull-man, expression more confused than afraid.

"What happened?" I ask. "I couldn't get the door open. Didn't you hear me calling?"

"Yes, and I'm sorry. I tried, but the handle got stuck." She watches her threading fingers, bottom lip pooching.

"Oh, no worries," I say, totally worried she'll cry. "Everything worked out. He's nice." I thumb over my shoulder at the bull-man.

"If you say so."

There's no point answering because unlike everything else here, her doubt is completely reasonable. Instead, I retrieve the bed slat, thinking it might come in handy later. "We'd better get going. Ferdy made enough noise with the door to call Pan down on our heads."

Rose floats toward me over the stone pavers in the courtyard. Her lips purse as she looks at the bar in my hand. "Ferdy?"

"Short for Ferdinand. Sorry, it's sort of a joke. He's just not what he seems." Or not *all* that he seems. The bull bumps my shoulder with his muzzle, and I scratch his head.

"Oh, I get it, from the children's book, right? That's cute. You must be an animal person."

I continue patting the bull's velvet nose, missing my little Edgar so much it hurts. "S'pose I am, but never on this scale. Then again, nothing here is normal, is it?"

She brushes her ghostly white hands impatiently. "Can we find the others now?"

"Definitely." One last scratch and I drop my hand. "Bye, Ferdy." He looks down his snout, intimidating as hell. I admit he still freaks me out a little. "Thanks for your help."

I head the opposite direction, Rose by my side, her movements are graceful in a creeptastic sort of way. "Do you know which way to go?"

"I see parts of the maze from my window. Woods are that way." She points behind us. "Hills and grass over there," she says, gesturing ahead. "But everything evaporates in fog at the borders. I don't know what's beyond them, maybe the real world."

Hooves pound distantly on the path behind us. I'm a little surprised, but assume the bull will lose interest after a while. I pick up the pace, eager to put more distance between us and the tower.

Rose concerns me. What if she's been here too long to release? She's sweet, but sometimes her words come out forced and unnatural. Makes sense if she's been isolated, and her knowing about the children's book is a good sign.

"We'll figure it out." My smile is meant to reassure. "Cole's been here before, and he'll get us out."

Her champagne-colored eyelashes flutter. "He's really nice."

I worried Cole might have unrealistic expectations concerning he and Rose, but her response is encouraging. "Yeah, he's pretty great. He—"

"Tell me about Gideon."

"Uh … " I feel the crease pinch between my eyebrows before I check myself. *Chill out, Rae.* She's talkative, friendly, outgoing. Things I'm not. It's natural to want to know who's risking their life for you.

Ferdinand bellows, and I startle like a jackrabbit.

Rose grabs my wrist and her feet materialize. "What's wrong?"

Our new friend stands beneath a cluster of trees. His ridiculously large head swings from side to side. Another moo and his hand plunders the leafy branch above. He's certainly excited about something.

"Apples!" I race to meet him. "Oh, you big, wonderful, hunk of bull, you." I can't remember the last time I ate anything. Literally. Ferdy pulls apple after apple off the limb. For every one he stuffs in his maw, another drops to the ground. "Rose, do you want one?" I ask, kneeling.

"No thanks. I don't really eat much."

Drat, I knew that. I feel like an insensitive jerk. "Sorry."

"Oh, that's okay, but shouldn't we keep moving?"

"We will. Give us just a minute." My attention is back on my apple. "Any worms, buddy?"

Frankly, the way he gobbles them, I don't think Ferdy cares. The apple skin is dark red, almost too perfect. A picture of Snow White crops up, but the needs of my stomach override possible treachery. I turn the fruit over looking for holes or rot. As I twist, a furry gray caterpillar crawls toward me from the other side.

Spiny tuffs of white fur stick up all over his back like feathers. A quill brushes my finger. The sting is immediate and worse than an oven burn.

I drop the fruit with a curse, then pop my finger into my mouth.

Pain and anger speed my breathing. I toe the ground near the fallen caterpillar, intending to bury the evil thing. Instead, I miss and my boot scratches a line six inches in the dirt. The soil unzips, exposing a small hole that devours the bug and seals shut again.

Whoa, what just happened?

The caterpillar is gone. Swallowed by the earth in seconds, and apparently, I made that happen. I glance at my boots, then the ground. Holy freaking crap. My chest rises, both with awe and some healthy caution. Seems I've discovered yet another skill that I'll have to explore later.

"What's the matter, now?" asks Rose. Her whine drags out, tone increasingly petulant.

Defensive, I respond with, "Nothing." Her eyebrows rise, and I hold out my swollen finger as if that explains. "See? A worm stung me." Since her mouth twists into an impatient frown, I see no reason to elaborate on the whole bug-eating-soil episode.

Ferdy bumps my hand with his muzzle. I think he's worried, and it's sweet—slimy, but sweet.

"Gross." Rose wrinkles her nose.

I don't know if she means the insect or Ferdy's dripping nose. Both qualify. Ferdinand holds another apple in his meaty hand, and shoves it at me with a grunt. Finding it pest free, I sink my teeth into the juicy flesh. My eyes close as tangy flavor explodes in my mouth.

More fruit disappears into Ferdy's gullet, juice dripping from his chin. We crunch away like two happy cows chewing cud. It isn't pretty. And I couldn't care less.

"What are you doing? Shouldn't we go?" Rose's tone grows more demanding.

"We are going. Chill *out!*" When she bites her lip, I instantly regret snapping. How long would I wait after being stuck in that tower? Her impatient glances might be fear Pan's following, and I feel like a jerk again. "I'm sorry. You're right. I'm tired and stressed, and when I'm hungry, I get cranky. In the South, we call that 'hangry.' Get it? Hungry plus angry is … " I smile. She doesn't. "No? Forget it. " So much for lightening the mood. "Let me just … yeah."

I pull my outer shirt off and sink to my knees. Scooping fallen apples, I wrap as many as will fit inside the dirty fabric and tie the ends together."

"Raven?"

Rose gazes down at me with icy blue eyes. Something about her strikes a familiar chord, but I don't know what it would be.

"I'm the one who's sorry. You've risked so much. Forgive me?"

"Sure. No problem." I lift my bundle. "I'm taking these for the guys in case they're hungry. See? We're going. It's all good."

Ferdy growls as though he disagrees before stuffing his cheeks with more apples.

Sorry, boy.

As we walk along, the bull-man's hooves beat the dry ground in hollow thuds.

Rose glances over her shoulder. "Looks like you've picked up a stray."

"Does, doesn't it?" A quiet smile breaks free. If Ferdy wants to tag along, that's more than okay with me.

Two hours of hiking and three apples later, I'm feeling better physically, but there's still no sign of Gideon and Cole. A purple dragonfly zips from cattail to thistle, keeping us company. I prefer the bull and bug's company to that of the incessant chatterbox next to me.

First Rose pumps me for information on the guys. Lonely or not, questions like are you and Gideon dating, is he a good kisser, and what's your bra size are none of her damn business. When she finally notices I'm not up for the role of *Gossip Girl*, she pouts. Unfortunately, she isn't quiet long before bringing up shopping, make-up, travel, and what model car I drive. I want to ask if she's seen the TV show *Keeping up with the Kardashians*, because that's who she sounds like.

She smiles and touches my arm a lot. In part, I think, because she's friendly. But also because her feet appear on human contact and that must be nice—to feel normal again. I've never been the touchy-feely type with my girlfriends, but I haven't been kept in a stone closet, either. I don't mind if it makes her happy. As Rose talks, I interject a word here and there so she thinks I'm listening, but I'm not; at least, not completely. She's got the energy level (and attention span) of a squirrel, and it's exhausting.

The landscape changes again, as it does so often here. The soil turns spongy, foliage drips with moisture. Tree varieties grow taller and more tropical. Towering palms with wispy fronds sway in the warm breeze. Flat bush leaves fan out in yellows and reds. A toucan or parrot or something else very un-South-Carolina-like calls its mate.

Despite the strangeness, our surroundings seem peaceful enough. Ferdy sends no impressions of impending doom. Still, around every bend in the road, I'm waiting for Pan to show up. It's too quiet. An ominous presence builds until I feel like goat-bait from *Jurassic Park*. I saw that movie too young and couldn't sleep for a week.

"Raven?"

"I'm sorry, what?"

"You're not listening, are you? I asked if something's wrong." Her gaze darts around. "And what's *Jurassic Park*?"

Did I say that out loud? "Sorry. It's just not like Pan to let me walk off with his prisoner and do nothing. He's got a bet to win, so I—"

"A bet? What sort of bet?" She sounds pissed off, and I don't blame her.

"If we make our way back out of the labyrinth together, Pan agreed to let us go. If not, we're stuck here as co-inmates."

She blinks. "That's it? That's your whole plan?"

"We'll get out."

Her laugh explodes harsh and cynical. "You'll never beat him."

I'm about to ask why she's so sure, and there he is. Ahead where the trail widens to a clearing, Pan astride the back of a triceratops.

Seriously.

Ferdy snorts. His hoof scrapes the ground.

"Speak of the devil," Rose says.

"You can say that again, sister." My fingers tighten on the metal bed rail in my hand.

"Ladies, how delightful to see you again."

The dinosaur pulls at the bit in her mouth. I say *her* because the animal's hide is lavender. I shiver, remembering my earlier comment about goat-bait and wonder if she's carnivorous. No way is this a coincidence. "What are you, some sort of clairvoyant?"

He smiles. "Ah, now that would be a trick. No, unfortunately I simply have excellent hearing."

He's listening? That's it! When I think back, some of the nightmares I experienced closely followed fears I'd expressed out loud. Desiree confessed to creating the same type of frightening visions to scare me away from Gideon. I'm guessing she learned from Pan—before her release and subsequent drowning, that is.

"So, you spy on us."

"Well, duh. You're a rather dull bulb today, aren't you?"

"Eavesdropping is so pedestrian, Pan. I'm shocked you'd stoop to something so unimaginative."

He rubs his stomach. "I'm not bothered by it. In fact, I've eaten quite well since your arrival."

I get his whole, horror show act now, and it's disgusting. He listens, makes his victim's worst fears a reality, then feeds off the suffering. It's true he said as much in the asylum, but I wasn't exactly coherent and wrote it off as part of my nightmare. My mind crushes him with a giant hammer. If I say that out loud, will it happen? Probably doesn't apply to his own pain. "Handy."

"Oh, indeed. You'd be surprised what nonsense people utter when they're under the influence. Now, where are you headed? To find your friends, perhaps? I thought I'd tag along."

Heavy footfalls inch closer until Ferdy's sticky breaths steam my shoulder. Bulls aren't known for staying cool under pressure, so I'm as surprised by his self-control as I am by the fact that he clearly stands with me and not Pan, whom I assume is his master.

Pan teleports off his dino-steed, and stands ten feet from me, ridiculous in his white tuxedo with gold trim and tails. On his head is a long, powdered wig straight out of the 1800's, a stuffed partridge nestled into the curls on one side. He looks more like a Mozart wannabe than sadistic ruler.

A dull ache starts in the back of my skull. To think this creep might eat my headache sends a shudder through me.

The dinosaur keeps her position up the path, though she tosses her head. We could use an ally. "Nice girl?" I say, reaching out with my mind.

"Uh, uh, uh. None of that," Pan says, wagging a finger as though I'm a naughty child. I make note of his three inch nails painted purple to match his ride. "You've already bewitched my Minotaur." He nods toward Ferdy. "The beast's job, Ms. Weathersby, was to skewer you with his rather impressive horns." He exhales in a dramatic sigh. "You've become most inconvenient." His smile is hard as flint, madness evident in his wild, red-rimmed eyes. I jump when he snaps his fingers. A small flame sparks and goes out in a puff of smoke.

Behind him, a ten-foot tall rabbit stands in place of the dinosaur. And it's pink.

The animals, his teleporting, the fire … it's obvious. "You control all four elements?"

"Imbecile. Of course! You single wielders are potent, but no match for me … " His fingers snap again. "I've been at it much longer, you said so yourself."

There's no time to react as willow trees erupt from the earth. Long branches snake around my limbs. We're established frenemies, and the willows ignore my request for help. The bed rail's torn from my hand. I cry out as metal slices the fleshy part of my palm.

Ferdy roars as several trees work to secure two thousand pounds of severely pissed-off bull. He's strong and doesn't know the word quit. Branches snap and break as he thrashes, but eventually, like a rat wound in a snake's coils, the willows win.

"Leave us alone!" *Ooh, good one, Rae.* If you're scolding your brother for interrupting a tea party.

Ferdy shakes with rage. His lowing echoes through the jungle.

Pan pantomimes a wide yawn before stepping forward. "Shall we go, *Rosamond?*"

I don't like how he says her name. I don't like any of this, but I can't stop him.

She doesn't resist as he tenderly wraps her waist. Or complain when he bends his head to whisper. Maybe she's used to this treatment, or believes it's useless to fight. Something feels wrong, though I can't say what. Poor Rose. Of course it's wrong. Everything's wrong!

He leads her toward the ginormous bunny that hasn't moved an inch.

With a swish of his hand, Pan evokes a twelve-foot wide hole in the ground. Grass, mulch, and dirt swirl together, creating a spinning vortex in the earth as smoothly as your grandmother mixes cake batter in her favorite bowl.

The vortex tilts, rising until vertical, like a penny standing on its side. Smooth gray stones form, lining the inner walls of a lengthening tunnel. Water gurgles along the floor, but none leaks outside the opening.

I strain against the willow limbs and catch a glimpse of a winding staircase. Steps curl around the walls and drown in the rising water.

A memory takes hold. I squint and see a door on the far wall—a green door.

My eyes widen. Rose's tower! Okay, not upright, as it should be, the structure's lying on its side, but that's sure enough her tower. Damn it! Pan is taking her back to jail.

He grins and waves before sending his prisoner through the opening ahead of him. Another swirl and the entire tower folds into the vacuous hole and disappears without a trace.

The moment they're gone, the trees release us and retreat into the ground. Good thing, or Ferdy might chop them to kindling with his ax.

A scream of frustration rips from me. The bull-man tosses his massive head in the air and trumpets. I stamp, and swear, and holler again. The Minotaur matches my tantrum yell for yell. I'm beginning to love this guy. No matter how miserable, it's nice to have company. When I'm done venting, I feel a little better. Not that my big show did me any good. Weary and defeated, I slump against the hairy mountain of bull-man.

A beefy arm comes around my shoulder, pushing my face into his underarm. The musk of wet swamp-rat might be preferable, but I couldn't care less. "Thanks, buddy," I say, as he releases me.

The rabbit's ears twitch. I'd forgotten about her. Or rather, I hoped she'd disappear, like her hideous rider.

Smashing rustles the palmetto bushes to our right.

What now, T-Rex, demon-possessed bulldozer, Jack the Ripper? Not that I'll guess anything out loud.

Ferdy tenses. I'm sure he senses my anxiety, not that he isn't shooting off waves of his own.

I squat, pick up the slat I dropped, and slowly straighten. Maybe three thousand pounds of rabbit will distract whatever's coming.

Two dark shapes burst from the jungle. At the sight of the Pepto-Bismol-colored bunny, they turn in unison, flinching again when they spot me. Well, and Ferdy, too.

The bones in my legs liquefy, and I stagger like a drunkard. A sob chokes anything I might say.

It's Gideon and Cole.

Chapter Thirty

Gideon

My throat dries. Every breath is a controlled effort as Raven stands sandwiched between two monsters. Relief she's still alive tag-teams with the fear she'll be killed any minute. My fists are instant balls of flame. Cole gathers wind around us, and I pull oxygen from his stores to fuel my fires. I don't know if it's the sight of my hands or the smell of smoke, but the alien-rabbit bugles like an elephant and thunders past us into the jungle. Trees snap in half and crash to the ground in its wake.

As the noise fades, I pivot to face the other threat. He's some kind of mythological hybrid of bull and man.

"A Minotaur," Cole says. "I've met one before. They're lethal."

Cole and I must share the same thought, because we break into a jog, readying for battle.

Raven darts in front of the beast. Her back to his ... chest? Both her arms stretch out on either side, warning us away, protecting him from attack.

Confused, I check my pace. Her lips are moving, but I can't hear her. And God, how I want to hear her.

The bull paws the ground and snorts. His eyes are red neon. Blood turns molten in my veins as I calculate how close she is to those deadly-sharp horns. When the Minotaur lifts his ax, I draw back my hand, the ball of flame ready to launch.

"Gideon, don't hurt him!" She gives me her profile and speaks low and steadily to the thing behind her.

Again, I slow my pace, keeping careful watch.

"Are you all right, Rae?" Cole expresses what I would say if I could find my tongue.

"Yes, fine. Sorry. He's a friend. Come and meet him just … walk nice, okay? You're scaring him."

"We're scaring him?"

My thoughts exactly.

We edge closer, moving slowly to honor her request.

My gaze sweeps the broad head of the bull, the arms and torso of a man that morph into animal legs with hooves. If the thing is Raven's friend, and helped keep her safe, then he's off my list to charbroil.

The ache I felt while she was missing amplifies now that we're together again. A drink of water set before a man dying of thirst, yet kept out of reach. I let Cole worry about the Minotaur while I indulge a moment, absorbing the sight of her.

Wild hair snakes out in all directions, framing a face with both a busted lip and fading black eye. There's a deep cut on her cheek and one through her eyebrow that will likely scar. Dried blood darkens the skin under her nose. Bruised knuckles, torn clothing, she reminds me of someone who's survived a war.

She watches me with stormy eyes, the details of her journey written on her battered body. A haunted expression assures me of the suffering she's endured and my will bleeds out with my heart.

In my mind, I'm on my knees before her in complete surrender, and then that's where I am. Head down, hands limp at my sides, staring at her boots.

"Gideon, thank God you're safe." She kneels, but doesn't touch me. Why would she? Her chin lifts. "Cole, sit down. You look ready to drop."

Cole obeys, and together we form a small circle. His smile is weary and fleeting. "It's good to see you, duck." Leaning over, he drops a quick kiss on her forehead. I don't miss the subtle wink he sends me as he straightens.

No spark of jealousy rekindles at their meeting. I feel nothing but gratitude everyone's alive.

Raven's hands tremble. As if she can't contain herself any longer, she throws her arms around the both of us and pulls us in for a hug.

I'm not a group hug kind of guy, but if it means holding Raven, I'll do it. My palm gently cradles her head. I lose count of the kisses I press to her temple.

"I'm so glad you're okay," she whispers.

I don't know if she's talking about me, or Cole, or both of us, and I don't give a damn. "You, too," I answer, words muffling against her hair. When I finally force some distance between us, I realize Cole has edged aside. He sits a little apart, pretending not to watch.

Rae studies my face. "What happened to you?" She glances at Cole, eyes narrowing over his shredded ear. "Tell me everything that happened."

"Not *everything*, surely." He pulls a face, but a smile leaks through.

"Yes, everything. I have news for you, too, and oh, wait … I have a surprise."

She springs up, excitement in her smile. I don't know where her strength comes from. She looks beat down, beat up, skin and bones, and she's the most beautiful sight I have ever seen. When she stumbles, I'm halfway up to catch her.

"I'm okay, Gideon. Stay there."

As I settle back down, I watch her search the ground a few feet away. She picks something up and stuffs it into her shirt.

Cole looks over, giving me one of his single shoulder shrugs.

The Minotaur waits near us, a formidable sentinel. One ear

twitches at a fly. His nostrils leak an impressive string of snot onto the ground. His gaze tracks Rae's every move. Instead of suspicion, I'm strangely relieved he's around.

Cole, however, glares at him. "Oi, remember me, mate? You tried to take my arms off once. Don't imagine I'll be forgetting it either."

Whether or not the bull remembers, he doesn't respond with more than a bored huff.

"Here we go, guys!" Raven says, striding toward us. It's so damn cute how happy she seems, dividing her treasure of apples between us, including the Minotaur. Her gaze keeps sliding to mine. Easily caught because I don't even try to pretend I'm not staring at her.

I smile as her eyes snap forward, but her cheeks redden, giving her away.

We crunch on apples and take turns relaying what happened after the Draugar separated us in the swamp. Cole recounts our run-in with the witches (omitting our embarrassing display with the sirens, of course). I talk about our increasing power.

When its Rae's turn, she folds up, resting her chin on her knees. My hands curl to fists hearing her story. Emotion weakens her brave front, and before long, her black lashes divide into wet, glistening spikes.

I need to hear this, even if the words flay my soul. I reach over and grip her forearm. The light pressure is meant to encourage. She laughs without humor and wipes her nose on her shirt.

After a pause, she shares how she traveled through the trees, and how some betrayed her. I marvel at her resourcefulness, but then, she's had to be. We all have.

"And now for the best part … " She calls to the Minotaur. Her *friend* lumbers over, and I'm forced aside to accommodate his mass. The animal drops to the ground between us, nudging her shoulder with his muzzle. Rae's arm wraps his thick neck and she scratches his wide, flat face. A smile lights her eyes. "Isn't he great? He loves it when you rub his head like this."

I won't be rubbing his head, no matter how great he is.

Cole shakes his head. "He's not a lap dog, you know." He slaps his thighs. "I can't bloody well believe it. You're mates with the thing that nearly tore my head off. He broke my leg!"

Rae frowns. "I'm sorry, but that was Pan's doing. Ferdy isn't like that. Not anymore."

"Ferdy? You two chat, do you?"

"No. Not like you and I do, but I understand him, and his moods, and he seems to understand me. Like with the trees, I sense their meaning. It's hard to explain." She hesitates. "There's something else. I've seen Rose."

"Pardon?"

She rubs the back of her hand under her chin. "I found Rose. Ferdy got her out of her tower, by the way, so maybe you'll like him better for that. Anyway … now don't freak out, but Pan showed up right before you got here. I think I know where he took her, but—"

Cole is on his feet, and I'm not far behind. "Let's go."

"Yeah, no. That's it exactly." She grabs his hand and tugs. When he hesitates, she holds a shushing finger to her lips, then points to the ground.

Halfway between a sit and a stand, I lower my ass again, torn between ending our mission, and heeding the stubborn set of Rae's jaw.

"What?" Cole peers both directions down the overgrown trail. A muscle in his cheek twitches, and I know exactly what he's feeling.

"That! The whole going off half-cocked thing, we've done enough of that. We need rest and a plan." She makes vague hand gestures in the air. I assume she means Pan, but she sucks at charades, and I'm really not sure. Cole seems as mystified as I am.

Blowing an impatient breath, she bends over, scraping mulch from the soil until the area is smooth. Pushing Ferdy aside, she tugs a stick from beneath his tree-trunk sized leg and starts scratching in the dirt. Cole and I crowd together reading Rae's message.

Void is wired. Pan hears all.
Suddenly, everything seems a whole lot clearer.

After admitting he was "knackered" and was going for a "kip," whatever the hell that means, Cole fell asleep. He lies on his side under a rubber tree leaf, snoring. I must have dozed off too, and I'm guessing for quite a while, because moonlight sifts beneath the rising sun, trimming purple clouds in gold.

Of the three of us, Rae got the least rest. She insisted on keeping watch, citing her new skill of leeching energy from the surrounding plant life does the same work as sleep.

I rise and head her direction. Bugs flit from my tramping steps, their wings little more than flashes in the meager light.

Raven's arms rise over her head, back arching like a taut bowstring. Even here in the muck and chaos, her beauty punches a hole in my chest.

"Hey."

"Hey, yourself." Her smile is quick, a fleeting spark and gone too soon. "Rested?" she asks, her tone overly polite.

"Yes. You?"

"I'm fine."

Fine. I gesture toward the pile of leaves at her feet. "Mind if I sit with you a while?"

She scoots over, though we have the whole jungle.

My ribs complain at the puncture site as I bend. The pain worsens every day, and I smother a grunt.

My head hangs back, and I study the sky. Faintly orange, the sun will make her appearance soon. In a few hours, we'll face Pan. I feel the truth of it, but whether we'll win or lose, I can't say.

Our plan, scratched in the dirt, is shaky at best.

I sneak a glance at Rae, watch the sky, her face again. The flush of her cheek is more complex than the colors painting daylight, her eyes more mysterious than the fading stars. "I'd like to talk to you, if that's all right."

She picks up a leaf, following the yellow veins with her fingertip. "I figured it was something like that ... confession, amends?" The edge in her voice is razor sharp. "It's not necessary, Gideon. We're cool."

This is every bit as bad as I imagined, but I gird my loins and head into the lion's den. "I have no right to ask, but I want to tell you something, if you'll hear me out." My lie stands between us, deep as an oceanic trench. I feel my racing heartbeats all the way up my neck. "Remember my last trip to New York?"

She doesn't answer. I can't read her and wish she'd look up, but she studies the leaf instead.

"I met with the board, and they explained changes happening at Maddox. Do you know what a hostile takeover is?"

Raven flips the leaf over.

"That's okay," I go on, nerves sparking when she won't answer. "It doesn't matter. The bottom line is ... that I don't have one anymore."

Her brow knits, clearly confused, but she still won't look at me.

"Bottom line ... you know, as in profit and loss reports, get it?"

Crickets.

"Sorry, lame joke." Oh God. *Shut up, fool!* Before I die of abject humiliation, I blurt the rest. "Raven, they took Maddox Industries away from me. I don't own it anymore."

I get my wish when she finally meets my gaze, the hurt inside her eyes is my crucible to bear. It takes every ounce of strength I possess not to turn away, but I don't. I owe her this.

"How can they do that?"

"I became a convenient scapegoat to cover theft and

mismanagement issues. I'm the sacrifice. Everything I had belongs to them now." Somehow, her trembling lip affects the wound in my chest. I break our gaze, but it doesn't ease the pain. "I can't fund your career or support you financially." When I pluck a weed from the ground, Raven winces. "I'm sorry. *Damn it,* I forgot." I offer her the broken plant. "I never meant to hurt you, and that's all I seem to do."

She quietly lifts the dying blade from my palm.

"They can't touch your tuition." Emotion thickens my voice as I mention her future. "At least you'll have that." When I shift, my wound stretches, and I duck my head, hiding the pain from her.

Raven tosses her head. "You must be furious."

"Hm. I was."

"Not anymore?"

"No." My fingers catch in my snarled hair, and I yank them free. "I'll survive." I find her eyes. "So will you. You'll be fine, better than fine. Raven, you should ... " I stop myself, disgusted how ingrained the urge to control everything is inside me. I came to set things right. I'm done convincing and coercing. Ordering people around like some delusional tyrant. I rub my jeans with my hands just to give them something to do. "Things I thought were important, and that I was sure I couldn't live without, have actually come to mean the least. Does that make any sense?"

"Yeah," she whispers. "It does."

"I'm sorry I lied. You deserved better, and one day I hope you can forgive me. It's no excuse, but when I lost everything, I panicked. I wanted to be fair to you and didn't know what else to do." My stomach churns with guilt and regret. I could use one of Dane's right hooks about now.

"It's okay. I think I understand."

Okay—she understands why I broke up with her, or *okay*— just stop talking and leave me the hell alone? "Thank you for that."

She whips her hair back, brushes her hands together. "Wait,

thank you for what? What is it exactly you want me to do with this information, Gideon?"

"I don't know if you remember, but last year we were in my study and we were arguing."

"Which time?"

"Point taken." I swallow around the nonexistent lump in my throat and find it won't move. "I'd screwed up again. You were leaving, and I stopped you, and I said, 'I'm new at this and not very good ...'" I motion between us with a finger. "At the time, I meant relationships, but now I know it's more than that. I'm not very good at being *good*. Not like you are."

She looks me dead in the eye. "And I said, 'I'm not good either. Only God is good enough to judge,' remember?"

"I do."

She'd said it first when we talked about the Artisans' brand of vigilante justice, pointing out the difference between making informed decisions and *being* "judgmental."

My hands lift in surrender, and I give her a sad smile, if such a thing exists. "All right, you are not good. What should I say instead? That you are kind and unselfish, talented and brave? Can I tell you that I love the sound of your laugh, and the way you stand on one foot when you brush your teeth? And last year, whenever you wore your messy, morning hair into my kitchen, the sight made me want to throw you over my shoulder and take you back upstairs."

Her cheeks, bronzed by the climbing sun, steals the air from my lungs. My grin comes easier as more adjectives scroll through my head to describe her. But she's best at managing monsters: an alcoholic stepdad, a ghost who became a friend, the Minotaur of the labyrinth—and then there's me.

Rae drops her leaf, then chooses another from the pile at her feet. "You know, when people meet, they bring their pasts with them. Every choice and situation lived becomes part of who we are." When I smile, her lips curve up. "You like that? My tenth grade guidance teacher shared that little nugget of wisdom."

"Very wise," I answer.

"I thought so." Her expression turns serious. "My point is not every moment is going to be a great or happy one. And that's okay. I can handle hard times if I love someone and commit to them. The thing is they have to be committed, too."

"You think I'm not committed to you?" My words are more statement than question.

"I think you mean what you say when you say it, until you say something else. And then you mean that."

Her words cut, but no more than I deserve. Another swallow of pride, and I answer. "You're right. Not about my feelings for you, but the rest. Raven, by the time I was eighteen, I thought I was invincible, that I could outsmart, or outmaneuver anyone. Last year, you said you needed time; that you weren't ready to be in a relationship. I never imagined that was true for me, too. I bullied you into being with me, because you're what *I* wanted. I'd already rejected my Artisan heritage, and part of my identity. Then I lost the money. I didn't know who I was apart from the monster, the ... machine my father built me to be. I wouldn't bend, so I broke, never once imagining that I could start over or be anyone else. Until now."

Rae stabs the dirt with the heel of her boot. "I never cared about the money, Gideon, only you. When you met me, I was sleeping in a storeroom." Her head dips. A tear slips down her cheek and guts me as it falls to the ground. "I get it, now. The fairytale only works if the prince lifts the kitchen maid out of poverty, but not the other way around. You never gave me the chance to ... " She tosses her head like she's clearing an unpleasant thought.

"You're right. I just couldn't see it before."

"Just tell me what you want."

You. Us. Everything.

I lean forward, cup her cheeks with both palms, gently forcing her gaze up. She doesn't stop me, though her eyes fill to capacity. "I'm sorry. I was a jackass, and I'll spend the rest of my life earning your trust back if you'll let me. I want there to be an *us*, Raven. When I broke your heart, I shattered mine." My hands fall away. "As far as what you should do ... I'm not giving any more ultimatums. No advice, or deals, or pressure. Drive your Beetle forever. Choose your friends, where you'll live, follow your own passions."

Just let me be a part of it.

"I wish I'd done that from the start." My voice is too low. I've never been so nervous, but I'm going to get this said. "I have nothing left to offer except the future we could build together if *you* want that, too. I wasn't ready, but I'm ready now. I love you, woman. Hear that, if you can't hear anything else. I've never stopped loving you, and I never will. Take your time if you want to think it over, as much as you need. I will always be here."

In my mind, she throws her arms around me, kisses me, and everything's forgiven. But in a world of fantasy and make believe, her silence is what's real. I told her to take all the time she needed, and I meant it. So though her continued quiet stomps the hope I have left, I force a smile. And leave her to her thoughts.

Chapter Thirty-One

Raven

For the second time, I skim along tree limbs as easily as any California-bred surfer girl—minus the tan and cool lingo.

Cole and Gideon don't fare as well with the whole tree-surfing thing. In fact, they aren't surfing at all. Without the gift of Earth element to supply a bond with the forest, the trees do their best passing my friends from limb to limb at my request.

When I suggested we travel by tree, the guys looked at me like I was crazy. I knew we could get to the tower faster this way, but I wasn't sure it would work. Gideon's body flops like a ragdoll being fought over by a group of girls at recess. Poor Cole actually shrieked when the first tree lifted him. I shouldn't have laughed, but he's hilarious in an unfunny sort of way. Perfectly safe, but this is new to them, just like it was to me. I would be more patient if I wasn't so keyed up.

Today, we're calling Pan out. Nerves chew at the lining of my empty stomach, turning it rancid. Our confrontation will decide Rose's fate as well as our own.

And then there's Gideon, the loss of his company, our break-up, and very unsure future. While I'm grateful he told me the truth, I'm not sure what to do about it. My head and heart fought this battle once before, and both lost.

I shove the thoughts to a hidden drawer deep in my mind. Today, I need focus. Tomorrow hardly matters if we don't escape The Void.

Species of tree change from steamy jungle to east coast woodland. Thick leaves filter sunlight, speckling the ground in light and shadow. I leap from pine to cherry tree, maple to cypress, the sensation as thrilling as the first time. I'm fearless in my jumps and swan dives, fully confident in the forest's willingness to support me.

Unfortunately, Ferdy refused the trees, and the vibe I got from the woods said the feeling was mutual. The bull ran beneath us for a time, but we move fast and he soon fell behind. I'm sad, but it's for the best. A Minotaur appears part man, but his mind is closer to an animal's. Pan used an innocent creature for evil, and that pisses me off.

I can't take him home. People would freak. The government would take him away, and the science community would probably pin him to a corkboard like some rare butterfly on display. A shudder riffles through me at the thought of him caged in a lab, afraid and alone. He should be munching apples and finding himself a she-cow somewhere.

The tower spire soars above the treetops signaling our destination. My tummy muscles tighten. Adrenaline spikes.

Hang on, Rose.

I send a message to the trees to slow our pace. Another peek at the tower—another stomach twinge. Instinct tells me I'll need all the energy I can get for this battle, yet I hesitate. The forest is strong, and vibrant, and lush. Asking them to share their power is weirdly like asking to borrow your best friend's expensive French perfume for a date. She's glad to share, but you don't want to impose or take too much.

I suck oxygen deep into my lungs as a sudden burst of

strength fills me. The woods must have sensed my thoughts and answered without me even having to ask.

Thank you. Thank you, friends. Brimming with fresh power, I ask the trees to lower us to the ground.

"Never again," Cole groans from the branch above me.

Our feet hit the earth at pretty much the same time. Gideon staggers, but catches himself. His expression's tense and winded, but Cole is positively green.

Guilt pings me. I should have gone slower. "We can rest if you need to, Cole."

He has the strength to look offended, but doesn't argue as he collapses under the shade of a nearby sycamore.

Gideon winks at me. "Wynter, you hungry? I have a protein bar in my pocket. Peanut butter and chocolate. Although, it's warm and kind of runny … "

Cole doubles over and vomits into the grass.

"That was really mean." I punch Gideon's arm, but he's laughing.

"To be clear … " Cole drags his sleeve across his mouth, "… I hate the both of you."

"Don't let a little motion sickness come between us."

"Sod off." Cole holds his stomach and balls up on the ground.

"Now that just hurts. You Brits are so fickle. One day, you're swearing secret admiration beside a Grecian temple, the next, it's all over."

"What?" I ask. Oh, there's a story here. Though, I'm honestly not sure I want to know.

"Prat," Cole says.

Gideon chuckles with a head shake.

I've always found his laugh sexy. Even now, his blond hair is dark with grime and sweat and my only thought is how can anyone make dirty look this good? His sea-blue and emerald gaze finds me. He casually lifts a hand to his ribs, and that's when I see it. This morning, the stain on his shirt was brown, not bright red like it is now. I thought it was mud.

"We've got to deal with that," I say, nodding.

He looks down to the hand covering his side.

I tear a strip of fabric from my shirt, and tie my hair in a messy bun behind my head. He can't fight if he's bleeding, and we need him, but the ex touching his naked torso seems out of line. Or is it?

Remembering what the plants did for me in the lake, I give an order. "I'll need you to strip."

"What?" both boys ask at once.

"Just the shirt, Gideon. You're obviously hurt." One golden eyebrow climbs higher but he makes no move to comply. "Well, come on," I say. "Take it off." The frustration lacing my tone is aimed at me. I'm worried about him and afraid what I'm planning won't work.

"You heard her, Maddox." Cole readjusts his position on the forest floor to watch.

"Well, yes ma'am!" Gideon grins like a wolf, but a wince steals the smile as he shrugs out of his clothing. From this angle, I can't see his injury. What I *can* see affects my already erratic pulse: toned body, broad shoulders, and the sharp cut of his abs made even more pronounced with weight loss. Everything about his movements suggests power.

I mentally slap myself. *Stop drooling, woman, you've got a job to do. You can help him, just be professional.* My fluttering nerves tangle when he faces me.

Cole whistles long and low. "Bloody hell, Maddox, you should have said something."

A puncture dents his right side making a black hole. Puffy, red circles form around it like Saturn's rings. We should have dealt with this sooner. Was he favoring that side of his body? Was I too angry with him to notice?

I take a calming breath. "It's okay. He's okay," I say, praying it's true. Ten steps and I drop to my knees at his waist. He shivers, skin pebbling under my searching fingertips. Definitely infected.

My chin tips up to find he's watching. "Lie down, okay? I

want to try something with you."

"Now? In front of the children?"

My mouth goes numb.

"Who am I to argue? I mean, if you want me this badly ... " He lies flat on his back. Arms outstretched as if I'm supposed to climb into his embrace. "Come here, baby."

Cole snorts. "Control yourself, will you, Rae? I've got unfinished business. A pretty girl to rescue, and if successful, some snogging of my own planned."

Gideon drops his arms, while my skin heats hotter than a summer sidewalk. I make a show of rolling my eyes so they don't think they're getting to me.

The injury looks serious. He could die from blood poisoning if I screw this up. "Be still, do you hear? Don't move at all."

"Why haven't we tried this before? I like you in the dominant role."

"Shut it, Maddox," I say, hating how breathy my voice sounds.

Something in my face must convince him, because his eyes soften.

A gentle breeze kicks up, warm and steady, and I silently thank Cole for his consideration. Gideon threads his fingers behind his head, but his gaze follows me. His breathing slows. We're ready.

My lids slide closed. I reach out to the surrounding forest with my mind. There's no water in sight, but I ask for healing anyway.

Thoughts pulse back and forth in steady rhythm between me and the local plant life. It's as though the woods and I share a heart, two chambers each, pumping energy over and under and through our joined consciousness. My spirit soars as I sense them responding.

"Hey, Raven," Gideon says, his tone careful.

My eyelids rise to view patches of leafy green herbs creeping over the ground to join those already surrounding us. When I lower my hand, a bunch of clover-like plants waddle onto my palm. Their roots tickle, and it dawns on me that's how they move, roots as feet. "It's all right. They're here to help."

Open. Open. The idea takes shape and grows inside my mind. Gideon tenses as the little plants scuttle across his torso. The scent of thyme fills my nose along with others I don't recognize. I count seconds in heartbeats. *Open* …

Open what? I don't see … Oh God. Open the *wound?*

How? With what? I have nothing sterile, no knife, nothing sharp at all. Wait … "Cole, can you help me?" I unbuckle my belt from my waist and pull it free. Once Cole is settled across from me, I lay the belt over my thighs. "This will hurt, but he can't move, understand?"

Cole scoots until he can clamp both hands over Gideon's shoulders. "You'll be right as rain, mate."

His smile is tight. "It's all good."

My hand finds his, and our fingers lace. "Try and hold still. I'll do the best I can."

He winks, and that simple gesture of trust closes my throat.

I release his hand. "Here we go." Thankful I used an oversized buckle when designing my belt, I take hold of the big silver frame and bend it back exposing the long metal prong.

The end is blunt and won't cut easily. My mind questions the earth again, but all I hear is, *open.*

The hole between Gideon's ribs might have been made by a bullet, it looks so deep. The skin is red and swollen with a yellow film covering the surface.

I place the prong at one end of the puncture and apply even pressure as though slicing with a knife. My hands shake as metal severs flesh. When his skin resists, I press harder. Gideon flinches as blood and pus run from the sore. Breath streams through his nostrils. I want to tell him that I'm sorry, and I only want to help, but he already knows.

Repeating the process on the other side of the wound, I create a three-inch incision. Sweat breaks out on my forehead. There's a crunch as Gideon grits his teeth. He's shaking, and a quick glance shows his lids squeezing shut. When he rolls his shoulders, Cole grips harder.

I sit back, finally finished with my gruesome task. The plants, which sat dormant during the "operation," march along Gideon's waist. Ridding themselves of soil encrusted roots and stems, the soft leaves twist together, vegetation darkening as tiny fibers release the medicinal oils inside. Their efforts create a pungent mash that seeps into the widened lesion. One layer burrows into the tissue while another forms a crust on top.

My head shakes in wonder. Right now, I don't care that I don't understand. I'm only grateful the earth made this sacrifice to aid the person I love most in the world.

We wait ten minutes, twenty. I'm not sure what happens next. Once covered in lake weed, I felt instant relief, but my scratches were nothing to his injury.

The sunshine grows warm and heavy on our skin. Cole stretches out a few feet away and drifts to sleep. Best thing for him.

Not a muscle twitches on Gideon's face. I lean in, hoping he's resting too, when his lids fly up. He bucks, releasing a noise between a cough and grunt. The green poultice molded to his skin boils and pops off releasing a stink worse than sulfur. I hope the plants have done their work, because whatever mash is left inside oozes from the wound and slides down his side.

We have no bandages, nothing to keep dirt out, yet I get an overwhelming sense we're to seal the hole. And there's only one way I know of.

"How you feeling?" I ask.

Gideon rests the back of his hand on his forehead. "Strange. Much better."

I release the breath in my lungs. "Good."

"No, I mean that was incredible. I can't describe the feeling." His gaze roams my face. "Thank you isn't nearly enough. You are the most amazing person I've ever known."

"I'm glad it helped, but it wasn't me. Anyway, you may want to hold off on the gratitude."

"Oh yeah, why's that?"

I can't bear to meet his gaze, so I take his hand. "I'm sorry. The plants say we have to close it." His brow creases. "You know, with your firepower? Can you, uh ... " My tongue bumps my teeth. "Ssssssss"

His "Oh" is less than enthusiastic. He eases onto his elbows before rising to his knees.

A snap of his fingers brings a flame to life. Fire dances fast and hot on the end of his finger. No hesitation, no warning. He sends the orange stream into his side, cauterizing the tissue. A long, drawn out curse leaves his lips, and it's over.

A wisp of steam rises from the burn. On instinct, I lean over and blow across the red, blistered flesh. "Damn, girl." He shivers, and I back off. Our eyes lock and hold with some invisible, tension-coiled spring. "The things you do to me."

Cole yawns and sits up. "What'd I miss?" His sleepy gaze drops to Gideon's ribs. Once healed, the scar will remain an ugly insult to his otherwise perfect skin. "You all right, mate? Because you look bloody awful."

There's a soft snort. "Thanks." Lifting his T-shirt off the ground, Gideon gives it a quick shake. I'm encouraged and surprised how easily he moves, as if there's no pain at all.

A hint of smoke lingers in the air. Cole rubs his palm over a darkening jaw. "Can you travel?"

"Soon."

The corner of Cole's mouth twitches. "Then put your shirt on, sweetheart, so we can blow that portal all to hell. Shouldn't keep a lady waiting"

The tower isn't visible from the path we follow. After ten minutes at a comfortable jog, we reach the cobblestone courtyard, and the reason becomes clear. The tower no longer sits upright at the center of the garden path, nor does it lie on its side as it did when Pan conjured the structure for his escape with Rose. Instead, a twenty-foot wide crater gapes at us where the pylon once stood. Row upon row of white stone disappears into the earth forming a deep well.

Pan inverted the tower.

Nothing should surprise me anymore, but his power is staggering.

Cole races to the edge of the hole and peers down. His chest heaves as he glances back, desperation reflected in his wild eyes. "It's dark, but the stairs are still there. Torches lit on the walls, as well, but everything's upside down." The wind picks up with a definite bite. Temperature change is a sure sign of Cole's agitation.

"We're expected," Gideon says.

"No way 'round it, mate." Without waiting, Cole picks his way down the first few steps.

I follow but am abruptly halted.

Gideon holds my wrist, his eyes reaching for the deepest places in my soul. "I love you. I hope you can believe that. No matter what, I love you."

My hand curls into his. Our fingers squeeze and let go.

A single beat of time passes and we're moving again, racing after our impatient friend. Gideon's hands torch, shedding light in the gloom. Cole's head bobs several feet ahead as he scurries down the steep staircase. "Hold up," I say, to no avail.

Massive roots have broken through the earth and mortar between the damp stones. They burrow between the steps in persistent snarls making our path uneven and slippery. Willow. I know without a doubt that Pan has requisitioned the one tree deaf to my influence. *Terrific.*

Water trickles down the walls, echoing in the cavernous spaces below. My feet slip. Off balance, my hand juts out to brace my fall, only the stone is slick and gooey. A giant eye protrudes from the wall, watching us. The lid blinks against my palm. I yelp and jerk away, elbowing Gideon's injured ribcage.

He grunts as all his air is expulsed.

"Oh!" I point to explain my actions, but the eye is gone. Nothing but a broken mirror hangs askew from a rusty nail. "Sorry. I thought … sorry."

I'm rewarded for hurting him when his lips brush my ear. "S'okay."

I fend off dueling emotions and descend the remaining steps.

At the bottom, more torches cast muted light on a circular enclosure. The sound of sluicing water grows louder, maybe from a nearby stream or well. Rusted, metal grates meant for ventilation now act as drains, marking the circumference every few feet.

Lumber, once joined to make roof joists and rafters, lies in ruins creating a floor of broken beams and rubble. Near the center of the crumbling room, a space is clear of debris, and within that small circle, Cole holds Rose in his arms.

I blink back the burn in my eyes at the sight of them together. Gideon's fingers press my shoulder, and I understand his message. "Better go, everybody."

Rose lifts her head. "Raven?" She squeals and holds out a hand. "Oooh, come here!"

Cole's positively beaming, so I take a minute we don't have to climb over heavy oak beams with Gideon close behind.

Rose grabs my hand, and with more strength than I thought her capable, topples me for a hug. Her neck stretches over my shoulder, and I realize she's trying for a better glimpse of our companion. I lean back as her expression twists into a funny smile. "Gideon … "

"Yes, I'm happy to meet you, but right now, we *must* go."

"Wait, just another moment, please. I have something to say." Rose stands. Cole's arm looped around her slim waist keeps her feet on the ground. She takes Gideon's hand, drawing him to her side opposite Cole, while I'm edged out. "Well, here we are—together again."

Again?

"My boys." Her voice takes on an odd inflection, deeper and more mature as she pulls them in tighter.

Wait, what?

"Isn't this sweet? I'm told revenge usually is, and best served cold."

Chains clink. A cacophony of machinery starts clacking around us—pulleys whir, gears click. Somewhere beyond our sight, a door slides shut with a terrific bang.

"Run!" I can't hear my shouts above the noise. As the flooring cracks and upends, Cole and I hit an invisible shield and fall on our butts, while Gideon and Rose stumble forward.

Droplets run down the wall's clear sides. Water rises at our feet, and I scrabble to a stand to avoid complete soaking.

One inch, two, three—liquid covers our boots. Cole bangs the glass with his fists but the barrier won't break. We hurl ourselves against the walls and find there are four to our cage.

And Gideon's on the other side.

The water is freezing, the air close and thin. I cough and suck an unsatisfying breath, wondering if I'm having a panic attack.

Gideon faces us. Rain falls from nowhere soaking him through, but thank God he's escaped our fate. He snaps his fingers repeatedly, getting nothing but wet sparks. He bolts forward, fists pressed against the glass. Veins bulge in his neck as he yells, "I can't get a fire going. Can you force the glass out with air pressure?"

Cole's already shaking his head. "Not enough oxygen."

Now I know why my head hurts.

Laughter filters through the chamber, as familiar as a recurring nightmare, though it isn't Pan's. Chill whispers brush my skin. The same corrosive breath a late frost employs to kill the last blooms.

"Desiree?" Cole asks, speaking the name on my lips.

Desiree drowned in the millpond last year behind Maddox mansion. But it's not Desiree who's laughing, it's Rose.

"What have you done?" Gideon shouts. Willow roots explode from the ground sending rocks and debris flying. Thrashing does no good as the trees hobble him like an animal. "It's impossible." Wet hair clings to his face. Thinner branches climb his shoulders and neck. Both his hands clutch the vine at his throat. His eyes blaze, but he can't defend himself.

"Is it?" Rose asks, hands clasping. "Is it, indeed?" Her silvery image shimmers on the far side of the room. A neon-blue glow surrounds her body as laser-like threads cut her apart. Limbs disjoint and dislocate, reorganizing themselves into someone else altogether. Rosamond is gone. But no ...

She never was.

This is Desiree. The other a lie built on the back of a damaged boy who only wanted to matter.

"How could you do that to Cole?"

"Yes, I'm sorry about that." Desiree pauses, thoughtfully studying the water at my knees. "In fairness, you were all warned. You left me no choice."

"But, you died ... " I sound like an idiot. Obviously, she didn't, as she's standing right here making our lives miserable again.

"Mm, seems *I* can't drown." Her smile spreads like a disease. "But you can." With a flip of her hand, a single wave in the tank pushes me down and holds me under. Just as quickly, the watery grip releases, and I break the surface, sputtering and coughing.

The night the Artisan curse was broken, the spell transferred power to four people, not three. Desiree died so quickly afterward, we never made the connection. But the fourth element *is* water, and Desiree clearly its wielder.

Squatting in the icy pool, Cole's hands disappear under the dark liquid. He frantically slides them along the glass, searching the perimeter. After a moment, he stands and wades toward Gideon who's still held beyond the barrier. "It's completely sealed off," Cole says. "There's nothing we can do. Get out if you can."

Gideon's headshake is violent. "I'm not leaving."

"No one's going anywhere," Desiree says, crossing her arms. "Though, I do enjoy a good drama if you'd like to try."

The guys argue as if no one spoke. When persuasion fails, they swear and hurl insults. Tears cloud my eyes. I don't know when or how it happened, but they're friends.

"It's suicide." Cole's frustration is evident in his glare. "You're a sandwich short of a picnic, you know that, Maddox?" He turns his back. "I'm done, then. Piss off."

As the water rises, something in my chest shrinks. I think it's faith.

Gideon works a hand free and presses his palm to the barrier. I fit my smaller hand inside his. *Go*, I mouth.

"The hell." His eyes narrow. I know that look.

"Please, *please* do this for me."

"Oh, enough already." Desiree lifts her chin. "It's time, Pan!"

Rain ceases outside the cage. A quake under our feet sends vibrations rippling through the water. The passage we came down cracks along the top, and sunlight cuts the gloom in sharp angles. Stone breaks apart as the tower splits into two even halves. Once the halves fall away, the exposed staircase bumps along the earth like the spine of a gutted whale left to rot.

Desiree hesitates near Cole. "Sorry, lover. You're just not my type." She frees a long root attached to Gideon's bonds, wraps it several times around her arm, and drags him from the ruined tower.

Without their captive, other roots sprawl uselessly across the floor. Dirt and gravel continue sifting like flour over the glass ceiling of our cage.

Water laps Cole's chest. He seems not to notice, just stares with a look of dazed horror.

"Cole?"

He startles before plowing both hands through his soaking hair. "I should have known. It's all my own stupid fault!" Rose's betrayal shows in his tortured eyes.

My heart cramps for him, but there's no time for blame. I grab both shoulders. "No it isn't. It's hers. Now, help me get out of here so we can kick her ass."

He glances again at the surrounding devastation, and I can only hope I've gotten through.

Desiree is planning who knows what for Gideon. There's a crap ton of water still rising, and our air's almost gone.

Think, Rae, think, think, think, think ...

My mind snatches at bits of information. What does it mean to control the elements? How can it help? Individually, we're weaker, but together we might be stronger.

"Cole, call the wind."

"I've tried."

"Try again! Reach past the glass. We can't give up." I close my eyes and search for the trees with my mind. No one is close, none but the willows who hate me. Then my mother's words find me again. *Miss Willow will betray you if she can.*

If.

You must bend them all to your will.

I concentrate on the willow roots. They snap and curl away at my beckoning, but the thought of Gideon only steels my will.

Come!

Begrudgingly, the roots make their way forward. I ask them to encircle the barrier. The more they balk, the harder my thoughts push. Howling wind strengthens my resolve, knowing Cole is fighting, too.

I open my eyes to a sea of roots wrapping around our jail. *Pressure,* I order. *Tighten, squeeze, smash my cage.*

The waterline ripples over my nose. We tip our heads back for air that's tepid and lean.

I appeal to every tree in The Void. Animals, plant life, soil, the earth itself, begging them to fight for us.

Willow roots flex and strain. Tiny fissures fork like silver veins of lightning across the glass box. The ground shudders. More roots tunnel up from the soil and butt against the clear floor of our prison cell. Glass snaps and crunches.

Our heads press the ceiling where there's a final gulp of air before submersion.

Cole takes my arm. Our eyes are open as we face one another. Black hair swims around his handsome face. He lifts a palm to my cheek.

I know what he wants. It's written inside his sad, weary eyes. Forgiveness. I take his hand in both of mine and give it, though there's nothing to forgive.

All the while, my mind chants. *Smash the cage ...*

The waters darken and blur. Cole's eyes roll white. His hand drops, and he falls away.

I'm floating. Weightless, my body drifts as though I'm made of nothing but foam. I'm a bubble riding the waves to the shoreline. It occurs to me I'm dreaming ... or drowning. My journey is peaceful until the surf changes. The ocean turns angry, wind bellows with a brave and vicious sound. Waves break me against an unyielding surface, and then I'm flung up and out of the sea, carried on the wind to freedom.

I'm not breathing, but I can't decide if that's important anymore. Enveloped in a cloud of sweet clover, I'm not unhappy.

A dull pain knocks at my chest as though I'm a door and someone wants in. *Thud. Ka-thud.* My body convulses. Another and another, though the pounding is more battering ram than polite knock. It almost sounds like a heartbeat. *Ka-thud, ka-thud, ka-thud.*

My lungs rip apart as air seeps inside. A cough blasts water from my throat. I choke and strangle and cough some more.

Ferdy's image wavers above me. He hits my chest with his fist, and I bounce.

"That's enough, mate." Cole's face bleeds into view across from the bull's head. Without a word, he lowers his mouth, fits his lips to mine, and gently breathes for me.

My limbs tingle, energy infuses my tired muscles. The clover covering my chest give their lives to renew mine. Power zings through my veins, heart, brain. Healing, rejuvenating, more plants come, replacing those that die until I feel as strong as ten men.

As Cole lowers his head again, my arms reach around his neck. "I'm okay," I whisper.

He straightens with a smile. "Rae, thank God. I was having kittens until your eyes opened."

"Thank you, bro. I'm all right, now." I sit up and throw myself onto Ferdy's body, hugging him with all my might. "You found us!" No matter what happens, he's coming home with me. Whatever it takes to keep him safe, it's done. I let my bull friend loose and bolt to my feet. We're still amidst the rubble of what was the tower. "Where's Gideon?"

"Out there, I think." Cole jerks his chin.

Ferdy moos low in his throat. Mucus plonks the floor.

"Your cow fished me out of the water tank, and then went back for you."

"Are you all right?" I ask.

"The air hit me straight away. I don't know how it works, but I feel strong as an ox."

Ferdy snorts.

"No pun intended."

We climb up the broken tower to the courtyard. As tense and ready as a cage fighter, a thundering crash only makes me move faster.

After crawling out of the hole together, we line up, shoulder to shoulder, and face our enemies.

But nothing could prepare me for the sight awaiting us.

Chapter Thirty-Two

Cole

Air element has darkened the sky in answer to my call, blotting the sun with gathering storm clouds. I felt the response, even from beyond Desiree's cell. Energy coursed through my body the moment the glass broke, as though the air waited impatiently to aid me.

Ferdy throws his head back and trumpets. If I could, I might do the same.

Thousands of trees gather at our right, towering over the tops of the hedgerow that make up the maze. Assembled in rows like wooden soldiers, they're impressive in number, and I assume here at Rae's request.

Gideon is missing, but Desiree waits to our left and behind her—a legion. Her blond hair whips in the breeze I've created. She pushes a few strands away exposing a small crossbow attached to her wrist. The weapon is laughable. What does the wielder of water need with a toy like that?

Her white dress flaps and molds itself to voluptuous curves. Such a waste. She could have started over, lived her life. Yet, her relentless need to blight the happiness of others sealed her fate.

I, for one, intend to make sure this ends. Today.

The army of Draugar part and something steps into view beside Desiree. The wind carries her greeting. "Hello, Pan. Dressing down today, are we?"

Pan. In his true form, I'm guessing. He's naked, which is disgusting, because from the waist up, his skin is smooth and chalky white. From waist to foot, however, he's covered in shaggy goat hair. Two thick horns protrude from his head, winding around his twitchy goat ears. Slanted, yellow eyes are wideset over a broad, flat nose. Though smaller, he and Ferdy pitted against one another would make quite a show.

Desiree inclines her head. "This concludes our arrangement?"

"It does."

"Our bargain?"

"Yes, yes, tiresome creature. The boy is yours, the others mine."

"Not the girl, the girl dies."

Raven tugs my arm, but I shake her off to listen.

"I think not," Pan answers. "I've decided to keep her, especially." There's finality, even masked warning in his tone. "With you and the Maddox boy gone, I'll need them both until I can appoint new Artisans and replenish my stores."

Desiree's white smile appears as sincere as a shark's. "Very well. So long as Gideon and I are free, what do I care?"

Pan waves a limp hand. As the Draugar trudge forward, Desiree and Pan slip behind the mob of undead. Bloody cowards.

I turn to Rae. "If they win, she gets Gideon. Pan wants you and me."

She nods. "We can do this." Lightning fast, she rises onto her toes and smashes a kiss against my cheek. "Survive." And then she's gone, running toward her forest.

The nearest oak bends and lifts her up. Damned if the thing isn't walking. All the trees are. They tear their roots from the soil and lumber forward to meet the Draugar.

Trees reach down, plucking zombies from the ground. Branches become arms, twigs work like hands and fingers, tearing dead limbs apart, ripping Draugar heads from their blackened bodies.

Fascinating as that is, I've got a band of stinking corpses moving my direction. I send a gust of wind and knock them down.

That's when I see Gideon.

Forty meters away, a large willow grows in the center of a concrete fountain. Reedy limbs bind our favorite firebug to her trunk. Roots gulp water and rain continuous moisture over him.

Clever. Too much moisture snuffs his ability to make fire. A fact we'd not known before today.

What my friend needs is a proper blow dryer.

Wind adjusts with my specific instructions. While a mild breeze blows over Maddox, I push a hundred times more force against the tree itself, keeping Gideon safe in the eye of my storm.

Leaves strip from the willow's slender branches. Limbs break and are carried off in the gale. Whenever a Draugar gets too close, I divide the wind at my disposal leaving one hand on the willow, while I blow the zombie away with the other.

It works until too many dead stagger my way, closing in from every direction. Their wrinkled skin resembles dried fruit, although a title like "giant prunes of death" really doesn't do them justice.

Ferdy takes up the cause, his ax severing the head of the nearest Draugar. Black slime sprays the garden as he lops the arms and legs off another two zombies.

Though I swore eternal hatred for cows, the smelly bugger's really starting to grow on me.

With the onslaught of dead managed, I angle back to Gideon and his lithesome jailor.

As Raven would say, *Let's do this!*

I send a wind blast strong enough to tear the top off the willow tree. Low light flares near her trunk signaling Gideon's dry enough to spark.

That's our boy.

Engulfed in flame, what's left of the willow falters like a drunken maître d'. Gideon leaps from the fountain and races through the maze, his body glowing like a small sun.

Unfortunately, Desiree spots him, too, and runs a course to intercept.

The great numpty doesn't notice her. He's too busy hurtling fireworks into the zombie ranks. Between his fire and Rae's homicidal trees, few Draugar remain.

Pan breaks from the remaining circle of zombies surrounding him. His hands combust and he hurls a bomb of his own.

The oak supporting Raven catches fire. Her scream sounds more angry than afraid as the flames spread.

Pan launches another comet into the moving forest. Smoke from burning wood blights the sky.

My throat tightens watching the old oak gently place Rae on the ground and out of danger. He rolls in the dirt to smother the flame. Mighty branches claw deep furrows in the earth. His twig-like fingers reach for his brothers, tremble and plead, but they can do nothing to save him. Since my element only feeds fire, I helplessly watch as more trees burn to death.

Gideon blasts Pan with an impressive bolide, and I'm shocked when the fur on his leg lights.

Expression clearly shaken, Pan seems as confused as I am. He puts the fire out and darts behind a row of hedges. It seems we're not immune to other wielders, but how does that work when we control the same element?

My thoughts are interrupted when Desiree calls water from the fountain and sends it over Gideon in a wide arc.

Raven approaches from the opposite direction, but the wind I send is faster. It nudges the flow of water aside where it splatters harmlessly to the ground. I'm jogging toward Rae, Ferdy's hooves clacking on the stones at my side. If we time this right, we can catch Desiree in a crossfire.

A long root lassoes Desiree's ankle and she face-plants.

Recovering with a guttural cry, she releases sheets of rain over Raven. The deluge swallows her, but also douses the trees burning nearby. Churning smoke hides Raven from my sight. A perfect time for Pan to attack, but he's gone missing, and Desiree's water trick destroyed the damaging forest fires—his best effort yet to stop us.

They don't seem unified. Confusion swamps me as I puzzle over their strategy, before it strikes me; they don't have one.

They never thought we'd get this far.

Spitting rain stings my skin, but I'm able to glimpse Raven emerging from the smoke in one piece. Desiree gathers water from the soaked ground and shoots Rae with the strength of a fireman's hose. I cringe as she goes down, and Desiree pounces.

Gideon is useless in this downpour, but no one told him. He's barreling through the hedges like a locomotive.

The monsoon blurs my vision. My feet stop moving, heartbeats race, as Raven's pulled onto her knees. Head forced back, throat exposed, clearly Desiree plans to finish her rival execution style.

My thoughts near hysteria; indecision and fear cripple my brain. That's when I see a dark shape charging through the rain toward them. Head down, horns pointed forward, the Minotaur aims for Desiree. With nowhere to run, her arm flies out. At first, I think it's a protective instinct, until I spy the crossbow on her wrist. The one I'd laughed at earlier.

Ferdy, no!

"Teleport!"

Gideon's yell works as well as a slap. *Shite! What am I doing?* My body vibrates, and I'm gone. Appearing beside Desiree, I lunge for her arm, my fingers wrapping her shoulder just as the arrow flies from the track.

The Minotaur buckles and falls, snout first. Momentum powers his enormous bulk forward plowing soil like a bulldozer.

Raven screams and throws herself. His weight could crush her, but she's beyond reason. Her arms wrap Ferdy's great neck.

She whispers between sobs, offering what comfort she can.

In my panic, I forgot to do the one thing that could have saved him. Now, his breathing comes in shallow pants, creating fog at his muzzle. The arrow protrudes above an eye, shaft buried deep. Blood runs from the wound, coating his face, staining the mud. Guilt sours my stomach. I failed him, and he's done for, poor bloke.

Rae grasps the bull's meaty hand with both of hers. I deflect the rain, using wind to create an umbrella above them.

Gideon crashes through the last hedge, his gaze falling on me and my prisoner, then the pair in the mud.

The fog at Ferdy's muzzle fades. His chest stops moving. Raven sniffs, gently lowering Ferdy's hand. Her fingers move six inches and curl over the bull's abandoned ax handle. She looks up, face hardened to flint.

Desiree jerks free of my hold and bolts, but Gideon blocks her escape. He wrestles her arms together, pinning her against his chest.

I know who commands the hedge that yanks its roots from the mire and sneaks up behind them. The thick shrub separates down the middle, leans forward, and swallows them both. I can't see a thing through the mesh of twigs and leaves, but like a heron regurgitating its dinner, the plant vomits Gideon onto the grass while holding onto Desiree. Trapped from the waist down, she fights like a cat until she's torn and bleeding, but can't break free.

Raven stands, ax gripped tightly in her hands. Red rimmed eyes tell the story of her grief as she faces the woman responsible.

Water answers Desiree's frantic call for help with a flash flood that drives us back. Raven's arm flies up, flagging the trees. They plunk their massive roots into the runoff to drink. A good idea, yet it won't be enough, because Desiree's already pulling more water from the ground.

Building her element in height and mass, she forms a static thirty-foot wall as easily as a kid stacks blocks. If I kill her, the water will drop and finish us.

I failed my friends once. I vow not to fail again. And as I study the towering black surf, I know the fight is mine alone. In physics, I never cared to understand turbine aerodynamics, never gave a shite about drag based wind, and now it doesn't seem to matter. I *am* wind.

Wind is force. It moves. I don't need to stop the water, just redirect it. I catch Gideon's eye. He steps forward, but I shake my head. "Leave her to me."

With a primal scream, Desiree releases her wall.

Impulses from my brain connect to my element sending hurricane force winds to divide the plummeting tsunami.

Water punches the earth on either side of us. It takes all of my strength to keep the crushing water out, but we're safe within my wind tunnel. As the water recedes, broken tree limbs stab the ground, bones of the dead pile at our feet, providing me with plenty of ammunition. Wind obeys willingly, lifting various items of debris with unseen fingers at my command.

"Pan, help me!" Desiree calls. When he doesn't appear, she turns to Gideon. "I know what I did was wrong. I know that, but if you let me go, I'll disappear. You'll never see me again, I promise."

"It's far too late for that now," I say.

Her blue eyes leak the element she wields. They widen as a dozen sharp objects hover near me. Whether because of her connection to Rose, or something else, I hesitate. I still see Rose's face, hear her voice. I know it's not true, but it's as if she died at Desiree's hand. The woman's hate is corrosive, all consuming. No matter what she says, she'll never stop hunting us. I have no choice.

Wind releases its arsenal. Whip fast and accurate, the tibia of a Draugar impales her torso, Ferdy's ax blade lodges between her neck and shoulder. She's run through with fragments of wood and bone until her white gown runs red with blood. Her eyes glaze before her head rolls forward.

The rain ceases with her passing. Clouds thin, allowing the sun to peek through.

A strange and sudden sensation leeches through my body. Growing more and more painful as it moves through my system, I double over with a cry.

"What's wrong?" Gideon asks, and then swears an oath.

The burn in my veins is acidic. I drop to the ground as Gideon crumples alongside me. Whatever's happening to us isn't affecting Rae, who crouches helplessly between us.

Is this Pan? A trick of the mind? I shut my eyes to what feels like crushed glass being forced through my arteries. I'm drenched with sweat. My stomach bloats. When I touch puffed-up fingers to my lips, I find them swollen, too. Waves crash against my eardrums. Water leaks from my eyes. Saliva fills my mouth, and I swallow only to have it fill again.

I'm drowning, or think I am. And just when I can't take anymore, the pain subsides. I lie still, feeling my body tissue absorb the excess fluids. It's over as fast as it began. Slowly, I open my eyes, and sit up.

"What the hell just happened?" This from Gideon, whose head I notice with some satisfaction is nestled on Raven's lap.

On a hunch, I raise a finger and point to a nearby puddle. Water jumps several inches. I glance up. "Can either of you … ?"

This time, I ask the trail of water to raise eye level before dropping again. Rae tries with no success.

"Interesting," I say, rubbing my itchy jaw. Can fire and water exist in one wielder? Pan manages. I lift a gallon or two of water from the ground and dump it on Gideon's head.

"Do you want to die?" he growls. "I was just drying out."

"Light up."

"The hell." He shakes his head like a dog sending muddy droplets flying. "You know I can't."

I think he can. In fact, he already did while fighting off the scorpion, we'd simply forgotten. The idea hit me when Pan was burned earlier. "Humor me. I don't know why, but I think our elements respond differently when we're fighting other wielders."

He argues first, because he's Gideon, but finally lifts his hand.

A snap of his wrist starts a flame reaching all the way to his elbow.

My smile is overly smug, but I really do enjoy being right.

"I'll be damned." A grin stretches his face. He turns to show Rae, but she's slipped away to sit with Ferdy's body.

"Maddox ... " No one feels worse than I do, but we can't stay here. "Let's go before Pan finds his balls." Since he doesn't like to lose, I'm guessing that won't take long.

Gideon's smile falters as his gaze skims the landscape. Severed body parts already twitch and hop, as though programmed to continue fighting no matter what.

I know he wanted Pan's head. We all did, but it's more important we survive. That was my promise to Rae, and I intend to keep it. "Not this time, mate," I say, by which I mean never.

Gideon catches my pointed stare. I don't try and persuade him, there's no need. Still, when he unclenches his jaw, my shoulders relax. His nod is quick before hurrying to Rae.

He will always put her first.

Chapter Thirty-Three

Gideon

Raven leans over her fallen warrior. Silent tears gleam as she says goodbye. "We should bury him." The words are rough-hewn and shaky.

"We should," I say, "but we can't afford the time. He would understand."

Her quiet sniff breaks my heart. If I had the power, I would make her pain mine. Carry her burdens, wear her tortured skin, breathe every anguished breath.

"One second, okay?" She hunches and using her forefinger, draws a line in the mud alongside Ferdy's body from his head all the way to his feet. Cole and I leap aside as the earth shudders open creating a hollow in the ground. A smothered sob escapes her as the Minotaur rolls into the twelve-foot crater she's made from *nothing!* A little rut in the dirt.

Her rise is unsteady. My arm wraps her waist, and I'm grateful she accepts my touch. Again, using her forefinger and thumb this time, she mashes her fingers together in the air. Another tremor taps our feet and the earth moves. Dark soil envelops Ferdy for an eternal sleep under a loamy blanket. A small rose bush responds to Rae's crooked finger and waddles from the maze. The thorny plant roots at the head of the gravesite and rests there.

Cole pats Raven's head. "Nice. What other secrets have you been keeping from us, little minx?"

She imitates one of Cole's one armed shrugs. "I couldn't leave him here like that."

Water fills a dozen circular puddles at our feet. As many reflections of the girl I love stare back at us from the ground, the silver sky her backdrop. I'm impressed, stunned by her expanding power. Yet that's nothing compared to the girl she's always been. My chest swells and aches at once.

"I'm sorry, Raven," Cole says. He scans the trees with something near loathing. "I can hardly believe I'm saying this, but we need the fastest route back to Gideon's mirror."

Mirror ... Truth flutters against the sticky web of memory. The threads vibrate alerting me to something important I'd forgotten. The watery puddles, silver skies, reflections, the Weird Sister's ramblings ...

"His power to see you lies in the ability to see himself. Pollute the silver circles. Blind him, and he will seek you no more."

Mirrors, that's it! Rose told Cole that Pan's mirrors were his view to the world, stored in different places and connected like a hive. That's how he *sees*. And ours is both mirror *and* doorway.

I release Rae and grab Cole's shirt sleeve. Confusion lowers his brow. An explanation's on my tongue when I remember Rae's warning. I hurry to the courtyard, dragging Cole after me.

He trips and lets fly with a string of British insults I'm sure would piss me off if I understood them.

I stoop for a broken stick, set the end ablaze, and then blow it out. Squatting over the stone courtyard, I scratch my message in soot. When the blackened end won't write anymore, I light it again, and repeat the process until I've communicated everything on my mind.

Cole slaps my back. His eyes light with understanding unsafe to express with words. When he motions for my stick, I pass him the makeshift pen, and he writes:

Brill, but forget Pan. Go home.

Raven is wild as she plucks the stick from Cole's hand. It won't write. I suppress a smile when she shakes it like a stubborn ballpoint, and I re-singe the end for her.

Stop him.

Gently, I take my pen from her. Our fingers brush and the contact jumpstarts my quiet pulse.

How?

Everyone goes still. How do you destroy an ancient magic? The portal is a mirror, but one made of liquid smoke. Raven extends a hand. Retrieving the stick, she writes once more.

Promise.

Her gaze hones in, steady as a missile locked on target. I'm sure her request is about more than shutting Pan in The Void. She's asking if I'm trustworthy, if I can keep my word.

I promise.

The sun ducks under a haze of thin cloud cover. Cole slaps two fingers across his wrist indicating his long lost watch. It's hard to gauge the time left until sunset, but no one wants to spend another night here.

Cole nods to Raven. "How 'bout a lift, luv?" He dares a smile, and I'm gratified to see her return one.

"Sure." She rubs her mud-coated palms on her equally filthy pants. "Will you gentlemen be traveling by tree or triceratops?" With that, she bounds off, signaling to a huge elm nearby.

"Are you mad?" Cole asks, once Rae's out of earshot. "You can't keep that promise."

I'm not arguing the point, so I answer with a question of my own. "If I fail, will you get her through the portal?"

His dark head angles from me to Raven and back, a grim expression coating his features. "You won't fail."

Once the ancient cypress deposits Cole's feet on solid ground, he promptly drops and retches. Though my reaction isn't as violent, I'm anxious, and sweating, and relived it's over.

"Now what?" Cole asks. He wipes his mouth and pushes to a wobbly stand.

We cluster together near the small pond where our journey began, and contemplate the door's destruction. The shimmering portal is so unlike the flip-side, where it masquerades as a harmless mirror in my father's study. Roughly twelve square feet, the portal quivers like heat waves off a newly tarred road. The gateway home is nothing more than a smear in the scenery. Yet, from this side of The Void, it sends a warning, emitting the subtle hum of a hot electric fence.

Raven tosses her head. "There's got to be a way."

I've both dreamed of and dreaded this moment, because I don't know the answer. The witch said to destroy it but didn't say how. Or did she?

Come on, Maddox, figure it out!

My brain fixates on the Weird Sister's instructions. I pace the length of evil shine, dissecting her words. "She said pollute … " My mind casts about for clues. "Taint, poison, contaminate … corrupt? If something is pure, a foreign substance will pollute it." We didn't kill the Draugar. In the end, we didn't need to. Slowing them down was enough. "Maybe we don't have to destroy the portal," I say. "Can we disable it?"

"Gideon!" Raven points indicating Pan is listening.

"I think we're past that now, don't you, luv?"

Cole's right. There's too much to communicate in writing,

and it's only a matter of time until he shows.

Urgency releases fresh heat in my veins. I shove a hand through the glass. The same sticky fluid as before covers my skin. A force I don't understand starts its subtle draw, pulling me toward the other side. When I resist, the mirror releases its hold, and my hand pulls free. "It's fluid, like liquid silver, nothing like real glass."

"Can't be shattered," Rae confirms. "What about using fire? Can you melt a mirror?"

Cole's headshake is anything but promising. "We tried once with a laser in Mr. Belfield's science lab. The glass bubbled, burned it a bit, but that's all." My frustration must show because he adds, "Don't panic. Let's review, shall we?" He holds up a finger. "The witch said Pan only seeks the living."

Raven nods. "He lives off their suffering."

"Right." Another finger goes up. "He watches our world and brings his victims here through the mirrors." A third finger rises. "We pollute them and he can no longer do either." Forth finger unfurls. "So, what's left?"

"The dead," I finish. "She said the dead may not enter. Blind him, and he will seek you no more. So who ... ?"

Raven snatches my arm. "My mother!" Her nails bite my skin as she stares straight ahead, unseeing. "I've been dreaming about her for weeks. Strange dreams that always end in nightmares about plants, and the earth—deaths, burials, and resurrections." She blinks, and that seems to snap her out of her trance. "I think she's been trying to tell me all along."

I gently pry her vice-like grip from my forearm. She folds into a sitting position at my feet, her shoulder blades poking out like wings.

"What are you saying?" Cole lowers himself to a seat next to her, and I do the same.

She makes a quick study of her bloody nail beds before raising her eyes. "Do you know anything about what happened to my mother, after she died?" There's barely a breath before she continues. "It was this huge scandal in our town. Turns out she was never cremated. The funeral home took our money, from other families too, and then dumped the bodies in a mass grave on their private property. We only found out because a storm unearthed them. Can you imagine what that was like for us? Driving down a flooded road and passing floating corpses everywhere? That's how people found out. The evacuation route went past the acreage where the bodies were dumped ... "

Her eyes glimmer, but she doesn't cry. She only waves her hand as if shooing a mosquito. "That doesn't matter right now. It's what I learned afterward that's important. State and federal laws exist about burials for a reason. The dead can spread infectious diseases, taint the ground, poison a well, or contaminate the air." Her laugh is brittle. "The dead *pollute*."

"The dead may not enter ... " Cole twists toward the flickering portal.

We're quiet together. Nothing but the quick sound of a squirrel up a tree and some fussing birds witness our collective ah-ha moment.

"That's it, then." Cole stands, brushing mulch from his pants. "We drag something dead through the mirror, and we're home!"

"Tsk, tsk. Always in such a hurry to leave me, eh?" Out of a nearby hedge walks Pan, calm and unremarkable as if he's out for an afternoon stroll. At least, I assume it's Pan. He's retaken the form of a man, shirtless with black leather pants and boots adorning his lower half. Stringy hair, white painted face, eyes blackened and running with makeup, he's a bad impression of Brandon Lee in *The Crow*. And adding insult to injury, the asshole's stolen my cane.

I'd like nothing better than to grab Raven and Cole and jump through the mirror to freedom, but I made a promise. My body heat rises as I brace for a fight. I concentrate the power around my organs. The sky darkens. Several trees appear above the hedgerow.

I arch my neck until vertebrae cracks. "We're done here."

"Indeed?" He smiles. "Certainly you may go, as soon as you decide who will stay."

Raven and Cole take their place on either side of me.

My chest is a furnace. "Never figured you for a welcher, Pan. The deal was to enter the labyrinth, locate the girl, and find our way out again. You knew Rose was a lie." When Cole flinches, I curb my speech. "Desiree is dead. Our deal is void."

"Interesting choice of words, dear boy, but they won't help you."

His gaze tracks Raven. "One *will* stay. I'm afraid we won't be denied. You can't kill the dead, and there's no escaping your own mind, am I right? Even the insane will tell you—wherever you go ... well, there you are." His strangled laugh ejects from his throat in a gag.

The maniac's confidence works in our favor. He thinks we mean to kill him, not trick him. The Draugar weren't alive either, technically, but we crippled them anyway. Too bad they aren't here. What I wouldn't give for one of their stinking hides right now—toss it through the portal—end of story.

Across the lawn, pond water stirs. Pan keeps his back to the ripples spreading over the surface in ever widening rings, yet his sick grin convinces me he knows what's coming. The water laps itself in waves until they skim the bank.

I step in front of Raven, ready for another scorpion. Her breath warms the skin of my arm. She's alive, and going to stay that way if I have anything to say in the matter.

Countless lumps boil under the pond scum until the surface resembles green oatmeal. When the lumps rise, I note their human shape. They're not Draugar. In each face, the eyes and nose are missing. Mouths are nothing but thin gashes sewn shut with black yarn, but if they're dead, they'll do.

Pan's new army aligns with him.

So be it.

I allow the heat begging for release to spread throughout my body. The sky mushrooms into chalky gray storm clouds.

Cole sends a message in his churning vortex of doom. Animals and trees break onto the scene. I'm no longer interested in solitude. This shared power with my friend and the girl I love makes me so much more than I am alone. And this time, I'm fighting on the right side.

Pan crosses his arms. "Come, come, children, who will it be? Monday's child—fair of face, Tuesday's child—full of grace? I prefer the girl, but the first to raise a hand will do."

Plants and wildlife loyal to Pan face off against Rae's band. Anxious expectation fills the air, then everything happens at once.

A moan echoes through the trees, quickly answered by one on the other side. Leaves quiver, moved by gusting winds. Timbers creak as opposing trees collide. Unfortunately, they're so busy fighting each other they cancel each other out as allies.

The faceless men march. I launch a firebomb in the shape of a burning lion. Cole rises two feet off the ground and feeds my flame more oxygen, tripling its size. My fire-beast lopes toward Pan's gruesome troops.

Pan spins, giving us his back. Hands in the air, he drains the murky pond sending gallons of liquid high into the air. The water gallops forward becoming a foaming, white stallion.

Fire and water arc toward each other. The elements hit in a brilliant head-on collision. Heat evaporates water. Water cools the blaze. Resulting steam hisses overhead, spreading on the wind in a cobra's pale hood before dissipating.

A willow tree breaks from the woodland skirmish. Long roots wriggle over the earth like octopus tentacles heading straight for Cole.

Raven dashes after him, in line with the accelerating willow. I let her deal with the tree, because Pan's mob is busy corralling me.

I whirl one hundred and eighty degrees, and shoot heat from my arms like a human flamethrower. Bodies blur inside a sea of red fire, but my exhale is premature. Charred and blistered, the faceless men pitch forward, continuing through the blaze.

With no eyes to see, they advance in slow, shuffling steps. Fire destroys the stitches sewn through their lips. Mouths hang open from nose to chin, the tattered, fleshy edges blowing in and out with every breath. The air fouls under their curse of decay and living death. Were they ever men?

In my years at school, I never attended any R.O.T.C. classes. I never went to boot camp. No one in my recent family history was in the military, or a cop, but everyone hears the stories. Their bravery and courage inspires us to leave no man behind ... I always admired them. People talk about how in the heat of battle, fear and confusion cause panic. I understand that now. Events unfold so quickly, there's little time to think. You react. Make mistakes. So your training better be thorough, ingrained, and damned smart.

In our reality, my friends and I are willing but untried and untrained. It's only now that I see our mistake. We've been separated.

I peer between the shoulders of two faceless men and locate Pan still standing near the drained pond. With a wave, he's gone, reappearing directly in front of Raven's path. Every heartbeat punches my chest as I watch her run right into his waiting arms.

If I attack him with fire, it could scorch her. In frustration, I send another missile into the approaching clones, charbroiling those closest. I need to put something dead through the portal, and fast, but not until my friends are through.

Cole grapples with a willow on the far side of the lawn. He's distracted by Rae's abduction and misses the writhing branch hovering at his back. Fear is a cold stab as I watch fine tendrils deftly wrap his neck. One quick snap and he drops, boneless as a sack of corn meal.

"No!"

Heat churns in my abdomen, fueled by fury, pain, regret. I release the power pent up inside me. The blast engulfs the next string of faceless in a second inferno, allowing me to break through their ranks. Cole hasn't moved. After all he's come through, to die in The Void …

I ask for help. Send the prayer I think Raven would. *God, if you can hear me. If it's not too late, please, don't let him die.* My blood pumps faster as I sprint.

Trees on opposing sides thrash each other in the distance, fully consumed in their own war. Trunks crack and split. A hemlock crashes to the ground and is mauled by the pulverizing limbs of a great oak.

A boom thunders across the field. The ground shakes as tiny cracks spread across the earth and widen.

Raven.

My head whips up as she bolts from Pan's grasp. He shrieks as mud gloms onto his legs and sucks him down.

Unlike the Minotaur's gentle burial, Pan's entombment is an ugly, violent thing. His hands windmill as he sinks. Caught between the will of two wielders, the earth first swallows Pan and then releases him with every alternating command. But who's stronger?

Safely out of reach, Rae turns, focusing all her attention on the hole Pan's clawing his way out of. Holding her hands high, she summons her element. Pale roots rise from the ground and curl around Pan's body.

A ten-foot wall of dirt and clay swells up like a muddy ocean wave hammering him deep into the tunneling pit. High and wide, more soil piles on until the mound becomes a knoll, the knoll a hill, the hill a mountain.

Seconds pass like hours until I finally reach her. Grabbing the arm of the goddess who is also just a girl, I wrench her around and pull her to my chest. The action is rougher than I mean, but relief drives me. My arms wrap her thin shoulders, but there is nothing frail about this girl. My eyes burn as I breathe her in. There's so much I want to say, but I only press my lips to her head.

"Gideon." She drags her gaze from Cole's still form. Water fills her eyes, polishing her gray irises until the tears break loose.

My thumbs brush the glistening trails from her cheeks. "Shh, I know." I scan the grounds. The dirt summit covering Pan hasn't moved, but the faceless have. While his army plods forward in drunken steps, I take Raven's hand and tug her toward Cole.

She pulls free and speeds ahead. Dropping to his side, Raven places her head on Cole's chest. Nerves jumping, I glance behind us. The willow has disappeared, but I keep an eye out just in case. The faceless aren't close, yet are tireless in their pursuit. Black and smoking, they swing each wobbly leg forward in a slow but steady motion. I lob another fireball.

"Rae … "

She straightens. Her eyes lit brighter than candles. "Gideon, he's breathing!"

I thank God for listening as I kneel and scoop an unconscious Cole into my arms. "Let's get him home."

I can only move so fast with my leg and wounded cargo, but we break for the mirror. The faceless change direction, but our lead gets us to the portal well ahead of them. Colors in the scenery shift and waver as we near the doorway.

"Rae, go on through." Her lips part, but I don't stop. "It will take one on each side to keep him from falling and splitting his skull. Once he's through, call 911."

She glowers at Pan's charred army.

"We're okay. I'm right behind you."

She reaches for my hand, and then she's gone.

Light refracts off her profile like a laser show as she enters the portal, and again as her dripping hands reemerge. I fill them with Cole's head and shoulders, and he passes for the very last time from Void to home.

Two down.

When I look back, one of Pan's men is almost on me. All I have to do is dive through the portal, and I'm free. I nearly do it. But the man's arm hangs in shreds at his side. Shattered bone protrudes from the blackened flesh. It's all I need to pollute the door.

I spring for the arm. Wrapping both hands around the elbow, I twist backward until I hear a crack.

His jawbone works up and down in a silent scream. His radius hangs at a wrong angle, but the ligament won't tear free. As I pull, the dead man's other hand grabs my throat with crushing strength. Fire is my element, so why does his touch burn? The rotting fingers on my neck sear my skin. The sensation is icy-hot, an anti-burn, as though the creature's coated in coolant—and my kryptonite.

I slam a flaming fist into his cheek. One last wrench and the arm rips free with a wet snap. Prize tucked into my side, I turn and plunge head first for the portal. My feet leave the ground. I'm flying, hurtling through the gooey plasma wall between worlds.

My head smacks a hard surface as I'm yanked short and stopped mid-air. Beneath the ringing in my ears, someone calls my name.

I've landed on my back, but can't roll over because I'm only partway through the portal. Everything below my knees remains stuck in The Void. I clutch the severed arm with one hand while Raven grabs the other and pulls.

A vice secures my ankles from the other side of the portal. Trapped by one of Pan's faceless soldiers, I wait for the punishing burn to begin. When I kick to free my feet, something sharp hooks my calves. Raven yanks until my shoulder threatens to dislocate, but we make no progress. And we're getting tired.

So close to freedom, our frustration merges. We color the air with swearing until a new weight crushes my legs from the other side. Pressure moves along my shins, over my knees and thighs, until a head pokes through the portal. Slowly, the face lifts. Dark hair, slick with oil from the mirror, recedes as two curling horns sprout on either side of a broad head. The nose elongates to a snout, pupils narrow to sharp slits inside yellow orbs.

Not a faceless ghoul, or a man, or even a mere magician.

Pan.

Heat fills my lungs, filters out to my extremities. His arms extend as he thrusts himself onto my torso and snatches at the severed arm.

My fingers slide over the burnt, greasy skin of the arm as I fight to maintain my grip. No way in hell is he getting this back. We play tug 'o war with the slimy limb, fire building inside me all the while. Rae and Cole are too close. I can't blast Pan without baking them or take the chance the portal will close with him on our side.

The goat-god's snarl exposes long square teeth. When his neck bends sharply to the side, I jerk to avoid a blow. Instead, his mandibles close over my hip. My scream echoes through the room as he rips out a chunk of flesh and spits it back into my face.

Raven's boot flashes over my head like a snake striking. Her heel connects with Pan's eye, plunging deeply into the socket.

Blood pours from the ruined orifice. The house shudders as he bellows, yet, he doesn't let go of the limb. Neither of us does.

Tree roots poke through the portal. I assume at Rae's bidding. They wind around Pan, covering his arms and neck. But one command from him acts like an electric shock, and the roots snap back through the door into The Void.

Rae kicks again and misses. His head dips. Catching his horn on her pant leg, it tears through the leather and into her thigh muscle. She shrieks and drops to the floor.

My heart falters as she does. I'm helpless, pinned by Pan's weight. The heat grows inside me to an unbearable level. A roar climbs my throat.

We're failing. Pan will continue his reign of torture if we can't stop him. My ancestors will never be cleansed of their atrocities. Rae and Cole will never be free.

I can't allow that, whatever the cost to me.

My mind revisits the honor of soldiers, their courage and loyalty to each other. How adrenaline makes a guy strong enough to lift a jeep off his dying friend. Constant horrors of war bind soldiers together so profoundly, throwing yourself on a mine to save the rest is automatic. Automatic …

"Rae." She lies on the floor near Cole's body, hugging her torn leg. "Drag Cole out of the room."

Her head tilts up, flashing eyes searching mine. I'm prepared for her stubborn objections, a debate. I get neither. Her gaze softens. Seconds pulse between us. Much as I try, I'll never know what she's trying so hard to say with her eyes. Does it echo what mine convey? *Forgive me. I love you. You're worth every bit of what I'm about to do.*

With a nod, she pushes to a rocky stand. Sliding her hands beneath Cole's underarms, she clasps them together, and drags him from the room.

Pan and I wrestle over the real estate of a rotten arm. This poisoned thing determines the future of the mirror, and with it, all of our destinies.

"Don't do this," Pan whispers, between labored breaths. There's fear in his eyes, even terror. "Please, please don't. Good boy. Have mercy. You don't know what it's like."

There's something truly panic-stricken in his tone that sends a chill through me. What's so terrible, even a sadistic madman fears it?

I give Rae as much time as I dare to reach a safe distance. A torrid force rises to the surface. I sense my actions copied by Pan. Together, we radiate the power of a quasar. Blood becomes magma, bones liquid steel, our eyes incinerators. The energy rattles the teeth in my head. I cinch the bone in my palm and release the beast I've kept chained inside for so long.

Pan bleats a low moan. "Don't leave me in there alone. It's dark, so terribly dark." His lids droop with his lessening grip, yet I grow stronger with each passing moment.

Heat warps the floorboards beneath us. Smoke rises, clouding the air. My enemy's eyes spark white, yellow, and red. The skin of his face blisters and peels. His fur singes—the stink musty and stale.

A sticky fluid seeps onto my fingers. The flesh on Pan's hands melts like hot glue. Knuckle bones poke through his fists. And he's laughing.

Sonic booms pound my eardrums. Once, twice, three times. Everything goes pyrotechnic white.

There's no pain. I might be dead. It's not as though I'd recognize the feeling. The weight flees from my legs. I turn and move freely, but I'm nearly blind and deaf. Nothing but a solid white sheet is cast in every direction, that and the ringing.

I'm on my hands and knees, crawling across an imagined floor. My fingers search for the missing bone that pollutes the mirror, but I find nothing familiar.

Two gentle hands clasp mine and stop my searching. Soft and cool they cup my face, stroke my head. Raven? I can't see her. I don't need to. Whether real or a dream, she draws me into her lap. One hand drapes my shoulder while the other continues its gentle sweeping of my hair. Definitely heaven.

You're safe. I think I hear. *Sleep now.*

And I do.

The Happily Ever After …

Chapter Thirty-Four

Gideon

When I wake, I'm home in my room at Maddox mansion. The room is dark, yet a slice of daylight peeks through the heavy drapery highlighting millions of swirling dust motes.

I try my limbs, fingers, and toes. Next, my head moves from side to side. Good. My sight is blurry, but my body works without pain. That seems wrong somehow. Am I dead, dreaming? Memories smear as I attempt to piece together recent events.

I struggle up, resting my weight on both elbows. I squint and ask the room at large, "What happened?"

A hand rests on my shoulder. "Easy, mate."

"Cole? You're alive?"

"Mm, thanks to you and Raven. Look, Dane's here with me, and Jamis—"

"I'm here too, sir." Jenny's plucky voice penetrates the gloom.

Everything comes rushing back in an instant. "Where's Rae? Is she safe? Where's Pan, did the portal seal?" As the fog lifts from my mind, questions pour out faster than anyone can answer.

"Rae's fine," Dane assures me. "She's been sitting with you

around the clock until Maggie finally threatened her—you know how she is. Rae agreed to sleep if we stayed."

"How long?"

"Three days."

"Damn boring, too," Cole complains, but his smile tells a different story.

I squint as Jenny opens the windows allowing more light into the room. My abdominal muscles tighten as I sit up. A growl rumbles from my stomach, hunger clawing at the lining.

"Now that's something I can fix," Jenny says. "I'll just pop down to the kitchen and see about getting you something to eat." She stoops over the bed, straightening the covers. Unshed tears gloss her aging eyes. "I'm awfully glad to see you up this morning, Mr. Maddox. Gave us all quite a scare, you know." Her enormous chest lifts with a sigh, and she pats my arm. "Right then. Mr. Jamis? I'll be needing your help, look sharp."

While Jenny is never happier than feeding the people she loves, Jamis won't be bossed, not even by her. He squares his frail shoulders. "*If* that is agreeable to Mr. Maddox?"

"Yes, it's fine, whatever she needs." I swing my legs off the bed. My head swims, and I wait for the vertigo to pass. "Jamis?" He and Jenny stop at the doorway. "I'm glad to see you. Thank you both for … for … " I care about them, and want to say so, but the words fail in my fast-drying throat.

"Good to have you home again, sir," Jamis answers. Jenny honks into her handkerchief as they exit.

As the door clicks shut, I scan the room for my jeans. "Tell me everything."

Dane steps to the bedside, blocking my view. "What are you doing?"

What does he think? "Going to see Raven."

Cole bounces onto the bed sending my head whirring again. "Not yet."

"Like hell."

"She's asleep."

"Then I'll watch her sleep."

"Brilliant, but first you need to eat something so you can stand without falling down. And bloody hell, take a shower, mate. You'll likely kill her with your stench."

He makes enough sense that my shoulders slump in defeat. I need to see her as much as I need sleep, or food, or air, but practically speaking, I'll wait a little longer. I scoot until my spine rests against the headboard. Once Dane sees he won't have to wrestle me to the floor, he plants himself in the armchair at my side.

"Pan?" I ask.

Cole pulls at a thread on his blue button-down. "Done. I woke just as Raven dragged me from your father's study. I saw you from the doorway, hanging from your waist through the mirror. Pan slobbering all over you with one eye hanging from the socket. One of the most disturbing things I've ever seen, I might add ... " A smile tips his mouth. "I wanted to help, but the minute Raven let go of me, I fell again, weak as a baby.

"I don't know how she got us both to the garden in time, but I think it had something to do with a tree. The air hummed and the whole house shook. I panicked thinking it was all going to blow—which it did, by the way. Big boom, nice mushroom cloud ... you razed your house, my friend." The mattress groans with his shift. "*After* you went nuclear, we dug up every bone in the bleeding graveyard. Made a pile, doused them with petrol and burned them to ash."

"We?"

"Cole called us," Dane says. "We drove up to get you, and brought you home. Doctor Dave's been here a few times to see you. Mostly exhaustion and dehydration ... you'll live."

"There's something else," Cole says, frowning. "When the portal blew, our powers went with it."

"What? No!" I snap my fingers over and over but produce no flame. The furnace in my chest is out. "You and Rae, too?"

He shrugs. "Seems so. We came home half-starved and

knackered, same as you, but with our injuries completely healed. The elements last parting gift to us, I suppose."

Dane leans forward. "Cole thinks the elements followed Pan back into The Void when you two blew apart. It's been quiet since you got back. Though there's a lawyer who keeps calling."

"What lawyer?"

Dane stares me down. His surly expression clearly states … *how the hell should I know?* "Windsor something or other. He showed up here day before yesterday. We keep telling him you're too sick to see anyone. He finally gave up and left a letter with Jamis."

Of course. Air exits my lungs in a noisy rush. "Final settlement papers for Maddox Industries." A dull ache starts at the base of my skull. I rub my eyes with my thumb and forefinger. "How long were we gone?"

"Seven days."

I drop my hand. "A week?" My shout hurts my head. "How is that possible? It felt like months." I bite my tongue remembering Cole was there four years.

"One of the many fun facts in The Void, every minute an hour, every hour a day."

"Really?" Dane asks.

"No." Cole answers dryly, then faces me. "Listen, I don't know what's in the letter Windsor brought, but I wanted to make you an offer regardless."

My eyebrows rise. Dane slumps in his seat with a huff, clearly aware and also unhappy about what's coming next.

"I've had a lot of time to think since we got back. I know what I want, and I've already spoken with Raven. My flight to France leaves at the end of the week. It's where I belong, and I intend to start my life over there. As you know, I'm extremely wealthy—even independently of what I'll inherit from my parents someday, I'm loaded." He says this without pride or guile, simply states it as fact. "I've been on the phone, making plans to finish school, and after that, start my own business. That's where you come in."

My pride rings a warning bell. "Cole—"

"Belt it and listen, Maddox." A cocky grin breaks free when I don't answer. "Good man." He leans back wrapping an arm lazily around one knee. "You have no family here, no ties any longer, but you have me. Sell the mansion, and sell the property at Grey Horse. The money will give you a start. Come to France. Bring Jamis and Jenny. I'll pay your way through school, plus whatever you need to live on. We'll call it an investment scholarship. When we graduate, if you want to, we can build something together. A start-up."

I glance at Dane having done the very same for his education last year. Based on my income, his tuition was pocket change, but it made a way for him and Maggie to be together. At the time, I did it for Rae, though it felt good to help someone. It's harder being on the receiving end.

"The money is nothing to me," Cole continues. "But Raven and you ... I meant what I said in The Void. We're brothers now. You saved my life." He shakes his head. "Neither of us has ever had a real family, but we could make one. Do whatever you want, mate, but think about it. Talk it over with Raven. I hope you'll say yes."

My fingers thread my hair and find it matted with grime and sweat. As God is my witness, I don't know what to do anymore. A grim smile twists my lips. Raven would say to ask God. "Thank you, Cole. I appreciate it."

"Is that a no?"

I lift my chin. "That's a thank you. I need to talk to Jamis, and to Raven."

"Talk about what, exactly?" This from Dane. I face him, and our gazes sync. "What happens the next time life gets hard? You gonna take her five thousand miles from us and leave her again?"

I deserved that. In his mind, I abandoned his best friend seven days ago and broke her heart. Surprisingly, his approval means more than I thought it would. "You were right, all the things you said to me that day at Grey Horse. I've done a lot of stupid-ass things in my life, and I may do more, but none worse than hurting her. So, if she'll have me, no, I won't ever do it again."

Seconds tick by. A breeze rustles the leaves outside my window representing two of the four elements we no longer control. We are free, but average. Mortal, but alive. It's enough.

Dane stands, russet dreads swing forward as he leans over and thrusts out a hand. I rise on shaky legs and take it. He slaps my shoulder so hard, I nearly fall.

Cole springs off the bed and meets us. I sway when Dane releases my arm and both he and Cole take a shoulder to support my weight. "All right, Romeo. Let's get you something to nosh on. Ugh, and for God's sake, take a shower. You can't romance a girl smelling like last week's pork pie."

My knuckles rap softly on the door of Raven's old room, and I enter, too excited to wait another minute.

She sleeps soundlessly on her stomach in the big white bed I had made for her last year. Her slight frame hardly makes a wrinkle under the blanket. Dark hair spills over the pillow covering her face. I designed the room with her in mind. We spent a lot of time here, and I'm a little sad to think of leaving despite the bad memories.

Maggie sits in a chair by the window, thick novel open on her lap. The trademark stripe in her blond hair is blue this week. She sets her book aside, rises, and meets me at the foot of the bed. Her eyes flicker as she studies me. A finger pokes my chest. "Does Dane know you're in here?"

"Yes." I lift the palm he pressed a short time ago—his way

of accepting my apology. My lips form a line as I prepare to give another. I've never apologized so much in my life. Then again, it's a practice long overdue. "I'm sorry, Maggie."

She releases a sigh. "I can't even ... " Her nose twitches as she tosses her hair. "I like you, Gideon. For a long time, I thought you were right for her, but then ... If Dane says you can be here, I guess that's good enough for me."

I suppress a smile as the little tyrant grants me permission to stay in my own house.

A sharp jerk on my shirt lowers my head. Maggie plants a soft kiss on my cheek. "Idiot." I straighten and peer down at her savage little face.

"Don't wake her up, she's exhausted and completely stressed out."

I nod obediently.

"And don't ever pull any stupid crap like that ever again. Ever."

"No," I answer.

She glares at me again before heading out. A quiet *snick* of the door closing seals Raven and me in together.

Taking Maggie's seat, I drag the chair closer to the headboard. I glance out the window as the breeze kicks up outside.

Sunlight reflects off the millpond in bright silver shimmers. Moss hangs from the live oaks, swaying in the wind. All four elements represented in the small span of my garden. I don't know how the others feel, but for me, the loss of my gift is like the death of a friend.

My gaze travels over Rae. Her steady breathing soothes me. I think about The Artisans, Pan's plea and banishment, Cole's offer, and a future with Raven. Can she trust me again? Would I if our roles were reversed?

She stirs and rolls over. A hand lifts the heavy curtain of hair from her face. Her eyes open. "Gideon?" She hitches up on one elbow. "How, uh, how long have you been awake? Her sweet southern drawl caresses my ears like warm sunshine. She rubs her eyes and sits up, looking around the room, but whether to get her bearings or in search of Mags, I can't say. And I don't care. Watching her is glorious. A privilege I thought I'd never have again. Finally, she faces me again. "Hi."

A slow smile tugs my lips. She's so damn cute.

"I'm glad to see you up. Doctor Dave said not to worry, but we did anyway. You slept for so long. He said that's all it was, sleeping, not a coma or anything bad like that. But it was scary. And oh, how long did you say you'd been awake?" Her eyes are overly bright as she fidgets with her covers. She's speed talking the way she does when she's nervous. A pretty pink hue colors her cheeks.

God, I want to kiss her.

"Have you eaten?" she asks her blanket.

"Raven … " My heart expands to fill my chest. I rise and step to the bedside, encouraged when she won't look at me.

"Because if you haven't, you should. I can make something or call Jenny?"

"Raven … " The mattress depresses under my weight.

She lifts her gaze. "Well, hey there, slugger. You're just going to sit down right there on my bed, aren't you?" She scoots away, giving me room I don't want. After a moment she says, "Yep. You're here. Looking like that. And I … " her eyes widen, " … have bed-head."

"You're beautiful. The most beautiful girl I've ever, *will* ever know." I can't help my chuckle as she flounces flat on her back.

Staring straight up at the ceiling, her eyes collect a watery sheen. I touch her chin with my thumb and forefinger, gently tilting her face toward mine. She doesn't speak. She doesn't have to.

I push her wild hair back from her face. "Raven." Hope arrests my lungs until her name is little more than a whisper. "Raven, I love you."

Chapter Thirty-Five

Raven

Months ago, Gideon said he loved me. Then he broke his word. In The Void, he said it again, and asked me to forgive him. I did almost instantly. It wasn't hard. I believe he meant what he said. Since then, I've had time to think about my issues with trust, fear, and loss. In the end, I figure we're both guilty. Gideon is as much to blame for being human as I am for not allowing him that privilege.

When did my fears become more valid than his?

Last year, fear of losing yet another person that I loved had me pushing him away. But he was hell-bent on us being together, so he made fast promises. I put all the pressure and responsibility on him to be perfect and perfectly keep his word. Never once did I consider the wounds he might still carry around on the inside from his past—painful baggage that he hadn't had time to deal with or heal from. I didn't think about what he might need from *me*. And in the end, what he needed was the space and freedom to fight his demons. Permission to try, succeed or fail.

Gideon's blue and green eyes watch me with the focused

intensity of an eagle. "I love you," he says again. "Forgive me. You mean … you mean everything to me. Raven, will you let me love you … can I come back?"

His voice trembles, thick with emotion. His words are clumsy and very un-Gideon-esque. He's vulnerable, and transparent, maybe even a little desperate as he searches my face for the answer he hopes to hear.

There's nothing left to consider.

"Yes," I say simply. "Yes, and yes, and yes." Tears threaten as I'm pulled into the circle of his arms. Warm breath falls on my hair as his kisses cover my head. The familiar scent of licorice and spice lingers on his skin.

"Forgive me." His arms tighten. "How could I have been such an idiot?"

"No." I shake my head, and he loosens his hold a few inches to look at me. "It's my fault, too. I wasn't being fair to you."

His eyes flash and darken. "Don't be ridiculous, woman!"

"Me? *You* don't be rid—"

Unable to wait, his mouth covers mine, crushing me with need, and want, and longing. My fingers tangle in his soft, golden curls. Pressure demands more and I open myself up to him.

He lies on the bed, pulling me down with him. Drawn under his spell, my body weakens, bones turn to syrup. He works his special kind of magic on me until I'm good and kiss-drunk. When I'm sure my lungs will explode from a lack of oxygen, he breaks away. Beginning at my jaw, he kisses a line along my throat to the hollow at the base, leaving a trail of heat across my skin. Embarrassed by my ragged breaths, I strive to slow them, and mentally order my frantic heartbeats to calm down.

He must sense something, because he lifts his head. The emotion in his eyes is exposed and raw—love, desire, admiration, devotion. He's as fierce, and volatile, and unpredictable as the element that chose him.

Heat blooms under my cheeks beneath his all-consuming gaze, and I glance away.

"Don't you dare hide from me, Raven Weathersby." When I look up, there's no impatience in his expression. His eyes are soft, sincere. He draws his thumb across the line of my eyebrow, down my temple. "Your passion was obvious the first time you walked into my office and told me off." His sexy smile produces tingles in my stomach. "Every single thing about you intrigued, teased, fascinated, and finally consumed me. I know who you are. I hope, in time, you'll trust me enough to be uninhibited, vulnerable.

"In fact," he kisses me, "I can hardly wait."

I smack his arm. "Dane's right, you are scary."

"Yes, but you like that about me, admit it." We kiss again until I feel his smile break out on my lips. "You're killing me, you know that?"

"Why, what do you mean?" I ask. And now I'm smiling, too.

He groans and rolls away from me onto his back. "Trust me. You don't want to know." The provocative timbre in his voice has me agreeing. "Hey, how do you feel about French weddings?"

A jolt runs through my veins. I shift to face him at the same time he turns toward me. His hand strokes my arm sending tiny shivers over my skin. "Depends on whose wedding you're talking about?"

"Ours."

Whoa Nelly. "I'm eighteen years old, for heaven's sake!"

"Yes? That's very good, Rae. What other tricks can you do?"

"Shut up." I shove his chest, which does nothing to move him.

His grin threatens my cool. "Do you want to move to France with me, Raven?"

"Do you?"

"Quit hedging and answer."

"Which question?" I'm teasing him back now.

"France, woman, France. You and me, baby."

"Do we have to decide right now? And did you just call me *baby?*"

He laughs. "No we don't, and yes I did. I plead temporary insanity, which is mostly your fault, by the way. Don't deny it. "

"Oh, I'm not arguing. You've always been crazy."

"Seriously, we could go to France, but only if that's what you want, too. As for marriage, I'll wait for you forever. I'm never going to want anyone else. But since we have no parents to object, and neither of us is young for our age, I don't know. Think about it?"

"Is that a proposal?"

"I guess it is."

"Well, it sucked."

His laugh is loud, and satisfying. I squeak as he grabs my arm and tucks me under his chest.

"Raven Weathersby, I love you to the point of absolute madness. You own me, girl. I want to be with you, love you, work beside you ... I never want to spend another night apart. Would you do me the incredible honor of becoming my wife?"

"As in married ... "

He grins. "That's usually how it's done, so yes."

When? My heartbeats snap and flutter like a flag in the wind.

Gideon answers as though I spoke aloud. "Now." He smiles. "Okay, someday, whenever you're ready. Here, or in France, or in the damn Congo, I don't care." His chest stills, and it dawns on me this incredible guy is holding his breath waiting for my answer.

"I will," I say, a little breathless. "Absolutely, someday, yes I will."

He bends his head, capturing my lips with kisses soft and tender. Every caress holds the promise of future passion and glory, triumph and heartbreak. What's life without risk? A year ago, I answered before I understood the question. But I'm ready now, sure of us. Hard times only highlight the good stuff. Real life is both, and I get to experience it all with Gideon by my side.

Chapter Thirty-Six

Cole

My new watch reads 8:45 as I pass through the door of my first tutoring session. Once I test out, I'll enter Uni next fall and do all the things normal, non-magical twenty-year-olds do.

Normal.

Whatever that is.

I choose a seat near the back of the library, because hey, some things never change. Scanning the room, it looks like we'll have nearly a dozen in the class, eight boys, and three girls. Most are younger than me, as expected.

Our tutor Mr. Brun sits at the front of the room behind a scholarly-looking walnut desk. Round, with a goatee and shock of fluffy red hair on top, he might be in his mid-forties. He pushes silver-rimmed glasses up his nose as he flips through some paperwork, ignoring us for another few minutes before class starts.

I don't care.

I don't care that my flat has nothing in it but a refrigerator and a bed. I have time to fill in the blanks. I don't care that I parked my motorbike illegally downstairs when I couldn't find parking and will likely get a ticket. I don't care that there are no girls in this classroom old enough to keep me out of jail or prettier than a doorknob to hit on. I have years to look for the right one. For the first time in my life, I have friends that are more like family. I'm happy to be in school, fully cognitive of the privilege it is to sit here as a free man with choices. I'm flying high.

The door opens and a last student walks through with a minute to spare. Long chestnut waves obscure her face as she focuses on the paper in her hand. Her body is long and lean in cut-off jean shorts, a black and white stripped tee, and black ankle boots. With an impatient toss of her head, her hair swings back exposing big, doe-brown eyes and a pouty, pink mouth.

This day just keeps getting better.

A quick peek at the room and she heads for the chair next to mine. "Hey," she says, dropping her leather bag onto the desk. "Anybody sitting here, yet?" Thick lashes shield her eyes, but her cheeks tint a healthy color. I'm guessing she's eighteen.

"Hello." I smile. "I'm Cole, and no the seat isn't taken."

"Great, thanks." She turns her little wooden chair backward and sits. Her fingers, covered in multiple bands of silver, tap out a beat on the top rung. I try and fail not to look at her shapely legs. My pulse gears up. "I thought I'd be late when I couldn't find anywhere to park my motorcycle."

No!

Mr. Brun stands, still studying the papers in his hand.

My new classmate leans over and whispers, "I don't know my way around yet, and I hate being late. Oh, I'm Camille, by the way." Her scent is fresh and floral, but not overpowering. Daisies maybe?

"Nice to meet you, Camille. Have you been here long?"

Her eyes roll. "Just two weeks. I'm from the states, Ohio. I don't speak the language and don't understand the way the city's laid out. I keep getting lost; it's so frustrating."

My expression hardens in mock seriousness. "That's terrible.

Locating the best *Le petit déjeuner* is extremely important. No Cheerios here, you know? I can show you sometime." I shrug. "If you'd like … ?"

Surprise widens her eyes, so I know she wasn't fishing for a date. She recovers quickly, playing with the ring on her pinkie. The fact she doesn't answer right away only peaks my interest. She's friendly, not reckless.

"Excuse me?"

I'm so caught up in our easy conversation, that it takes me a minute to realize Mr. Brun is addressing me. Or us.

"Pardon?" I straighten and face front.

Our tutor's nostrils flare in exaggerated irritation. "I simply asked whether Mr. Wynter and Miss Johnson were ready to join the rest of the class?"

I glance at Camille. She stares at her hands, cheeks flaming, which for some reason gives me tremendous satisfaction. "Apologies, Mr. Brun." I wave a hand. "Do carry on."

The class snickers, but Brun sloughs it off and passes out our syllabus for the term.

Camille tears a page from her binder and scratches a few words. When she passes it to me, I regress to year nine as I unfold the note and view her message.

Are you going to be trouble for me, Wynter?

My lips curve. I slip the pen from my notebook and answer.

I hope so, but only specializing in the fun, B-grade stuff.

I pause and then add …

Actually, I'm a very trustworthy guy, Camille.

After reading, she carefully folds her paper and tucks it inside a pocket in her binder. I'd think she was blowing me off if not for her occasional, quiet smile. For the remainder of class, she doesn't look at me, and I battle to keep from staring at her.

An hour passes too quickly, and Brun ends the class. Face flushed again, Camille is up and out of her seat in a flash. Arms clutching her bag like a life preserver, she exits the room and is gone.

I stand and heft my pack over my shoulder. As I stroll into the hallway chatting with a few remaining students, it strikes me the act is as average and mundane as any other human being experiences on the planet. The air passing through my lungs feels like true freedom.

A pretty girl with wavy chestnut hair glances my way before pushing through the double glass doors at the front of the building. There's mystery behind that quiet smile.

Until tomorrow, Camille.

I'm definitely up for the challenge of knowing her better ...

... and I've got all the time in the world.

The End

Acknowledgments

Hi!

This is the part where I thank the talented and selfless people who helped make this book a reality. A part I really like, but since you may not recognize the names, let me tell you what they did for me ...

For the folks listed below, and because they've been so amazing, virtual balloons, chocolate cheesecake, and miniature horses all around! Yeah!

A heartfelt thanks to Georgia McBride and everyone at Month9Books for loving my story and giving me the chance to share it with others.

To my editing team: Georgia McBride, thank you for your wisdom, direction, advice and encouragement, and Cameron Yeager, who put up with me, told me the truth, and helped make this book so much better than it would have been without her, thank you. You both rock!

To J. A. Belfield, Stephanie Judice, Colleen Spencer, Blake Reece and Jennifer Jenkins, thank you a million times over, for reading (and rereading—ad nauseam). There is simply no way this book would exist without your creative input, patient support, and friendship. Try not to think about all those times the revised manuscript showed up in your inbox *again*, the hand holding you did, the many panic attacks you warded off ... Just know that I love you all so much. It's impossible to thank you enough.

To Jamie Arnold: thanks for being a fantastic publicist and all around great person, (the girl's so sweet, I want to dunk her in my coffee). Also, doxies rule!

To the always amazing Jennifer Million: thanks for not plotting my murder when I email with too many annoying questions. Thank you Bethany Salminen, for treating my comma phobia. Your eagle eyes are the best! And again, to the amazing Georgia McBride for my drop-dead gorgeous covers.

Thanks to my entire family, for your faithful support.

To my husband, love of my life, and best friend, thanks for every single minute.

Maddie Mae, for never doubting.

Thanks to Ronen, for modeling the joy and wonder of simply being alive.

… And Manny.

And to you, wonderful, lovely reader, thank you *so* much for buying and reading this book. I wrote it for you. I love inventing people and places, creating adventures and romances, and then telling you wild stories about what happens next.

Thanks for letting me.

XOXO

Julie
www.juliereece.com

Julie Reece

Julie Reece was born in Ohio and lived next to her grandfather's horse farm until the fourth grade. Summers were about riding, fishing and make-believe, while winter brought sledding and ice-skating on frozen ponds. Most of life was magical, but not all.

She struggled with multiple learning disabilities, and spent much of her time looking out windows and daydreaming. In the fourth grade (with the help of one very nice teacher) She fought dyslexia for her right to read, like a prince fights a dragon in order to free the princess locked in a tower, and she won.

Later, she invented stories where she was the princess ... or a gifted heroine from another world who kicked bad guy butt to win the heart of a charismatic hero. Who wouldn't want to be a part of that? She moved to Florida where she continued to fantasize about superpowers and monsters, fabricating stories (her mother called it lying) and sharing them with friends.

Then she wrote one down ...

Hooked, she's been writing ever since. Historical, contemporary, urban fantasy, adventure, and young adult romances, she loves strong heroines, sweeping tales of mystery and epic adventure ... which must include 'a really hot guy'. Her writing is proof you can work hard to overcome any obstacle.

OTHER MONTH9BOOKS TITLES YOU MIGHT LIKE

THE ARTISANS

EMERGE

GENESIS GIRL

PRAEFATIO

Find more awesome Teen books at http://www.Month9Books.com

Connect with Month9Books online:

Facebook: www.Facebook.com/Month9Books

Twitter: https://twitter.com/Month9Books

You Tube: www.youtube.com/user/Month9Books

Blog: www.month9booksblog.com

Request review copies via publicity@month9books.com

THE ARTISANS

JULIE REECE

MER CHRONICLES
BOOK 1

She will risk
everything to stop him
from falling in love with
the wrong girl.

Emerge

TOBIE EASTON

"The most fun I've had reading in a long time!" —Wendy Higgins,
New York Times bestselling author of the *Sweet Evil* series

Their new beginning
may be her end.

BLANK SLATE: BOOK 1

GENESIS GIRL

JENNIFER BARDSLEY

PRAEFATIO

A NOVEL

"This is teen fantasy at its most entertaining,
most heartbreaking, most compelling. Highly recommended." –Jonathan Maberry,
New York Times bestselling author of ROT & RUIN and FIRE & ASH

GEORGIA McBRIDE